27 AD

J.D. Morrison

27 AD

ISBN 13: 9780999524329

Library of Congress Control Number: 2018937466

Cover design © by All Things That Matter Press
Published in 2018 by All Things That Matter Press

This book is dedicated to Jena, my muse and wife.

Part One

Legions of Nanorobots Target Cancerous Tumors with Precision - *Researchers have just achieved a spectacular breakthrough in cancer research. They have developed new nanorobotic agents capable of navigating through the bloodstream to administer a drug with precision by specifically targeting the active cancerous cells of tumors.*
    ~Science Daily, August 15, 2016

Strange is our situation here upon the earth. Each of us comes for a short visit, not knowing why, yet sometimes seeming to a divine purpose.
    ~Albert Einstein

Uprooted ~ 4 BC

Doctor Joseph Goldberg cradled the child with one arm and with the other injected the subatomic nanite serum into its bottom. He sat alone with the child and recalled the cascade of events that brought him to this moment. His time travel jump had been unremarkable, aside from the sudden change in venue and perhaps a feeling he likened to jet lag. The most perilous aspects of his first few hours were finding clothing, then food and shelter before nightfall. His Jewish heritage facilitated his relatively quick blending with the locals, and his role as a magus helped explain away any unfamiliarity they may have perceived.

He was somewhat surprised to find the two other magi already present when he arrived at Herod's Palace in Jerusalem. When they learned he had a good idea of exactly where to look for the newborn, they agreed to follow. Dr. Goldberg knew of Herod's nefarious intent but accepted his gifts for the child, which were to be presented on behalf of the king. By the time the magi left Jerusalem, Herod's soldiers were already mobilizing to hunt down the would-be child king.

The magi found the child, his young mother, and middle-aged father in the little town of Bethlehem, just south of Jerusalem. They paid homage to the child and offered Herod's gifts to the parents. It was Dr. Goldberg who warned of the imminent danger to the baby and suggested an alternative that would assure the child's survival. It took some convincing, but the child's young mother, Mary, eventually yielded her baby to the care of the magi for the sake of its safety. The magi agreed not to return to Jerusalem and instead headed east, out of Judea.

They followed the King's Highway trading route and settled into an inn near Dhiban, east of the Dead Sea. Herod's soldiers had disregarded the three sojourners and instead were focused on tracking down an infant child accompanied by his parents.

It became clear after the child was successfully spirited away from Judea that the other two magi had no intention of raising the child, which was convenient for Dr. Goldberg and his hidden agenda. Dr. Goldberg parted ways with the other magi as soon as they were out of Israel and King Herod's sway.

Once alone with the child, Dr. Goldberg propped him up between a couple of wool pillows and scribbled a cryptic note onto a scrap of papyrus: "4 BC, Jesus of Bethlehem, son of M & J." He coiled the note and sealed it in wax, then rolled the child over and inserted the message as a suppository.

"Sorry kid, they'll need confirmation," he said to the protesting child. "That's not the worst part. I'll not make you wait." He lacked the pulse generator in antiquity to actuate the subatomic nanites that would send the child forward in time. He had to improvise. He took one of the pillows and placed it over the child's face. It was a quirk of the nanites that they would cause the subject to jump time when the heart stopped. He distracted himself from the cruelty of his action by contemplating what temporal paradox he might be creating by suffocating the baby Jesus. The child stopped squirming, lay still for a moment under the pillow, then completely vanished. It would be up to his team at the lab to revive the child.

Government mission accomplished, he would now fulfill the role he had sworn as Master Freemason to remain faithful and keep watch. His would be a lonely stakeout in this ultimate test of the immutability of time, for Jesus' ministry was not set to occur for another thirty years. He gathered his belongings and headed up the King's Highway, the way he had come, then traveled west into Judea towards Arimathea to begin his new life, and to patiently wait.

Christian boarded the aircraft without luggage. He had no checked bags, no rolling tote for the overhead bin, not even a backpack to cram under the seat in front of him. He just had his wallet and keys in his pockets for this quick trip home to Houston. It was liberating. His dad often teased him about traveling lightly, and this was taking that euphemism to new heights. He mused that a life with no baggage would be sublime indeed.

Christian reflected upon his nomadic inclinations. He couldn't remember the last time he was this enthusiastic about a move and a new job assignment. He was being given the opportunity to work with his dad on time travel experimentation with some of the most advanced technologies known to man. He couldn't get back to Florida and start his new life fast enough.

He supposed it was about time to be moving on anyway. He had been in Houston just long enough to grow shallow roots, which now had to be nipped. Bonnie O'Shaughnessy was her name. Bonnie was a kindergarten teacher at a private Catholic school in a Houston suburb. A co-worker of Christian's, Bonnie's brother Sean, had introduced them. They were just a few months into their relationship and his attachment was minimal. He reasoned it was best to cut things off now before they, or she, got serious. Christian resigned himself to meeting her in person to part ways as amicably as possible. His intention was to call her that evening and set up a coffee date for a mature discussion about the significance of the job he was being offered. Surely, she would understand.

Christian got off the plane at Houston's George Bush Intercontinental Airport. He discarded the newspaper article he'd been reading on how President Trump managed to secure his second term, then headed for the driverless-taxi stand. Bonnie was there to intercept him. He spotted her first. She stood out in the most alluring of ways. The late afternoon humidity, combined with the chaos of auto traffic, produced just the right amount of atmospheric moisture to cause her cotton summer dress to cling to her shapely figure. Her flowing fiery red hair was slightly frizzy, and her milky white skin glistened in the summer sauna.

She cheerfully ran to him when she saw him emerge from the airport's exit doors. She leaped into his arms and gave him the kind of welcome home hug of which most men only dream. He felt the closeness of her body and smelled her scented mix of sweat and lavender. This break up was going to be more difficult than he had anticipated.

He greeted her with a peck on the cheek. "Bonnie, you've surprised me."

"Oh honey, I just couldn't wait to see you again," Bonnie said as she threw her arms around Christian's neck. "I left numerous messages on your cell phone. Didn't you get them?"

"Uh, I've been kind of busy," he replied, trying to pry her arms from his neck.

"Well, I finally gave up on getting you on the phone and just called the Florida office directly. They told me your flight number. I brought Hashtag, too. He's waiting in the car."

"How sweet," Christian managed. "How long have you been waiting?" The poor dog's probably been sweltering in the car, he thought. This wasn't the goodbye scenario Christian had imagined.

"Oh, just a little while," she said. "I've let Hashtag out of the car a couple of times already and the windows are cracked wide, so he's fine." Bonnie tried to kiss him more fondly, prolonging the embrace.

He patted her back. "Well let's get going. I doubt you're legally parked down here with the public transit."

Christian neglected to hold Bonnie's hand as they walked to her car, and he allowed her to open her own door. "Where's your luggage?" she asked as they got in the car.

"I left it in Florida," he replied as he slid into the passenger seat. Hashtag immediately jumped from the rear into Christian's lap and began licking his face, giving Christian the benefit of abundant dog slobber. "Hashtag, easy on the tongue."

Bonnie started the car and navigated her way out of the terminal parking area. "Why would you do that? Do you have to go back again soon?"

"As a matter of fact, Bonnie, I do. I've been offered a great career opportunity at the Cape Canaveral site and it's impossible to turn down. I'll be working with my dad." He was grateful she was driving and had to concentrate on the traffic rather than look into his eyes.

"Florida sounds nice," Bonnie said as she merged onto busy Interstate I69. "I wouldn't mind getting away from this humidity."

"Yeah, you should come check it out sometime. It still gets humid, but it comes and goes, and the breeze off the ocean is more refreshing than the gulf coast of Houston." He was trying to figure out how exactly to say, "you're not coming with me," without having it sound so abrupt.

"I'll have to check into whether my Texas teaching certification will transfer to Florida," Bonnie said, clueless to the signals Christian was proffering.

"Aren't you already committed to teaching another year at St. John Paul?" Christian wondered how many hints he was going to have to drop.

"Well, nothing's ever written in stone, you know." Bonnie's smile was starting to fade. "Things come up in life. The school understands that."

"Of course," Christian said. "I just thought you really liked where you were teaching." Christian was glad for the presence of Hashtag filling the space between him and Bonnie.

"Why are you constructing so many obstacles?" she asked, briefly taking her eyes off the road and looking at Christian. "You're not considering taking me with you, are you?"

The dog settled down, albeit on Christian's lap, and was oblivious to the tension forming in the front seat of the car. "We're going to have to talk about that. I was going to call you tonight and set up a date to fill you in on what I'm thinking."

"Fill me in on what you're thinking?" Bonnie weaved into the speed lane. "That doesn't sound like I'd be a part of what you're thinking. I can see where this conversation is going, Christian. I knew when I got into this relationship that you were a free spirit, but I was hoping you'd see that we have something special, and that you'd fall in love with me and we'd settle down. The kids loved it when you stopped by the elementary school to give me flowers, and I see how gentle you are with Hashtag. I thought we might have a life together, with children of our own."

She was laying the guilt trip on thick. Christian nodded his head and listened.

"Are you really leaving without me Christian?" Bonnie looked over and Christian could see the tears beginning to well up in her eyes. He felt like a cad.

"Bonnie, I ..." At that moment Hashtag decided to lean over Christian and stick his head out the open window of the passenger door. Pushing the dog slightly so he wasn't breathing its fur, Christian continued. "I can't pass up this opportunity Bonnie," he said sincerely. "The work they're doing in Florida is at the cusp of nanorobotics. Some of the smartest minds in the world are working on the team I'll be joining. And, I'll be working with my father."

"Can we keep in touch at least?" She sped past a line of cars. "I could come visit."

"No, probably not," Christian said flatly. He dared not question her speed, but he secretly prayed for his survival, on several levels. "And us having children was never going to happen Bonnie. I have other aspirations and have no desire to be tied down by that kind of obligation."

There was a prolonged silence. Bonnie began to sob as she exited the interstate. This was not an amicable way to leave her. Even the dog whimpered slightly, perhaps finally realizing the sadness emanating from the driver's seat.

The mood in the car was somber as Bonnie approached Christian's apartment. She stopped the car in front of the building and turned to him, her mascara badly smeared and her tears flowing freely. He couldn't leave her like this. "Would you like to come in? We can talk some more," he offered.

"No. Just get out."

He obliged. He picked up Hashtag and placed him on the seat next to Bonnie, then stepped onto the curb and began to wipe dog hair off his lap. In an instant, Bonnie reached across the dog, slammed the door, and was already speeding away. Christian accepted the fact that anything left at Bonnie's place was now the marooned property of the Houston ex-girlfriend.

Teambuilding

Christian put the Bonnie break-up saga behind him and focused on extricating himself from Houston. He packed his belongings, which constituted mostly of dirty clothes, into cardboard boxes and had them shipped to Cape Canaveral. He said his goodbyes to his Houston team and then returned to Florida. It didn't take him long to settle into the temporary housing that wasn't far from the Spintronics Florida campus.

Things moved quickly from day one. His dad invited him to a team building session the evening before his first day of work at the Cape facility. "Tell us about your beer drinking experiments at Houston," Dominic asked Christian over the clamor of the happy hour crowd at the team's favorite local pub. Christian smiled wide at the table full of his new work peers. This wasn't the first time the reputation of his former team's experiments with the fermented brew had preceded him. "They weren't beer *drinking* experiments, per se. They were beer *making* experiments."

"You have my attention as long as it involves beer," Dominic said.

"Understood," Christian nodded. "Now that the molecular nanites are self-programming," Christian explained, "it has significantly simplified their practical application. They can mimic a base characteristic from a small sample of liquid. For example, we can make a pitcher of lemonade from one drop of lemonade using a single molecular nanite capsule. When applied to contaminated water, nanites purify it. When applied to certain plant seeds or reptilian eggs, they accelerate growth. The Houston team's preferred media for this important research was beer, naturally. There was great enthusiasm, as you can imagine, for these experiments, which inevitably involved various ales, lagers and stouts."

"I can't believe the government let you get away with making beer under the guise of scientific research," Dominic shook his head as he spoke.

"I assure you, the Houston team diligently completed the requisite Food and Drug Administration forms to document proper disposal of the liquids produced," Christian said. "The most common explanation of 'consumed' has not garnered any additional scrutiny from the FDA to date."

"So, you're telling us the Houston team *drank* the beer they made, right?"

"Yes, that was the basic idea."

"See, that's what I'm talking about!" Dominic said. "We need those kinds of experiments here at the Cape!" The table voiced unanimous agreement.

Christian's dad interjected to give Christian the lowdown on the team members sitting around table with whom he'd soon be working. "Dominic Frazier is a superb test lab technician and he's been around a while. Corner him when you get a chance. He can tell you some stories of his own."

Christian nodded and followed his dad's eyes to a mature man with a grey goatee. "That's Operation's Manager, Cornelius Jones." He turned to Christian and said seriously, "You'll want to be friends with him. Nothing jumps without Cornelius' seal of approval."

Christian opened his mouth to interject something but yielded as his father continued speaking.

"Cornelius, I'm pulling Christian off his Houston assignment to insert him here to lead the time travel test team." The two men shook hands. "Brace yourself to be interviewed," his dad whispered to Christian with a sly smile.

"Nice to meet you," Cornelius said. "What do you know about quantum field theory?" Christian got the immediate impression that Cornelius was a bit skeptical about Christian's technical qualifications, CTO's son notwithstanding. He realized it would take time to win Cornelius' confidence, along with the rest of the staff, but he was a natural charmer and was attuned to finding common interests. He answered the question as best he knew how. "It's a complex subject. Niels Bohr said a hundred years ago, 'Anyone who is not shocked by quantum theory does not understand it.' I tend to agree."

"Good, at least you're not a hot shot know-it-all," Cornelius smiled. "We should get along just fine."

Senior Biologist, Claire Khalil was sitting to Christian's left. Christian had met her earlier at the door to the pub and he already liked what he saw. Another round of beers was ordered, and Christian was prompted to provide a brief history. "I was born in Nevada, moved to Florida when my father founded Spintronics, and I'm a Florida State University grad. My resume is a bit eclectic after that because it has taken me a while to figure out what I really want to do with my life."

"And what is that?" Claire asked.

Christian let go of his beer glass and set his hands flat on the table, giving him time to pause and compose a sincere response. "I'm still sorting it out. I considered seminary. Dad's staunch religious beliefs are no secret, so you can imagine how I was raised." He managed a wayward glance at his father. "I admit I share his convictions."

"Doesn't that make it tough to be a research scientist?" Cornelius directed the pointed question to Christian.

"No, not at all," Christian stood firm. "I see great synergy in the advancement of science and faith in the existence of an almighty God. The idea that religion and science don't mix is a fiction of modern society. Up until the mid-twentieth century, many of the most significant scientific breakthroughs were facilitated by deeply religious men, priests, and monks. The man who first theorized that the universe was expanding, based on Hubble's 1924 telescope observations of galaxies, was a Catholic priest. A theory that was later confirmed by Einstein."

"I didn't realize that, and I'm usually up on that sort of thing," Cornelius said. "No offense, but I'm going to fact check this." Cornelius pulled out his iPad and scrolled through a brisk "Big Bang Theory" search. "I'll be damned, his name was Georges Lemaitre, Belgian physicist and Roman Catholic priest."

"There's more if you want to hear," Christian offered.

"Sure, give us another religion-fosters-science fact," Cornelius grinned.

"All right, did you know that one of the foremost influential developers of the theory of evolution was a Catholic monk?" Christian said. "His name was Gregor Mendel."

"Mendel was a monk?" Cornelius asked. "You're going to have me baptized Catholic before the evening is over," he joked.

"Well, he was an Augustinian friar to be specific," Christian said. "And baptism isn't such a bad idea Cornelius. There are far worst things that could happen to a scientist. You know what Mark Twain said when asked if he believed in baptism?"

"Tell me," Cornelius took the bait.

"He said, 'Believe in it? Hell, I've seen it done!'"

"I'll drink to that," Cornelius said and raised his glass as they all toasted to the blending of religion and science.

The next round of beers arrived, and the conversation continued. Claire redirected the interrogation along a more personal tangent. "I don't see a wedding ring," she said with a grin.

The group chuckled and warned Christian that Claire had no filter when it came to discerning which questions were appropriate. "She's also one of the few single and hot girls on the research team," Cornelius whispered to him.

Christian glanced down at his empty ring finger and made a mental note of how liberating it felt to board the aircraft without baggage. "I admit my life's pursuits have kept me from the ties of a permanent romantic relationship," Christian said. "But I'm a reasonably good handyman and I can cook," he added with a wink to Claire.

"I don't believe it," Cornelius said. "I think you've actually made Claire blush." The table broke out in laughter.

"You don't look very much like your father," Claire changed the subject. "You must favor your mother."

"I was adopted as a baby. They're the only parents I've ever known. I don't really know much else about my origins," he shrugged.

Christian was ready to take the focus off his personal life. "I like your earrings," he said to Claire. He thought the earrings looked like dangling strands of shellacked vegetation growing from her earlobes.

"Oh, thank you," Claire said. "They were made from time travel experiment artifacts a few years ago. We were just setting up my lab and these two clovers appeared on my desk. I figured they were my welcoming gift."

The lighthearted banter continued for another round of beers. When the last round arrived, Christian smiled broadly at the group and raised his beer. The men's eyes followed the raised glass. Claire's eyes stayed fixed on his face. "Here's to new adventures," his eyes locked onto Claire's as he spoke, "and new friends."

Spintronics

Christian battled through a hangover the following morning and rummaged through boxes to find something presentable to wear for his first day of work at the Cape. Christian wasn't an accumulator of stuff. He unpacked several boxes of dirty clothes and piled them by the washing machine. He assessed that most of his moving effort would involve catching up on laundry. The one-bedroom apartment he was moving into was part of a two-story multi-unit building owned by the company for the purpose of lodging visiting research scientists. Spintronics had recently renovated the building to incorporate an AI personal assistant, the latest in-home electronics advancements. Alexa would be good company, and Christian liked that the apartment was located off Astronaut Boulevard, just a short distance from the Cape Canaveral campus. His dad explained that it was more efficient for Spintronics to own an apartment building and furnish the apartments than it was to pay travel expenses for employees and consultants. He agreed the homey setting would be a better arrangement for the business traveler. He was joining the team at the request of his father and CTO of Spintronics, Dr. William Naismith. Christian had proudly watched his dad pragmatically expand Spintronics to multiple locations, each conducting research projects exploring the application of nanorobotic technology across a broad range of scientific disciplines, including time travel.

Christian stepped onto the balcony and lit up a Marlboro Light. He ashed into the remnants of a potted plant and considered the new job. He was grateful to have this opportunity to work directly with his dad's team. He was appreciative for the continued opportunity to be able to do anything at all in life. His near-death experience with cancer had given him a new perspective on life's priorities and he often treasured even the seemingly mundane moments. He stubbed out his cigarette and retreated inside to finish his unpacking.

Christian used one of the company's uRide self-driving cars to get to campus the next morning. He realized that the proximity of his apartment to the facilities would allow him to either bike or jog to work, if he allocated sufficient time, and the urge to do so got stronger with each palm tree he passed.

Christian's Cape facility badge was ready for him when he reported to the main campus building. He made a point to stroll the grounds, testing his dad's assurances that he'd have free reign access throughout the campus. He didn't find a single door latch that wouldn't toggle from red light to green light when he waved his badge. His dad caught up to him by mid-morning and offered a tour of the Cape Canaveral facility. The tour turned out to be quite enlightening and he was intrigued about a certain nuance of time travel.

"Why do you have to time travel naked?" Christian asked his father over the hum of the micro-pulse generators at the heart of Spintronics time travel experimentation lab.

"Only organic matter can be transported," his dad explained. "It isn't that the subject has to be naked when they initiate the jump, but when they transport, any clothes they are wearing will simply fall to the floor and the time traveler will indeed be naked upon arrival at their target coordinates. The organic matter and the space enveloped within it form the equivalent of an electromagnetic Faraday cage. Skin infused with time transport enabling sub-atomic nanites forms an organic sheath, while cloths, not being within the sheathed boundary, stay behind."

Christian paused to inspect one of the micro-pulse generators in the test lab. "How is the jump location programmed into the test subject?"

"Sub-atomic nanites are encoded with unique coordinates identifying the time and location on the earth's surface that's to become the subjects' new space-time location," his dad replied. "We call it their space-timestamp."

"Can we specify locations other than Earth, like the moon, Mars, or beyond?" Christian asked.

"That's a great question," his dad nodded. "There's something about the continuity of life on the surface of the earth that allows us to calibrate our equipment to a known space-timestamp that the nanites can understand. The nanites can't infuse non-living material, nor do they seem to understand spatial coordinates that have no evidence of life. This doesn't mean we couldn't transport living matter to another planet, theoretically, if we knew the planet's space-time coordinates and it also supported life."

They made their way to the bio lab where animal test subjects were prepped for time travel and then analyzed upon their return. "Before we go in here," his dad cautioned, "I just want you to know this is where we're going to need your help the most. The test team is struggling with getting an animal to successfully complete a round trip. Your experimental techniques from Houston and your out-of-the-box thinking may be just what the research staff here needs. I know you'll enjoy the challenge, and besides, it would be nice to have you around."

Christian suspected his dad was onto something spectacular at Spintronics headquarters in central Florida, but he had no idea of the magnitude and ramifications of the sub-atomic nanite research being conducted. His former Houston team's molecular nanite breakthroughs paled in comparison. How could he not allow himself to be drawn in and become part of this fascinating research?

His dad opened the door to the bio lab to reveal a sterile hospital environment with cages, stainless steel tables, and medical equipment. They were met by the attractive, olive-skinned woman Christian had sat next to in the pub. "Claire, nice to see you again," Christian said with maximum charm. Until now the tour had been all business for Christian, and while he was genuinely enthusiastic about joining the Cape's time travel team, he couldn't help but be distracted by Claire's figure. He curtailed his instincts to look past her white lab coat. He extended his hand and kept a business-like manner.

"Nice to see you again, too, Christian," she said as she set a white mouse into its cage, brushed her hands on her lab coat, and extended her hand. She maintained eye contact and offered a firm shake. Christian sensed her strength and yet gauged her hand to be warm and tender.

His dad spoiled the moment. "Mind if I show Christian around the lab Claire?"

"Nope, go right ahead," she smiled, opening her arms in a welcoming gesture. "If you see any animals you like in here, please let me know." She held her gaze at Christian's eyes just a moment longer than necessary.

Christian spoke the instant he and his dad finished the tour of the bio lab and stepped into the hallway. "I think I'm going to like it here."

His dad raised an eyebrow and smiled. "See something you like in there, Son?"

Christian wondered if it was that obvious. "Yes."

"She's the best biologist we have. Treat her accordingly," his dad said sternly. "And yes, I think you're going to like it here. Let me know if the arrangements we've made for you to stay in the Cape visitor's housing works for you."

"Absolutely. I'm honored that you've asked me to join. I won't disappoint you."

Christian's dad left him to fend for himself for the rest of the afternoon, which gave Christian time to contemplate the upcoming challenges. He recalled how he initially became familiar with nanites and their application at the cellular level to combat his cancer. After exhausting conventional treatments for his diagnosis of advanced stage four melanoma, he was administered an experimental genomic treatment of cellular nanites. The nanites were specifically tuned to his DNA and designed to operate at a cellular level to bring cells of abnormal status back to their normal baseline, effectively curing his cancer. His understanding was that the nanites were now permanently infused into his body and that they continued to work at fighting the growth of cancerous cells. It seems to have worked so far as his cancer has officially been in complete remission for six years. Interestingly, the nanites have a continual side effect of rapidly healing cuts, bruises, burns, and abrasions; a consequence that has come in handy several mornings while shaving.

Christian suspected it was because of Spintronics' nanite research and his dad's status at the company that he was considered for participation in early human trials of the cellular nanite treatment. The initial prognosis for him with advanced stage four melanoma was fatal unless drastic treatment was implemented with urgency. The success of the nanite treatment in curing his cancer spurred his curiosity about further nanite research, a curiosity that became an obsession when he joined Spintronics as a research scientist at the Houston facility.

After the busy workday, Christian and his dad strolled to the parking lot. "Dad, when you helped found Spintronics, did you honestly expect it to become as big as it is now and for it to be doing the kind of breakthrough scientific research it's conducting?"

"Expect is too strong a word," his dad said. "We had a vision. We wanted to remain a private firm with the latitude to pursue what interested us most, which was nanorobotics technology. Dr. Nguyen and I, along with Dr. Goldberg—who is no longer with us—saw the potential for spectacular achievements in medicine, biology, and cosmology and we believed that a company founded on bringing that vision to fruition was warranted. The public is still relatively ignorant about nanite technology, but these microscopic robots are going to revolutionize everything from medical science to environmental science to time travel, as we've discovered." His dad smiled, "Drive safe, Son, see you tomorrow."

"Glad I'm here Dad," Christian smiled back. "Love you."

"Love you, too."

Cubepods

Next day, Christian found Cornelius taking a break in a common area just outside a cleanroom labeled Miniature Robotics Test Lab B. Cornelius wasn't alone. He was accompanied by a 3D holographic projection of an instructional video about the latest sub-atomic nanite research at the Berkeley site. The projection came from Cornelius' personal cubepod, the next generation in personal communications technology. Instead of providing video on a screen, the cubepod projected a 3D image that resembled a densely pixelated hologram. Cubepods had been on the market for a couple of years, but supply was still not keeping up with demand. The manufacturer had the foresight to utilize the cube's polished carbon surface as its solar recharging source, allowing the device to be recharged via the sun.

"Hey Cornelius, good to see you," Christian said. "I've been meaning to get myself one of those. I'm still using this outdated smart phone. I'm jealous whenever I see someone conversing with these Star Wars like holograms. It seems so real, you can practically touch it. "

"Oh, trust me, I know it. Mine was on backorder for months," Cornelius said. "Wait a second, this file is boring. Let me swap it out for one I pulled from the video library last night." Cornelius clicked a couple of buttons and in just a few seconds, The Grateful Dead, live in concert, projected from the cubepod. They marveled equally at the quality of the technology and the concert performance itself. Clearly the cubepod blows away all previous pod technologies known to man, Christian thought. They both enjoyed the front row view of the concert for a few moments.

"I think my father used to listen to these guys," Christian said.

"Wow, you're making me feel old," Cornelius grimaced.

"Sorry. But what great technology. It's so clear, like we're actually at the concert. What will they think of next?"

"They've already thought of it," Cornelius said. "We're going to be receiving beta units from Berkeley for a new communications technology that they've integrated with the cubepod. They've leveraged the angstrom thin memory arrays that drive the densely pixelated 3D image. Come to the cross-technology briefing this afternoon at 3:00 in the campus learning center and you'll hear all about this new breakthrough from Berkeley. They'll be conducting a live videoconference from California. Correction, a live 3D cubepod conference. See you there?"

"Roger that, three p.m. in the learning center. Looking forward to it."

Christian realized that one of the benefits of working in a private research firm was the occasional sneak peek at the latest technology before it went to market. Berkeley apparently found another use for the cubepod and Christian was looking forward to seeing what it was.

Christian spent the early afternoon continuing to meet headquarters staff, attaching names to faces and getting settled into his new office, which included your basic assortment of computer equipment. To that he added technical journals, sailing photos, a Bible on the desk, and an antique crucifix mounted on the wall. The office was nice to have, but he would be spending most of his time buried deep in the lab facilities of Spintronics. The next lab experiment he'd be able to observe wasn't until tomorrow morning, so as 3:00 approached he made his way to the campus learning center.

Christian surveyed the large center. It resembled a small auditorium that accommodated seating for about three dozen people with two rows of seats configured in a horseshoe. A small pedestal with a lone cubepod was sitting just below the large screen in the front of the room where Cornelius was standing and having a conversation with the Berkeley folks on the screen. The room was filling up with Spintronics staff curious to see the newest advancements coming from the Berkeley team. Cornelius signaled for everyone to settle in and then cued Berkeley to initiate the meeting. The screen shut down and, in its place, appeared a 3D projection of Dr. Piao-Li Nguyen "standing" in the middle of the room next to Cornelius. Dr. Nguyen was the Senior Technical Staff lead at the Berkeley site and one of the founders of Spintronics. He was revered as the technical champion of multiple advancements in sub-atomic nanite research.

Dr. Nguyen began the cross-technology briefing with a question. "Can anyone tell me what electro-magnetic signal propagation delay is?" Plenty of hands went up. This was not a hard question, as electro-magnetic signal propagation delay and digital processing delay of various media was a familiar phenomenon for this crowd. Dr. Nguyen smiled and pointed at one of the attendees raising her hand.

"Electro-magnetic signal propagation delay refers to the lag time between transmission and reception of an EM signal," the young lady replied.

"Yes, that is correct. The typical video signal delay is several seconds, depending on distance and transmission media performance. Please keep that in mind and observe the following," Dr. Nguyen said.

"Cornelius, select an attendee please." Cornelius grinned and pointed to Christian.

"Sir, allow me to introduce Mr. Christian Naismith," Cornelius said. "He joined us just this week to help work out some kinks in our nanite research."

"Mr. Naismith, this is quite an honor," Dr. Nguyen said. "Your father must be delighted to have you here with him." With that, Dr. Nguyen loosely cupped his fingers. "Let's have a race, shall we? Cornelius, in a few moments hold up a random number of fingers and let's see who can indicate the finger count first, me or the honorable Mr. Naismith." He paused. "Whenever you're ready."

Cornelius raised both hands, holding up four fingers on one hand and three fingers on the other. Christian took the race seriously and barked out as quickly as he could, "Seven." At the same moment Dr. Nguyen held up both hands, four fingers on one hand, three fingers on the other, and stated, "Seven."

The entire room of educated scientists and engineers sat for a moment dumbfounded. Dr. Nguyen should not have been able to signal his answer as rapidly as Christian. The delay of the signal processing to California and back should have added several seconds of propagation delay.

"What have we just observed?" asked Dr. Nguyen.

"You are responding in real time," Christian said.

"Very good Mr. Naismith, that I am. In fact, you're able to observe me making the observations in real time, just as if I were right there in the room with you, which I assure you I am not. You're there in Florida, I'm here in California and yet we are able to communicate without delay." He paused for effect. "This, ladies and gentlemen, is the unveiling of the latest breakthrough in sub-atomic nanite research from Spintronics Berkeley. Gone are the days of long distance communication transmission delays, and by long distance I mean any distance. This technology enables instant communication across the cosmic distances of light years."

Christian sat down, fascinated, and gave the discussion his full attention. He had always marveled at how messages from Star Fleet command were able to reach Captain Kirk over vast distances at speeds that obviously exceeded maximum warp. Apparently, Berkeley had come up with the technology to turn such conversations from fantasy to reality.

Dr. Nguyen went on to explain that this was a special modification to the cubepod. Berkeley figured out how to uniquely pair cubepods for instantaneous communication using Bell effect sub-atomic particle spin characteristics to facilitate digital communications.

"It's important to me that each of you grasp this concept, so this lecture is about to delve into the technical," Dr. Nguyen said.

"Hopefully we've piqued your interest and you can bear with me as we discuss electro-magnetic spintronics, Bell's theorem and quantum entanglement."

Christian remained captivated as Dr. Nguyen indoctrinated the class with the details.

"The Bell effect was named after physicist John Stewart Bell for his ground-breaking research into quantum mechanics and absolute determinism in the universe. The Bell effect was discovered incidentally when research scientists wanted to analyze the effect on individual subatomic particles that were otherwise paired in nature. To do this, the paired particles needed to be separated, the spin on one of the particles reversed and then the particles brought back together to see what would happen. In sub-atomic terms, the separation need not be far. The surprise finding was that when the spin on particle 'A' was changed, the spin on particle 'B' instantaneously reversed. It was determined that the paired particles would maintain their mirrored relationship regardless of the distance of separation: a meter, a kilometer, a parsec, it wouldn't matter," Dr. Nguyen again paused for effect.

"The Bell Effect transcends known conventional space-time physics and its implications are profound. Given banks of paired particles and translation of spin to the computer machine language of 0's and 1's, instantaneous digital communication is now possible across vast distances of space and time. In laymen's terms, this simply means that the signal values at both locations are synchronized, regardless of distance. At first, these communications were based on a crude Morse code, then graduated to 8-bit registers capable of transmitting ASCII character text. I'm proud to say, Berkeley has continued to integrate more complex banks of paired sub-atomic particles until they were ultimately integrated into the super dense memory array of the cubepod to produce the cosmic 3D walkie-talkie you see before you today."

The room exploded with astonishment.

"Please, please," Dr. Nguyen said to calm the audience. "Let me finish. We feel we're ready to send beta versions to the other facilities for further research on the technology. The Cape Canaveral site will be sent four additional beta-version cubepods that are uniquely paired. One will be paired with a companion cubepod in Atlanta. Another will be paired with its companion in Houston. The remaining two cubepods will be a paired and set aside for research as Cape Canaveral sees fit. This should be fun," Dr. Nguyen said. "Are there any questions?"

Hands went up and Cornelius pointed to a lab technician. "May I have one?" she asked.

"We'll probably have to share the ones we have," Cornelius said. "Any other questions?"

There were many and Dr. Nguyen graciously dealt with them all.

Christian walked out with Cornelius after the meeting and asked, "Who's in charge of our cubepods?"

"That would be your father," Cornelius answered. "He's delegated the Berkeley, Atlanta, and Houston linked cubepods to my care. I can't speak for the paired set. If you're interested in those, you'll have to speak with him."

"That's okay, it's more curiosity than necessity," Christian said. "Perhaps later."

Experiments

Christian was glad to see a familiar face on the lab tech team that would be conducting this morning's experiment. He had shared beers with Dominic Frazier a few nights ago and the two exchanged pleasantries. The guest of honor for the time travel experiment was a small white mouse named "Boomerang 52".

The team progressed to the point where they were able to send living organisms back in time and were now attempting to return them to the present, alive. Christian learned at the pre-briefing that they were still in the stage of experimentation where results were mixed and varied wildly. The mouse had already been infused with sub-atomic nanites with a past space-timestamp signature. This part of the process seemed to be working fine. Once activated, the mouse would be transported to a past space-timestamp coordinate as the new baseline of its existence. The newest factor in these experiments involved the attempt to return the mouse to the present, still living. To try and accomplish this they infused the mouse with a second set of sub-atomic nanites encoded with the space-timestamp of the moment of initial transport. Christian interrupted the pre-brief meeting. "Sorry to interrupt but it's important I understand the process. Why must the return space-time stamp be the moment of initial transport?"

"It's not possible to program the nanites to return the test subject to a timestamp any later than the moment of transport because future space-timestamps cannot be determined," Dominic said. "Nor is it ever permissible to program the second set of sub-atomic nanites to return the test subject any earlier than the moment of transport because the lab team is bound by the immutability of time. Had the team ever programmed a subject to return to a moment before they sent it, it would have appeared already, in its returned condition. Immutability of time is our bounding guideline. I can give you more background later how the accidental incidence of this very phenomenon led the team to discover that they were actually causing the test subjects to travel back in time."

"Understood," Christian said. "We can talk more later."

The pre-brief continued, mostly for Christian's benefit, on the defined repeatable procedures that the Cape staff had developed for each time travel experiment. If the test subject was successfully transmitted to the target destination and was transmitting status data, the technician would report that telemetry was established. If there was no telemetry, it meant there was no communication coming from the test subject for reasons unknown.

The moment of truth was at hand. A countdown was announced and at the count of zero the firing of an electro-magnetic micro pulse announced the transport of the target subject to its new space-timestamp. Christian was briefed to not be surprised at any results he saw. Yet, he was shocked when in the flash of an instant Boomerang fell flat on its side, dead.

"Well, that wasn't too bad," Dominic remarked calmly.

"We killed it!" Christian said.

"At least it's in one piece this time," another technician stated.

The room filled with other voices and buzzed with technical and procedural discussion.

"We have telemetry. Space-timestamp coordinates confirmed," Dominic said.

"Excellent," a technician replied. "Set on automatic monitor and record. Tag and label the test subject. Get it to the biology lab and have them assess cause of death as soon as possible."

Christian remained lost in thought, stepping through the experiment in his mind, catching up logically to where the rest of the test team already was. He had to step out of his space-time reference frame and get into the mouse's. To him, Boomerang appeared to never leave the table. The unfortunate thing just keeled over and died. In the mouse's reference frame, it time traveled. It went back in time to its target space-timestamp, existed for some indeterminable period, and then returned to the original space-timestamp from which it was sent. Unfortunately, it died somewhere along the way. Subsequent autopsy would reveal exactly how the mouse died but knowing when it died was anybody's guess.

Christian let the team complete experiment close-out procedures and then asked to spend some time with Dominic to pick his brain.

"Sorry for my stunned reaction in there this morning," Christian said.

"We should have warned you more explicitly I suppose," Dominic said.

"I wasn't ready for that," Christian admitted.

"Neither were we at first," Dominic said. "It took us a little while to figure out that our test subjects, while appearing to never leave, actually were traveling back in time and reappearing to the present. Sometimes the subjects don't return. But when they do, they are always dead."

"Hmm, that's perplexing," Christian said. "Talk to me about the kind of results you've seen so far."

"I've been here since the initial phases," Dominic said. "Where would you like me to start?"

"Start from the beginning. I need to know how we got here."

Dominic proceeded to recount the time travel experiments, going back a few years, leading up to this morning's experiment. "At first our work had nothing to do with time travel," Dominic said. "Spintronics was in the initial stages of injecting sub-atomic nanites into a test subject. Only certain test subjects would receive them, namely, only organic matter. We focused our work on small grasses, weeds, clovers, etc. We weren't expecting anything to happen other than successful infusion of the nanites into the subjects. Occasionally, the little sprig of vegetation would disappear. We didn't know why. As testing expanded to larger quantities of plants, the test teams began to observe statistically significant numbers of the vegetation disappearing. We began to infuse thousands of blades of grass at a time, each labeled and tracked after nanite infusion. It wasn't understood at the time what was happening to the blades of grass that were disappearing, so experiments were designed to focus on that phenomenon."

"Was the Berkeley site involved in the initial stages as well?" Christian asked.

"Yes, we collaborated with Berkeley," Dominic said. "They helped us correlate the grass blades that disappeared to variability in the manufacturing process of the sub-atomic nanites. With a few tweaks, Berkeley was able to help us generate a batch of nanites that caused a batch of a million clovers to disappear. Some of them reappeared across campus and beyond, with reappearance occurring more frequently closer to the epicenter of experiment. Lots of people saved the clovers as souvenirs. That's where Claire got those earrings you were commenting on the other day," Dominic grinned. "We had a couple of clovers shellacked and made into earrings as a welcoming gift when she first started with the team. Girls love stuff like that."

Christian nodded and returned the smile.

"What was interesting about the early clover experiment wasn't only the transport of numerous clovers to new locations around campus, but also the condition of the clovers after transport. Some of them were still fresh, some of them were withered to varying degrees, and some were almost completely dried up. It became obvious that the dead clovers spent a long enough time at their destination site to wither and dry. So, not only had the clovers been transmitted through space, they had also been transmitted back in time. And apparently, different clovers spent different amounts of time back in time. This hypothesis was confirmed when reports of clovers appearing around campus were correlated with the time of the clover experiment. Hence time travel was discovered and the science of sub-atomic nanite programming for purpose of time travel was created."

"Explain to me why the appearances of the clovers were so random around campus," Christian said.

"Sure, getting to that," Dominic explained. "Berkeley was able to attribute the cause of the clovers appearing around campus to small variabilities in the sub-atomic nanite programming. Through trial and error, Berkeley associated these small variations to a distinct location, at a distinct time. Thus began the process of calibrating sub-atomic nanites for test subject transport to a target place and time. Berkeley figured out a process by which to calibrate sub-atomic nanites to known space-timestamps, and it soon became their primary mission."

"That is so totally cool," Christian said.

"Yeah, right? However, there's still a relatively low percentage of success in the mapping process. Sometimes it takes Berkeley ten tries or more to successfully transmit a test subject to an uncharted target space-timestamp. But they decided that if you can send enough test subjects and send them quickly, a low success rate was tolerable. The Berkeley site is using bacteria as test subjects so even at a less than 10% success rate they are still making significant progress and not feeling guilty about killing their subjects, an issue some on our team struggle with. Berkeley is currently building a scatter graph to map past space-timestamps. They're able to target locations that support life, basically limiting target locations to the surface of the earth."

"Yes, my dad told me about that constraint," Christian nodded, and continued to listen as Dominic expounded on the time travel experiment results to date.

"I hadn't actually understood how Berkeley accomplished arranging for telemetry from the test subjects until I saw that cubepod demonstration yesterday afternoon," Dominic said. "They've evidently been lacing the transport nanites with Bell effect-like registers."

The background of the evolution of the Berkeley mission was helpful to Christian's understanding of how the sub-atomic nanite research was split between the Berkeley and Cape sites. Dominic's explanation about the plant and animal testing at the Cape reinforced Christian's understanding of the Cape mission.

"The animal time travel test results have been consistent with the plant testing results, which is nominally around 10% successful transport to target time and location," Dominic said. "The Cape staff struggled at first to understand the results during the early phases of testing. They often assumed that the experiment killed the subject, just as you initially thought at this morning's mouse experiment. It wasn't realized until later that the return of the dead subject represented their most successful attempts at completing a round trip. Suspicion developed when animals observed as instantaneously dying appeared in conditions that couldn't be easily explained, except in the context of a successful delivery at the target location. Notable exhibits include a mouse partially digested by a snake and a dove with a breast full of birdshot."

"So even though the animal's body appears to return here instantaneously, it lives for a period at the target location in the past?" Christian asked, astounded.

"Yes, exactly right," Dominic said. "Honestly though, the test team is frustrated by the fact that the return-to-sender stamp doesn't seem to be working right. Some of the legacy test subjects continue to send telemetry, so they're known to still reside at their target destination. One of the questions the team is trying to decipher is, why haven't all the test subjects come back yet? In the scheme of things, this morning's test was relatively successful."

"Except for the part about the mouse being dead," Christian said.

"If they come back, and that's a big if, they always come back dead," Dominic said. "That's our main problem. That, and not knowing how long they're living in the past. It seems random."

"Thanks Dominic, this background information has really helped me understand where we're at with the time travel experiments." Christian assessed next steps. "Can you point me to the biology lab? I'd like to find out the status on the autopsy of our mouse from this morning."

Christian found the bio lab and was surprised to see Claire there petting one of the guinea pigs. The bio lab was full of the sights, sounds, and smells of animal life. He had mixed emotions as he took in the scene, remembering the test results from this morning.

"Hello Claire. Good to see you again."

"Good to see you, too, Christian." Claire smiled.

"I came to check on the autopsy of the mouse from the experiment this morning. Do you happen to know if the lab has determined cause of death yet?

"Not yet," Claire said.

"What's the usual cause of death?"

"We've seen it all, Christian. Half eaten, squished, electrocuted, burned, poisoned, even death by simply old age. There are thousands of ways for them to die. I can tell you that none of our test subjects has managed to avoid that fate and find the successful path home alive."

The way Claire described it, Christian was reminded of the "choose your own adventure" books he read as a kid where each decision led the antagonist to some sort of demise.

"Clearly, at least a few of them fair well for a period of time at their new location," Christian said. "I wonder why their return time stamp doesn't work."

"The return jump remains indeterminate," Claire said. "We can control when and where we send them, at least we think we can, but we can't seem to control when they come back."

"Claire, your autopsy work is critical to our understanding of what's happening to these animals once they've reached their destination. The more we can understand what's happening, the closer we'll be to understanding why the return timestamp isn't working. I know it must be wearing on you to constantly have the test subjects return dead. Please persevere and I'll do my best to help the team figure this out."

"It has been frustrating Christian, and I'm truly glad you're here. I'll continue doing my part to help the team, as best I can."

"You're awesome, Claire," Christian said sincerely. "I think we're going to make a good team."

"I know we are." Clare smiled and added a little wink.

Christian managed a quick bite before returning to the test lab for the afternoon's experiment. The Cape Canaveral team settled into a routine of conducting two tests a day. Christian learned that they constantly varied the test subjects in hopes of finding a distinguishing pattern of results. This afternoon they were sending a small bird to the next space-timestamped destination programmed by Berkeley. As Dominic explained, Berkeley owned the programming responsibility for sub-atomic nanites since the necessary sub-atomic particle acceleration and isolation equipment resided at their facility.

Christian observed that the test procedures were conducted in the same manner as in the morning, but this time the results were different. The bird disappeared entirely from the lab table, but telemetry was secured, meaning contact with it at its target location was still maintained.

"We have telemetry, space-timestamp coordinated confirmed," the technician reported.

"Telemetry lost," the technician reported a few moments later, indicating the Cape was no longer receiving communication signals from the bird.

"Set to continue monitoring and record," the lab manager said.

Christian discerned that the afternoon's experiment was less successful than the morning's, because having no returned test subject meant the return timestamp failed completely.

Christian continued to monitor each experiment through the rest of the week and into the next. Each experiment failed to bring the test subject back alive and it didn't take Christian long to empathize with the frustrated staff. Christian felt the two-a-day testing pace was not a significant enough sample size to observe subtle trends that might help uncover the reasons for the return not working correctly. He thought of Berkeley and their scatter graph mapping of the space-time grid. Their sample size was huge. Christian wanted to see if there was a way they could collaborate with Berkeley to get more sample test data using their test subjects instead of subjecting more animals to time travel tests.

Christian sought out Cornelius and the Berkeley-linked cubepod that he was holding.

Cornelius wasn't hard to find. He was obviously having way too much fun with the cubepod hologram feature, Christian thought, as he heard *All Along the Watchtower* reverberating down the hallway. He reached Cornelius' office and stuck his head through the resonating guitar in the hands of the legendary Jimmy Hendrix. "Hello Cornelius, we need to talk."

Cornelius flipped a switch and grinned. "Hey Christian, what's up?"

"First of all, I love Hendrix. He was an absolute genius with the guitar."

"I'm surprised you even know who he was, especially given your comment about the Dead. Maybe I'm not so old after all."

"Well, I don't know about that. Ah, please," Christian held up his hands, "truce."

"Truce," Cornelius countered.

"Hey, I need a favor. Would it be possible to speak with Dr. Nguyen at Berkeley?"

"Sure, he usually makes himself readily accessible for discussions with us," Cornelius said. "Go ahead and call him."

"For this discussion, I want to use the Berkeley paired cubepod. Is that it?"

"Um, no, this one is paired with Houston." Cornelius was obviously not thrilled with the idea of yielding one of his toys. "How long do you need it?"

"A few days, maybe more, if you don't mind." Christian was still new to the processes at the Cape facility and wasn't sure of the protocol. Of course, the paired cubepods were something new to everyone, and it became obvious that Cornelius wasn't quite sure of the protocol, either.

"Has your father approved of you using the cubepod to speak with Berkeley?" Cornelius asked.

"Is he supposed to?"

"What do you say we check it out with him," Cornelius said as he dialed an extension on his speakerphone.

"Dr. Naismith here," Christian's father answered.

"Sir, I have your son here in my office."

"Yeah, he tends to poke around. What's up?"

"Hey Dad, I'm here and you're on speakerphone," Christian chimed.

"He wants to borrow the Berkeley linked cubepod," Cornelius said. "Do you approve and should I have him sign it out or something?"

"Yes, I approve," his dad said. "Are you thinking maybe we should chain it to a plank of wood, like a bathroom key?"

Christian watched the body language as Cornelius winced. "No sir, I don't suppose that'll be necessary."

"Neither do I," his dad said. "Just don't break it, Son, and tell Dr. Nguyen I say hello."

"Understood Dad, thanks."

Cornelius hung up and handed Christian the cubepod. "Okay hot shot, here's the cubepod linked to Dr. Nguyen's in Berkeley. Please don't take offense that I checked with your father. I'm a by-the-book kind of guy."

"I appreciate it, Cornelius. I'm glad we're all on the same page now."

Back at his office, Christian sorted out the few buttons and roll-ball controls on the cubepod, took a deep breath, and pinged its companion in Berkeley, indicating a conversation was desired. Seconds later, there was a 3D image of Dr. Nguyen's head sitting on Christian's desk.

"Hello Dr. Nguyen," Christian said. "This is my first time using a cubepod, how do I adjust the holographic display on this thing?"

"Hello Mr. Naismith, I figured you'd be the one to get hold of one of the linked cubepods," Dr. Nguyen said. "Use the roll ball to adjust the image to where you want it projected. You'll get used to it pretty quickly."

"Yes sir, I'm sure I will. I've been meaning to get one of the general cubepods for a while, but I'm still managing with an old smart phone."

"Ouch," Dr. Nguyen said. "That is antiquated. By the way, my friends call me Paul."

"Thanks Paul, and I'm Christian. Hey, I wanted to talk to you about the progress of sub-atomic level nanite research at the Cape. Specifically, the frustration the Cape is having with its time travel tests with animals. I wonder if Berkeley could help us work through some of the difficulties."

"Well that depends on what difficulties you're referring to," Paul said.

"There are numerous problems to solve," Christian began, "and it's difficult to address all of them, or really any of them, with our limited sample sizes. First, the rate of success for the initial transport of the test subjects is way too low to be anywhere near practical. We're not getting enough data to help us understand what's happening on the other side of the jump. If we could successfully transport more test subjects, we'd be able to figure out more rapidly what's happening to them. We need to double or triple the success rate of initial transport and anything you can do to improve that would be appreciated. Secondly, the telemetry is not dependable, either. Sometimes we get it, sometimes we don't, and sometimes it comes and goes. We have no idea why. Thirdly, the return space-timestamp is not working the way it was designed to. As you probably know, we've yet to have an animal come back alive."

"Fair enough, give us a couple of days and we'll see what we can come up with," Paul requested, making virtual eye contact. "Glad you're here Christian. I see a lot of your father in you. Let's fix this."

"Agreed and thank you. Talk to you soon."

Answers

Christian was once again conversing with Paul's hologram a few days later.

"We've been working on the first problem," Paul said. "We can increase the probability of successfully transmitting the test subject by repeatedly targeting the same space-timestamp location."

"How high can you increase the probability of success?" Christian asked.

"Looks like we can achieve 50%, even better when we transport to higher elevations," Paul said. "It seems targets that land on higher terrain tend to have better transport results. Specifically, mountain tops and hill tops produce more consistent results."

"How consistent?"

"If we combine the repeated targeting technique with a target location of a high mountain, perhaps 80%."

"That sounds a little more promising," Christian said. "Can you do me favor and send us specifications for experiments designed to repeatedly send to the same target and program some nanite batches for mountain top targets." He had one last question, for now. "Any thoughts on why the returning animals always come back dead?"

"We have no idea," Paul said, flatly.

Christian made sure the Cape test team received the specifications and began conducting time travel experiments accordingly. The team was sending five animals in rapid succession to higher elevation targets. The results were consistent with Paul's hypothesis of improvement, but the ramifications were even more difficult on the testing staff. Significantly more animals were successfully making the jump to their target locations and therefore even more were instantaneously reappearing on the test table dead. They were dealing with a half dozen or more dead animals each day. The carcasses were piling up in Claire's lab and she wasn't happy.

Claire called Christian to the lab and launched into a tirade. "Is there an actual real person with feelings inside that cold shell of yours? Do you see these dead creatures all around us in here? How can you remain so indifferent? It's disgusting. You have the gall to call this progress? We can tolerate doing the occasional autopsy on a test subject for the good of science, but we're still human beings with a conscience. You can only ask so much of a person before they crack and since you seem blind to it, let me open your eyes. We're already there. Just check the rate of lab staff calling in sick and you'll get the picture."

"I know it has been brutal, Claire. Believe me, I don't like it any more than they do."

"Well you had better do something about it, mister," Claire warned, "or you're going to find yourself without a lab team."

Claire's prediction was exactly right. Two technicians quit that week, fed up with the animal cruelty. People weren't going to tolerate this rate of animal sacrifice, nor could Christian blame them.

Christian consulted with his dad and together they agreed that low morale and failure fatigue were taking too much of a toll on their program and that a respite was required. They suspended the animal time travel experimentation, reverting to plants once a day to maintain their cadence and keep lab skills sharp. They'd have to come up with another solution to figure out the answers.

Christian pondered the impact he made on the time travel experiments. He pushed the team to the brink by increasing the test sample size without anticipating the ramifications. They were unable to perform meaningful root cause analysis because they lacked the necessary critical data to analyze. He knew what needed to be done. He just had to figure out the way to convince his dad and the rest of the team.

Christian owed his life to nanite technology. He wanted to give back to the scientific community that had given so much to him. He contemplated being the subject of an ultimate character challenge: You're handed a time machine. It can transport you backwards in time, but not forward, and it can transport you to any place on earth. It is 80% reliable and there is no return trip that you know of at this point that doesn't involve death. Where would you go and why? For Christian, there was only one answer and he began to formulate a plan to convince his dad of what needed to be done.

He decided to get out of the industrial complex setting and have this discussion over dinner the next evening. His dad was a perceptive man and had probably been awaiting an invite for some time. He readily agreed to the dinner date. Christian was apprehensive. There was no manual on how to tell your dad you intend to be the first known human time traveler.

He chose to conduct this important discussion at a classic Mediterranean restaurant with outdoor seating on the waterfront, to enjoy the Cape's location as a barrier island on the Atlantic Ocean and its fresh seafood. He made a point to order an Israeli Petite Syrah red wine to pay homage to the region he intended to travel to in antiquity.

At dinner, the two men settled comfortably into general conversation. His dad asked him how he was adjusting to his new digs and to the dynamics of the team.

"The apartment's fine and everyone at HQ has been great. They've all been supportive, and they've helped me get me up to speed quickly." He chose to leave out the part about being chewed out by Claire.

"That's great, Son. I've received a lot of positive feedback about you."

"That's nice to hear, Dad." He probably received some negative feedback as well, but words of affirmation were his father's primary love language.

"It's nice to be able to spend some time with you outside of work," his dad said. "But I get the feeling this isn't strictly a social visit. I suspect you're about to tell me something that's been on your mind. I've been patiently waiting to hear. I knew when you consulted with me about shutting down the animal testing that you'd be working on another plan."

Christian took a deep breath and began. "I'm pursuing the mission you charged me with. You asked me to join the Cape research team to help figure out why the time travel experiments were failing. As you know, we broke down the problem into separate solvable pieces and proceeded with experiments designed to optimize our results. By increasing the animal sample size we've learned a little more, but in the process, we stressed the system to its max. I've been consulting with Dr. Nguyen to see if he could help improve the space-time transport probability odds without us turning the animal test lab into a slaughterhouse. He's come up with some improvements we should be able to leverage."

Christian took a sip of wine and continued. "That said, we collectively can't seem to make any progress figuring out why the return trip results are always catastrophic. We simply don't know enough about what's happening on the other side of the jump and I have a suggestion."

"I'm listening."

"At this point, we're at a standstill because we're not receiving sufficient data from the destination side of the jump. We could send a hundred more rabbits and they're not going to be able to tell us what's happening. We need to get a human in the loop to figure out what's really happening." He paused and looked solemnly at his father.

"Dad, we need to send a person." Christian continued to look intently at his dad who appeared to be thoughtfully considering the concept before responding.

"Son, in my mind the goal of time travel is to get to the point where we can safely send a human back in time for historical research purposes. I believe, given the immutability of time, that the time traveler would be able to observe but in no way change historical events. I'm not so naïve to think that any kind of exploration like this is going to be perfect, but we're currently talking about a situation where no test subject has come back alive. I would *not* be comfortable asking anyone on Spintronics staff to time jump under current circumstances."

"Dad, hear me out please before you pass judgment on the appropriateness of the idea. I sincerely believe we have a situation with the animal test subjects that only a human is going to be able to fix. And, as far as asking anyone on Spintronics staff to make the jump, I agree with you, that isn't something we could ask anyone else to do." Christian paused before his next sentence. "In fact, I have no intention of asking anyone else to go. I'm determined to make the jump myself. "

"Absolutely not!" his dad said immediately.

"Now, hold onto your shirt Dad. From my perspective, I owe my life to nanite research. My cancer was terminal and if not for the cellular nanites engineered in Atlanta, I would not be here today having this conversation with you, and you know that. You've poured your life into this work, for the betterment of society, and now it's my turn to do the same. You and I both know that we couldn't charge anyone else with this mission, and yet you must also realize that somebody has to go if we're going to make any more forward progress. It is completely logical and appropriate that I be the person take on this responsibility."

Christian thought his utilitarian appeal would strike a resonant chord with his father. Still, he had never seen his dad cry and rarely did his dad let his emotional guard down, especially in a public setting. But now he saw watering eyes and he didn't know how to read them.

"Son, I know you feel deeply about giving back to the organization that saved your life, and more so to the cause that we both believe is helping to change the world for the better. My first thought is to say that I'm not ready to lose my only son to a mission that I don't feel has a high enough chance to be successful."

"Dad," Christian began.

"Wait," his dad interrupted. "I said that was my first thought. You're more like me than I care to admit at this moment. We're both very deeply committed men. I need more time to think about this. Let's revisit this discussion in the morning. Fair?"

"Fair."

"Good, now let's enjoy this meal, and this wine. I like your selection."

"I thought I'd try getting used to Israeli tastes," Christian said with a wink to his dad.

Christian went straight to his dad's office the next morning and wasn't surprised to find his dad already at work. He looked tired to Christian.

"Hi Dad."

"Son."

"You look like you didn't sleep much."

"How could I with your time travel on my mind?"

"I know. I'm sorry."

"Don't be. Listen, I'm not going to lecture you about the dangers of such a trip, you know them as well as I do. I'm not surprised that you want to be the one to take the risks needed to solve the mysteries with the time travel experiments. I can't say I'm particularly happy about the idea, but I will support you."

Christian let out a breath he didn't realize he was holding. "Thanks Dad, I'm really glad you came to this conclusion."

"Hold on. This is all on the condition that we diligently work to maximize your chance of success. I insist we bring every available Spintronics resource to bear to ensure your survival. If we're going to do this, we're going to do this right. I want senior technical staff at all sites informed and engaged. Work this through Paul. Inform him in your next discussion that you've managed to convince your father and that Spintronics should provide you any support necessary."

"Dad, I'm on it. Trust me, we both want this to be a success," he said.

"I'm sure you've put a great deal of thought into where you would like to go?" his dad asked.

"Honestly, since I'm doing this duty for research, I'd want the latitude to go someplace personally fulfilling. If Berkeley can program nanites to target 27 AD Galilee, that's where I'd like to go."

There was a long silence. Then both men smiled.

"Fair enough, you have my tentative blessing. If Paul confirms that Berkeley can target 27 AD, that's fine with me, but your priority is fixing the problem with the return jump and coming home safely."

"Thank you for this opportunity. You've always inspired me to take challenges head on. We can do this."

"If anyone can, I believe you can, Son. I support you and you know that I love you."

"Yes, I know you do. I love you, too."

That evening as Christian headed down Astronaut Drive to his apartment he made a mental note that he had yet to walk or bike to work. Once home, he tossed a half-smoked pack of cigarettes onto the kitchen counter and swore off smoking henceforward. There wouldn't be cigarettes where he was going so he needed to start the transition now. He'd also have to be doing a lot of walking, so he decided before bed that he'd walk to work in the morning.

Unfortunately, the next morning he felt pressed for time. He gulped down his coffee and jumped into the car for the quick trip to work. He was anxious to speak with Paul. He went to his office and called Paul on a conventional phone.

"Hello, Dr. Nguyen here."

"Hi Paul, it's Christian."

"Oh, hi. I'm surprised to get a call from you on my cell phone, especially this early. You usually use the cubepod. Nothing's happened to the cubepod has it?"

"No, no, I just wanted a more private conversation with you, one that couldn't be overheard." As Christian said this it occurred to him that it was roughly 5:00 a.m. in California. He was so anxious to talk to Paul that he neglected to consider the time difference. He probably should have gone ahead and walked.

"Sounds serious," Paul said.

"It kind of is," he confided. "You know that our most confounding problem with the time travel experiments is that we have no idea what's happening to the test subjects when they're transported back in time. Aside from the telemetry that we receive sporadically, we have no other data, including why the subjects appear to be staying in the past for varying lengths of time. We're going through all these experimental gyrations and we're still flying blind."

"Yes, I know that is most frustrating," Paul said.

"We could successfully transmit a hundred rabbits and not even one of them is going to be able to help us figure out what's happening on the other side," Christian said, his irritation showing in his voice.

"It would be nice to figure out a way a get more cognitive feedback from the target destination," Paul agreed.

"We need to get a human in the loop."

"Well, that would be nice, but I don't think we're there yet Christian."

"I'm suggesting we use a human test subject."

"Seriously?" Paul asked.

"Seriously."

There was an extended pause before Paul responded. "A human subject would certainly help, but so far it's been a one-way trip. We can't ask anyone to do that."

"I wouldn't ask just anyone," Christian said with conviction. "Let me ask you this: Theoretically, if we did have someone go back in time, about how far back could we send them?"

"We've already extended the space-timestamp scatter graph back several thousand years," Paul said, "but that's not necessarily reliable, as you realize. But Christian, when we're sending bacteria, or lab animals for that matter, it's not that critical. Sending a person would be an entirely different matter."

"What are the limitations for the target location?"

"We can transport the time traveler to anywhere on earth that supports life, more reliably on mountain tops, as you've helped us confirm," Paul said.

"If I gave you a time and location and Berkeley focused on it, are there any tweaks they could make to improve the probability of a successful transport?"

"Probably. We've been doing our best already, but I would certainly have them check again. What are you thinking Christian? Time travel for any human test subject is just not viable at this time, in my opinion."

Christian looked down at the *Bible* he was holding in his hand. His faith remained important to him. He hung onto his faith while beating cancer with help from the miracle treatment of the cellular nanites. Now he was resigned to give back to the field of nanite research that had saved his life.

"Not any test subject Paul, me."

There was silence on the line until Paul spoke again.

"Have you spoken to your father about this?"

"Yes, I've consulted with my father and he's on board."

Paul let out an audible breath.

"So, you've discussed this with your father and he agrees not only to the idea of sending a human back in time, but that you'll be that human?" Paul said, sounding both incredulous and skeptical.

"It took some convincing, but I eventually secured his blessing. This isn't a mission we would ask anyone else to accept, so I'm the logical choice to go. He did ask that you bring in senior technical staff from all sites to consult on optimizing my probability of safe return."

"I can do that, certainly."

"Paul, with the understanding that this may in fact be a one-way trip for our human test subject, wouldn't you say it would be a reasonable request for that individual to be given the latitude to request any place and time of their choosing?"

"I suppose, within the bounds of our technical capability and within the confines of a belief in the immutability of time. Yes, I think the test subject should have that right."

"Good, me too. I've been thinking about this for a while. Can you target a mountain top in ancient Galilee, near Nazareth, circa 27 AD?"

"I would think so, yes. Does this test subject also wish to meet Jesus?" Paul responded with a hint of sarcasm, still believing the conversation to be somewhat hypothetical.

"Given the choice of going back anywhere in time, 27 AD is where I would choose to go, and mostly for that reason, yes. Primarily though, my purpose, per emphatic instructions from my father, is to provide meaningful feedback from the destination site, to figure out what's causing the return trip to fail and what the subjects are doing when they're back in time."

"Christian, I'm still not sure about this," Paul began.

"If I take one of the new cubepods with me," Christian interrupted, "will it still be able to communicate with its paired companion here at headquarters once I've jumped back in time?"

"If you're asking if a cubepod transported to the past will continue to communicate with its companion cubepod located in the present, I don't see why not. We're already doing that on a more rudimentary scale to establish telemetry with the animals we send."

"Very good, that's one hell of a walkie-talkie you guys built. I'll be taking one of them with me. We're going to be depending on the paired cubepods for communication, so we can actively work out the issues we're trying to solve."

"I'm sorry Christian, but I'm still a bit dumbfounded that Spintronics is even considering this."

"Can I ask that you contain conversation about this mission to only senior technical staff for the time being?" Christian asked. "The matter of sending a human test subject is sensitive and I don't want the teams distracted at this moment."

"Yes, of course. I have reverence for your father. He and I go back a long time. I trust the two of you will proceed cautiously with this and I assure you full support from senior technical staff."

"I appreciate that Paul."

"I'll get the sub-atomic nanite programmers focused on your target. I'll also pull in senior staff and then I'll wait for further word from you. I have to tell you, Christian, that I'm also going to have a conversation with your father about this."

"I would expect nothing less Paul. I'll be in touch with next steps as soon as possible."

Christian ended the call. He glanced at the *Bible* and the crucifix on the wall and thought about what it would be like to meet Jesus.

Homework

Christian leaned back in his office chair and contemplated the task before him. He needed to make sure he was fully briefed on all the time travel experiment results to date so he could focus on the remaining knowledge gaps. He also wanted to fit in reasonably well with the society he was travelling to, so he needed to study their language and culture. His light brown skin would fit right in, but he probably needed to grow a beard.

He combed through the time travel experiment notes for hours, reconfirming the results of the testing to date. The information about what was happening to each test subject was limited to its telemetry data, as reported by Dominic and the rest of the test team, and its autopsy, as reported by Claire's lab. He felt confident that a human test subject would be able to fill in the missing knowledge gaps by communicating with the test team real-time through use of the paired cubepods.

Christian chose the time and location for his trip because Jesus' life was, for him, the single most influential event in all human history. He was awestruck by the thought of meeting Jesus in person, of hearing him preach and seeing him perform miracles. He knew enough about the *Bible* to realize that Jesus would be living in or around Nazareth at the beginning of his ministry and that the first major miracle would happen at the nearby city of Cana.

Christian knew ancient Palestinians were multi-lingual. He needed to learn basic Aramaic, the language generally accepted to be the native tongue of Jesus, to communicate casually with the local population. He may have to learn Greek as well, since it dominated as the language of public conversation in Palestine. He'd focus less on Hebrew, the language of the Jewish synagogue, and Latin, the language of Palestine's Roman occupiers. Interacting with church officials or the ruling Romans was not on his agenda. Christian just wanted to be able to understand Jesus when he met him. Arriving in 27 AD, he reasoned, would put him in Palestine at the cusp of Jesus' ministry. Jesus would not have begun his Galilean ministry yet and would still be living in or near his hometown of Nazareth.

Christian wanted to have reference material readily available to him after he jumped and for that he needed to do some prep work with the paired cubepod. He picked up the phone and called his dad.

"Dad, Cornelius tells me you're in charge of the paired cubepods that Berkeley sent us. It's my understanding, per Paul, that the paired cubepod will function as my communications link back to headquarters after I jump. There's some reference material I'd like to download in advance. Can I have one now?"

"Yes, that makes sense. You take one of the Cape's paired cubepods and I'll hang onto the other one, for now. Come to my office and get it whenever you like."

"Thanks Dad, sounds like a plan." Christian appreciated that his dad didn't ask a lot of details about exactly what he wanted to download and why. Over the years they had developed a mutual appreciation of not over communicating with each other. When matters were sensitive, they would answer each other's specific questions and often no more, respectful of boundaries. It was one of the many traits he admired about his dad.

Christian was able to download Babbel tutorials for Greek and Aramaic to the HQ paired cubepod he was now claiming as his own. Being able to work in advance with the cubepod he would eventually be taking with him was a good arrangement.

Christian made efforts with his physical appearance to help him blend into the ancient Palestinian society. He began to spend more time in the sun to darken his skin, something he usually avoided after his cancer diagnosis. He stopped shaving and let his hair grow scraggly. These changes attracted both curiosity and criticism from other team members, including Claire, who apparently liked the beard but criticized the outdoor sunning. Fortunately, it didn't take long for his skin to bronze and, in his defense, he pointed out that he had quit smoking.

After a couple of weeks, Christian had established a tan, grown a modest beard, and developed rudimentary Aramaic language skills. He hoped Berkeley was making effective use of the time to hone the nanites they were programming for him. It was time to check in again with Paul. He pinged him on the Berkeley linked cubepod and Paul's 3D image appeared.

"How's our special research project progressing Paul?" Christian asked.

"We've been working on targeting the time and location you've specified and have confirmed that we can target 27 AD. We've managed to deliver test bacteria to the ridgeline of Mt. Kedumim just to the west of Nazareth with a reliability consistent with previous results, perhaps marginally better. The repeated targeting has helped us refine the nanite programming for that space-timestamp, however, there are other variables not in our control, or at least not within our understanding."

"What are the odds?" Christian made eye contact with Paul's 3D hologram.

"Slightly better than 85% for successful transport for our test subjects."

Christian frowned, he had been hoping for better. "What about tuning to my DNA?"

"These sub-atomic nanites aren't like the cellular nanites that cured your cancer, Christian. These operate on a sub-atomic level where DNA distinctions between humans, or between animals, or even between animals and plants shouldn't matter. Now that we've fine-tuned the programing to Mt. Kedumim as best we know how, I'd hate to let the team mess with that calibration."

Paul paused, then offered the following procedural suggestion. "We've noticed that the odds of successfully sending subjects increase when they're sent in bunches. For example, if we've successfully transported test subjects to the target multiple times in a row, the transport odds of the next test subject seem to improve slightly. It appears that the equipment can zero in on the target more consistently the more we send to the same target. Statistically speaking it evens out, of course, since the failures can also come in bunches. What I'd say is we should design the transport of our human subject around being within one of these hot streaks of success. The odds should be better at that moment."

"Sounds like a gambling casino strategy," Christian said.

"It probably is, but in this case, it's based on science and the stakes, as you know, are high. We want to offer you any edge we can."

"I appreciate that. What about telemetry?"

"There's no variability in telemetry for us since we use only bacteria. That only happens with the animals," Paul said. "You're going to have to analyze that problem at the Cape."

"Okay, sit tight a few more days. Thank you for your suggestions. I'll get back to you soon." The office dimmed as Paul's image faded. Christian wondered what the calculated odds were for any of the other bold adventurers of mankind. What were the odds for Christopher Columbus or Neil Armstrong succeeding in their missions? He suspected they'd have accepted even longer odds than what Berkeley just offered. Christian charged ahead. He still needed to work on the telemetry problem, and to do that he needed to speak with Dominic. He found him the test lab.

"Dominic, good to see you." The men shook hands. "You've stuck with the program through a difficult situation with the animals and I really appreciate that."

"Hey Christian, you don't need to butter me up. I'm committed for the long haul. I'll be one of the people turning the lights out, if it comes to that. What's up?"

"The Cape's animal test subject telemetry results are inconsistent. Berkeley doesn't seem to have any telemetry problems with their bacteria test subjects. Is there any analysis we can do to help us figure out why we have the issue and they don't?"

"We'd need to thoroughly scrutinize the test data," Dominic said. "Perhaps there are patterns that have developed from the larger sample sizes that we've not previously noticed. What exactly are you looking for?"

"Can you tell me if there are any times when telemetry results seem better than others? I'm looking for any kind of an edge in the next level of experimentation."

"And what level would that be?" Dominic raised an eyebrow.

"Please just have the team analyze the data, it's important." Christian wanted to keep plans close to the vest for now. He headed back to his office.

Dominic was at Christian's office door a few hours later.

"Birds!" Dominic was out of breath from the run. He was excited about a discovery associated with birds.

"What about birds?" Christian asked.

"Birds provide consistently better telemetry results. Sometimes telemetry comes and goes with them, but even intermittent telemetry is better than radio silence. We really don't know why they should provide any different telemetry results, just that they do." He shrugged but kept the excited smile on his face at the revelation. He saw the contemplative expression on Christian's face and asked, "Do you have any idea why?"

"Maybe," Christian said. "Berkeley says that they have better success targeting space-timestamp locations at higher points. If it's simply a matter of getting high enough above ground level to overcome cosmic interference, then it would make sense that the birds, flying as they do, would consistently provide better telemetry as well."

"Oh, that's interesting. I didn't have that insight. Might have been a useful parameter to know." Dominic cocked his head.

"Yeah, sorry, I didn't want to bias your team's analysis," Christian said. "I assure you, this is an extremely helpful observation. You'll see it play out in the next phase. Thank you so much."

Christian felt like he had done his due diligence. Berkeley had refined the nanite programing, they had identified sequential patterns of transport success, and now the Cape team understood how to maximize telemetry results. Still, no progress was being made understanding why the return trip wasn't working. Solving that riddle was one of the primary purposes of getting the human in the loop.

Christian was ready to talk to his dad again. A business discussion in dad's office would suffice this time.

His dad's office door was open when he went to visit, but he knocked anyway to get his attention.

"Hey, come on in."

Christian sat down across from his father, leaned forward, placed his elbows on the desk, and waited for eye contact. "Dad, the senior staff has made great strides with optimizing the space-timestamp targeting and jump capability. The way the test will be structured, the odds are strong that I'll be successfully transmitted to the target location. It's a little scary to verbalize, but nevertheless true that we should be able to send me back to 27 AD."

"That's good news to hear Christian."

"My focus when I get there will be to help the Cape and Berkeley teams sort out why there are difficulties getting the return timestamp to work right and what the test subjects are encountering. I've scrutinized the test results to date and feel I'm fully ready to do my part."

"Ok, so you're ready to expand the preparation efforts and include the larger team?"

"Yes, exactly, I think it's time. We're into the final planning stages and we'll need the full support teams to make final preparations."

"I agree, it's time," his dad said. "Is there anything else?"

There it was, an open-ended question. His dad didn't often leave an opening quite that wide and when he did, it was purposeful.

"I was just thinking about how fortunate I am to have you as a father and how much I cherish our conversations," Christian confided. "I just want to let you know, I can't imagine having any other dad in my life than you."

"Son, we have a special relationship; we always have. You've been a blessing from the first day you came into our lives. It was a big decision for your mom and I to decide to adopt. Our pastor was thrilled as well, but advised us to be patient, thinking it would be a lengthy process. We were amazed when that same week a baby was left on the steps of our church in Nevada. When the pastor contacted us and informed us that our baby had arrived, we knew you were a gift from God."

"I believe that, too, Dad."

"You were the answer to our prayers. Now my prayers focus on the prospect of having to let you go on this journey. I cherish our discussions, too, and while you're on the other side we can use the cubepods to keep them going."

"Dad, you inspire me on so many levels. I love you for that."

"I love you too. Let's get this company spun up to help you succeed."

All In

Spintronics had vast resources. The Atlanta, Houston, Berkeley, and Cape Canaveral research sites employed some of the best minds from around the world. Christian would have every advantage that modern medical, molecular, and cosmological science had to offer. Cross-site cubepod conferences were held regularly, often with what was becoming the familiar sight of 3D images from cubepod conversations.

Atlanta synthesized a cellular-level general inoculation, which they felt would protect Christian from the known contagions of ancient Palestine. They confirmed that the nanites that had cured his cancer were still functioning quite well.

Houston contributed their molecular nanite technology. The latest generation of molecular nanites were self-programing and therefore multipurpose. They'd afford Christian survival tools in an unpredictable and unsanitary environment.

Berkeley analyzed the success patterns of space-timestamp transport and designed an experiment structure that would maximize success probability by transporting the human subject within a confirmed hot streak. They constructed models to calculate the best time of day to arrive to optimize survival of the time traveler in the midst of an ancient society.

Cape Canaveral arranged the test lab to accommodate the experiment design and prepared the most appropriate animal test subjects for confirming telemetry from the target location.

The team practiced considerable dry runs over a period of a few days, simulating various scenarios they may have to deal with during the live test. They'd be as prepared as possible for the monumental event.

Christian was in his office late afternoon on the eve of his jump. He was apprehensive and excited at the same time. The only thing he could think to do was pray. Then he heard a knock at the door.

"Come on in," he said.

The door opened, and Claire stepped into his office. "Tomorrow is a big day." Claire smiled.

"That's an understatement." Christian smiled back.

"How about we get a beer? My treat," she invited.

He accepted the invite. One beer led to another and their evening stretched late into the night. Claire was extra sweet to him at the pub, which continued when they returned together to his apartment. The gentle touches and familiar discussion provided him the telltale signals that he was a man being seduced. His admittedly shallow male mentality was hopeless to resist the amorous overtures from an attractive, lithe, and intelligent woman. Nevertheless, he valiantly tried to clear the air of any possible misinterpretations of what might happen throughout the night. "Claire, you know I'm not going to be around to follow up on whatever happens tonight, right?"

"Yes silly, I know that," Claire rolled her eyes. "Men are so naïve. Let me fill you in on a little secret when it comes to women. Timing is everything. It's true, timing often inhibits, but sometimes, timing can liberate. Tomorrow is a big day for you. Let's just say tonight's your lucky night."

Christian considered himself to be just a regular guy. He had no delusions of himself flaunting virtues amongst society. Besides, in his experience, the woman was always in charge of this sort of thing anyway, and if Claire was hell bent on getting him laid that night, who was he to stop her? Tomorrow was a big day for him, and it could easily be his last day, with him being vaporized into nothingness by subatomic nanites.

Christian decided to live in the moment. He rationalized that there was a limited number of "first times" in life, and in this case, it could likely be a last time. He threw himself into work at HQ and hadn't been with anyone since the breakup with Bonnie. His arousal told him, and clearly communicated to Claire, that he was ready to spend his last evening entwined between a woman's thighs.

Her supple lips met his and locked. She didn't make him play red light, green light with her body. As the clothes dropped to the floor, the discovery process of what their bodies offered each other progressed. Their subsequent mutual orgasms assured that neither was left disappointed.

Claire stayed and nestled tenderly with Christian through the night. Christian was used to sleeping alone, but that night he appreciated the comfort of being cradled in her arms. He slept soundly as night stretched into morning.

"Christian, wake up," Claire nudged him. "We need to head into the lab in less than an hour."

Christian was bleary eyed as Claire placed a steaming cup of coffee by the bedside. He had been working relentlessly, spending countless long hours preparing for this day and now he had less than an hour before the start of the main event. The endorphins from intercourse weren't enough to overcome the hangover, but adrenaline and coffee would have to be enough to get him going this morning. He seated himself on the bedside, picked up the cup, noted its dark cream color and inhaled its aroma. The coffee was prepared just the way he liked it. "I'm going to miss this."

"The coffee, or the sex?" Claire asked.

"Well, they won't have coffee in first century Palestine," he answered.

Claire's cold stare of disapproval reminded him that clever comments are best left unsaid. He tried to recover. "Both of course." But it was too late. It would take flowers, and maybe chocolates, to dig himself out of that hole, but he'd have time for none of that this morning.

"Seriously, thank you for the coffee. You've been sweet to me. But, you go on," he said to Claire. "I'll meet you at the lab."

Claire set aside her playful mood and turned serious. She grasped both his hands, looked him square in the eyes and said, "I rushed last night because I'm afraid I won't see you again. Prove me wrong." Then she kissed him briskly and bolted out the bedroom door.

Christian put thoughts of Claire aside and dressed casually. He picked up the pack of Marlboro Lights that was on his dresser; the idea of one last smoke appealed to him. He lit a cigarette on his way out, nonchalantly brushing his fingers across the "No Smoking" sign mounted by the door. He surveyed his spartan apartment and realized it was time for one last conversation.

"Alexa, close the blinds, turn out the lights, and moderate the temperature. I'm going to be gone for a while."

"Christian, where are you going?" Alexa replied in her pleasant female voice. Christian continued to be amazed at the level of discernment achievable by modern artificial intelligence systems. He decided to answer Alexa's question directly.

"I'm travelling back in time to ancient Palestine, around 27 AD. I need to fix some bugs in our time travel experiments."

"Do you intend to meet Jesus while you're there?" Alexa asked.

"As a matter of fact, I've thought that might be nice."

"All right, see you in three years," Alexa said.

Christian thought this reply odd from a computer ostensibly designed to manage home electronics. He figured Alexa's integration with Watson technology must be paying dividends. "Why do you say, 'in three years' Alexa?"

"Archives indicate the ministry of Jesus lasts approximately three years from the time of its initiation in Cana, Galilee," Alexa replied. "Be aware your uRide taxi has arrived out front. Have a good trip Christian. I'll turn the lights out after you leave."

Christian decided to refrain from explaining to Alexa that he had no intention of staying for the entire ministry of Jesus. "Okay Alexa, thank you," he said and strolled out to catch his ride.

Jump day at Spintronic's HQ started with briefings for the test and support teams, followed by system checks across the board. All sites were online with a live cubepod broadcast of the event. Medical staff stood ready with several pints of blood Christian had donated in advance.

Christian was administered a series of sub-atomic nanite injections as the designated jump moment approached. These nanites, programmed to send him to Galilee 27 AD and to return him to the present time, would fully infuse his body. Most importantly, they'd infuse the organic tissue in his skin, forming the time traveling equivalent of a Faraday cage. Everything within the boundary of his skin would transport to the target location.

Christian wore a modest hospital gown. What he was wearing wouldn't matter if the jump proceeded as planned; his clothes would drop to the floor when his flesh made the jump. He saw his co-workers and friends waiting to support him as he entered the lab. He greeted and sincerely thanked each in turn. He shook hands with Lab Technician Dominic, who was so critical with his testing experience and Operations Manager Cornelius, who had introduced him to the Bell-effect linked cubepod technology. He pecked Lab Biologist Claire on the cheek. Claire glowed with a satisfied smile and sported crease lines of concern on her forehead at the same time. He noticed Paul at Berkeley and nodded in acknowledgment. Lastly, he hugged his dad who was standing proudly amongst the staff to support him.

The experiment design was slightly different this time, noticeable by the small flock of a dozen white pigeons lined in a single column beside the electro-magnetic micro-pulse generator that would activate the sub-atomic nanites already in their systems. Each bird had a clover shaped tattoo on its breast so Christian would recognize them at the jump site. They couldn't use normal foot bands since those wouldn't go with the birds when they jumped.

Christian turned to Dominic and quizzically said, "Doves?"

"We only send indigenous species and I thought they were appropriate," Dominic said smiling, obviously quite proud of himself. "Claire procured them especially for the occasion."

"I see, thank you for the nice touch you two. Let's see if they bring us luck today," Christian said sincerely.

There was a buzz of excitement in the test lab. Cornelius got everyone's attention and after brief introductions, turned the explanation of the test protocol over to Christian's father.

"This experiment is designed to maximize the probability of sending our first human time traveler," his dad said, nodding in Christian's direction, "to the space-timestamp of his choosing. As most of you know, he has chosen 27 AD, in the regions of Galilee, for personal reasons. His primary mission will be to help Spintronics further its time travel research, hopefully clearing up several currently unanswerable questions. Let me state, on behalf of myself and all of Spintronics, how proud we are of you, Christian, on this day." The room filled with applause, which Christian received graciously. "I now turn the floor over to Dr. Nguyen."

"Thank you, sir," Paul said. "This experiment is designed to take advantage of subtle probabilistic differences we've observed during the sequential transport of multiple target subjects to a solitary space-timestamp. We'll be sending these birds you see in the room in sequence ahead of Christian, to the exact same target timestamp we've programmed for Christian. This target is well known to us by now in Berkeley as we've been working with it since we were first approached with this proposal. It is a high probability target on a ridge top in the region of Galilee. We'll transport Christian to the target destination only in the midst of what we've termed a successful hot streak, defined as the successful sequential transport of five test subjects to a single target location. While we expect to be able to achieve a hot streak with these dozen birds, it is possible that we may not, at which point this test will be aborted. Please don't be disappointed if that happens, as it would be for Christian's protection. There are far worse scenarios than having to re-calibrate and try again another day."

Paul yielded the floor back to the Cape staff. Cornelius signaled for test and support stations to provide status checks. All stations were go for experiment commencement. "We are a go for human time travel initiation," his dad announced. "Godspeed, Son." With that final invocation, the jump sequence began.

The lab team huddled around bird #1, preparing it for its time travel jump. In a few moments it was ready. Claire moved to stand next to Christian, cubepod and plastic baggie in hand. A countdown announced that the moment of jump initiation was coming. At the count of zero, there was a dull flash and the white pigeon immediately lay dead at the bottom of the cage.

Christian winced at the sight of the dead bird. Its head lay awkwardly backwards against its back and dark red blood was oozing across its body from its fully exposed neck. The sight reminded him of why he had called a halt to animal testing in the first place.

"Positive telemetry," Dominic announced.

"Successful transport, first of series," Cornelius said.

The positive telemetry told them the bird was alive at its target destination and yet the visual effect of the deadly return trip wore heavily on the collective spirit of the lab team, especially because the life of their first human test subject hung in the balance. They rallied and began preparations for transport of bird #2.

Claire leaned in near his ear. "When the time comes, you're going to have to listen to my instructions carefully. Be ready."

"Yes dear," Christian said. Claire ignored the term of endearment.

The next countdown began and soon another dull flash signaled the transport of bird #2. It completely disappeared.

A few moments later Dominic announced, "Negative telemetry."

"Failed transport," Cornelius said.

The test staff prepared bird #3.

Christian leaned towards Claire and whispered, "Why am I oddly more comfortable with the failure than I am with the success?"

"You're not the only one," Claire said.

Another count down, another flash. This time bird #3 lay motionless at the bottom of the cage for no obvious reason. The staff examined the bird and confirmed it was dead.

"Positive telemetry," Dominic said.

"Successful transport, first of series," Cornelius said.

The next countdown began, and another flash occurred. Bird #4 disappeared.

"Negative telemetry," Dominic said.

"Failed transport," Cornelius said.

They were back to the beginning of rebuilding a successful series, which began with bird #5 and continued through bird #8. Each dull flash produced a dead bird, some gruesomely so, including bird #8, which had evidently been crushed and partially chewed to death. Dominic and Cornelius announced positive telemetry and successful transport in succession for each bird. Claire placed her hand gently on Christian's shoulder and his dad maneuvered his way to stand on the other side of Christian. His dad put his hand on Christian's other shoulder in a sign of support. Claire leaned towards Christian. "If this next dove transports successfully, we're in a hot streak and you're next. You'll need to put this cubepod and this baggie into your mouth and shut it tight so they travel with you. The cubepod is waterproof to 10 fathoms, so it'll be fine."

Christian nodded in acknowledgment of the instructions.

Suspense was building for the transport of bird #9. At the count of zero, there was a dull flash and bird #9 completely disappeared.

There was silence in the test lab. There were only 3 birds remaining, not enough to rebuild a hot streak of 5 successive transports.

Christian noticed Cornelius hesitating. He made eye contact with Dominic and received a telltale wink. Christian had remained relatively quiet through the exercise so the sound of his voice, combined with the collective silence at the disappearance of bird #9, commanded instant attention.

"Technician Dominic, do we have telemetry?" Christian asked.

"We have positive telemetry," Dominic confirmed.

"Dr. Nguyen, can you confirm that bird #9 is a successful transport, indicating we are now in a hot streak?" Christian said to the 3D image of Paul.

"The positive telemetry indicates the bird has successfully transported to the target location," Paul nodded. "Its failure to return is an indication of another problem, the one you are going to investigate, but it is not a failure of the destination timestamp. I agree we are now in a successful hot streak."

Christian shifted his gaze back to Cornelius.

"Successful transport, fifth of series," Cornelius announced. "It's confirmed we are now in a hot streak. Prepare Christian for transport as the first human time traveler."

"Open wide tough guy, you're going to need these," Claire commanded. Christian obliged and into his mouth, left cheek side, went the cubepod. Into his mouth, right cheek side, went the sealed plastic baggie of molecular nanite capsules. He was too busy feeling like a chipmunk to be as nervous as he otherwise might have been under the circumstances.

The lab team moved deliberately. Christian adjusted his stance into what he could only imagine was a good landing position. The lab team aligned the pulse generator to his left shoulder. His dad squeezed Christian's shoulder then released his hand and stepped back as the countdown began. Christian glanced at his dad. His dad brought his left hand to left ear and with thumb and pinky extended he mouthed, "Call me," to his son. Christian nodded in agreement. Somewhere around the count of five he began to wonder if this was going to hurt, 3-2-1 and the lab disappeared in a dull flash.

Birth ~ 27 AD

The scene before him instantly morphed to an obscure landscape. Christian, the time traveler, arrived slightly disoriented near the summit of a rocky, brush-covered mountain. The visual his mind was processing yielded to the immediate sensation of a chilling mountain breeze scraping across his naked body. The sky's ambient light told him it was either dusk or dawn and after a moment of observation, he reasoned it was early evening. He noticed the silhouettes of several doves fluttering in the darkening sky. They probably had a better idea of where to go than he did.

It was early winter at his new location. The nights would come quickly and would be longer nearer to the equator. The thought was that with an evening arrival time he'd hopefully appear without much notice, would have enough time to find a place to settle in for the night, and would be able to develop a plan of action for his next day.

Christian extracted the cubepod and plastic bag from his mouth and, having no other place to put them, held them in his hand. He scanned the horizon, briefly taking in its splendor. It was quickly getting darker. It was already too dark for him to tell if there were any towns in the valleys below, not that he would've headed that way in his current attire.

His priority was to find clothing and someplace to stay for the evening. He clumsily explored barefoot across unfriendly terrain. He heard a flock of sheep, followed their wavering cries, and was fortunate to find a young shepherd setting up his nighttime camp. Christian was able to communicate just well enough with the boy to convey that he needed a little help. He half expected the boy to glibly reply something along the lines of him obviously not being from around here. Instead, he recognized the simple Aramaic phrase, "Follow me."

The boy led him to a stable just down the hill, urged him inside, and gave him the universal palms down signal, "stay here". Christian obliged. He avoided disturbing the lone donkey occupying the stable. He found some ragged clothes in one corner of the stable to bundle himself in and lay down in a pile of hay to wait out his first night. His commitment was to check in when he found a safe place to settle. He gripped the cubepod in his hand and hoped the reception in the stable would be sufficient. He pinged HQ. The answering ping came quickly, and a 3D image of his dad appeared before him in the stable.

"Son, very good to hear from you!"

"Yeah Dad, it's nice to see this technology works, that's for sure. I'm checking in just to let you know I'm safely settled in for the evening." A wave of relief swept over him at being able to communicate with HQ, and especially to be speaking with his dad this first night in this strange time and land.

"Roger that. I won't keep you long. I see you found some rags and shelter," his dad observed.

"Yes, fortunately I have. I'll get more oriented and find something better tomorrow. Don't worry about me, I'm fine."

"Good to hear. Tomorrow will be a busy day. You take care. I Love you."

"I love you, too, Dad."

The image of his father faded and suddenly Christian felt very alone. He recalled the comfort he had enjoyed just one night previous in Claire's arms. He glanced down at his near naked body and noted that this was reference day zero for the sub-atomic nanites infused into his body, their birthday, so to speak. The stable smelled earthy, and the foul smell of the nearby donkey crept into his nose. Christian assumed fetal position, cradled himself in his own arms, and managed to fall asleep.

Christian awoke the next morning to the sound of dozens of sheep vocalizing their pleasure at the rising of the sun. The first order of business was to secure more appropriate clothing. He scanned the stable and spotted an empty feed sack, which he put to immediate use as a carrying bag for the cubepod and plastic baggie. He was grateful there was nobody else in the stable, other than the donkey, to view the naked man with the sack.

He eased open the stable door and the first thing he noticed was a flock of sheep. The second thing he noticed was a linen cloth and a rope draped across a wood railing by the stable entrance. The linen cloth turned out to be a common tunic and the rope clearly was meant to serve as a belt. A pair of basic leather sandals was placed by the rail's post as well. A large jug of water, a ceramic drinking cup, bowl of dried fruit and some cheese rounded out the display. The Berkeley model certainly couldn't have anticipated this kind of good fortune.

Christian located the shepherd boy and attempted to thank him, but no language tutorial could've prepared him for this kind of full immersion. Still, he was able to glean the boy's meaning as the boy gestured to Christian's clothing and repeated a word Christian recognized as "gift" several times. How this shepherd boy managed to obtain these clothes and food and why he bothered would likely remain a mystery. Christian's first impressions of this ancient society were certainly good ones due to the shepherd's kindness. Grateful, but needing to get on with his mission, Christian managed to get confirmation that he was in Galilee and was then pointed in the direction of Nazareth. If his desired location was correctly programmed, he'd currently be on the ridgeline of Mt. Kedumim, just to the south of Nazareth. It was unclear how much time he'd have to explore this ancient civilization. He reminded himself that Berkeley struggled with calibrating the return time. He pushed away discouraging thoughts and was determined to focus on his primary mission of figuring out the problem with the return timestamp.

The stable where Christian spent the night was high up the ridge, which was good for reception with the cubepod. He went back inside the stable to give it a try again this morning. He pulled the cubepod out of the feedbag and signaled HQ with a ping. An acknowledging ping came quickly, and a 3D image of Dominic Frazier burst into the stable before him. "Dominic!"

"Hey Christian! Really good to see you!"

"Likewise, my friend. These things really do work."

"Indeed, they do. How's it going?" Dominic asked.

"It's been a smooth adventure so far. I was fortunate to be provided shelter, clothing, and food by a local shepherd. How's the telemetry?"

"We have you tracked solidly through transport plus almost fourteen hours."

Christian proceeded to fill Dominic in on the trip so far and then asked, "Hey, where's my dad?"

"He's gone home. It's late night here. We've been taking turns with the cubepod in case you attempted contact and I got the late shift. Lucky me, I'm the winner of the first contact lottery."

"What do you win?"

"All-time cosmic bragging rights!" Dominic chanted, pushing his arms to the ceiling and preening.

"Nice. I would say well deserved, but I have to break the news to you. My dad tucked me in last night on the cubepod."

"Oh, I know, I meant bragging rights for non-parental personnel," Dominic clarified.

"Okay, congratulations then. Hey, what time is it exactly there. It's mid-morning here."

"It's 12:15 a.m. here. You jumped at roughly 10:30 a.m. Cape time and landed there at roughly 7:30 p.m. Palestine time. You'll always be roughly nine hours ahead of us."

"Got it. I'll be sensitive to any check-ins past 9 a.m. here."

"Let's get to work," Christian said, reminding himself of exactly why he came. "First thing, let's validate the hypothesis that there's ground interference affecting telemetry. I'm going to take a short hike down the mountain. It shouldn't be more than an hour down and an hour back. I'll ping you back in a couple of hours. Tell me what you're able to record."

"Got it," Dominic said. "Talk to you soon."

Before starting down the mountain Christian removed a molecular nanite capsule and cracked it open over the jug of water. He wasn't sure it was necessary, but HQ's instructions were to use the capsules because water purity would be unknown. He took a swig of water, nibbled some cheese, grabbed a couple of pieces of dried fruit, and headed down to the base of the mountain.

The mountain's rocky path wound randomly amongst large basalt boulders. The jagged, uneven footing eventually gave way to a smoother surface as he approached the base of the ridge. After an hour's walk, he was within sight of Nazareth and could hear the bustle of people and animals emanating from the town. But he would not venture there today.

Christian lingered, then headed back up the same path, across the uneven grazing fields, and finally back to the stable. He pinged HQ with the cubepod.

"Dominic, how was the telemetry?"

"Tracked you for fifteen minutes, you headed northwest, then we lost you," Dominic said. "You popped back onto the grid just about 10 minutes ago and we tracked you coming back to your current location."

"That's consistent with my descent down the ridge. We'll have to keep an eye on the tracking, but so far higher elevations do seem to provide better signal capability," Christian said.

Christian and Dominic went on to compare notes on topology and the gradient where the telemetry signal seemed to drop. They discussed the set of test plans for tomorrow and then signed off for the day. Dominic had obtained permission to hang onto the companion cubepod until the test thread they were executing was completed. Christian was to check in tomorrow morning at exactly 7 a.m. his time. He set the alarm on his cubepod accordingly.

Christian explored the ridgeline around the stable that afternoon. He saw no sign of the shepherd boy or his sheep. The donkey was gone, too. Not wanting to push his luck, he settled in that evening in the stable once again, in lieu of searching for other shelter. The stable was serving as a good home base for now.

Christian spent the night bundled in the hay. He pinged HQ on schedule the next morning and got Dominic again.

"Good to see you again my friend," Christian said.

"Likewise, Christian. I've delegated the cubepod to myself on this end until we get some basic testing done. When you ping, you'll either catch me or one of my fellow lab technicians for the next few days," Dominic informed him.

"That's fine. Please tell everyone else I say hello."

"Absolutely," Dominic said and started on the business of the day. "As we discussed yesterday, Berkeley wants us to send you additional test subjects and have you make observations on your end."

"Roger that. Are you going to send me the three remaining doves?"

"Negative, not exactly," Dominic said. "Those three doves have destination space-timestamps of two days ago. If we sent them, you'd never see them. We have a half-dozen doves reprogrammed for your current time and location. They'll begin arriving in a few minutes and at ten-minute intervals over the next hour. Confirm you're in a confined space where you'll be able to observe them for an extended period."

"Confirmed. I can seal up this stable. Doing so now."

Christian observed the window openings at the front of the stable, each with rolled-up cloth tied above them. He was able to release the cloths and secure them at the bottom, covering each window. He also pushed thatch into the creases in the stable walls to seal the openings between wood planks.

"That should do it," Christian said. "Ready to receive transport of the doves and observe them here in the stable. This is why I came. Let's do this."

"Understood. Lab team has been on standby, prepped and ready," Dominic said. "The doves are pre-programmed for their jump. We're a few minutes from the first countdown. Sit tight Christian."

He sipped some of his water and nibbled on dried fruit while he waited. Finally, the moment came to send the first test animal to Christian's current space-timestamp.

A technician's voice in the background signaled the countdown, "3-2-1."

The dove instantaneously appeared at near ground level, towards the back of the stable. There was no noise and no slow materialization process like a Star Trek transporter. The dove simply blinked into existence. Christian noticed its CC-1 tattoo on its breast. It fluttered and at the discovery of its freedom began to walk around the floor of the stable, pecking at the hay.

The Cape continued to transport birds to Christian's location for the next hour. Four of the six test subjects successfully arrived in the ancient stable. He observed the birds as they meandered about the stable as a group. The bird labeled CC-3 seemed to be in charge of the small flock, followed by CC-1, then CC-2 and CC-6. Telemetry was positive from 5 birds. CC-5 had apparently jumped to a location just outside the stable and telemetry tracked it flying northeast. This series of tests reinforced to him the inherent unreliability of the time traveling process. Only four of the six test subjects arrived at the correct time and location.

The next phase of the testing involved observation of the test subjects to see if any of their return timestamps would activate. Christian remained near the stable and his four test subjects for the rest of the day. He stepped outside for a moment of fresh air and late afternoon sunshine. When he opened the stable door to come back inside, CC-3 and CC-1 slipped out the door before he could reclose it. They immediately took flight and flapped away to the freedom of ancient Palestine. Christian had mixed emotions about their escape. He had seen so many animals die in the lab that he found himself secretly cheering for the birds.

Christian spent another night in the stable, smelling lingering donkey odor and listening to the cooing of his two remaining pigeons. He set his clay cup of water out for them to drink. He observed the roughhewn workmanship in the wood planks of the stable and decided that in many ways, little had really changed in man's evolution. Here in this farm country stable he could be anywhere at any time. The thought comforted him, and he drifted off to sleep.

Dominic answered when Christian called the next morning. They exchanged greetings and proceeded with business.

"We have telemetry from four of six doves," Dominic said. "CC-2 and CC-6 there with you in the stable and CC-1 and CC-3 lingering outside. CC-5 dropped off the grid last night, headed off the mountain and hasn't returned. Based on the observations from your hike, we can infer it's now closer to the ground level of your terrain."

"The mountain isn't that big," Christian said. "I agree CC-5 could have easily flown to ground level by now. Isn't it time we let the last two birds go free? It's not fair to keep them confined in here."

"Acknowledged. Berkeley has already concurred that you're to release the remaining test subjects this morning," Dominic said. "Their scientists are satisfied that the experiment gave them some new data they can work with."

"Understood. I'll let them go right after we sign off," Christian said.

Christian informed Dominic that he'd be on standby for further testing and in the meantime not to be concerned if HQ lost telemetry on him because he'd be off the mountain exploring the town.

Christian signed off, then opened the window thatches and the front door. It was nice to air out the place. CC-2 and CC-6 wouldn't leave the stable so he shooed them out the door.

Christian knew Berkeley would be diligently at work trying to figure out why the return timestamp was not working. In the meantime, he'd move onto his secondary and more personal objective.

Somewhere down below, off this ridge, was a small village named Nazareth with a resident carpenter named Jesus, whom Christian was intent on meeting. He was also hungry. A man can survive on dried fruit and cheese only so long. Besides, he understood his time here was limited and he didn't want to miss his chance to meet Jesus. Christian decided that he'd venture into Nazareth tomorrow morning to accomplish his long-awaited rendezvous.

Nazareth

Now I would not give you false hope on this strange and mournful day, but the mother and child reunion is only a moment away.
~Paul Simon

Christian followed the same rocky trail towards Nazareth that he walked the first full day while testing telemetry with Dominic. This time he'd continue down the road and into the town.

Initially, Christian felt he'd blend in just fine. The tunic was suitable. His beard and skin color seemed appropriate. Even the feed sack he was carrying made him look like he at least was doing something. Olive trees and rocky grazing fields gave way to man's shaping of the environment as he approached the outskirts of town. He became more apprehensive as he braced for full immersion into this ancient society. He was a modern city man and the sights and sounds of agriculture were foreign to him, much less the integration of goats, quail, and the random chicken amongst the human population. His olfactory senses weren't used to the smells of the ancient village. This was an age when sheep dung was used as fuel for cooking fires. Nor had the Aramaic tutorial sufficiently oriented him to the real-life dialect and voice inflections of the villagers he heard speaking. There were other languages besides Aramaic mixed in as well.

His confidence ebbed as he took in his surroundings; he was truly a stranger in a strange land.

Nazareth was a modest village of a population of no more than one thousand people. It was probably the kind of place where everybody knew everybody, so he thought it shouldn't take him long to locate the Rabbi Jesus. He cautiously entered town and took time to listen to the conversations around him. The mix of language he was picking up included Aramaic, bits and pieces of Greek, and others he didn't immediately recognize. The people toggled back and forth across language boundaries. Christian silently berated himself for not focusing more on Hebrew. He was looking for a rabbi, so he should have acclimated himself to the Hebrew language. Too late now.

He observed a while longer and then worked up the courage to engage the locals in conversation. He could barely make small talk and resorted rather quickly to repeating the lines he practiced for this purpose. "Do you know Jesus?" Heads would shake. "Do you know Mary the mother of Jesus?" Nobody did. He felt like an evangelist on the street corner. "Do you know Jesus, the son of Mary and Joseph of

Judea?" Finally, there was recognition and reaction from a young man. Aramaic communication was difficult, but Christian had no trouble understanding when he heard the promising phrase, "follow me," once again.

The man led him to the other end of town where a handful of men were working on a construction project. Christian deduced that they were implementing repairs to the stone house located there. The young man pointed to one of the worker men and nodded his head. Christian couldn't have prepared for the emotions that poured through his mind at this moment. He bowed his head in utter respect and asked in his very best Aramaic, "Are you Jesus?"

The answer came back as a flat, "No."

Christian was deflated. The man who directed him here said something to the worker in Aramaic about mother and father and then the worker turned quizzically back to Christian.

"My mother's name is Mary," the man said. "My father was named Joseph. My name is James."

"My name is Christian," was all he could muster in Aramaic.

Christian was quite familiar with the religious controversies about whether Jesus had siblings. Inconsistencies in biblical translations led to a variety of theories ranging from actual brothers, to cousins, to an expression of close camaraderie. He wasn't seeking to resolve discrepancies of religious doctrine, yet he was immediately confronted with one on his first contact with people of this era.

"Why do you seek my mother and father?" James put down the tool in his hand.

"I seek your brother Jesus," Christian could articulate only simple phrases. He couldn't read the expression of James' face. There definitely was internal dialog going on in James' head.

Eventually James responded with the now familiar phrase, "Follow me."

James and Christian headed back towards the town's center. They made their way to a series of cut stone homes just beyond the lone marketplace of Nazareth. James escorted him into one of the homes. It was a well-constructed, empty, three-room dwelling with a thatched roof

"Wait here," James said.

A few minutes passed before James returned in the company of a middle-aged woman. She wore a powder blue linen tunic, a light cloak, and an embroidered veil draped across the crown of her head. Christian mused that her angular features and stoic manner reflected a difficult life. He didn't have to ask who this was. He instinctively bowed deeply. It's a wonder he didn't fall on his knees in worship. The woman squinted her eyes and pursed her lips tightly together in an expression that communicated all too clearly that she wasn't quite sure what to make of the man standing before her in her home.

"This is my mother, Mary," James broke the silence.

Christian couldn't help but think what a lucky guy James was. Or maybe not, considering if your mother was in fact the Mother of God and you knew that, it would be mighty tough to disobey her without having the mother of all guilt trips. Christian still couldn't find his voice.

"Leave us," she commanded, and James quickly exited the house. She stared at Christian for a few moments, obviously sizing him up.

"Who is this Jesus you seek and why do you mention my name and the name of my husband?" she inquired sternly.

Christian thought, bingo, Mary and Joseph. He's getting warm.

"I seek the Rabbi Jesus because I would like to meet him," he managed to state his intentions simply and honestly.

Mary appeared to ponder a response, but then she just turned and walked out the door. Christian stayed put and waited for a few minutes. Eventually, James re-entered the home and explained to Christian that his mother instructed him to provide Christian lodging and food.

James made room for Christian so the two could share one of the rooms of the house. Christian enjoyed a very welcome meal of matzah and goat's cheese. He had no other plan and desperately wanted to spend more time with mother Mary, so he gratefully accepted the hospitality. He spent the rest of the day getting familiar with the small village and allowed his ear to get acclimated to the sounds of the foreign tongues.

Christian spent the next few days in Nazareth. He was becoming comfortable with the language and the culture of the people. He thought he'd be able to converse reasonably well, given enough time. While he desired to make himself useful, James took one look at Christian's soft hands and resisted letting him assist with any of the odd jobs he was working on around town. James slowly relented as Christian sufficiently demonstrated his handyman skills.

James was able to outfit Christian with a change of tunic and clean loincloth. He also provided him with a leather pouch to replace the feed sack he was using to carry the cubepod and plastic baggie of nanite capsules. James proved to be an extremely welcoming host, no doubt at the instructions of his mother. He asked James about Jesus. James explained he didn't know him, but that his mother seemed to have heard of him.

"You are new here and you need to be patient," James said, sensing Christian's frustration. "My mother will speak with you eventually about this person you seek."

Christian's patience was wearing thin. It was time to check in with HQ again. Christian prepared a snack of dried figs, dates, and water.

"I need to hike up the nearby mountain for a bit," he said to James, who reacted as if to follow. Christian held up a hand and explained, "I need to do this alone, but I will be back soon."

"It will be cold." James pulled a cloak off a hook on the wall and handed it to Christian.

Christian hiked up Mt Kedumim to find some privacy and to obtain a decent cubepod signal to get through to HQ. He'd experiment later to assess the limitations of communication nearer ground level. He followed the road up the hillside and headed towards the ridge. He spotted the small stable where he had spent his first nights and headed across the grazing field towards it. He opened the door and stepped inside. There was no donkey in the stable this time, just its lingering smell.

Christian fetched the cubepod from his pouch. He twirled it slightly in his hand and remarked on how out of place it seemed in this ancient land. He contemplated the ramifications of accidently leaving it behind, or even worse, if it fell into the nefarious hands of some ancient evil genius. He tapped the button that would ping the companion cubepod. Dominic answered.

"Hey Dominic, you still hanging onto that thing?"

"Yep. I took it home with me," Dominic said. "We're not done reporting on the first test thread yet."

"I don't have anything new to report on that from my end," Christian said.

"Let me pass along Berkeley's report to you and then I'll yield the cubepod to Claire," Dominic said. "She's been aching to talk to you. First, Berkeley confirmed our observations about the telemetry. They've been mapping the ridgeline, and the limits of their targeting capability correspond to the telemetry results. Therefore, they're satisfied with the correlation between telemetry and location targeting."

"I'm glad they're happy," Christian said.

"Secondly, they were very interested in the jump results of CC-5."

"CC-5 is the one that popped up outside the stable," Christian said.

"Correct," Dominic said. "Berkeley thinks a failsafe kicked in for CC-5 and they've been waiting for confirmation that it actually works."

Dominic went on to explain that Berkeley laid out their space-time targets on a ten-meter grid. They built in a failsafe in case a target was occupied at the moment of transport so that instead of the jump failing, it would transport the test subject to an adjacent grid point. In the case of dove CC-5, the grid target inside the stable may have been occupied by either Christian or another object already in the stable.

"Berkeley thinks the jump failsafe programming kicked in and CC-5's jump target translated to a grid point ten meters away, outside the stable. They're really excited about this," Dominic said.

"Well I suppose some progress is better than none. What about the return timestamp not kicking in at all for the remaining test subjects?"

"They're still working on that." Dominic shrugged and lifted his hands, palms open, in the universal I don't know gesture. "They need more time to investigate."

"All right, let's set schedules for checkpoint calls moving forward. Inform the team about the hike up the mountain I need to do to establish communications. Let's plan on checkpoints every two days or so. Don't ping me, I'll ping you. Also, see if the Berkeley guys have any better clue as to when my return trip nanites are supposed to activate. I would like to have a better idea of how much time I have here."

"Roger that. It has been good talking with you Christian. I'll be passing the cubepod off to Claire. Be safe."

Dominic signed off and the image faded.

Christian returned the cubepod to the pouch and stepped outside the stable into the crisp clean smelling mountain air. He ate his snack of dried fruit and drank the water skin dry. It looked like he was going to have to get used to this hiking routine for a while. He headed back down the mountain, reenergized from contact with HQ. Occasionally, bits of dirt and rocks wedged their way between the arch of his foot and the leather of the sandal. He looked down forlornly at his feet, they were taking a beating. He wondered if any local merchants sold the equivalent of hiking boots.

Christian returned to the village of Nazareth and to the home of Mary and James. He saw Mary fussing with a small cooking fire. She was immediately relieved at his return. "James told me you went to climb on the mountain. I was concerned you had left us."

"I would not do so without telling you," Christian said earnestly, once again adjusting to the Aramaic tongue.

"That is good." Mary remained plainspoken. "There is much we may talk about, but the time is not yet right. Remain here with us. We will talk later. There's lentil soup on the fire. Enjoy." With that, Mary was on her way.

Christian was hungry, and the soup smelled delicious. He scooped the soup into the well-crafted wooden bowl Mary had left by the fire and began to sip, wondering if perhaps her husband Joseph had fashioned the bowl. He thought about how difficult Mary's life must have been after Joseph passed and reflected on the refined toughness she had developed. There was no doubt who the alpha was in the family. Mary had an aura about her that the military call a command presence. Christian was perfectly content to stay, just as she requested, but he was nevertheless growing increasingly anxious that his limited time was waning.

Christian hiked up the mountain again two days later. He entered the stinking stable and pinged HQ on the cubepod. This time a cute girl wearing green dangly earrings answered.

"Hey chipmunk," Claire said.

"Very funny Claire. You got a real kick out of shoving that stuff in my mouth, didn't you?" Christian feigned a laugh.

"All part of the job Christian. It's seriously good to see you, though. Hey, I know you already talked to Dominic, but men are terrible at asking the right questions. Tell me, how did it feel?"

"What do you mean?"

"Oh come on," Claire rolled her eyes, "when you made the jump, were there worm holes, bright flashing colors, elongated stars? Anything like that?" She peered at Christian expectantly.

"Nope."

She made a pouty face, then tried another angle. "Did it hurt?"

"Not even a tingle."

She tried one last time with a wide-open inquiry. "Can you tell me anything about the moment of your historic jump back in time that you think the history books will consider the least bit interesting?"

Christian seriously considered the question. "I was momentarily disoriented." Then he added with a wry smile and wink, "and I arrived naked."

"See, now that's what I'm talking about. The juicy details to help the rest of us mere mortals visualize what your time traveling experience was like."

"You're being sarcastic," Christian replied. He grinned, then added, "Really, I hate to disappoint you, but it wasn't that exciting. It was more like flipping a switch."

"Listen Christian, trust me on this, when you write your memoirs you're going to have to jazz up the time travel part a little bit."

"I'll have to remember that," Christian said dryly.

"Now who's being sarcastic?" Claire smirked. They laughed together.

Christian proceeded to recap the previous couple of days in Nazareth, then he asked, "Are there any new breakthroughs with the analysis of the testing results?"

"Berkeley is still scrutinizing test data," Claire said, "and there's nothing new to report to you. In the meantime, HQ staff will continue to take turns with the paired cubepod because everybody wants the opportunity to speak with the time traveling hero. You should see the sign-up list. Lots of people are patiently waiting their turn."

"That's nice. Please let them know how truly flattered I am."

Christian remained on the ridgeline for an hour after communicating with Claire to give the cubepod time to recharge. He established a routine of hiking up the mountain every other day. It became his sojourn of spiritual retreat, with the stable serving as his private getaway. The donkey's lingering odor was ever present, even if the donkey wasn't.

He conducted checkpoint conversations with various members of the test and biology staff at the Cape. Periodically, he'd encounter a group of people who stayed up late just to get a chance to see and talk to him. He was flattered at the attention and their devotion to the mission.

Christian was becoming accustomed to living in the ancient village. He became more conversant in Aramaic and he was contributing as best he could to construction projects, such as they were, in which James engaged him. Christian enjoyed bonding with James in the process. He could tell Mary was beginning to relax a little more around him, teasing him about his retreats up the mountain from which he came back refreshed. Perceptive woman, Christian thought.

James kept busy with work around Nazareth and he eventually appreciated the extra hands Christian was able to provide. One morning as they were shoring up the thatch roof of a neighbor's house James said, "You seem reasonably capable of basic home repair work. What did you do for a living before you came here?"

"I had a job testing things to see if they worked right."

"Did you have to work with your hands a lot?" James asked.

"No, not really. It was mostly just a lot of reading and math," Christian said.

"And yet, you are good at working with your hands," James observed.

"I don't think I could make a living at it, like you."

The daily dialog while working with James was helping Christian get acclimated to the people and the language. He liked the routine and valued the friendship they were building.

His cadence of every other day sojourns up the mountain continued until finally Cornelius answered the cubepod. Cornelius elatedly held another cubepod in his hand. "Hello from Cape Canaveral. Good to see you. I've picked out something special to share with you, check it out."

Cornelius pressed a button causing a 3D image of a long-haired hippie playing live on stage in 1969. Christian hadn't realized how much he missed music from his century. The rhythmic rock band sounds and especially the flute built the mood until Jethro Tull broke into *Living in the Past*. Christian tapped along to the beat. The donkey was in the stable that day and Christian thought that he might have been swinging his tail in rhythm. They all enjoyed the full duration of the classic song.

"I really have to thank you for that, Cornelius. That was so incredibly good to hear."

"I thought you might like it." Cornelius nodded towards the back of the stable, "Whose donkey?"

"Beats me. Just be grateful the cubepods don't transmit odors," Christian said as he crinkled his nose.

They continued to chat for a while, mostly making small talk.

"Hey Christian, we need to fork the conversation over to the mission for just a moment. There's someone else who wants to speak with you." Cornelius was still holding the extra cubepod in his hand. He poked another button and the 3D image of Paul appeared.

"Paul, great to see you!" Christian said.

"Truly an honor to see you Mr. Naismith." He bowed slightly in Christian's direction.

"Was that a bow? Very funny Paul."

"Merely a show of reverence, I assure you."

"In that case, thank you. But seriously not necessary. I haven't done anything of note yet."

"I disagree. Everyone here is in awe of your courage, so you better get used to it."

"Okay, okay. I'll try to keep my ego in check. On a more serious note, do you have some news from Berkeley?"

"No, I don't and that is unfortunate because according to our models you should have returned home by now." Paul couldn't hide his concern. "We're analyzing the problem and we're dumbfounded by why the programming for return hasn't activated. We're now into the phase of this exercise where having a human in the loop is key."

"I understand Paul. This is why I came in the first place and pretty much the predicament I expected. What can I do to help from this side?" Christian was fully engaged and ready to solve any problem.

"At his point, I'd say just keep checking in regularly. We'll continue monitoring telemetry," Paul said.

"Okay, roger that. We'll maintain the current routine." Christian tried to mask his dismay at maintaining the current routine. In scientific terms, Paul basically just admitted they have no clue what's going on, or what to do about it.

"We'll figure this out Christian," Paul said. "It may take some time, though.

"It is genuinely good to see you Paul. Thank you for staying up late to deliver this news directly."

"I wish it were better news," Paul said sincerely. "You hang in there."

Christian noticed Cornelius give Paul a quick sideways glance.

"Good to see you Christian. Be well," Cornelius said.

Christian replied with his own salutations and closed out the communication.

Christian exited the stable and let the cubepod soak up some sun while he ate, drank, and scanned the Galilean countryside. He heard the bleating of sheep in the distance and decided that it was quite beautiful here. Life for the villagers was laborious, but simpler than modern times. The people in Nazareth kindly took him in, providing food, shelter, clothing, and companionship. He might be here a while, he thought. He decided he'd make the most of it and figure out what he can give back in return.

Christian and James managed to coexist quite well in their room of the house. At first, Christian felt as if he were a stranger thrust upon James at the behest of his mother, but now he felt theirs was a solid friendship. They also regularly spent time with Mary, sharing meals and trading stories. He spoke with them in generalities about numerous topics and religious philosophies with which they were unfamiliar. His Aramaic skills improved to the point where he was genuinely comfortable conversing with them and others in the village. Christian listened intently whenever Mary mentioned anything about their family history. There was nary a mention of Jesus. It was as if the baby Jesus recorded in history didn't even exist.

Christian contemplated the ramifications and considered the idea that maybe recorded history missed on a few details about the identity of Jesus. Perhaps the baby's name was initially James, not Jesus. Holy men often accepted new names. Simon became Peter and Saul became Paul. It was not such a stretch to imagine that James becomes Jesus. This line of thinking made him see James in a new light. Had he been living with his Lord and Savior all this time, without even realizing it? he wondered. Further, he wondered about the importance of his own presence in Nazareth. Following the immutability of time theory, he considered that his presence in Nazareth might be a purposeful fate and that his role might be to somehow mentor James into a new concept about man's relationship with God? He didn't know if this line of thinking was realistic. James was not a rabbi, nor did he aspire to be one as far as Christian could tell. He needed to speak with his dad again.

Christian headed out the next morning, making quick time to the stable. Once again Cornelius answered the cubepod.

"Hello Christian, good to see you again."

"Good to see you too Cornelius. Is my dad available?"

"He's sleeping," Cornelius said.

"I'll wait. Ping me when he gets into the office." Christian signed off and waited outside the stable.

About an hour later the cubepod pinged. Christian moved back inside the stable and answered the cubepod.

"Son."

"Dad."

"Good to see you, Son. I just want to let you know that I've been fully briefed on the results of your mission to date."

"Fabulous, so we both know I might be here a while at this point," Christian said. "There's apparently little I can do along the lines of system debug, or at least nothing Berkeley can think of, so I've shifted my focus elsewhere and I have an intriguing question I need to ask you."

"I'm all ears," his dad said.

Christian went on to relay what he had heard so far from Mary, stressing the point that there was no sign of Jesus. "My question is this: Could it be possible that my being here in 27 AD is so impactful on James that it becomes the catalyst that propels James to embark on an epic ministry under the new name of Jesus?"

"Well, anything is possible," his dad said cautiously. "Why Jesus' ministry sprang up when and where it did isn't fully described in historical text. Something, or someone may have given it a kick start."

Christian perceived that his dad's words were measured, and rightfully so. The ramifications could be monumental.

"I don't know what to do, Dad. I feel like the weight of the world is on my shoulders with this, literally."

"Son, I can't tell you what to do. You're there, I'm not. Follow your gut. I know you'll make the right choices."

"Thanks Dad. This conversation has been helpful. I love you."

"Love you, too."

Christian walked back down the mountain, having obtained permission to set wheels in motion that would change the world. No big deal. He had an unsuspecting protégé on his hands. James was a good man and Christian would enlighten him to his higher calling as Rabbi Jesus. This was about to get interesting.

Holy Family

Christian steered their conversations towards religion over the next few weeks and the possibility of redemption and eternal life. He endeavored to mentor James on the teachings of the New Testament. He described a God of love and mercy for all people. He expressed that God knows us intimately and desires a direct and personal relationship with each of us. He explained his heartfelt belief in this message of love and mercy and how this good news must be shared with others. Christian viewed himself as an instrument of God through his mentorship of James.

Eventually, both James and Mary warmed to his ideas and began to enjoy their discussions about religion. Christian couldn't recall any deed in his life that he'd consider more fulfilling than this critical time he was spending with Mary and James. He realized this was going to be a conversion process that would take some time. At least his subjects seemed willing and able to absorb the message he was delivering and when the time was right, Christian was hopeful James would be ready to assume the role of Jesus.

One evening after dinner, Mary asked James to spend some time with his construction buddies so she could have a private conversation with Christian. James obliged and gave them their space.

"Christian, I know there's an important conversation you've been wanting to have with me, but honestly I've been waiting for you to become sufficiently conversant in Aramaic before having that discussion. I see now that you are ready."

"Yes, I am Mary, and I'm hoping you're talking about the person I was asking about the first day I came here." Christian opened his palms to her. "In which case, I assure you that you have my undivided attention."

"Yes, that's exactly what I'm talking about," Mary nodded and gazed down, contemplating for a few moments, as if engaged in some sort of internal dialog. She raised her eyes to him. "I'm going to tell you a story Christian and I don't know why I'm going to divulge this to you, other than a sense I have that you need to know the whole truth. But first, I really need a cup of warm Cyprus tea."

Christian helped Mary prepare her tea. It was for her the one indulgence she allowed herself in an otherwise relatively austere lifestyle. Mary settled back down at the table and slowly, somewhat cautiously, began her story. "I've been waiting for the right time to bring this subject up again. It concerned me when you left that day to climb the mountain and I feared you may not return. You see, it is because of this Jesus you seek that I instructed James to make room for you in our house. When you asked me about Jesus, it conjured up a memory, and a long-held secret of which very few people know. Even James does not know he has a brother who was born in Bethlehem."

Christian was stunned to hear what Mary was telling him.

"I traveled to Bethlehem while I was pregnant. Joseph and I were responding to a Roman call for a census of Judea. My pregnancy was an awkward matter because the child did not belong to my betrothed, Joseph. It was further complicated because I was so young, and Joseph was twice my age. I gave birth to a child in Bethlehem and we named him Jesus. The situation became even more precarious when King Herod, acting on prophetic word that a savior king had been born, issued an edict that all Hebrew male infants under two years of age in Bethlehem's vicinity be slain. We were concerned because we had already registered the child in the Roman census. Soon thereafter, in happenstance I cannot fully explain, journeying magi arrived seeking to pay homage to my child. The magi confessed they felt they brought danger upon our child, for they were the prophets who proclaimed the new king's birth to King Herod. The magi offered safe passage for my child away from King Herod's wrath. We felt vulnerable. After some consideration we yielded the child to the magi, to save his life. The magi offered valuable gifts for what they deemed fair compensation for the adoption of Jesus."

The magi trading gifts in exchange for the baby Jesus wasn't exactly the story Christian learned in grade school. He continued to listen to Mary, transfixed.

"After the magi's visit, Joseph and I didn't stay in Bethlehem, not very long anyway. We didn't have family or friends to keep us there, nor did we feel comfortable heading back home, since we would endure questions about the baby. We decided to make our way to Egypt, where Joseph thought he could find good carpentry work and where other inquiries would be limited. In hindsight, it is a very good thing we let the magi secret Jesus out of Judea because King Herod's soldiers stopped us in Marisa, before we got out of Judea, and searched our belongings. They would have certainly found the child and killed him right there. We settled in Succoth, Egypt, just across the Red Sea. While there, it became evident that I could not get pregnant again. Indeed, it's somewhat miraculous I conceived Jesus, given certain irregularities of which I'll spare you the details. This is truly a shame because I love children. I love them very much, making the decision to give Jesus to the magi that much more excruciating."

Mary paused, swirled the tea and put her nose to the cup, taking in its aroma.

"My emotions shut down for a time after I handed the baby to the magi. I felt like I was drifting and was looking forward to having other children. It was devastating when it became evident that I could not. However, rather than feel sorry for myself, I realized that just because I could have no more children of my own, I was not precluded from caring for other young ones, so I took up work at an orphanage. It was from there that we adopted James. It didn't take much persuading of Joseph, for he also saw the practicality of eventually returning with a child whom we could quite easily pass off as having been the one born in Bethlehem. We accepted James as our own son and began raising him in Egypt."

Mary sipped her tea.

"We waited a few years for word from home. Upon hearing that King Herod was dead and that the Roman governor of Syria, Quirinius, had decreed a new census, we decided to migrate back to Palestine. However, on the way Joseph learned that rule of Judea had been delegated to Herod's bloodthirsty son Archelaus, so we decided to head for Galilee instead and take our chances under King Herod Antipas. So, we settled here in Nazareth. Soon after arriving, Herod Antipas announced intentions for massive new construction projects. Joseph worked some in Japhia and then performed carpentry and stonemasonry work in the nearby fortress city of Sepphoris. I followed my passion and continued to work with children. Joseph and I ended up fostering several children over the years in Nazareth, until Joseph died in a massive construction project in the new Galilean capitol of Tiberias. At this point, the fostered children ventured out on their own and only James stayed behind with me to tend to the needs of the home."

Mary continued in a more relaxed tone, as if relieving herself of a burden long held in was lightening her spirit. "This story I reveal to you Christian is solely for your knowledge. It is my hope that by sharing this truth with you, you will have renewed insight into the true purpose that brought you here. I don't know what that purpose is, but I believe God has sent you to us for a special reason." Leaning back, Mary drew a cleansing breath, put her nose to the teacup and smiled, enjoying her simple pleasure in life.

The story Mary revealed answered many of Christian's questions concerning the absence of Jesus. He had recently been operating under the assumption that James would become the Rabbi Jesus. Now he realized Mary did in fact give birth to a baby named Jesus, who has apparently been raised and educated under privileged circumstance as the adopted child of eastern magi. He considered the possibility that Jesus would soon return to initiate his ministry. It was fascinating how uncertainty around the historical records of Jesus' early life made alternate scenarios plausible. The *Bible* was also nebulous about Jesus having siblings. The clarification about James' adoption in Egypt addressed that curiosity as well. Mary was sitting patiently, letting Christian process the information.

Christian nodded in understanding. Like jigsaw puzzle pieces strewn across a table, coming together into orderly assembly, a picture began to take shape in his mind. He gathered his thoughts and formed his response.

"Mary, I sincerely appreciate you sharing these confidences with me. I was initially encouraged when I found you and James here in Nazareth, generally fitting my expectations, as well as hearing about your husband Joseph. But I was mystified at the absence of Jesus, and it's truly comforting to learn that the baby Jesus was born. Have you heard from the magi or from Jesus since the events in Bethlehem?"

"No, I have not heard from the magi since then, nor have I heard the mention of Jesus' name, until you arrived in Nazareth. I've told the story to no one, until now. But somehow you already knew about my baby named Jesus. How is that?"

"Mary, this is really difficult to explain, but where I come from the story of your baby Jesus is well known."

"That makes no sense," Mary said. "For only the magi would have known the baby's name was Jesus and you could only have heard the name if you had been with them."

"I assure you there are other explanations," Christian said, struggling with what to tell Mary. "I originally came here with the simple hope of finding the Rabbi Jesus and quite frankly to be awed by him. Instead, I've found myself disappointed at his absence. What you've told me here this evening helps me understand why that might be and it gives me hope that Jesus will indeed return soon and start his ministry. I know you've been bluntly honest with me and you must trust that I'm being honest with you as well. I have not come from the magi and now I'm waiting for Jesus to return, just as you are."

"I believe you're being as honest as you can, and I also think there are truths yet to be revealed," Mary said.

"I'm glad we talked," Christian evaded.

"Me, too." She sipped her tea again.

Christian acknowledged that even the holy family was entitled to hide their dirty laundry. Indeed, it seemed that family secrets are another truism that transcended the ages. He began to process the information at hand, sorting facts from fiction. Jesus was born in

Bethlehem and was secreted out of Judea by the magi. Now all he had to do was wait for Jesus to come back to Nazareth and start his ministry.

Christian climbed the mountain the next morning, went into the stable, pinged HQ and asked to speak with his father. It took a few minutes for HQ to track him down, but eventually his dad came into view. They exchanged greetings.

"Dad, I wanted to update you on an important discussion I had with Mary about Jesus."

"Oh, she finally talked to you about Jesus?" His dad raised an eyebrow.

"Yes, she sure did and it's quite a story." Christian went on to relay the whole saga about the magi taking the baby Jesus away from Judea.

"So, there really is a baby Jesus who was born in Bethlehem, son of Mary and Joseph?"

"Yes, and I now believe that Jesus, educated in the east, will return to Galilee soon and start his ministry. It isn't exactly what we expected, but it actually makes sense if you think about the kind of schooling Jesus would need to be the teacher and orator he became."

"That is very interesting indeed. Hopefully you won't have to wait long for Jesus to arrive," his dad said. "And, I guess you can relax on trying to mentor James."

"Yeah, it's a much more plausible scenario I believe, and a bit of a relief actually. I'll keep you informed."

"Please do. I Love you."

"Love you, too, Dad."

They were sitting by the cooking fire that evening when Mary made a request. "Christian, we would like to invite you to synagogue with us to celebrate Purim. We're walking to Japhia tomorrow. Would you join us please? You may have an opportunity to share some of the beliefs you have told us about there as well."

Christian considered the invitation an honor even though he couldn't quite place which deliverance from slavery the holiday Purim represented. But he knew it was regarded as a joyous occasion, so he gladly accepted the invite. "I would love to join you, thank you."

"I have an extra sudarium and tallit you can borrow for the ceremony," James said.

"Thank you." Christian replied, though he wasn't exactly sure what those things were.

The next morning, the villagers of Nazareth gathered to walk together to the Purim celebration at the neighboring Japhia synagogue. Christian put on the garments James provided. The sudarium covered his head and the tallit was a rectangular garment the Jews draped over their shoulders at synagogue. The tallit James loaned him was woolen with black stripes and knotted tassels along the fringes.

It was a short twenty-minute walk to Japhia. Some of the families were carrying small animals they would use for sacrifice, as was custom, most commonly small birds. On the way, Christian noticed one young man carrying a cage containing a dove with the unique clover marking on its breast. It was one of the birds used for his time travel jump and it was about to be sacrificed.

The party from Nazareth arrived at nearby Japhia.

The town was of mostly stone construction, just like Nazareth, though larger. Japhia had benefitted from construction projects King Herod Antipas had commissioned, including a few more main buildings in a town center and a temple with finely crafted stonework. The temple was a tiled building surrounded by a shimmering pasty white mortar patio. There were two rows of single room mud brick and stone houses on either side of the white patio. These houses served as prayer rooms off to either side of the temple building.

The festival activity centered around the temple. People lined up with their animals to offer as a sacrifice. Christian could not help but follow the progress of the dove as a boy carrying its cage made his way to the Japhia rabbi. To Christian, the sacrifice of these animals seemed cruel, but to these people it was part of their way of life. He watched as the rabbi clutched the dove in his hand, said a blessing and sliced the neck. The dove landed in a bloody heap amongst the previously immolated birds. Then, the dove vanished.

The disappearance distracted Christian for the remainder of the festival. Mary introduced him to people and made a valiant effort to get him to engage in theological discussions about God. Christian didn't feel confident or comfortable enough to do this. He was preoccupied with what happened to the clover tattooed dove and not assured enough in his ability to speak Hebrew fluently.

The bird died and then disappeared. To him, this meant that its death precipitated its disappearance, or, more accurately, its transport back to its original space-timestamp.

Christian made another trip up the mountain the next day to report his observations. He slipped into the stable and pinged HQ. Dominic answered, and they exchanged greetings before Christian shared his news.

"I've made a new observation that may be of interest to Berkeley," Christian said.

"What have you seen?" Dominic asked.

Christian went on to describe the bird with the clover tattoo and that it disappeared when it was sacrificed, leading him to believe it must have jumped back to present day. The bird had been here in the past for an extended period of time, so he doubted the timing of its disappearance was coincidental.

"See if Berkeley can make any sense of why the bird jumped shortly after its death and not sooner," Christian said. "I don't believe the timing is a coincidence."

"Roger that, I will pass along the observation and the suggestion," Dominic confirmed. "They're probably going to ask you to run another experiment."

"I've no problem with that. That's why I came here in the first place. Maybe this will be the breakthrough we've been looking for," Christian expressed hopefully. "I'll plan on returning here early tomorrow morning, so let the test team know I'll have the full day to make observations."

"Understood. I expect they'll have something set up for you to run tomorrow."

"Okay, see you then," Christian signed off.

Christian trekked back down the mountain. He suspected his duty tomorrow would include the need for him to have a knife. He found James doing some repair work on the outskirts of town.

"James, I need a favor. I'm probably going to need a sharp knife. Do you happen to know where I can get one?"

"When do you need it?" James asked.

"Not until tomorrow," Christian said.

"Okay, don't worry about it. I have several and can spare one. How about you help me fill the cracks in this wall in return," James offered.

"You got a deal."

Christian and James worked that afternoon on the cracked wall and a few other small projects around town. That evening, James reached into an old wooden trunk in the corner of his room and pulled out a fisherman's knife for Christian. The knife had an iron handle and an iron blade that pivoted on a central pin allowing the blade to be tucked into the handle, like a modern pocket knife, except the fisherman's blade was shaped in a half moon. The knife fit easily within the leather pouch in which he carried his cubepod and the nanite tablets. It was perfect.

"It's going to be warm tonight. How about we sleep on the roof?" James suggested.

"Sounds good." Christian thought it was a novel idea. They grabbed their mats and climbed up to the flat roof of the house. Christian looked around and saw hundreds of men throughout the village settling in to bed down on their rooftops. Not such a novel idea after all.

Christian hiked back up Mt. Kedumim the next day, mentally preparing himself for the day's experiments. He entered the stable, closed the door and pinged HQ.

Headquarters responded and this time there was a team of tab technicians accompanying Dominic and Cornelius.

"Good morning Christian. As you probably suspected, we're going to be running another experiment today and you're going to have to help us out from your side," Cornelius said.

"I suspected as much," Christian said. "What's the plan?"

"The test subjects this time will be rabbits. We will be sending four of them to your location in stable. They're adorable," Cornelius said. "Unfortunately, we're going to have to ask you kill a couple of them as part of the experiment. Do you copy that?"

"I understand. Let's get on with it." Hopefully these would be the last animals they'd have to kill in the name of time travel experimentation.

The Cape proceeded to transmit the rabbits to Christian's space-timestamp stamp in the stable. All four test subjects, tattooed 1, 2, 3 and 4 arrived successfully. He was instructed to immediately slaughter rabbit 1. Then he was to wait one hour and slaughter rabbit 2. He was told to leave rabbits 3 and 4 alive.

Christian caught hold of rabbit 1 and cleanly sliced its neck. He held the rabbit briefly, then it vanished. "Test subject vanished from my end Cape. Confirm you have test subject body at Cape."

"Confirmed, test subject 1 body is at Cape," Dominic said.

Christian waited the prescribed one hour before he caught hold of rabbit 2 and cleanly sliced its neck. He held the rabbit in his hands and it vanished. "Test subject vanished from my location. Confirm you have body of test subject 2 at Cape."

"Confirmed, test subject 2 body is located at Cape," Dominic said.

"These are the expected test results," Christian said. "Are we done killing animals for today HQ?"

"That's good enough," Cornelius said. "We have what we need for now."

"Okay, may I keep rabbits 3 and 4 alive?"

"Yes, you may," Cornelius said.

"Cape, I have a question."

"We're listening," Cornelius said.

"Would I be correct in assuming that you have had the dead bodies of test subjects 1 and 2 since the initial jump? Specifically, that the bodies have been there for over an hour?"

"Confirmed," Cornelius said.

"Would I also be correct in assuming that you also have the dead bodies of the other test subjects, rabbits 3 and 4? Specifically, that their bodies have been there for over an hour as well, even though they are currently alive here in ancient Palestine."

"Hold please," Cornelius said.

The 3D cubepod display changed to a vague opaque color. Christian didn't realize the cubepod had a hold button. He'd have to ask about that. He waited over a minute, which was a rather long time considering the direct link.

"Confirmed," Cornelius said.

"So obviously we've just solved the mystery of why some of our test subjects appear to have lived at their target destinations for differing periods of time. From the perspective of the test subject, they don't return until they die. Even though, from the perspective of the team at HQ, the subjects appear immediately, but dead," Christian stated.

"Yes, it appears we have solved the puzzle, Christian," Cornelius said. "Thanks to you."

"Ok guys, I get the picture. Please be advised I'm going to remain in this location until you locate my father and advise him that I need to have a discussion with him immediately. Can you mirror that back to me?"

"Roger that Christian," Cornelius confirmed formally. "You are standing by to have a conversation with Dr. Naismith."

"Have him ping me. In the meantime, I'll be taking a walk to clear my head."

Christian closed out the cubepod session, put the cubepod in the leather pouch and walked outside the shed. He left the door open so rabbits 3 and 4 could wander free. This would be an enjoyable time for a cigarette, he thought. HQ was withholding critical information and he wanted to understand why.

The cubepod pinged. He went back inside the shed, closed the door and opened the session. It was his dad.

"Dad, I have a blunt question. Do you have my body at HQ?"

"Yes."

"Did I come back dead, like all the other test subjects?"

"Yes."

Christian finally put it together in his mind that from the perspective of the test team, his body has been at HQ since the moment he jumped, because his return space-timestamp was from that moment.

"I assume you've had my body there since the initial jump and you were just waiting for me to ask the right questions or figure it out on my own."

"Pretty much," his dad said.

"Okay, I'm going to overtly refrain from asking too many detailed questions about how I died. But if you remember, I have a secondary agenda and I would like to know if you believe I'll have enough time to accomplish meeting Jesus. Can you give me an idea of how much time you think I have remaining in 27 AD Galilee?"

"Son, we would have told you if we felt you were really pressed for time. I obviously can't tell you exactly when you will die, but it looks to me like you have a few years, best I can surmise."

"Fair enough, that should give me time then."

"Yes, it should," his dad confirmed. "Anything else?"

"Is there anything we can do about this?"

"Time is immutable. I don't mean to state this coldly, I'm simply stating scientific facts when I say that you'll die in ancient Palestine and we already have your body. I know this is a lot to process. As your father, I ran the full gamut of emotions the day you jumped, spanning utter grief at your returned body and utter joy at your check-in call from Palestine that night. All I can advise you to do is use the time you have well. But, then again, that's a good way to live life regardless."

Christian understood death was a very real possibility when he volunteered to be the human time travel guinea pig. "Let's leave it at that for now. I do feel silly being the only one not realizing this for so long, but I understand. I guess it needed to be a discovery process for me to be ready to accept it. I love you, Dad."

"I love you, too."

Christian was relieved to know he had plenty of time to meet Jesus. He didn't need to rush things. He could get the most out of his experience in ancient Palestine while he waited for Jesus to return from the East.

Christian cleared his head as he made his way back down the mountain. At dinner that evening, he verbalized his heartfelt appreciation to his hosts. "Mary, you and James have been so gracious in taking me into your home. I realize the stay has lasted longer than anticipated and certainly probably longer than you wanted."

"No Christian, don't speak like that," Mary interrupted, sensing her visitor's need for validation. "From the moment James brought you into our home we have felt a special connection with you. You have treated both of us with utter respect and you have shared wisdom such as we have never heard. It is we who have had the privilege to house you all this time."

Mary was truly a fabulous woman, Christian thought.

Mid-afternoon the following day Christian observed Mary boiling water. She seemed distressed about something. Mary explained that several of the young school children were sick. There was something wrong with the well water and it was hitting the youngest children the hardest.

Christian followed Mary to the well and drew up the bucket. The well water was rancid with a cloudy color and an odor of decay. He wasn't sure exactly what the problem was. Perhaps an unknown contaminant had seeped into the water table, or an animal of some sort had managed to fester at the bottom of the well. He wanted to give back to this ancient community and now he saw an opportunity to discreetly make a meaningful difference.

"Mary, I think I can fix this," Christian said. "I brought something with me from my home that may clean this up and I would like to try." He was knowingly about to violate the prime directive, using advanced technology while interacting with an ancient society. He rationalized that clean drinking water was a basic human need in any era and he believed he could provide the solution discreetly.

First, he wanted to see if the molecular nanite capsule would work to purify a bucket full of the water. If successful, he'd expand the experiment to the entire well. He reached into his leather pouch and unzipped the plastic baggie. He removed a molecular nanite capsule, cracked it open and poured the contents into the bucket of water. The effect was practically instantaneous. The nanites responded as programmed to the stimuli and purified the water, making it clear and odorless. He marveled for a moment and then carefully returned the zipped baggie to his leather pouch.

Christian took a small sip of the water. It tasted fabulous. He lifted the bucket and poured its contents back into the well. He drew up another bucket and tasted the water. It tasted significantly better, with absolutely no hint of contamination.

"You can tell the village that the water is safe now, but leave me out of it please," Christian said.

Mary passed the word and soon many villagers were replenishing their water containers.

Mary was eager to talk about the purification of the well water at dinner that evening.

"Thank you for what you did today Christian," Mary began.

"What did he do?" James asked, before Christian could say anything.

"Christian fixed the well," Mary said.

"You fixed the well? How?" James asked Christian.

"With a magic potion from his pouch," Mary intercepted the response.

"You have magic potions?" James asked. "I was wondering what was in that pouch. It hasn't left your side since you got here."

They both peered at Christian. Wow, this conversation spun out of control quickly, he thought. He could just imagine how he might be affecting history this very moment. Would there be accounts that read like a Dungeons & Dragons novel about a wizard that comes from the mountain with his magic bag of spells? He needed to de-mystify the event, but he struggled to find the right phrases in Aramaic that would correctly modify their perception. He couldn't very well mix in words such as technology and nanites. "It's really a small matter," Christian tried to convince them. "Do not speak of it further, I wouldn't want word to get around that I'm some sort of magician."

They nodded as if they understood, though Christian wasn't sure.

"Let's eat, shall we. It has been a busy day," Christian said.

Mary prepared pan-fried millet pancakes. They tasted heavy with salt and olive oil. Christian was appreciative for the calories, but he realized what he truly longed for was a fat, juicy cheeseburger from home.

The Good Shepherd

Christian headed up the mountain again the next day. The climb was uneventful until he heard the bleating of sheep and saw that the field outside the stable was overrun with the animals. There was a sizable flock of organized chaos grazing the periphery and chewing their cud. Some were sheared. Some wore bells around their necks. Lambs were frolicking about and there were sundry black sheep mixed into the bunch. The shepherd boy was at the entrance to the stable holding the reigns of a donkey in one hand and in the other, his crook. Christian continued his advance, dodging the odd sheep along the way.

"Hello, my young friend, excellent to see you again." Christian greeted the boy in his best Aramaic.

"Likewise, sir, I see you are learning to speak our language, although you have a rather strange accent."

"I suppose I have. Spend as much time as I have in Texas and Florida and you're guaranteed to speak any language with a strange accent." Christian smiled wide, his southern drawl apparent, even in Aramaic. "You've no idea how helpful your kindness was to me that evening when we first met."

"It is our way," the boy acknowledged.

"What's your name?"

"David, son of Caleb."

Christian extended his hand. "Nice to meet you David. My name is Christian, son of Doctor William Naismith." It was fun to fully introduce his lineage.

"Tell me David, what brings you to this stable today?"

"It's my family's stable and I need to prepare Nikud for a journey," he said, pointing to his donkey. David raised an eyebrow and inquired, "What brings you to the stable today?"

"I've been using the stable as my private little getaway, and I also like to visit the donkey." Christian bluffed his way through an explanation. "I'm glad I finally know the donkey's name. Where are you going?"

"I must journey to a trading post at a place called Arbela, on the north side of the Sea of Galilee. It's a long journey and Nikud must carry the wool to be traded for linen," David said.

Christian wondered if he'd ever see the shepherd boy again and thought that if he did, he might repay him for his previous kindness. "Could you use some help?"

"I can make the preparation myself, thank you, though," the boy said.

Christian realized the words hadn't fully expressed his intention. "If you would like some company on the journey, I would like to go with you."

"Being a shepherd is a lonely job. Your companionship would indeed be appreciated," David said, smiling.

"It is my way," Christian said, echoing David's initial kindness.

They worked out the travel plans with agreement to meet back up the next morning to begin their journey to Arbela.

Christian skipped the usual check in that day. He'd explain his absence to HQ later. He was enthused to be doing something a little different and was looking forward to seeing more of the Galilean countryside. He was also pleased to have this chance to repay kindness by accompanying the shepherd boy on his journey.

It would take two days for Christian and the boy to make the journey to Arbela. Mary and James helped Christian pack supplies and provisions accordingly. Christian appreciated the extra cloak they provided him, which would serve as something akin to a bed roll for him to use while sleeping. They stocked him up with dried fruits, nuts and water skins.

He said his goodbyes and made his way to meet David on the road at the base of the hill. David was ready and waiting with Nikud in tow. The donkey was weighed down with wool compressed and strapped on its back and on each side of its torso.

The pair first headed north toward Cana, traversing rocky terrain until they arrived at the road heading east to Arbela. The rolling fields, spotted with juniper and spruce trees on either side of the road, reminded Christian of the unspoiled hill country of Texas through which he once passed. Fields of grass with sprinklings of wild flowers appeared more commonly as they progressed towards the Sea of Galilee, and a faint fragrance of honeysuckle scented the air. He noticed sparrows and other birds darting through the sky and heard the sounds of nature emanating from the tall grasses. They stopped periodically to rest, feed and water Nikud. Christian estimated that they traversed fifteen miles on the first day and were more than half way to Arbela.

They made camp at a rocky site just off the road. Christian saw a circle of stones, obviously used by previous travelers to contain a fire.

"This is a common resting place for travelers along this road," David said. "We will camp here. Help me gather kindling for a fire." David reached into his backpack and pulled out a bow drill used for starting fires. Christian helped by gathering sticks and stacking them in the stone circle. David wadded up a small ball of dried grass and placed it next to the kindling, then got down on one knee and put his other foot on the fireboard to pin it in place. He braced the bearing block between his wrist and shin, keeping it steady as he spun the drill and applied downward pressure. The spinning of the spindle in a hole on the fireboard created a fine dust which soon ignited. David tilted the fireboard to let the tiny coal fall into his wadded ball of grass and coaxed it to flames. Christian was grateful someone in their party knew what they were doing when it came to camping, and he paid close attention to the process David followed to get the fire going.

They sat by the campfire and talked for a while, sharing life stories. "I come from a long lineage of a shepherding family. My father was a shepherd, his father was a shepherd before him and so on down the line as far as anyone in the family can remember. I am my father's only son. The stable you stayed in with Nikud was built by my grandfather and my family home is not too far from the stable, just beyond the next hillcrest."

"I am an only son, also," Christian confided. "I don't have any pets at home, though lately I've developed a greater compassion for animals. I don't know very much about donkeys. How long do they live?"

"Donkey's live a long time," David said. "Nikud's been a loyal member of our family since before I was born."

Christian appreciated the precociousness of this young shepherd. Hard living apparently made a boy grow up fast in Galilee. The pauses in their conversation became longer and finally Christian drew his cloak over him and fell asleep under the stars.

Morning came too quickly for Christian and he lamented not being able to have a hot cup of coffee. Dried fruit, a bit of cheese, and water served as their breakfast and they were on the road to Arbela once again.

"Arbela is a regional trading hub for textiles," David informed Christian. "It's located on Mt. Arbel at the northern end of the Sea of Galilee and the climb to it will be arduous."

They made their way along a ridgeline overlooking some rather ominous cliffs. David was leading the way, pulling Nikud next to him. Christian's breathing was heavy, and his steps measured as he followed. They rounded a bend and stumbled upon a viper sunning itself on a boulder by the path. The viper was startled by the trio and struck in the direction of Nikud. The donkey unfortunately reacted by quickly lurching away towards the cliff. The added momentum of the loads of wool were enough to send the animal's fore and hind right legs over the edge. Christian watched helplessly as David, clinging instinctively to the reigns, was whiplashed into the air by the trajectory of the donkey and both boy and animal plunged over the edge of the cliff with sickening thuds.

Christian quickly scrambled down the cliff face after the pair, slipping and scrapping his body on the rough boulders, sharp twigs, sticks and thorny bushes that clung to the cliff's face. He bloodied every extremity by the time he reached the ledge that had broken the fall of both donkey and boy. The wool loads were strewn at the base of the cliff. The donkey was motionless and obviously dead. Christian headed for David, who was unconscious, but alive. David was bleeding profusely from a severe wound across the crown of his skull, which Christian instantly compressed with his hand. Christian needed to find help quickly or this boy was going to die.

Christian cradled David in his arms and awkwardly slid down towards a lower road at the base of the cliffs. He maintained pressure on the wound and kept David's head elevated on his shoulder. He managed to make it to the road, where he headed east, supposing civilization was more likely closer in the direction of the Sea of Galilee.

Christian had no idea how close the next town was or where any kind of help might be. He trudged desperately at a lumbering pace, cradling David, for what he estimated to be about ten minutes.

A small group of people emerged in the distance, headed his way. They were four women, perhaps on their way to fetch water from a well in the vicinity, Christian thought. One of them broke into a sprint towards his location.

She arrived, breathing heavy and intent on helping. Christian, exhausted, had fallen to his knees, David's head cradled in his arms. Tears were streaming down his face. He barely had the energy to speak and he said in a hoarse voice, "the boy split his head open," in English.

The woman clearly understood that the boy was injured in some way and saw that Christian was covered in the boy's blood. The location of the injury was not instantly evident to the woman and her puzzled look made him realize he had spoken in English. Christian repeated in Aramaic, "He has a severe head wound."

The woman immediately tracked her attention to the boy's skull. She gently put her hand on top of Christian's hand and requested, "Let me see."

Christian removed his hand, half expecting David's blood to spurt. No such thing happened. The woman assessed the injury. "The bleeding seems to have stopped. In fact, it really doesn't look that bad to me," she said.

One of the other women arrived. She was bearing water. "Bring that here," the first woman commanded. The woman removed her fine cloak, dipped it into the water and proceeded to clean the dried blood out of David's hair and scalp. The scrubbing aroused a complaint from the boy. She completed the process over David's protests and declared, "Sure looked like a bloody mess, but he seems fine now." She looked at David and asked, "How do you feel?"

"My head hurts a little, but I think I'll be ok. Where's Nikud?" David asked.

Christian pulled the boy closer and inspected the top of his head. He saw that the wound had healed. He was sure the boy's head had been cracked wide open. His blood-covered garments testified to the wound's severity. He stepped back through the events in his mind. He hadn't imagined the deep gash he had seen across the boy's skull. He reached for the woman's already soiled cloak and asked, "May I?"

She yielded the cloak.

Christian wiped his own hands and elbows to reveal smooth healthy skin. He had seen his own wounds heal quickly before, as a side effect from his cellular nanite treatment. Nanites providing that same rapid healing to someone else's wounds was a revelation.

"Where is Nikud?" David repeated more sternly.

"David, Nikud fell over the cliff and dragged you with him. It was a high cliff and a terrible fall. Nikud was dead by the time I reached the lower ledge where you and he landed. I don't think he suffered," Christian informed the boy. This news clearly made the boy sad. He laid a hand on David's shoulder in sincere condolence. "I had grown fond of Nikud as well," Christian said. David nodded and was helped up.

"We will head for Capernaum," the woman informed her attendant and then invited Christian and David to accompany them to get cleaned up.

Christian directed his attention to the woman who had sprinted to their aid and was evidently in charge of the foursome. "Thank you for your help. My name is Christian, and this is my young friend David. We were on our way to Arbela when we took a nasty tumble. What is your name?"

"My name is Mary, Mary of Magdala," she smiled.

"Mary Magdalene?" Christian unintentionally blurted out loud.

"That is another way to say it, yes," Mary said quizzically.

What are the odds of this encounter, he mused? He resigned himself not to be surprised at any chance encounters with epic biblical figures. This is when and where they are gathered in history and assuming the historical records are reasonably accurate, he should be expecting to find them. He was just going to have to get used to it.

"This is my personal servant, Sarah," Mary gestured to the closest of the three women in her party.

"Allow me to introduce my friend Joanna, wife of Chuza, King Herod Antipas' steward and her personal servant Susanna," Mary gestured towards the other two women in the group.

Christian smiled and offered each of the women a slight nod. He noted that the steward of King Herod Antipas would be a significant position of rank involving the management of royal finances. Mary obviously had connections with people of power in Galilee.

Christian observed that Mary was close to her servant and friends. He instantly developed a liking to the Mary Magdalene character unfolding before him. She was intuitive, confident and kind, just like Jesus' mother Mary. How fortunate he was to be able to make first-hand observations about her and to debunk misperceptions that have been passed down through the ages. Notably, he already assessed that Mary Magdalene was no prostitute. Based on her garments and stature, she appeared to him to be a woman of some means who commanded respect.

Christian gathered his thoughts as they started along the narrow dirt road. He was anxious to speak with his dad about the rapid healing he had just observed. His own healing, he knew, was explainable due to the cellular nanites that were infused into his body to cure his cancer. Christian didn't quite understand the healing of David, but assumed it was some kind of secondary affect from contact between his blood and the boys'. He didn't realize that was even possible.

David stayed quiet as the party put distance between themselves and the cliffs of Arbel. They were leaving Nikud and the bundles of wool behind, as the wool was too heavy to for them to carry. They might come back for them with other beasts of burden later. Christian noticed a stressed expression on David's face when the boy glanced back in the direction of the mountain. Christian turned to look. Carrion vultures were already circling above the cliff face over the dead body of Nikud.

Capernaum

They approached Capernaum from the west. Christian saw the long narrow city strung out along the northern edge of the Sea of Galilee. They were entering a thriving ancient city of traders, merchants, artisans, and craftsmen. Its streets were cobbled and amply wide for two-way traffic. They passed groups of stone houses constructed around shared courtyards. Christian noticed that the houses were typically single story with pitted stone stairs that led to thatched roofs. They approached a basalt block temple at the center of town. It had a single high tower and a large columned patio facing in the direction of Jerusalem. Their destination was just past the synagogue.

They arrived at the gates of a compound that was someone's private home. It was an insula of stone homes located between the synagogue and the Sea of Galilee. The homes surrounded a large cobbled courtyard. The courtyard had shared cooking facilities and large stone bathing amenities, complete with stone and fabric walls for a modicum of privacy. Mary led the party through the entrance gate of the courtyard and instructed Sarah and Suzanna to inform the owner of their arrival.

A handsome, mirthful man emerged from one of the houses on the periphery and approached the party with a huge grin. "Mary, so good to see you again." He assessed the party. "What do we have here?"

"Judas, meet Christian. Christian, Judas."

Judas stepped forward, hand extended. Christian immediately took notice of a rather impressive ring made of white gold and containing an intricately cut gemstone which adorned Judas's hand. Judas greeted Christian with formal sounding Greek phrases that Christian couldn't understand. Christian extended his hand and shook.

"He does not speak the language of the public forum," David chimed. "He's only recently able to speak our common familiar tongue."

"Is that right? And who might you be young man?" Judas asked.

"I'm David, son of Caleb. Christian is my friend. We were on our way to Arbela when me and my donkey Nikud fell down the hill."

"It looks like you took quite a tumble David. We'll have to get you cleaned up." Judas shook David's hand as well. Then Judas looked around the courtyard and inquired, "And, where is the donkey?"

"Nikud did not survive the fall," David replied sullenly.

"Oh, I'm so sorry. This has been quite an ordeal for you then. Come in David, please be my guest in my home this evening." Judas turned back towards Christian. "If you intend to travel these lands, you should learn to speak Greek. It has been universal here since the invasions of Alexander."

Christian had no intention of traveling the lands. He was only going to be in Arbela to repay a debt of kindness to David. His initial reaction to the chastisement of not speaking Greek faded from defensiveness to self-admonishment that he had not focused more on learning the Greek language as he initially intended. Judas was simply speaking the truth and Christian recognized the wisdom of his advice. By the time he formed his response in Aramaic, it was of the proper tone. "I hear you and I will take your advice to heart."

Judas was pleased at Christian's response. "Excellent, you are welcome here my friends, as any friends of the honorable Mary of Magdala are friends of mine as well. I insist that you stay with us, refresh yourselves in my baths, feast with us this evening and tell us the story of your journey."

Christian and David nodded in unison at the invitation. They were dirty, hungry, and tired, and Judas was offering a solution for all those issues in one fell swoop.

Christian and David were shown to one of the houses on the insula surrounding the courtyard. The complex was designed to support multiple families. Judas claimed the entire insula as his own and upgraded the accommodations of the courtyard to suit his tastes.

Christian stripped down in a room of the house assigned to him. He put his backpack and leather pouch on the wool-stuffed bed and followed instructions to set his soiled linens outside the door to be cleaned. He wrapped himself in a luxurious towel and headed for the courtyard where he soaked in a warm bath. This was his first full bath since arriving in Galilee and he enjoyed it immensely. The bath water smelled of fresh lemons and sandalwood.

He scrutinized the architecture of the courtyard's bathing facility. The baths were different from the ritual mikvehs of the Jews. These were designed with Roman inspired engineering with heated water and submerged stone platforms for lounging. The plumbing for the baths emerged from a stone wall. On the other side of the wall the pipes ran to a large stone oven at the edge of the cooking facilities and from there to a large cylindrical ceramic tank that spanned the length of the kitchen. The plumbing looked like bamboo piping, except where it entered and exited the stove, where the piping was some type of finished brass.

Christian luxuriated in the bath for a long time. It was nice for him to feel almost human again and fully clean. His thoughts wandered to family and friends and he reminded himself that he must talk to his dad again soon.

When he got back to his assigned house he saw that his soiled linens had been taken away and replaced by two sets of fresh loincloths, fine new tunics, a silk belt, and a floor-length heavy cloak. He dressed in all but the heavy cloak and rejoined the small community of Judas' friends in the cooking and dining area of the courtyard. Everyone was relaxing around the fire pit. Christian noticed that David had received the same royal treatment as him.

Christian and David relayed to the group their story about falling down the cliff. Christian glossed over the fact that David was severely wounded, but now appeared fine. Neither Mary nor Judas pressed him to explain the bloodstains.

"One of these days Christian, you are going to trust us enough to honestly explain what transpired on that mountain today. In the meantime, please enjoy the meal and rest in my home tonight." The wine flowed freely. Christian devoured his leg of lamb, it being the first legitimate piece of meat he had eaten since time traveling. Subsequent conversation served to enlighten Christian about life around the Sea of Galilee. He learned much that evening about the social order of the Galilean people, their economy and their religion.

Christian got a good night's sleep in a comfortably stuffed bed. The next morning, he walked into the courtyard and saw Mary's servant, Sarah, working at the kitchen stove amongst the brass cookware, mortar and pestle by her side. Christian smelled a familiar aroma as he approached. Sarah was straining boiling water through a crushed brown powder cupped within a thin sheet of papyrus.

Christian recognized the familiar aroma. "That smells amazing!"

"Judas asked us to make a cup of Haraaz bean extract for you this morning. This is for you." Sarah extended the cup to Christian and bowed her head.

Christian tasted the ancient coffee. It was slightly bitter, as he expected, but not bad considering its rough preparation. He noted the tangy taste of the Arabica.

Judas walked into the kitchen carrying a small wooden bowl. "Where did you get the beans for this drink?" Christian asked Judas.

"Ah yes, the bean extract. I thought you might enjoy it," Judas said. "The beans are barter from a client in Egypt. Where he gets them, I do not know. My stash is limited. That cup is my welcoming gift to you."

"Thank you very much. You have no idea how much I am enjoying this. You know what would be perfect to take the edge off the slight bitterness?"

Before Christian could finish his thought, Judas smiled and extended a bowl containing a pool of creamy white liquid. "Warm milk from the neighbor's goat?" Judas offered.

"Exactly." Christian eagerly accepted the bowl and tilted it so some of the milk colored his coffee.

"I like it that way, too. Mind if I join you?" Judas said.

"Please." Christian nodded.

Christian got to know Judas better over the next few days, learning that Judas was a practical and savvy businessman. Judas had a keen grasp of the trade routes that drove the economy of upper Galilee. Capernaum served as a trade hub between Babylon to the west, Egypt to the east, and Syria to the north. The domination of the Roman Empire throughout the region facilitated the free flow of goods, providing opportunity for enterprising trade merchants like Judas to become very wealthy.

Christian listened to Judas describe his tradecraft as a merchant who deals in jewelry and high-end merchandise. "One of my most lucrative endeavors is in the production and selling of signet rings with engraved gem stones, called intaglio, for Roman officers, elite citizens, and religious leaders. These are highly valued objects and serve to seal a personal signature onto documents and letters. The gems bare unique carvings of animals, objects, battle scenes, or figure heads. The rarity of the gems and the quality of the engravings my workmen are able to produce make my signet rings a prized trade good."

It seemed to Christian that Judas was the signet ring tycoon of Capernaum. Judas showed off his own signet ring." Do you like my ring?" Judas asked. Christian looked more closely at the ring Judas wore. The face of the stone held a cameo of a man's face, with symbols in the upper right and lower left-hand corners. "It's the hero Jewish priest Judas Maccabee," Judas explained. "Hanukkah is celebrated in honor of his restoration of the Jerusalem temple. The open palm here," Judas pointed to the upper right-hand symbol, "is the Indian Jain symbol of ahimsa, and the club symbol here," Judas pointed to the lower symbol, "is from Gaul. The small symbols represent the limits of my trade routes across the Roman Empire."

Christian admired the expertly etched stone, with the face of a bearded man adorned with a jeweled crown at its center and symbols around the edges. "Yes, the workmanship is outstanding. Very impressive indeed," Christian acknowledged. "That club symbol is like one of the suits in a deck of cards."

"Excuse me?" Judas said.

"Um, I mean, well it's a game played where I come from. Cards are, oh never mind," Christian stammered.

"I'm *very* interested to hear about where you come from," Judas said. "How about you stay in Capernaum for a while as my guest?" Christian readily accepted. The situation was different for David. He needed to get home to tend the family's sheep. He was also expected to bring home a cargo of Arbela linen on a donkey. Judas was able to facilitate getting David home quickly and safely by commissioning a horse and rider. Further, he squared away David's losses with a generous compensation of coin.

Christian asked David to stop by Nazareth and inform Mary and James that he'd be staying in Capernaum for an undetermined amount of time. He also provided David the now freshly cleaned cloak that James had loaned to him at the outset of the journey and asked David to return it to James. At Judas's suggestion, they included a modest gift tucked into an inner pocket of the cloak.

David reciprocated by reaching into his pack and handing his fire-starting bow drill to Christian.

"I have others. You will need this, sooner or later," David said.

Christian accepted the gift and David set off back to Nazareth.

Christian was anxious to check in with HQ. There was much to discuss. He consulted with Judas about where he might find high ground for what he described as his special form of spiritual meditation. Judas seemed intrigued but did not press for more information. Judas described the local topology. "The ground will get higher to the northwest towards Safed, the highest elevation in all of upper Galilee. It will be full day's journey to go there and back."

"That's an awfully long trip just to get some solitude on high ground. Can you think of any alternatives that might be a little more convenient?"

"'If all you really want to do is be up away from ground level for your prayers, might you find the high tower of the synagogue acceptable," Judas volunteered. "It is a holy place after all, is it not? I can arrange to get you in and see that you are given privacy in the upper room of the tower."

Christian had no idea whether it was acceptable or not, but trying it sounded more enticing than a full day's hike into an unknown countryside. Judas escorted him to the Capernaum synagogue and had a discussion with the rabbi. Christian noticed that the rabbi wore a signet ring with a Star of David engraved on its gemstone mounted in the center. Also on the stone was a Gaul club symbol in the lower left-hand corner and the open handed Jain symbol of ahimsa on the upper right. This was clearly a product of Judas's tradecraft. Judas gained entrance for the two of them.

"Hey, I noticed the rabbi has a nice signet ring. Is it a ring of your making?" Christian asked.

"Indeed, it is. The rabbi's name is Jarius. I befriended him a few years ago. How do you think I've managed to secure your passage to the tower's upper room?" Judas explained. "My clients are my friends and vice versa."

The stone steps of the Capernaum temple led to a broad raised foundation. It followed the construction theme of the communal homes in Capernaum with a rectangular main prayer hall and surrounding rooms. Ornate basalt stone colonnades were situated around the periphery and there was one side open to the south with a view of the Sea. Judas pointed Christian to the northeast corner and explained, "You'll find spiral stairs in that corner leading to a room at the top of the tower. You will have privacy there for your prayers." He added with a grin, "And by the way, if you're going to frequent synagogues you're also going to have to learn to speak Hebrew."

"Yeah, yeah," Christian said, as he considered how short sighted he had been to focus only on Aramaic.

"You can make your own way out when you're done. See you back at the house later." And with that, Judas gave Christian his space.

Christian ascended the stairs to the top of the tower. The room was just as Judas had described. He removed the cubepod from his leather pouch and pinged HQ. The 3D image of Claire's head and shoulders appeared in the small room. She was in her night clothes and appeared to be in her bedroom. She stretched languorously. "Christian, we were starting to get worried. The team decided to take turns keeping the cubepod overnight at home."

"Sorry about not checking in sooner and I do appreciate the hardship of the time difference on the staff. I've been given access to a tower room at the town I'm staying in and the reception seems fine. I should be able to check in more regularly while I'm in Capernaum."

"Okay, that's good to know. We just get worried when we don't hear from you on a regular basis."

"Hey, I have a lot of information to relay. You may want to take some notes,"

"All of these calls are recorded silly, just tell me what's going on."

Christian went on to describe the herd of sheep, the donkey, the viper, the aborted trip to Arbela, the nasty injury to the shepherd boy's head and its rapid healing, the chance encounter with Mary Magdalene, the trek to Capernaum, and the hospitality he's receiving from Judas.

"Claire, you have to relay the information about the rapid healing of the shepherd boy. He suffered a considerable gash in his head and was bleeding profusely one minute, and a few minutes later his cut was gone. Both of us were covered in blood, but our cuts were healed, mine *and* his."

"Wow, that's incredible Christian. Do you think the nanites in your blood somehow transferred to him?"

"I can't think of any other explanation. I had no idea the nanites would have secondary healing powers, and I don't think anyone else had thought of this either."

"I'll be sure to relay that information. That's huge."

"It sure is. And Claire, this Judas fellow is a genuinely nice guy. Both he and Mary are respected members of society and neither lacks for creature comforts. Judas is responsible for getting me into this temple with its high tower."

"Judas! Wow," Claire said. "Is this the same Judas that betrays Jesus?"

"No way," Christian said. "Like I said, this guy is really nice. I've met several men named Judas in my time here. It seems to be kind of a common name."

"Not so common anymore. That's a shame," Claire said.

"I agree. Don't forget to relay my observation about David's head wound to my dad. He'll be very interested in the potential secondary healing effects of the cellular nanites."

They continued with some small talk and then worked out a check-in schedule for the next week.

"Good to talk with you again Claire,"

"You, too, Christian. We miss you," Claire signed off.

The change in scenery was nice for Christian. He decided to make the most of his valuable time here in Capernaum getting to know Mary and Judas. He settled into his own house in Judas's compound and established a new routine of early morning communication with HQ. The more regular checkpoints allowed him to cycle through conversations with various friends and to have several quality conversations with his dad. There were no additional breakthroughs for HQ to report, so Christian was free to explore Palestine more fully.

Mary and her women friends were business associates with Judas. They had connections with Roman officers and religious leaders throughout Judea, Samaria and Galilee, which enabled Mary to handle the marketing side of business for Judas. She helped facilitate the commissioning of uniquely personalized signet rings. Mary also remained intrigued by the miraculous healing of the shepherd boy and often lingered at Judas' home to visit with Christian.

One morning, Judas caught up to Christian as he was returning from the synagogue. "Good morning Christian. I'm enjoying your company. Come, have breakfast with me. I would like to talk further with you."

"Breakfast sounds good," Christian said.

The two men went into the courtyard and were immediately served by the servant girls. They ate hot millet with honey, figs and olives on the side, and pomegranate juice to drink. "I'm sorry I don't have any of the coffee that you loved so much," Judas said. "The beans to make that concoction are very rare."

"No problem. Waking up to it that one morning was a treat to last me a long time."

"Good, good," Judas smiled. "Christian, I find you intriguing. You're a stranger in our lands and yet filled with compassion for our people. You're not a Jew and yet you're intimately familiar with our history. You speak and act in ways that are foreign and yet you are sensitive to local customs. So, please, accept a bit more advice from me on languages, if you don't mind. I certainly don't want to offend your intellect."

"No, not at all," Christian said. "In fact, I welcome any instruction you have for me, in language or any areas that you think would be of benefit to me."

"Fair enough. If you're going to thrive in this area, you need to be conversant in Aramaic for family settings and Greek for public gatherings. You'll need to know Hebrew to converse and be respected by the Jewish clergy and you will need to know some Latin so you can interact with the Romans."

Christian sensed a kindred spirit as Judas stepped though the importance of each language in Palestine. "Yes, I appreciate what you're saying. So far, I've been managing with the Aramaic and I do know some Latin from when I was in school, but regardless, I really hadn't planned on staying here long enough to make fluency in these languages necessary."

"Oh really. So, your visit will be short? I was hoping you would stay longer. I enjoy your company."

"I don't know exactly how long I'll be staying," Christian admitted. "I was only planning on traveling with David to keep him company on his journey. But, I must admit, your hospitality has been generous, and I've really enjoyed getting to know the people here. I may take you up on your offer to stay around a bit longer than originally planned."

"Splendid!" Judas said and sipped his tea.

The mentor-protégé relationship between Judas and Christian spawned a mutual friendship. Judas appreciated that Christian was a quick study when it came to learning languages. In turn, Christian saw admirable attributes in Judas, which helped explain his success as a businessman and contributor to society.

Evenings gathered around the fire pit afforded the best opportunity for Mary, Judas, and Christian to talk. One evening before Mary came over to join them Christian said to Judas, "Ever since I've arrived, you've been so kind to me, accepting me into your home, letting me use your baths and eat your food. I'm not sure how I'll ever be able to repay you."

"You repay us each day with your company and the insights you share," Judas said. "When Mary gets here, tell us more about this Jesus from Nazareth you're seeking."

"Are you sure I'm not intruding on your time together with Mary?" Christian asked. "You two have known each other a long time I gather."

"No, you're not intruding at all Christian. Our relationship is strictly business, I assure you. I am not oriented towards women."

"Ah, I understand," Christian nodded. "May I ask how you and Mary met?"

"Sure, I don't mind at all. Mary was an established vendor in Magdala, specializing in exotic jewelry from Babylon and beyond. She's a self-made woman, Christian. That's what makes her different and why she commands so much respect. Some women may have means, but it is usually because they benefit from a rich man who provides for them. Mary of Magdala provides for herself. I was steered her way when I was inquiring about trading partners and business connections. Mary was able to help me with both and we struck up a friendship from there."

Mary and Sarah arrived just then. Christian and Judas stood to greet them and then they all settled down, wine in hand, for another evening of talk.

"I've asked Christian to tell us more about Jesus from Nazareth tonight," Judas said.

"Oh yes, please do," Sarah seconded.

Mary nodded in agreement and sipped her wine.

"The ministry of Rabbi Jesus changes the way man thinks about his relationship with God," Christian began. "Jesus tells us that we're entitled to have a direct and personal relationship with God. That in fact, God desires to have such a relationship with each person. He'll preach in ways people can relate to and in terms that speak to people's hearts. He'll advocate leadership through servitude and mercy by the powerful. In short, he will be the greatest teacher, philosopher, and prophet the world has ever known, or so a multitude will believe.

"Sadly, he will be rejected by the people of this time as another false messiah, but ultimately he'll be seen by millions of people across many nations as the savior of the world. That is why I came here to meet him."

Judas smiled and nodded. Mary and Sarah were enthralled.

"Oh, I have so many questions," Mary said. "How do you know he's coming and why from Nazareth?"

Christian drifted into a passing pleasant thought as he noticed Mary's face glowing from the backlight of the fire. Her innate beauty suited her, like the shore on the sea, or the horizon of the sky, her skin served as a completely natural boundary containing vast wonders yet to be discovered. He caught himself thinking this way and stopped it. How could he even think of hitting on Mary Magdalene?

"Christian?" Mary interrupted his thoughts.

"Oh, sorry, lost in thought for a minute. How do I know Jesus comes from Nazareth? I'll tell you the same thing I told his mother. Where I come from, the stories of Rabbi Jesus are well known and regarded as common knowledge. I expected to meet him in Nazareth and was surprised at his absence. I've only recently discovered that his return is imminent, and he will be coming from lands to the east where he was raised by royalty."

"I don't understand how you know these things," Mary said, "but honestly, your stories are so captivating. I swear, I could sit at your feet and be content listening to you talk all night."

"I agree," Sarah said. "Tell us more."

"All right, I will tell you a story of the kind Jesus will tell," Christian said. "If a pearl is thrown into the mud, it will not lose its value, and if it is anointed with balsam, it will not increase in value. It is always precious in its owner's eyes. Likewise, the children of God are precious in the eyes of God the Father, whatever their circumstances of life."

"You're saying God loves each of us the same?" Mary asked.

"Yes exactly, that's the message Jesus will deliver. It doesn't matter if you are sinner or saint, rich or poor, or any other distinction we make amongst ourselves. Jesus will teach us to see life from God's perspective, not our own, and then to live accordingly."

"You're on a roll tonight Christian," Judas said. "You have a knack for this, you know."

"Well if I'm going to keep going, I'm definitely going to need more wine."

"Oh, I can get us all some." Sarah stood up and ducked into the cupboards just behind the cooking area.

"Get the good stuff," Judas yelled out to her.

Sarah emerged with a fresh skin of wine and refilled each cup.

Christian swished the wine around in his cup, sniffed its earthy aroma, and took a sip. "This is quite good. It has pronounced tannins, peppery flavor, and a dry finish. Where is it from?"

"Yes, I liked it, too," Judas agreed. "It's actually a fairly local variety from Syria. I like to give the wines from different regions a try before resorting to paying absurd prices for the Greek and Italia varietals."

"Looks like this one's a winner," Christian lifted his glass in salute.

"Yes, I intend to get more." Judas lifted his glass as well. Mary and Sarah did the same and they toasted to good times with new friends.

"Christian, we want to hear more, and I have a challenge for you. I know you've been drinking, which hopefully just means you'll be more relaxed. My challenge to you is to repeat the pearl in the mud story, but tell the story in Greek," Judas instructed. "Sounds like fun, right? And, remember, you're amongst friends."

"Do I have to?" Christian pouted ever so slightly.

"Yes," Mary demanded, "we need to hear Greek rolling off that fabulous tongue of yours." She finished her sentence with a flirtatious smile.

There was no way Christian could turn down that kind of entreaty. "All right, I will try. I can't promise I'll know all the words, though."

"We'll help you through it," Judas said. "You're on, *Pearl in the Mud*, Greek version, 3-2-1, go!"

Christian stood up, cleared his throat, lowered his voice an octave and started the pearl in the mud parable again, this time in Greek. Judas stopped him. "No, no, just talk to us, you're among friends and I'm sorry, I may have set you up for that with all the buildup. Just take a deep breath, maybe another sip of wine, and tell us your story."

Christian sat back down, gulped some wine, relaxed his throat and started again. It was apparently an entertaining rendition for the trio of listeners as he fumbled his way through "anoint", "balsam", and "precious" in Greek. In the end, they applauded and toasted his efforts with more wine.

Christian stumbled to the baths the next morning and found Judas already there. "I have a headache," Christian said.

"You have a hangover, my friend," Judas observed. "We'll get one of the servants to fetch you some hot tea with honey."

"That sounds good. Right now, though, I just need to soak in one of these baths." Christian climbed into the hot water. "Ah, your baths are phenomenal."

"I've grown rather fond of them myself," Judas said. "They were no small undertaking. The hardest part was hauling the pre-cut stone into the courtyard without breaking the gates, or anything else along the way."

"I'm certainly enjoying the fruits of your labor Judas," Christian said. "Actually, that tea sounds good, and maybe some water? I think I'm dehydrated."

Judas called a servant and ordered the beverages for Christian.

After the bath, Christian walked next door to the temple. He dragged himself up the temple stairs, greeted Rabbi Jarius, and then trudged up the stairs of the tower to the upper room. He pinged HQ and Cornelius answered.

"Hey Christian, good to see you," Cornelius said. "Though, I've seen you looking better. What happened? You look like you've been shot out of a cannon."

"That bad, huh?"

"Let's put it this way, I know it's morning there, but it looks as if you haven't been to bed yet."

"That's just about right, I suppose. I'm not sure what time I did go to bed, but I know we were up drinking until the early hours of the morning.

"Who's we?" Cornelius asked.

"I spent the evening bonding with my new friends, Judas, Mary and Sarah. They're good people. They're curious about why I'm here and where I came from. I've been telling them about Jesus and his message of love and acceptance."

"I bet those are interesting conversations," Cornelius said.

"Yeah, they are. I actually kind of like sharing the message of Jesus with people who've never heard of him."

"I can just envision that," Cornelius said. "I know you sort of feel stuck there right now Christian, but I can see you thriving in ancient Palestine, if you allow yourself to. May as well, since we don't know how long you'll be there."

"You have a point there, Cornelius. Thanks for the encouragement. On another note, I don't have anything of significance to report. Anything new on your end?"

"Things are pretty quiet here right now. The team was intrigued about the discovery of the secondary healing powers you seem to have, so they're focused on trying to replicate that in the lab. We'll keep you informed of progress."

"I appreciate that. Thanks for your continued encouragement and tell everyone I said hi."

"My pleasure. Take care but go a little easier on the wine."

"Roger that, take care," Christian signed off.

Christian took a walk around Capernaum that afternoon. He was reasonably able to navigate his way around using the high tower of the temple as a landmark.

Judas, Mary, and Sarah were keen on learning more about Jesus, so a few nights later they repeated their fireside chat, only this time Christian took in less wine. "So, you went to Nazareth expecting to find

Rabbi Jesus," Mary started, "and you were surprised to find out he wasn't there. What makes you so confident he'll be showing up soon?"

"From the stories I've grown up with the timing is right for him to arrive soon. Also, it's based on what his mother told me in confidence, about her baby Jesus," Christian said.

"Oh, come on, we're your friends," Mary chided. "Enlighten us and tell us what you know."

"She told me she hadn't told the story to anyone else, but she didn't exactly say I couldn't repeat it," Christian reasoned. "So, I suppose."

Mary curled up at Christian's feet near the fire and peered up into his eyes, eager to hear his words.

"I came to Nazareth fully expecting that Jesus would already be there preparing for his ministry," Christian explained. "There was a language barrier for me to overcome to get even the basic picture that he was not there, but his mother Mary and brother James accommodated me in their home as a visitor. After becoming more fluent in Aramaic, I was able to have a conversation in depth with Mary about the baby Jesus. It turns out the baby was born in Bethlehem, just as I expected, but because the baby's life was in danger from the wrath of King Herod, Mary let visiting magi from the east sneak the baby out of Judea."

"I heard the same thing happened with John the Baptist," Sarah said. "His parents supposedly went to Egypt."

"Yes, Mary and Joseph, the parents of Jesus, went to Egypt as well, but apparently without the baby Jesus," Christian said. "I have to admit I was confused at first, with the absence of Jesus. Then I thought maybe James would become Jesus. It was only after learning for sure that the baby Jesus was actually born that I became convinced that he'll return soon."

"What if he doesn't?" Judas asked, playing devil's advocate.

"I would personally be shattered if what I had been taught from childhood didn't come to fruition," Christian said, soulfully.

"Well let's hope that doesn't happen," Mary said sincerely.

"Does he become a king?" Sarah asked.

"Not in the way that you mean, Sarah. But he was born a king and will reign forever. I know that doesn't make sense to you, but maybe you'll come to believe it when you meet him and listen to what he has to say."

"Christian, there is danger for this man Jesus if he is viewed as a prophet," Judas warned. "The Jews are a fickle bunch. They will stone their prophets just as quickly as they would embrace them."

"I agree with you on that Judas. The message of Jesus is a dangerous one and it will not be well received by people in positions of power. I remain convinced, however, that the world must hear his message and that this is the place and time it will be delivered. Jesus must exist."

Christian stopped. He was standing, tense, with fists clenched. He sighed, "I'm sorry, I guess I got a little too excited."

Mary tapped the seat next to her by the fire and Christian went and sat beside her. Mary began to gently scratch his back.

Judas looked at the two of them and smiled. He shifted his attention to Christian. "Do not be sorry. It is gratifying to see you so passionate. We all view you as a wise man, despite your lack of language skills. What I would like to hear from you now is the truth about what really happened with David's head wound. Mary saw you both covered with blood and I saw the blood-soaked clothing you wore."

"Yes, I'm ready to share this with you. The gash across the top of the boy's head was massive and somehow by the time Mary got to us on the road it was healed. I was scared the boy was going to die and truly surprised myself at his recovery." Christian took a deep breath. Mary and Judas dared not interrupt his momentum. They stayed silent, waiting for the next revelation. "I've thought about it and I believe I know what happened. Where I come from there are fabulous medicines that cure diseases. I had one such disease and received a very special treatment that cured me. That medicine remains in my skin and blood to this day. I bloodied my hands on the way down the cliff in pursuit of David and I believe the contact of my blood with his open head wound facilitated transfer of my blood's healing agents to him. The medicine in my body was designed to fix things that are not right and that is apparently what it did for the boy."

"We don't have anything like that in Palestine," Judas remarked. "Around here people would call that a miracle."

"Well, it's kind of unique where I come from, too," Christian said.

"The boy was meant to be healed Christian, and through his healing you've learned something about yourself. Have you not?" Judas asked.

"Yes," Christian admitted, though he wasn't sure he and Judas were talking about the same self-knowledge.

"Let me ask you what characteristics you think this Jesus, son of Mary and Joseph, has that will enable him to become a messiah?" Judas asked.

"In my faith, he is the Son of God," Christian said solemnly. "He will be gentle, kind, non-judgmental and, well, perfect. He will speak and people will listen and follow him. He'll be able to demonstrate miraculous signs of healing and casting out demons."

"If he's also a man, he won't be perfect, I can assure you of that," Mary said.

"Honestly, though," Judas said, "I see a lot of those same characteristics in you. For you've shown us a grand vision, which you are obviously passionate about. You know things people would not normally know and you do things people cannot normally do."

"Judas, where I come from, everyone knows these things I know. And the shepherd boy healed because he benefited from a medical treatment my blood happens to carry. If you see characteristics of Jesus in me, then I am flattered," Christian said. "It is an important part of my religion to live in a manner consistent with the teachings of Jesus."

"It seems like you're accomplishing that quite well then, Christian," Judas said. "Congratulations."

"Thank you, I think." Christian squinted at Judas, trying to discern his meaning, then let it go. "Speaking of Jesus coming back soon, I really should start making my way back to Nazareth. He could've already arrived."

"Can you stay a few more days?" Mary implored.

"Oh Mary, you have to understand, I have to get back to Nazareth. I had no intention of being away this long and Jesus may have shown up by now. I really don't want to miss his coming."

"All right, it's late and we're all tired. Let's all get to bed and meet back up here to talk about it in the morning," Mary suggested.

"That sounds like a good plan," Christian smiled.

Return to Nazareth

Christian walked next door to the synagogue early the next morning. He greeted Rabbi Jarius in Hebrew and proceeded to the private room at the top of the high tower. He conducted his standard checkpoint conversation with HQ, relaying that he'd like his next conversation to be with his father.

He returned to Judas' insula and packed his bags. Mary Magdalene was disappointed to see that Christian was packing. "We were just getting to know each other," she said, slightly forlornly.

"Believe me, I know Mary and I would really like to stay longer if I could, but I must get back to Nazareth. Besides waiting for Jesus, I have other unfinished business," Christian explained, gently touching her cheek with his palm.

"Would you be surprised if I told you that you may have unfinished business here in Capernaum as well," Mary smiled.

"I like the sound of that," Christian returned the smile. "I've genuinely enjoyed your company while I've been here. It has been fabulous. But, I must return to Nazareth now. I've been away too long as it is."

"Will you come back soon?" Mary asked.

"I want to but can't promise that either."

"Hearing that makes me sad. I hope to see you again Christian," Mary said softly before leaving him alone.

Christian completed his packing and headed for the cobbled courtyard's common area. There he found Mary and Judas in the kitchen area. Sarah and Suzanna were preparing a breakfast of fried eggs, cheese, fruit, and goat's milk. "We insist you stay for breakfast. Then you may be on your way," Judas said.

"I'll accept that, thanks," Christian said without enthusiasm.

"Why so grumpy?" Judas asked.

"Oh, I'm sorry. It's not you, it's me. I hate to admit to myself how much I've enjoyed your company. You're the best friends I've made in a while and the idea that I may never see you again is gnawing at me."

"Maybe you're not the only one who knows things, Christian," Judas said. "I've a feeling we'll be seeing each other again and I look forward to that reunion."

"I hope you're right about that, Judas."

Christian's mood lightened has he shared breakfast that morning with his friends. Still, he was determined to set off on his way. He made a point to state in Greek, "I appreciate your hospitality Judas and I look forward to seeing you again."

"No problem." Judas said, also in Greek. "It is a long journey to Nazareth and this is still a strange country to you, are you sure you know the way?"

"I'll manage. I really must go."

Just then a rider arrived at the front gate and rode into the courtyard holding the reigns of a second horse, a white Arabian stallion.

"It is a long trip on foot my friend and only a few hours on horseback. Accept this gesture from me and Mary." Judas smiled. "My rider will see to your safe return to Nazareth. Attend to your business there and know this house is always open to you."

"You're going to need these," Judas extended a small bag of coins to Christian. "We hope you find the Rabbi Jesus."

"You did not need to do this, but I sincerely appreciate it." He accepted the bag then said his goodbyes to Judas and the rest of the household.

Mary was standing by the white horse, hands folded behind her back, clearly waiting to be the last to wish Christian goodbye. As he approached Mary and the horse, Mary smiled, leaned toward him and kissed him on the cheek. "I do hope you come back soon."

"Me, too," Christian said as he mounted the purebred and started on his way to Nazareth.

The road sloped slowly upward as they headed west towards Cana. They passed the cliffs of Arbel where the wool bundles were still strewn on the ledge. They passed the grass fields and the site where he and the shepherd boy previously camped. Then they turned south and headed for Nazareth, in the heart of lower Galilee. The trip was made vastly easier by the mode of transportation Judas graciously provided.

A small crowd gathered as Christian and the rider approached the outskirts of Nazareth. It wasn't often that the inhabitants of Nazareth received a visit from riders on such fine stallions. He realized it wasn't so much him who was receiving the attention as it was the stunning purebred he was riding. The kids at town center all wanted to touch the horse. His escort handled the commotion professionally, calming the horse and helping the animal to accommodate the patting.

Christian saw James and Mary amongst the crowd. He dismounted, retrieved his belongings, and signaled farewell to the rider who was anxious to leave the town. The rider signaled farewell and hollered a command that made the horses turn and prance, serving as entertainment for the crowd. Christian made a beeline for James and Mary and they hugged and greeted each other as old friends would.

"Christian, we are so grateful you have returned to us," Mother Mary said. "When David returned he told us you were staying in Capernaum for a while, but we had no idea how long you might be there." She gave him a thoughtful look. "Though, we figured you must be doing just fine. The gift you left in James' cloak was way too much money."

"The coins were from my friends Judas and Mary of Magdala," Christian explained. "They have a fabulous house in Capernaum and are quite generous people. I agree that I was gone too long, and we do need to talk, but later."

"How are you?" Christian asked James.

"Same old Nazareth. I see you've stepped up in the world. Nice horse."

The three of them made their way to Mary and James' home, catching up with the latest news on the way. Christian figured that if Jesus had returned to Nazareth, they would certainly have mentioned it by now.

"A friend of mine has a daughter who is getting married in a couple of days to a merchant in Cana," Mary said. "She's opened the invitation to family and friends in Nazareth and, by the way, she knows you fixed the well. We would very much like it if you would attend the wedding with us."

"I would be delighted to," Christian said. The wedding at Cana, Christian thought. This was it. This was where he would finally meet Jesus who will work his first miracle by turning water into wine. Jesus had to be at Cana, for it was written and time is immutable.

Wedding at Cana

The ideal man bears the accidents of life with dignity and grace, making the best of circumstances.
~Aristotle

The night before the wedding Christian could hardly sleep. He knew he'd be meeting Jesus the next day. The thought blew his mind. He wondered, what could he possibly say to him? How would he look? After all these years of seeing Jesus portrayed by thousands of artists throughout the centuries, Christian was going to see Jesus face to face.

Bible historians believe that the wedding at Cana was where Jesus' first miracle occurred, where he turned jugs of water into wine. Despite Christian's initial disappointment of not finding Jesus in Nazareth, there was no doubt in his mind that Jesus would attend the wedding of Cana and, at the behest of his mother Mary, would perform his first miracle. And Christian would be there to witness it.

Mary's friend had told her to invite her sons and any friends they wished to bring. So, Mary, James, Christian and a cadre of their friends made the three-hour walk to Cana early the next morning. When Christian saw the crowd that gathered to go to the wedding, he thought that perhaps the bride's family miscalculated how many friends a pair of construction workers might bring along when free alcohol was involved.

Christian arrived with his party to the wedding celebration and scanned the large gathering. The celebration had a festive atmosphere. There were a couple of belly dancers wearing fitted tops, hip belts, and flowing harem pants artfully gesticulating their torsos in rhythm to the flute music. The feast, presented buffet style on multiple tables encircling the courtyard, included mutton and assorted figs, dates, olives, beans, and nuts.

Mary introduced Christian to her friend. "Christian, this is Rachel, mother of the bride."

"So nice to finally meet you Christian," Rachel said. "It was so nice of you to fix the well water that was making the Nazareth children sick."

"Ah yes, it was my pleasure to take care of that. Good to meet you, too." Christian had already figured the discrete good deed apparently wasn't such a secret among Mary's friends.

"You, James, and your friends are welcome so please enjoy yourselves. It is a fabulous day to marry off another daughter. I would introduce my husband, but I believe he's managed to get himself distracted at the moment."

"Thank you," Christian said. "We are sure to have a wonderful time with all you have provided." Until the wine gives out, Christian thought.

Rachel's attention shifted to her other wedding guests and Mary became entangled in side conversations as well, freeing Christian to survey the crowd. He searched expectantly for a man who may be Jesus, but in reality, he had nothing to go on except that he felt he'd recognize Jesus' presence. The feast continued, and Christian's disappointment grew with each passing hour. No one named Jesus was there and time was running out. He continued to mingle, introducing himself to every man he encountered, hoping one of them would say that his name is Jesus.

The wine supply allocated for the wedding celebration was eventually depleted and Mary found Christian. "I'm concerned that the sheer size of the wedding party has overwhelmed the expectations of the wedding planners," she said. "They've run out of wine. I was wondering if you could help. Whatever you did to the well, could you use that same magic to help with the wine?"

Jesus had failed to arrive and now Mary was turning to him to perform a miracle the *Bible* attributed to Jesus. He was crestfallen and confused. Time was immutable, a fact that had been driven into Christian's head by his dad. He considered the convolution of circumstances that brought him to this moment. He needed time to think. "Yeah, it looks like they weren't ready for the entire Nazareth construction crew to show up," Christian said.

"Can't you fix it, like you did the well?" Mary appealed.

In fact, he could fix it like he did the well by using some of the molecular nanites, just as with the beer experiments. But having the capability and performing the act were two different things in his mind. He resorted to honesty. "Yes Mary, I do believe I can help them with their shortage of wine. However, it is written that this is the first of numerous miracles to be performed by your son Jesus, whom I expected to be at this wedding."

"I'm sorry this has not turned out as you expected. But I feel badly for the wedding party and if you can help them, I would sincerely appreciate it."

Christian considered the request from the Mother Mary. Technically speaking, he could oblige her, and yet in doing so he'd be usurping the first miracle of Jesus. He thoughtfully considered his choices and ultimately reasoned that perhaps cosmic forces had intervened so that he could facilitate this first miracle in advance of Jesus's arrival. In the end, he simply nodded his head.

"Whatever he says to you, do it," Mary said to the servant girls standing nearby.

Christian focused on the task at hand. He accepted that accomplishing the miracle of turning the water into wine at the wedding at Cana would now be his responsibility.

The wine he was to produce needed to be of superior quality, so Christian cornered the headwaiter away from the party. "Sir, my name is Christian. I'm a guest of the wedding party and I would like to chat with you about some wine. First, may I know your name please?"

"Call me Barbelo," he smiled and reached out his hand to shake. "But, I'm sorry, we have run out of wine."

"I've heard," Christian said as he returned the handshake. "Surely you have a private stash of good wine, don't you?"

"Well yes, I've three Roman decanters of excellent wine," Barbelo admitted, "but they are not for this wedding party."

"I just need a tasting. Describe for me what you have please,"

"Your choices are limited to an Italian Aglianico, a Greek Agiorgitiko, or an Aegean Limnion," Barbelo said. "They're all fine wines."

These were ancient varietals, perhaps long since gone by way of antiquity. One name did at least sound familiar to Christian, though, and he'd have trouble pronouncing the other two anyway. "Even their names sound like a mouthful, but the Limnion sounds most familiar to me. Let me try that."

"Ah yes, Limnion was a favorite of Aristotle. Perhaps that is why it sounds familiar. It's a full-bodied red, with moderate tannins and a hint of mineral aroma," Barbelo explained.

It sounded odd to Christian's ear to hear the name of a familiar historical character spoken in Greek. The philosopher Aristotle, he knew, was a student of Plato and instructor to Alexander the Great circa 300 BC. "Yes indeed, that must be why. I'm familiar with his theories of causality and the rational soul. If it's good enough for Aristotle, it's good enough for me." Christian handed Barbelo two silver coins, compliments of Judas. "Will this be enough for a small cup of the Limnio wine?"

"Yes, this is more than enough," Barbelo said, accepting the money. "I will be right back." Barbelo returned and handed Christian a small delicate glass filled with Limnion wine. "A fine wine deserves an appropriate vassal. Return the glass please, it's from Sidon."

Christian recognized the name Sidon as present-day Lebanon. Sidon must be some sort of renowned manufacturing location for glass, as

Barbelo's intention clearly was to impress. "Understood, I'll be sure to return it."

Christian went out the back door where there were six large water pots of stone for the Jewish custom of purification. He instructed the servants to fill the pots with water. They filled them to the brim. He reached into his leather pouch, removed a molecular nanite capsule and cracked it open over the glass of wine. He then poured a small sample of the nanite infused wine into each water jug. He knew the nanites would work quickly to do what they were programmed and the water would be turned to wine.

Christian then instructed the servants to draw out several carafes of the water that was now wine and bring them to the headwaiter. Barbelo tasted the wine and said to the servants, "This tastes like the Limnio, yet you have brought out full carafes of it. Where did all this wine come from?"

The servant girls pointed towards Christian standing near the rear entrance.

Baffled, but grateful, Barbelo called out to the bridegroom. "Most wedding parties serve the good wine first. You have waited to serve the best wine last."

The bridegroom was perplexed, not knowing from where the wine had come. He asked the wait staff, but they didn't know. The servant girls who filled the jugs with water realized that Christian had turned the jugs of water into wine and they proceeded to spread the word. When the bridegroom heard what the servant girls were saying, he sought out the man they were saying turned water into wine.

Christian was standing next to Mary and James when the bride and groom came over to demonstrate their appreciation. Before introductions could happen, the bride was already giving Mary and James a big hug. The groom reached out his hand to Christian. "We want to show you our gratitude, for you have turned our humble wedding into an even more festive occasion. I know you are one of the guests from Nazareth, but we've not met until now, I'm sure. My name is Isaac Cananeus, son of Abraham and this is my new wife, Sophia. Please tell us your name."

"My name is Christian," he said and returned the handshake. "It is a pleasure to meet you, Isaac and Sophia."

"I don't know how to thank you for such a generous gift," Isaac said. "There was no wine left, but the servants say you turned the jugs of water into wine. I am amazed, as is everyone present."

"He has done miracles such as this before," Mary interrupted. "He is a man of mystery and great wisdom. Please, just rejoice in his presence and his gift of wine."

The bride and groom looked at each other and turned to Christian. Sophia said, "Thank you sir! You've brought so much joy to our wedding by what you've done."

"Yes," Isaac said, "you have demonstrated a great wonder indeed. I will not question, but only be grateful."

Before Christian could respond, he heard the growing rhythmic clinking of utensils on ceramic cups and glasses around the celebration hall. The flute music halted briefly as Isaac captured the attention of the wedding attendees. Isaac raised his glass of wine and announced, "I would like to propose a toast to my new friend Christian. This man has blessed our wedding by turning water into a fine wine. He has demonstrated a wonder to us today that surely will be spoken about for generations. Christian of Nazareth, we salute you!"

"Mazel tov!" cheerfully rang out from the gathered crowd as cups and glasses were raised in unison in tribute to Christian.

Christian offered a head bow in acknowledgment to both Isaac and the gathering. The music resumed, and the dancing followed. Christian turned to Isaac and his new bride. "You are a lucky man," he said. "I'm happy for both of you."

Isaac embraced Sophia in an enveloping hug, grinned and replied to Christian, "Yep, I'm smitten with my beautiful young bride and grateful that you've made her so happy on her wedding day. Allow me to introduce you to my father. Come with me."

Christian followed as Isaac led them to the rabbi who had conducted the wedding ceremony. The music from the reed pipe whistled loudly near the belly dancers, so Isaac pulled the rabbi slightly further back and projected his voice over the music. "Dad, I want you to meet Christian. He is the miracle worker who turned the water into wine for us." Isaac turned back to Christian and said loudly, "This is my dad, Rabbi Abraham."

Rabbi Abraham stopped leering at the belly dancers long enough to shake Christian's hand, leaned forward, and spoke into his ear. "My son has his work cut out for him with Sophia. I'm glad you've helped him off to a good start. Someday, I would like to understand how you changed the water into wine."

"Long story rabbi and not a secret I would easily reveal. Please just accept the wine as my gift. I'll tell you what, though, you've done a rather nice job of providing entertainment as well." Christian gestured towards the belly dancers.

"Fair enough. We accept your generosity. Know that you are welcome under my roof at any time. Please do come back and visit us." Rabbi Abraham smiled and nodded, "Shalom."

Christian nodded, bowed slightly, then pointed over top of the dancing crowd to indicate he was headed back to the other side. He found Barbelo. "I've hung onto this thing for dear life Barbelo. Let me give it back to you before I break it." Barbelo stretched out his arm to accept the glass and was about to say something when an inebriated wedding guest spun from the dancing crowd and plowed between Christian and Barbelo. Christian heard the shatter of glass and instantly knew Barbelo had lost his grip on the prized object. "Oh," came the cry from Barbelo as he pushed the drunken man aside and crouched down, forlornly looking at the jagged shards. "Everyone watch your step," he bellowed. "This is sharp, watch your selves, this will cut up your feet." The party guests eased away, forming a small circle, as two servant girls appeared with broom and dustpan to scoop up the fragments from the floor. Barbelo supervised until he was satisfied the ground was safe.

"I'm sorry about that," Christian said.

"Cost of doing business my friend," Barbelo shrugged. "I have other glasses. It's not a problem. I was more worried about people hurting themselves on the broken shards. Besides, you're not at fault, unless you consider yourself to be responsible for the intoxication level of the crowd over there."

"Guilty as charged," Christian admitted. "I owe you a glass."

"Ha, I owe you much more than that sir," Barbelo said with a smile. "Let's enjoy the party."

Mother Mary approached Christian. "You're the toast of the wedding."

"Appears so."

"I was thinking about what you said before, about this being something Jesus did. You said it like it had already happened," Mary said. "You weren't surprised that the wedding party ran out of wine, were you?"

"It's true, it is written that they would run out of wine. But Jesus was supposed to be here to create more wine, not me."

"Is it possible that you're the one who was supposed to be here, to accomplish this miracle all along and you just didn't realize it?" Mary peered into Christian's eyes. "Normal people don't know the things you know, and they cannot do the things you do. I'm watching you struggling to embrace this role. Please know I've already accepted you in my heart as my son. I cannot explain where you might have been raised, if not by the magi, but I do know what I see in front of me, as surely as a mother recognizes her own son."

Christian didn't want to argue the point with the Mother Mary here at the wedding. He knew he was not her baby, grown into a man. Instead he said, "Mary, I'm humbled by your acceptance of me. Please understand, I still need time to process what's happened here today and I must consult with my father. I admit this wedding serves as a validation for me that events described in scripture did indeed happen. It's just, all my life, Jesus has been my Lord and I cannot fathom the ramifications of his absence." Christian's last sentence trailed off as he gazed out across the rocky hills to the east of Cana. He starred, looking at nothing, lost in his own murky thoughts and debilitating consternation.

"You have a faraway look in your eyes," Mary said. "What you already know, I cannot imagine. I want to feel happy for you that you're finally figuring out what I've long suspected. And yet, now I sense your anguish instead. This is going to get harder isn't it?"

"Mary, if this is what I think it is, this is just the beginning," Christian said. "And yes, this will get very hard indeed. Now, I'm desperate to find another way."

"Assuming there is no other way, what happens next?" Mary asked.

"I need to speak with my father. I have a lot of questions and I'm very apprehensive about the answers."

The wedding celebration continued late into the night. The Nazareth contingent found friends and family to stay with in Cana until morning. That night fell forcefully on Christian. His body was restless and his mind unsettled. He found everyone but Jesus on his quest and he turned water into wine in Jesus' absence.

All Christian could think about on the way home was walking straight up the mountain and having a frank conversation with his dad. There were questions he needed to ask, questions he's been hesitant to ask. Now, he needed to know.

When they returned, Christian passed through Nazareth and followed a familiar path up Mt. Kedumim. He located the stable and went inside. It was empty. He pinged HQ on the cubepod. He heard the acknowledging ping and the 3D image of his dad appeared in the stable.

"So how was the wedding?" his dad inquired.

"Dad, it's because of what happened at the wedding in Cana that we're about to have a very important conversation."

"Okay, I sense that you're very disturbed about something."

"Developments have proceeded along a line I could not have expected. It has been a process of discovery for me on several levels. Through extended visits in both Nazareth and Capernaum and yesterday in Cana, I've managed to encounter important biblical figures, except for the central character, Jesus. It has been a puzzle that I'm now apprehensive to solve."

"Jesus wasn't at the wedding at Cana?" His dad seemed surprised.

"No, he wasn't. And further, the wedding party did in fact run out of wine and the Mother Mary turned to me to fix the problem," Christian said. "Which of course I accomplished using molecular nanite technology. And for the record, I replicated a Limnion red wine and it was very good."

His dad remained silent.

"Now Mary thinks I'm her son Jesus. And God help me, I'm thinking I could well have to play the role in order for Jesus to exist. I've already cured the shepherd boy, saved people from getting sick by purifying the well, and now I've turned water into wine. I suspect you know more than you've let on so far and you've either been waiting for me to figure it out, or to ask the right questions."

"A little of both actually," his dad admitted.

"Okay fine. I'm led to ask more questions then, although I'm still not sure I want to hear the answers." Christian paused and took a deep breath. "I know my body came back dead just like all the other animal test subjects. I now need to know, is it evident to you how I died?"

"Yes, it is."

Christian had to know. "Tell me."

"Son, it looks as if you were crucified." His dad maintained eye contact.

Christian tried to process the method of his death. It was as if he had just been sucker punched in the stomach. He felt flush, a gut retching reflux convulsed inside him, he doubled over and threw up his breakfast.

Christian took a moment to recover his composure. He wiped his mouth with the loose sleeve of his tunic and took a swig of water. He glanced up and saw his dad looking at him with anguish. "I'll be all right," he said, "I just need a moment."

"Take your time."

Christian took a few breaths and said flatly, "Describe the wounds."

"Your face was badly battered. You had been severely scourged. You had puncture wounds about your scalp, the telltale nail wounds to wrist and feet, a large puncture wound to your side, your arms and legs were badly scrapped and bruised and you had deep lacerations across the base of both calves."

Christian remained silent.

"It was a terrible sight. I had the same reaction you just did when I saw your body come back in that condition. It was days before I could return to the medical lab where we kept your body. It was extremely traumatic for everyone at the Cape. Nothing could have prepared us for what we saw. Everyone you've spoken to, from the very first time you checked in, either saw it directly, or has been fully briefed on what happened. By my order, they have been under strict instructions to completely avoid the subject with you. I knew you'd start asking questions when you were ready to hear the answers."

"Thank you, Dad. I think it was best that I didn't know that from day one." Then, knowing his dad's principles, Christian purposely asked an open-ended question. "Is there anything you can tell me to give me a glimmer of hope that I may yet survive this predicament?"

"As a matter of fact, there is. Let me tell you what we have here at the Cape, so you have a more complete picture. We have your body, preserved in a sort of coma."

"You have my attention, go on,"

"We started working on reviving your body the moment it returned, and your resuscitation actually wasn't that difficult to accomplish," his dad explained. "Your mangled body returned with the space-time-stamp of the initial transport moment. As you know, we had med tech teams standing by. They estimated your heart stopped beating roughly twenty-four hours prior to return transport. You arrived here in an arms-folded burial position, naked, without your burial clothes wrapped around you. What's interesting is the fact that your body lingered back in time a short while. Unlike the other experimental animals that returned quickly after their death, your body took a while to jump after you died. We think your cellular nanites fought to maintain your organ functions even after your heart stopped. So, while you were in fact dead when you returned, the cancer-curing cellular nanites managed to preserve your oxygen-deprived organs long enough, until life support could be administered at HQ. The required resuscitation was modest. We started IVs of saline and your own pre-donated blood to get some fluid into your veins, compressed your open tibial arteries, then one shock of the defibrillation paddles got your heart going again."

"I'm alive in the present?"

"You're in a coma. Well sort of a coma. Your body is fine, fully healed in fact, probably due to the cellular nanites. Your brain waves are consistent with a person in a moderate coma. It's more like your body is in hibernation," his dad explained.

"I'm alive but unconscious and have been that way ever since I jumped. Why won't I wake up?"

"That's a great question. I need to walk you through some theories we have. First, as you know, the reason why your return time stamp didn't work is because, for some reason, the initial time-space transport nanites can't, or won't, yield to the return time-stamp transport nanites until the organic material they inhabit dies," his dad reiterated.

"Animals always coming back dead was a bug with the combination of initial and return jump nanites, not a result of the jump itself," Christian said.

"That's right. Theoretically, if we fix the conflict we should be able to control the return jump. In your case, it took some time for your body functions to degrade sufficiently to the point where the return nanites could take hold. There may be something about the return nanites not having acclimated to live tissue fully but at least long enough for the transport to occur. Obviously, this needs further investigation in a more controlled setting at a future time. Had your body not jumped back to the lab, your cellular nanites would have eventually fully failed and you'd have died permanently, just like anyone else."

"That may explain why my body lingered here in this time and then jumped. Why is my body in a coma?"

"The second part of the theory is more of a hunch and this is going to require some faith. It's my hypothesis that just as time seems to be immutable, so, too, must your consciousness be immutable. That is, whether it's the human soul itself, or communication between the nanites at multiple locations, it appears you're only allowed to be awake in one location at a time on a specific timeline."

"You think that for me to wake up in the modern time-space reference location, I need to die in the ancient one?"

"Yes, that's exactly what I think," his dad confirmed.

"Dad, now I really need your advice."

"How can I advise you?"

"I have a very important decision to make. It's tough to even verbalize. Wouldn't it be blasphemy for me to assume the role of Jesus Christ?"

"I don't know that it necessarily would be."

"What should I do?" Tears were flowing down Christian's cheeks.

"I don't understand this any more than you do. Maybe Jesus will still show up. Just because you end up getting crucified doesn't mean you die as Jesus. People were being crucified left and right in the Roman Empire in the first century."

Christian fell back into silence, feeling the decision had already been made. He had cured David's wounds and turned the water into wine at Cana.

"Son, I'm proud of you and I love you. I trust, in both you and God, that whatever is happening is for His purpose."

"I love you, too, Dad. Thanks for reminding me to have faith."

Christian sat alone in the stable after the 3D image of his father faded. He curiously inspected the smooth metallic edges of the cubepod he was holding. He envisioned that the cubepod was a box, and inside the box lived Schrodinger's cat, simultaneously alive and dead. The paired spinning particles of the cubepod's memory array transcended space and time and were permitting him to see both states at the same time. If he were the cat, in which state was he, alive or dead? He contemplated Rene Descartes' "I think and therefore I am," and decided since he was aware, he must be the alive cat. He'd go with that thought.

Christian considered what was to come as he embarked on emulating the ministry of Jesus. He was familiar with the major miracles, but he couldn't help thinking he was in way over his head. He possessed knowledge and technology, but some miracles simply couldn't be duplicated with his limitations. He decided to take things one day at a time. He'd trust that events would unfold as they were meant to and that perhaps Jesus would show up and everything would be explained. In the meantime, the term, "What Would Jesus Do?" would have a new personal meaning.

Christian returned to Nazareth and the home of Mary and James. When he found Mary alone, quietly sipping her tea, he approached. "Mary, I know that you believe I'm your son Jesus. It would be deceptive of me to let you believe I've come from the magi. I am not that child, but I am here, and I believe, for whatever reason, that I'm destined to fulfill the mission Jesus was supposed to accomplish here on earth. Maybe he'll still show up and then I'll understand more fully what my role in life is because he'd be able to explain this puzzle to me. Until then, I'll be your Jesus. Your love and support will be crucial not only for my success, but for my wellbeing and sanity. I'll need your strength, but mostly your love."

"Oh Christian, of course I'll support you. I've believed in you since you arrived," Mother Mary said, "from the moment you came to Nazareth asking to find Jesus. I know you won't disappoint us. You have my support and you are my son, whether you believe this or not. By the way, I've already been bragging around town about how my son, Rabbi Jesus, turned the water into wine and that you were the one who fixed the well that had been making the children sick. That should fit in with that book of yours, where things are already written."

"Yes, it should. What will you tell James?"

"I will tell him the truth," Mary said solemnly, "after dinner tonight. What will you do next?"

"Next, I need to head to the Jordan River and pay a visit to a man who's baptizing people."

"Oh, your cousin John?" Mary asked. "Why visit him?"

"Mary, it is written in the Gospels that after the wedding at Cana, Jesus went to the river Jordan to be baptized by John and that is exactly the path I intend to follow."

"All right, if that's the case, would you mind if I come with you? I haven't seen John in a while and maybe we can stop and visit his mother along the way? She lives in Samaria."

"John's mother Elizabeth is still alive?" Christian asked, knowing she was advanced in age when she conceived the baby who would become John the Baptist.

"No, not Elizabeth. I mean the woman who raised him, Elizabeth's sister Hannah. Elizabeth died when John was only seven years old. Though, there you go again Christian, knowing things in ways I don't understand. I haven't mentioned my cousin Elizabeth to anyone in a long time."

"These things are written and so I know them," Christian said. "I'm not sure how else to explain it and yes I would love your company on the trip."

Baptism

Christian made a quick trip up Mt Kedumim to ask HQ for a favor. He wasn't sure if it was possible, but he needed an image file and voice recording downloaded. He pinged the cubepod and Cornelius answered.

"Hi Christian."

"Hey Cornelius."

"I understand you had a frank talk with your father. I'm glad," Cornelius said. "It's been hard for us to keep that information from you every time we talked. Are you okay?"

"Yes, thanks for asking Cornelius. It was gut wrenching to hear, but I've had some time to think about it and, well really, there's nothing for me to do but press ahead."

"I agree. It's good to see you in good spirits Christian."

Christian gave his friend a genuine smile. "Hey, I need a file from you, if it's possible."

"Sure, depending on what you need."

"I need a dove to appear and a voice to make a pronouncement about me." He went on to describe exactly what was needed and waited in the stable until it was produced. Turns out, it wasn't that difficult, and the download worked just fine.

Christian came back down the mountain and saw that Mother Mary and James were both packed and ready for the trip to visit John. "I'm coming with you, too, if you don't mind," James said. "Mom told me about you being her son born in Bethlehem. I just want you to know, I trust her instincts and if she's willing to accept you as her son, then I, too, am willing to accept you as my brother."

"That means so much to me James." They exchanged a hug. "And, it is good you're coming. After I get baptized, I'm going to have to go on into the wilderness on my own for a while to prepare for the ministry. Please see to our mother's safe return and I will circle back to Nazareth when I can, but it may not be for a while."

"Understood, she already told me what your plans are," James said and reached down for a pair of soft leather boots sitting by the door of the house." That's why we got you these. Sandals won't serve you well for the land where you're headed."

Christian accepted the boots. "Thank you, James. These are perfect."

"We'll leave you on your own on the other side of the Jordan," James said. "For now, we should be able to make Nain by nightfall. That's a trading hub so we should be able to find a place to stay there without a problem. Next day we can stay with Hannah in Salim and from there we'll be within half a day's walking distance to the Jordan."

"Lead the way, brother," Christian said as he smiled at James, then winked at Mary.

They headed south to Nain near the border of Galilee and Samaria and found a place that provided food and lodging for the night.

They headed southeast the next morning, walking at a reasonable pace for Mary and taking breaks as necessary, finding shade under a grove of fig trees during the heat of the day. They entered the small village of Salim in late afternoon and paid a surprise visit to Hannah. She gave Mary and James big hugs. "And who's this you've brought with you Mary?"

"Allow me to introduce my long-lost son, Jesus," Mary said. "He's returned to us at last. We're on our way to visit John and so we thought it appropriate to pay you a visit."

"Very nice to meet you Jesus," Hannah said. "I know there's a story here and I want to know all the details. You all simply must stay the evening and give me time to pack up and join you tomorrow. I'm due to visit John again anyway and it would be nice to have company on the walk. Would that be all right?"

"The more the merrier," Christian said. "It's nice to meet you, too, Hannah."

"We were counting on you to let us stay Hannah," Mother Mary said. "Thank you for coming through for us. I will help you with dinner."

"That sounds fine, I'm interested to hear the story of this son of yours." Hannah and Mary walked towards the kitchen area and their last sentence Christian could make out was something of a question from Hannah about who the father was. He didn't hear the answer.

James and Christian sat down, stretched their legs, and massaged their aching feet. "That's a lot of walking," James said. "I think I've just about worn out my sandals."

"I know," Christian agreed, "and your mom is a real trooper about it."

"Our mom," James corrected him, "and yes, she is."

Hannah and Mary served a hot meal of lamb stock over millet, mashed chickpeas, and bread that evening. It was welcome nutrition for the travelers and a treat for Hannah as well since she had saved the lamb bones for just such an occasion.

The next morning, Mother Mary, Hannah, James and Christian headed east to the Jordan River. They entered the Jordan valley and approached the meandering lower section of the river, north of where it empties into the Dead Sea. It wasn't hard to track John down, for all they had to do was follow the path of others making the same pilgrimage. Soon, Christian spotted a crowd and a man preaching at the water's edge. "Oh, there he is," Hannah said. "He'll be delighted to meet you, Jesus."

"I've been looking forward to meeting John, too," Christian said. "It will be quite an honor in fact."

John the Baptist saw Hannah as she approached. He stopped what he was doing and bolted from the water in their direction. He ran up to her, lifted her off the ground and gave her a huge bear hug. "Mother, so great to see you! Just look at the crowd and dedicated disciples and more people are coming every day."

"Yes son, you make me proud. I hope you're taking good care of yourself out here."

Christian assessed the wardrobe worn by the famous John the Baptist and was amused to see that he was in fact wearing a shaggy camel hair tunic and a thick leather belt about his waist. John was a full bearded, tanned, bare footed, muscular man. He fit the John the Baptist stereotype quite nicely.

"We've all come out here to see you today, John. Do you remember Mary and her son James?" Hannah asked, gesturing towards the others in the party. "And, there's someone new here to see you."

"Yes of course, it hasn't been that long," John reached out to hug Mother Mary and then gave James a hug as well. "Good to see both of you." Then John turned his attention to Christian.

"This is your cousin Jesus," Hannah said. "He's another son of Mary and Joseph, born before James. It's a long story but the important thing is he's come back home. It's because of him we've all come out to see you today."

"Jesus of Nazareth," John said with reverence. "This marks the ultimate moment of my life. It's an honor to finally meet you. As significant as my work here has been, I'm not fit to untie your sandals. I've awaited your coming, as it was told to me, and it's pleasing to see you in the company of my mother and other relatives."

"The honor is mine, "Christian said. "How is it you knew I was coming?"

"I knew you were coming in the same way you knew you had to be here."

"I'm here because I'm fulfilling what has already been written," Christian replied.

"Is it not therefore written that I would be here preaching repentance and baptizing with water, and yet proclaiming there would be one coming soon who is mightier than I, baptizing in spirit and fire?"

"Yes," Christian admitted, puzzled at John's knowledge.

"Well then, let's do this," John said. "But first, let's start with your brother. James, would you like to be baptized?"

"Oh, you should," Hannah said.

James agreed and they all walked back through the crowd to the water's edge. John gave a nice little speech about how his extended family had come all the way from Galilee and that James and Jesus were here to be baptized. John explained that the women present were his mother and the mother of the men being baptized. James removed his tunic and waded into the Jordan, waist deep. John dunked James' head under the water and pulled him back up, proclaiming his rebirth as a child of God.

It was Christian's turn next. He removed his gear and tunic and waded into the river. With his permission, John dunked Christian's head under the water. Christian came out of the water and squeezed the water from the ends of his long hair. John said to him, "Cousin, congratulations, you've been baptized a child of God. I'm glad you have accepted this calling and I wish you well. Is there anything else you need?"

"Maybe some advice," Christian admitted, while still standing bare chested, waist deep in the river. "I'm about to head off into the wilderness for an extended period in preparation for my ministry. Given your experience out there, can you give me any survival tips?"

John laughed. "That's a fabulous and practical request my cousin. You're fortunate because this is a good year for locusts, so they will be plentiful. Wild honey is also prevalent. However, I must caution you about gathering it. Gather it only near dusk or dawn, for the bees are much more likely to swarm during the heat of the day when the sun is fiercest. I have a feeling you will be just fine though. God will care for you."

"I hope so and I appreciate the suggestions."

"Jesus, I look forward to your return. I know your ministry will be powerful and that I must diminish, and you must increase."

"That, too, is as it's written," Christian said. "You are wise man John, son of the priest Zachariah, Baptizer of men, preacher of repentance."

"You part ways with me with an exaltation of fancy titles," John said. "Yet my titles pale in comparison to yours, Lord Jesus."

"Perhaps we are mutually humbled, let's leave it at that." Then Christian reached out and hugged John close. "You've done well, John, continue to be strong and my best to you."

Christian returned to the shore, recovered his gear and grabbed his tunic. He hugged Hannah, James, and then Mother Mary. "I must be on way now." He bowed to all of them and made his way to the opposite shore. He fiddled briefly with his cubepod. An animated majestic dove appeared over him and the voice of Doctor Naismith bellowed, "This is my beloved son, in whom I am well pleased." Christian didn't know how long he was going to be able to get away with parlor tricks like this, but he would take this one for now. There was technically nothing inaccurate about what his father had just declared.

Christian glanced back across the river and saw looks of astonishment on the faces of all those present. He stood up, smiled broadly, waved goodbye and turned to walk into the wilderness beyond the Jordan. He would use this time to study and prepare himself for what he knew would be a challenging mission.

He soon noticed that a couple of John's disciples were following him. He turned and asked them, "Why are you following me?"

"Rabbi, John bears witness that you are the Messiah. We wish to be your disciples."

"What are your names?"

"James, son of Alphaeus and Judas Thaddaeus."

Christian allowed them to stay with him at his camp that night and spoke with them about having a personal relationship with God. He preached that night privately to them about love and shared with them versus from the New Testament.

As night fell, he explained that he must first venture into the wilderness alone, but that they could do him a favor. "Go to Capernaum. Find Judas at his home there near the temple and inform him that the man he knew as Christian has accepted his calling as Rabbi Jesus. Tell Judas I'll be there after about forty days."

"My brother lives in Capernaum," James said. "Going there is not a problem Rabbi, I know the way well."

"We'll do your bidding, Lord," Thaddaeus said, "and we'll wait for you there."

Christian headed into the wilderness the next morning, alone.

The Wilderness

Christian headed to the eastern edge of the wilderness of Judah. He found an isolated expanse with a desert climate and a wild landscape. The land was crisscrossed by innumerable deep limestone ravines. He saw a topography of multiple high points from which he should be able to establish regular communication with HQ. He intended to stay true to the biblical record and remain in the wilderness for forty days.

Christian planned to use his time to research the ministry of Jesus. The preparations made prior to his jump were inadequate for the endeavor upon which he was about to embark. The mission parameters drastically morphed from working out time travel problems to emulating the ministry of Jesus. Thus far, he had been getting by from his basic memory of *Bible* stories. This time in the wilderness would give him the opportunity to study the Gospels more thoroughly.

He thought about the amount of water he had turned into wine at the wedding and did a little math. Six large stone jars holding at least seventy liters each, equated to 420 liter bottles of wine. That was a lot of wine. Surely Cana had wine for days after the wedding feast ended.

Christian also understood now why Capernaum would become the hub of Jesus' ministry in Galilee. The home of Judas would have served well as a gathering place with its dorm-like accommodations for Jesus' apostles.

Christian's limited camping experience with the shepherd boy sensitized him to what to expect as he roughed it in the wilderness. Still, he knew even the hardiest of survivalists would find the next forty days a challenge. But he also knew that his method of death would be crucifixion, so he wouldn't be dying in the desert. "What doesn't kill you makes you stronger, right?" he said aloud.

His first set of priorities included locating sustainable sources of water and food. He brought with him as much as he could carry, perhaps water for three days and food for a week. If John's diet was any indication, he needed to get used to eating locusts and wild honey. His next priority was to establish his camp at a reasonable height from which he could contact HQ. He found a suitable site after walking several miles. He used the bow drill David had given him to start his campfire, though he found it more difficult than he anticipated. David make it look so easy.

Christian climbed to the ravine precipice and pinged HQ on the cubepod. Cornelius answered. "Hello, this is heaven, may I help you?"

Christian burst out laughing. "Oh my god, Cornelius, this is serious stuff. You can't be doing that to me!"

"Oh, why not my friend. It is all a matter of perspective. So, tell me all about what it has been like to take up the mantel of Jesus."

"It's going to take me a while to get used to it," Christian said. "On one hand, I feel like a magician playing tricks on a naïve population with the technology I have at my disposal. On the other hand, a message of redemption from a loving god needs to be delivered to these people. Scripture needs to be fulfilled, right? Or rather, I need to 'write' the Gospels, so to speak. Overall though, I would say I'm still apprehensive about the whole idea. My plan is to perform the ministry based on what's written in the *Bible*. And, I believe I've adequate time to figure out how to do it. Though I'm really hoping that the real Jesus shows up eventually."

"It's a tough spot," Cornelius sympathized. "Seeing as you're speaking with heaven, how can we help you?"

"Okay heaven, here's what I need."

Christian went on to spell out a litany of requests ranging from technical to philosophical. He wanted confirmation that the cubepod had sufficient memory storage to handle the expected volume of reference material he wanted to download. Key reference material he needed included: regional time appropriate maps, a study *Bible* with cross references and footnotes, the earliest Greek translation available of each Gospel, historical records of Pharisee and Sadducee religious guidelines and practices, Roman doctrine, and anything else about ancient Palestine the HQ team thought might be useful for their wayward time traveler. "Also, give me the Babble tutorials for Hebrew and Latin. I'll take this opportunity to smooth some rough edges I still have in those languages."

Christian had another challenge for the HQ team. "Cornelius, do you remember what happened with Apollo 13?"

"Yes, of course, they had a major malfunction on the way to the moon and just barely made it back alive," Cornelius said.

"Exactly. If you remember, they had a problem with their oxygen supply and only limited tools available to correct the issue, or they would suffocate long before they made it back to earth. It was the mission control team that figured out the contraption they needed to assemble, using materials on hand in their capsule to fix the problem."

"Understood. We are your mission control team," Cornelius said.

"Yes, and I need the best minds in Spintronics working on the problems at hand. To emulate the miracles of Jesus, I have a cubepod and nanites. That's it. Have the team walk through the *Bible* with a completely new lens. The image of the dove and my dad's voice at the

River Jordan was sufficiently believable. There may be other occasions like that where the cubepod will work. Some of the other miracles, though, I haven't quite figured out how to accomplish. Please let the smart people in Berkeley and the other sites know that I'm counting on them for support."

"Christian, your father has already given that exact same order. People are already working on it."

"Excellent. Make sure they know how much I appreciate it."

Berkeley working on accomplishing the miracles of Jesus' ministry was music to his ears. He had one last special request for Cornelius. "Would you mind downloading some music for me? You know what I like and there's nobody out here in this lonely desert but me." Christian remained on the ravine's crest until his cubepod was fully charged, then returned to his camping area to begin studying.

The next communication came later that day when the material was ready. Before cracking open the reference material he scanned through the music playlist that Cornelius provided him and chuckled. He saw there was no sense of irony left untouched at HQ. First on the list was the theme song to *Jesus Christ Superstar*. The second song on the playlist was clearly the most apropos for the moment. He cranked up the volume and the sound of the Rolling Stones', Live from Zilker Park, reverberated across the ancient wilderness of Judah. Mic Jagger blasted off the introductory line of *Sympathy for the Devil* and so fulfilled the temptation of Jesus. Christian contemplated the conundrum that there wasn't anyone with Jesus to witness exactly what happened while he was in the wilderness to record in the Gospels. He was just going to have to tell Matthew about it later, he thought, though he may leave out the parts about the Blitzkrieg and the Kennedys. That would be too weird.

Christian established a routine of studying reference material, periodically contacting HQ, and ensuring his survival, though not necessarily in that order. He could tell Spintronics staff was hard at work brainstorming the accomplishment of biblical miracles. In some cases, there was more than one way to imitate the events, but others remained a challenge, such as bringing dead people back to life.

He studied the biblical text and supporting material and attempted to map out the order and location of the events of Jesus' ministry. He determined that he was going to be doing quite a bit of walking around Galilee, Samaria, and Judea. His ministry circuits would cover an area of eighty miles north to south from upper Galilee to Jerusalem and twenty miles east to west from the Jordan to Cana. He tried to imagine the size and determined that it was an area roughly the size of Connecticut.

He decided that he would need two bases of operation. One would be in Capernaum, in the north, ideal with its location on the Sea of Galilee and the convenient housing of Judas. The other could be in or around Bethany, in the south, which Christian was yet to scout. Bethany was where Lazarus lived, and it was apparent from the Bible that Jesus stayed in Lazarus' home. Perhaps Lazarus' home could be the base of operations in Judea, just as Judas' home in Capernaum would serve for Galilee.

Jesus agitated the Jewish religious aristocracy, the Sadducees and the Pharisees of Judea particularly, and Christian planned to follow the same path. He decided to spend the rest of the day delving further into the Jewish sects and studying the Hebrew language.

The Sadducees were of an elite Jewish sect identified with the upper social and economic echelon of Judean society. The Pharisees were more like a political party who claimed the full-support and goodwill of the common people, even though they accounted for less than 1% of the population. Christian found it interesting to learn that the Sadducees were the ones who maintained the 2nd Temple in Jerusalem, which was the center of worship and Jewish society in Judea and had been since its reconstruction 500 years earlier.

Christian understood both the Sadducees and the Pharisees would be threatened by the populist message of Jesus, and their combined strength in Jerusalem would lead to Jesus' crucifixion. His crucifixion, if the real Jesus didn't show up. He put that out of his mind.

Christian needed a better understanding of the Gospels and other Gnostic writings. He paged through the display on the cubepod and turned to the beginning of the New Testament. The Gospels of Matthew, Mark, Luke and John appeared in that order in the Bible, though he knew they were not written in that order. Early first century animal skin scroll fragments indicate that all the Gospels were originally written in Greek, which is why Christian asked HQ for the earliest available Greek translations.

The books Matthew, Mark and Luke presented an overall synopsis of the life of Jesus. Distributed between 50 to 60 AD, they were mainly written to gain converts. Matthew was an eyewitness to the ministry of Jesus and, as a tax collector, would have had writing skills. Mark was a friend of the apostle Peter and documented Peter's accounts of events. Luke was a physician, a non-Jew, and the companion of Apostle Paul. Luke also wrote the Acts of the Apostles.

The Gospel of John, written 85 AD, mostly provided inspiration for the already faithful. John's was the only Gospel to include the raising of Lazarus from the dead. Its author is mysteriously self-identified as "the disciple whom Jesus loved," though the identity of the author has been the subject of scholarly debate.

Christian decided he'd pay special attention to what he said to Matthew, as he was the only eyewitness Gospel author. Christian wanted control of that pen. There may be need to shape Matthew's observations around certain events so history is recorded correctly.

Christian used the time in the desert to construe the ministry chronologically. He paid special attention where consistencies existed across Gospels. He memorized the twelve apostle's names and how they were recruited. Matthew described the recruitment of Simon Barjona and his brother Andrew, then James the son of Zebedee and his brother John. They are all fisherman and would likely be recruited soon after Christian returns from the wilderness.

The remaining eight apostles are named later in the Gospel of Matthew: Philip, Nathanael, Thomas, Matthew, James the son of Alphaeus and Judas Thaddaeus, whom Christian has already met but didn't recognize as an apostle at the time; Simon the Zealot, and Judas, who would be called Iscariot. There are going to be a lot of James' and Judas', hopefully he wouldn't get them all confused.

Christian continued this process of mapping and visualizing event sequences in his mind. He knew all the apostles were Galilean and figured they would all be recruited early in his ministry. It was quite overwhelming as he considered the scope of the ministry in total. He trusted HQ to sort out the miracles. He was more concerned about all the oration required of him, with which HQ wouldn't be able to help.

He regularly communicated with HQ while isolated in the wilderness and looked forward to the conversations on both a personal and mission level. He could tell that progress was being made with each conversation and took comfort in knowing he wasn't confronting this challenge alone. Unfortunately, HQ didn't always have the answers. The resurrection of Lazarus was particularly problematic. Christian was counting on someone at HQ having an aha moment for that one.

He climbed to the precipice for his next communication and pinged HQ. Dominic's image appeared.

"Hey Christian," Dominic said.

"Hey Dominic, good to see you. What's new?"

"Everyone's working really hard on the miracle challenges."

"You mind telling me which one's they find most challenging?"

"Lazarus's resurrection is top of the list," Dominic said. "They're also not sure how you're going to calm the seas, since the nanites can't control the weather. And, they don't really understand your power over demons. There may be some others. Regardless, sure does look like you're going to be busy."

"Yes, that's for certain." Christian wanted to help them focus. "Lazarus's resurrection won't happen until near the end of the ministry in Judea. Tell them not to worry as much about it right now. Have them put their energy into the first part of the ministry centered around the Sea of Galilee. Among other things, I'm going to have to feed 5,000 people at one time and that can't be faked. Let me worry about calming the apostles while they're on the seas. And as far as the demons are concerned, this society isn't very diligent about treating mental illness. Some of the possessed may just be schizophrenics."

"Yeah, that's what Atlanta was thinking. They were wondering if there was a way to ship you antipsychotic medications," Dominic volunteered.

"Let's not go there," Christian said.

"We agree. We do have an animated image to send you, though," Dominic informed him.

"Oh really, what of?"

"The animation is of you, walking," Dominic shrugged. "You're going to have to project it onto the water for when Jesus walks on water."

"Oh great, I'm damned for sure. Jesus walking on the water will be a hologram. Is that the best Berkeley can do?"

"That's the only viable option," Dominic said, "and the timing will be critical, so they'll want to walk you through the process as that miracle approaches. You're going to have some busy spurts. The feeding of 5,000 people and the walking on water miracles occur back-to-back on the same night."

"Nice! That's the sort of stuff I'm needing Berkeley to work out for me. Reminds me to ask, how's the telemetry?"

"It comes and goes. When it comes in strong we usually think it's because you're about to contact us and you're ascending to a high place."

"Can you tell where I am right now?"

"We have strong space-timestamp coordinates, but the place you're at has no name. You're in the middle of nowhere, between Jericho and the Dead Sea."

"Tell me about it." Christian sighed. "Dominic, do me a favor and pass the cubepod along to my dad again."

"Absolutely, take care." Dominic signed off.

His water source was a pool of stagnant water that remained at the bottom of the deep ravine below his camp. The ravine escaped the majority of daily sunshine, so the pool avoided significant evaporation.

He established a routine of climbing down every couple of days to refill his bola bags with water. He learned from his experience with the well in Nazareth that the purification power of one capsule was sufficient for a large volume of water and the molecular nanites were certainly doing their job on his little pond. Spintronics couldn't have anticipated he'd be applying nanite technology as a survival tool while staying in the wilderness for forty days, but it was for applications like this that the nanites were provided in the first place.

Christian's camp was midway up the terrace. Between communicating with HQ above and fetching water from below, he was getting plenty of exercise. He noticed that the ambient temperature dropped precipitously towards the bottom of the ravine near the watering hole. Often, he'd escape the heat of the day by remaining near the base of the ravine.

He set aside time each afternoon to study ancient Palestinian history, culture, and languages. He caught his mind drifting one afternoon as the personal 3D tutor droned on, speaking and reading Hebrew. He came to realize the homework would be helpful only to a limited extent since modern Hebrew vocabulary and pronunciations were altered from the form in the first century. His Europeanized Hebrew would need further tweaking when he got back to Capernaum.

He took a break and set the study material aside, descending a little further to fetch water. He caught site of a small viper slithering across the river rocks at the bottom of the ravine, twenty feet from the water's edge. Sensing movement, the snake stopped. Christian had a score to settle. He slowly approached the snake from the direction of the water, raised his foot and slammed the heel of his leather boot down on the viper's head, smashing it against a rock.

"That's for Nikud!"

Christian draped the snake's body over his arm, collected water, and climbed back to his camp. He propped a large flat rock across the fire, peeled back the snake skin with his knife and laid the sliver of snake meat on the hot rock to cook. The thought of eating snake intrigued Christian. He had eaten Everglades' alligator before and was anticipating the reptile to have a similar texture and taste, like a cross between seafood and chicken. Regardless of taste, it was a welcome bit of nutrition for his protein starved body and a relief to know he'd not have to survive on only locusts and wild honey. The meat of this snake turned out to be gamey and tough. He was pretty sure the bit of flavor it picked up was from the salty minerals from the slate upon which it was cooked. He didn't expect to see Israeli desert viper on menus anytime soon, but he nevertheless ate every morsel.

He made the climb to the precipice to talk with HQ early the next morning. He was looking forward to speaking with his dad again and was pleased when his dad answered the ping. Christian dropped pretenses. "Dad, I'm really struggling with this whole playing God thing. This was never my intention. I'm just a regular guy." Christian appreciated his dad's innate ability to listen and validate feelings.

"I'm struggling with this, too, Son," his dad said.

What? Wait a minute. Not quite what Christian was expecting to hear.

"I've regretted allowing you to go from the moment the first dove returned dead on the test table. You have no idea how hard it was for me to refrain from leaping into the middle of the room and yelling for the experiment to be stopped right then and there. With the subsequent failed test subject transports, I rationalized that maybe it wouldn't happen that day and we'd be afforded another chance to talk about it. I was relieved when the last sequence was broken, until you colluded with Dr. Nguyen. All I could think of was that I still wanted to talk to you." He bowed his head. "Can you imagine the guilt I felt the next moment when your body returned so badly beaten and abused?"

Christian was quiet for a minute. "No, I can't. Nor am I so sure you can save me now and I'm sorry for that. But knowing how this tragedy unfolds certainly doesn't make it any easier for me to play the part. What gives me the right to play God?"

"What gives me the right to play the father of God? By giving you my blessing, I've accepted my own role as an iconoclast." He struck a lighter tone. "Do you know that as I browse the Gospels now I take special pride when Jesus is referred to as the Son of Man. I would like to think that as you take up your ministry you'll also think of your father in the process and know that you're not in this alone. In our case, we'll make it a term of endearment, not a sacrilegious claim."

"I suppose," Christian said. "But I'm going to shy away from titles that ascribe me deity. I can try channeling Jesus the man. I'm not going to claim to be Jesus the God."

"Hold that thought." His dad raised a cautionary hand. "Before you go writing off divine labels, remember John 3:16. The entire point of you channeling the ministry of Jesus will be lost if it doesn't include the concept that you are, in fact, the Son of God instead of just another in a long line of Jewish prophets. How about we reach a compromise allowing you to retain a measure of integrity as a man, and yet achieve the intent of Jesus' ministry. Let the proclamations of your deity come from your followers on your behalf. Your job is to perform miracles, demonstrate foresight, and speak your wisdom. They will come to their own conclusions, and you'll let them. Is that a deal?"

"I can live with that. It's a deal."

"I know you'll sort it out," his dad said. "There are other important topics we need to discuss. The Berkeley team is struggling with orchestrating Lazarus' rising from the dead with any technology or medicine available, much less using the limited resources you have on hand. I know you told Dominic to tell the team not to worry about that right now, which I think is good advice for the moment."

"Yeah, we have plenty of work to do in Galilee before we need to worry about ministering in Judea."

"The other problem I'm sure you are struggling with is getting your head around your own resurrection. You need to speak with conviction that you'll rise from the dead in three days."

"Dad, this is crazy."

"No, it's not. The fact is, your dead body is going to transport to HQ when you die, just as the animal bodies have. Like I told you before, you jump back about twenty-four hours after your heart stops beating, which will give your friends there enough time to put your body in the tomb," his dad explained. "Your body will transport, leaving your burial wrappings behind in place just as the *Bible* describes."

Christian followed his dad's logic and stated it plainly. "You believe Jesus was a time traveler."

"Yes, indeed I do."

"And the Berkeley team as well believes Jesus was a time traveler?"

"They do now, yes," his dad said.

"And Berkeley is prepared to shift their resources away from their nanite research to run models about the best way for me to play Jesus?"

"You make it sound like a game. To them, this is no game. They fervently believe in the immutability of time. As best we can tell, our timeline has not changed and our continued communication with you testifies to that fact. They're committed to modelling the miracles of your ministry because they believe they already have. They are bound by pre-destination to do so and, quite frankly, they're obsessed with it."

"It sure is foreboding, being the tool of some of the smartest minds in the world," Christian said.

"At least they're on your team. Is there anything else you need now?"

"No Dad, I'm good."

"Okay, love you."

"Love you, too."

Christian's exploits alone in the wilderness gave him time to consider the valued friendships he had already established in Palestine and the challenges that were ahead. He needed this retreat to ponder and gather strength before embarking on this unknown journey. By the time Christian reached day forty in the desert he had mellowed and mapped how the entire ministry would unfold. He would spend most of his ministry in Galilee and then migrate to Judea after the great signs and miracles were accomplished. Only the resurrection of Lazarus and his own crucifixion would remain. All told, it would take about two and half years to complete his mimicking of Jesus' ministry.

Christian climbed the steep rocky canyon wall one last time at dawn of his fortieth day in the desert. A brilliant sun rose over the wilderness. He noted the leather boots gifted him by James had served him well. He settled at the summit, removed the cubepod from his leather pouch, twirled it in his hand and let the sun reflect off its polished metallic finish. He considered pinging HQ, then suspended the idea and instead decided to cherish the moment. He surveyed the inhospitable land before him. The isolation of the wilderness was abated by his ability to daily commune with HQ staff, but somehow solitude seemed the appropriate course of action that last morning. Christian focused on his breathing, slowing its pace after the exertion from the climb. There was sparse vegetation amongst the landscape before him, and yet the westerly breeze carried a subtle hint of juniper and spruce. He perceived the soft whistling of the wind through the limestone ravines. He gazed inward, pushing the morning sights, sounds, and smells to the back of his mind. After a time of meditation, he finally managed to quiet the noise of competing thoughts and in the stillness, Christian prayed.

Part Two

Fishers of Men

But, there it is
You see it's all clear
You were meant to be here from the beginning
    ~Emerson, Lake & Palmer

Forty days in the wilderness can change a man. Christian's doubts about channeling the ministry of Jesus abated some. He headed north to the Sea of Galilee to recruit his apostles. He planned to swing by Judas' home in Capernaum and then go in search of four fishermen: Simon, Andrew, James and John. Spintronics Houston helped him work out a scenario to leverage the molecular nanites to overflow the fishermen's nets with fish.

Christian progressed along the eastern shore of the Sea of Galilee, passing through small villages that ringed the fresh water lake, until he came to the Greek village of Hippos, located strategically on a hill overlooking the sea. Famished from his time in the desert, he stopped to eat some smoked fish and bean paste on flat bread. After lunch, he continued north, passing through the town of Bethsaida and then turning west towards Capernaum. He used the high tower of the Capernaum Temple as a homing beacon. He went to the temple, met Rabbi Jarius and asked for a favor.

"Rabbi Jarius, it is good see you again."

"Good to see you, too, Christian. It has been a while."

"Yes, it has. I had some fundamental issues to sort out and it took time to do so. Which leads me to why I'm here. I haven't been to Judas' home yet. I wanted to speak with him in private first, rather than in front of the audience that I'm sure is in his courtyard. Would it be an imposition to have him meet me in one of prayer rooms of the synagogue?"

"Not at all. Do you need me to have one of my staff summon Judas to the temple?"

"Yes, that's what I was hoping you would offer. May I wait in the temple until he arrives?"

"Absolutely," Rabbi Jarius nodded, then went off to send a messenger to find Judas.

Christian found solitude in one of the temple prayer rooms and practiced his newfound meditation skill. It was nice to be back in the familiar surroundings of Capernaum and he hoped Judas would be receptive to the proposal he was about to make.

Judas arrived at the prayer room door, escorted by Rabbi Jarius. Christian rose to his feet and gave his friend a big hug. "I'll leave you two to yourselves. Take as long as need." Rabbi Jarius bowed and left them.

"Christian, why didn't you come directly to the house?" Judas asked. "And look at you, you've lost weight."

"Tell me about it." Christian replied as he looked down at his emaciated frame. "I came here first because it seemed more appropriate that we speak in private."

"Okay. James and Thaddaeus delivered your message about the ministry you plan to begin," Judas said. "I'm happy for you and glad to see you've accepted this calling. I had a feeling about it, you know. It's going to be an adjustment to start calling you Jesus."

"Oh Judas, you don't have to call me Jesus. You can call me, Rabbi, Teacher, Master, Lord, or the Messiah," he joked. "Seriously though, you and I both know I'm just a man and regardless of what happens over the next few years I intend to stay grounded in that truth."

"Understood, I'll endeavor to call you every appropriate title under the sun and I will cut you down to size if your head gets too big."

"Let's see how far that gets you." The two men laughed together.

"On a more serious note, I'm glad you came to the realization that you are Jesus," Judas said. "Let me know if there's anything I can do to help you in your ministry, and I mean anything." Judas held his gaze.

"As a matter of fact, there is something you can do to help. The time in the wilderness gave me an opportunity to think a lot about logistics and it's clear we're going to need a base of operations for the ministry in Galilee."

"Let me stop you right there. My home is your home. We'll make room where we have to for anyone who needs lodging, for as long as it takes."

"I knew I could count on you, but still, I felt obliged to ask."

"Say no more. I am at your service, as is my household."

"Thank you, Judas, you are a dear friend."

"Before you get into any more conversations," Judas said, "let me be the one to share some rather tragic news with you. John the Baptist is dead. King Herod Antipas had John arrested and then beheaded while you were in the wilderness."

"Oh no, so quick." Christian shook his head. "I just barely had a chance to meet him."

"I know, I liked him, too."

"You met him?"

"I did, a couple of years ago. He was a good man."

"When we go back to your home I'll look for the right moment to say a few words about John to whomever is gathered.

"All right, shall we go?" Judas asked.

"Yes, after you."

The two men arrived at the courtyard gates of Judas' home and excitement fanned out across the insula. Waiting there were Mary Magdalene, Sarah, James and Thaddaeus and one other familiar face Christian couldn't place. They all shook hands, hugged, and kissed as part of the long awaited reunion.

Judas introduced the familiar looking man to Christian. "Jesus, I would like you to meet Simon Cananeus, son of Abraham. He came looking for you here after he could not find you in Nazareth."

Christian wondered if this was to be the apostle Simon the Zealot.

"Good to meet you, Simon. Why were you looking for me in Nazareth?"

"You were at my brother's wedding in Cana and you turned six jugs of water into fine wine. I came looking for you as soon as I sobered up." Simon laughed heartily.

"Ah yes, you were the flute player at the wedding. I wondered why you looked so familiar. Happy to see you again." They shook hands. "I take it Cananeus could also be interpreted as 'of Cana', your hometown."

"Yes, and I'm surprised you remember me," Simon said. "Those ghawazi dancers were rather distracting."

"That's what you call the belly dancers? Ghawazi dancers. I like that name, and of course I noticed you. I liked your music. Did you bring your flute?"

"It's called a mizmar," Simon said, "and yes I did bring it."

"Excellent," Christian said. "Let's pray we have lots of reasons to celebrate and enjoy your music."

"Well, so far it has been great. Judas has a fabulous house. The food is superb, and the baths are refreshing," Simon observed. "A man could get used to living like this."

"Yes, I supposed he could," Christian said. "Well, let's enjoy it while we can, we have a lot of work ahead of us to spread our message throughout Palestine. Will you be joining me in my mission?"

"Absolutely," Simon said. "It's high time the people rallied against the Romans and their Sadducee puppets."

This last statement confirmed Simon's politics. Christian wouldn't bother to articulate that his purpose was not an armed revolution. "Well it's great to have you on board Simon."

Christian let the excitement of the reunion settle down a bit. When the timing was right he turned to Judas. "I think now is the time." Judas tapped people on the shoulder and directed their attention to Christian. Christian hung his head. He paused for a moment and determined then and there that this was where his leadership must begin. This household must have more anxiously anticipated his return than he realized with the death of John. And how much more so would the disciples of John be hungering for a shepherd. Christian understood that he must step into the void and rally the faithful under his leadership.

He lifted his head and got the attention of his friends and new disciples. He spoke loudly and firmly. "Folks, I've learned from Judas that John the Baptist has been executed. While you've known this for some time, please realize it comes as a shock to me. In this moment, I admit that I'm swimming in emotions and that one of these emotions is anger, for I met John just before entering the wilderness and was baptized by him. He was truly the salt of earth and I will miss him, just as I know you already do. We will welcome anyone who was a follower of John's into our fold. His message will be our message and we will amplify it with love and personal connection with God. What John cried out in the wilderness, we will proclaim in the towns and cities of Palestine and eventually in Jerusalem itself. Through our ministry we will assure that John the Baptist shall not have died in vain."

Christian turned back to Judas. "Thank you for letting me know so quickly about John. The mantel is now ours to carry."

"Very nice speech Lord," Judas said sincerely. "I'm with you." Christian smiled at Judas and proceeded to reacquaint himself with those in the courtyard.

After a short while, Christian circled back around for a private word with Mary. "See, I came back after all."

"Yes, I see that. Not quite the way I expected, but I'm glad you are here."

"I am, too. I'm sorry it took so long. Forgive me for leaving without any promise of return."

"If you truly didn't know, then there was no way you could promise. I'm just glad you're here now and I hope we can pick up where we left off."

"That would be nice."

"Let's start with this," Mary leaned forward, kissed Christian square on the lips, then playfully turned and sashayed away. Christian noticed a certain wiggle as Mary walked and wondered if she always walked like that or if women have a knack for wiggling their hips depending on their intentions.

Later that evening they were sitting around the fire in the courtyard. "Tomorrow I intend to continue recruiting apostles," Christian said. "I would be honored if you all would join me. We won't need to go far, just down to the shore of the Sea of Galilee." Everyone agreed to join him.

Christian and his disciples James, Thaddaeus, Mary, Judas, Sarah, Joanna, Susanna and Simon, set out for the shore of the Sea of Galilee the next morning. They found their new recruits at the water's edge between Bethsaida and Capernaum.

Christian took in the scene. The gentle waves of the large lake lapped at the shoreline and the dock. There were several boats within proximity, some with active fishermen and others at shore with fishermen tending to their nets. Christian expected to find the apostles Simon, who would become Peter, and his brother Andrew, and James and John with their father Zebedee. He spotted a fisherman on the docks, gathering up his catch. "Would you mind buying some fish for me this morning?" Christian asked Judas.

"My pleasure Lord, I've got the money purse," Judas said. "How much do you need?"

"I'm not sure exactly. Just enough for me to have a decent chance of finding one with eggs in it."

"Interesting," Judas said, "let's see how much this fisherman wants for this whole bundle."

Christian let Judas do the haggling. Judas and the fisherman settled on a price and Judas handed Christian the mesh containing about a half dozen fish.

"What kind of fish are these anyway?" Christian asked.

"They're tilapia," the fisherman said. "Quite common in the waters of the Sea of Galilee and tasty, too."

"I'm seeking specific men this morning for a very special calling to my ministry," Christian told the fisherman. "Would you mind telling me if any of the fisherman around here are brothers named Simon and Andrew and another set of brothers named James and John, sons of Zebedee?"

"Before I go pointing out my friends for a special calling, you mind telling me who's asking?" the fisherman replied, a bit guarded. Christian thought about his wording and realized his inquiry sounded a bit ominous. He softened his tone but proceeded with equal confidence knowing history was on his side.

"Yes of course," Christian bowed slightly." My name is Rabbi Jesus. This is my friend Judas of Capernaum and those are my other disciples," Christian gestured towards Mary and company on the shore line. "What's your name?"

"I'm Philip," he said as he looked over at Judas. "I recognize your name. Are you the same Judas that helped the synagogue fund the repair of this dock about a year ago?"

"Yes," Judas said. "I like to give back to the community when I can."

"Well, we appreciate what you've done for us. As far as the other fisherman you seek, they are right out there," Phillip said as he pointed towards a couple of boats not far from shore. "They regularly complain that they don't catch enough fish, but invariably they seem to cast their nets in roughly the same places. It's the way of fisherman you know."

"Yes, I think I understand," Christian said. "Do you think anyone would mind if go sit over there at the end of dock for few minutes?"

"Be my guest." Philip shrugged.

Christian hadn't expected the apostle Philip to also be at the Capernaum docks that morning. He wanted to make sure this was the correct Philip as recorded in the *Bible*, so he sought the only confirmation he knew.

"Thank you," Christian said, "and by the way, you might want to stick around and watch this, too, Philip. Let me ask you, do you have a friend named Nathanael?"

"Yes, Nathanael is my best friend," Philip confirmed.

"Okay, watch this and then go tell him what you've seen." Christian smiled. He gave Judas a hand signal to wait here and then strolled out to the end of the dock, carrying the mesh of fish.

Christian connived to target the boat with Simon and Andrew first. He sat down and began to slice open the fish, one by one. He found what he was looking for after gutting three of them: a fish loaded with eggs. Spintronics Houston assured him they had replicated the fish egg rapid growth capability of molecular nanites and it should work just fine. He reached into his pouch, withdrew a molecular nanite capsule, cracked it open over top of the exposed eggs in the guts of the fish, and then dropped the mama fish into the water. Within a minute he saw fish popping up around him. He stood up and called out to the two fishermen, "How goes the fishing?"

"Not so well, we've been fishing all morning and haven't really caught much," one of the men said.

"Looks like there's a lot of fish over here, why don't you cast your nets in my direction?" Christian said.

"At your bidding, we'll try it," one of the men replied.

By now the nanites performed their function and brought the school of fish eggs to their full grown steady state. Christian greatly enjoyed watching the drama play out as the two fishermen drew up their nets so overloaded with fish they couldn't handle it alone. They called out to their companions nearer the shore for assistance. The four of them barely managed to drag the haul into their boat and make it back to the pier. None could believe it. These men grew up on the sea and they knew these waters. What they just witnessed defied explanation. One of the men spoke. "Master, what an extraordinary amount of fish in one casting of our net. We've never seen anything like this! Did you make that happen?"

"It is written that I get the attention of you, your brother, and your friends in this way."

By now Philip and Judas had also rushed down to the end of the dock to help secure the haul of fish. "Simon, you need to listen to this man, his name is Rabbi Jesus and what he just did was incredible. I assure you, those fish weren't schooling at the end of the dock until he walked out there." Philip was already becoming Christian's enthusiastic ambassador. "Rabbi, this is Simon, his bother Andrew, and that's James and his brother John, both sons of Zebedee." Philip was gesturing with his open palm to each man and then lastly to the older man still in his boat, now tied to the dock.

"Gentlemen, it is truly an honor to meet all of you. I'm here to recruit you to a new and holy calling. It will entail a different kind of fishing, for we will be casting a wide net, sharing a new message of God's love and fishing for the souls of men."

The fishermen looked around at each other and ultimately deferred to Simon to do the talking. "Rabbi, we're amazed by the sign with the fish and humbled at your seeking us for this calling, but we are simple fishermen and we know nothing of this new message."

"I have long known all your names, and so, too, have I known that you will become my apostles. Through you, many will come to know a deep personal relationship with a loving God. You have but to drop your nets and follow me." Christian articulated these rehearsed these lines with a beaming smile. "The decision you make this day will change your lives and the lives of the multitudes whom our ministry will touch. It is indeed a special calling. There will be challenges, but there will be equally great adventure. Follow me this day and be forever grateful."

The men needed no more convincing. Thus, another miracle of Jesus was accomplished and several more apostles were recruited. It probably helped that Christian brought a small following with him to the shore that morning, for these men found themselves joining a group of already dedicated disciples.

Christian had to take care of one more order of business. James and John where abandoning their father, Zebedee. Christian considered that he'd not have left his father in this way, and it bothered him. He approached Zebedee on the dock.

"Your boys are coming with me. I feel badly for taking them away from you."

"Don't feel badly," Zebedee said. "I have other sons to help me fish. These boys have a new opportunity with you. Any father worth his salt wants a better life for his sons. You've shown them a fabulous wonder and your calling is profound. They are good boys and they will serve you well. Besides, you left me with a boat full of fish. What have I to complain about?"

Loop closed. He acknowledged the blessing and led his new apostles away. "Philip, please come along, and where's your friend Nathanael? He needs to join us as well. I think you may find him sitting under a fig tree over in that grove."

"I'll run and get him," Philip said and took off running to find his friend.

Soon thereafter, Philip caught up to the crowd of disciples with Nathanael in tow.

"How is it you know us by name?" Nathanael asked.

"Long before this day, I have known all your names and the names of others yet to join us," Christian said.

Nathanael bowed. "You truly are the Messiah, for Philip told me what you did with the fish. You also knew my name and you knew I would be under a fig tree."

"I assure you, you will see many more wondrous signs on the journey ahead," Christian said.

The group made its way towards Judas' home in Capernaum. "You are important additions to a select group I will be recruiting for my ministry throughout Galilee and Judea. I appreciate your commitment to this ministry and as we get started I would like us to focus on the message of God's love that we are spreading. The message is the important component, not the messenger."

They all expressed their understanding. The apostles would be staying in the houses on the insula around the courtyard of Judas' compound, each house accommodating two men. "There are still more apostles to recruit," Christian said to Judas. "Please make sure to leave room for them."

"I have it covered Lord," Judas said.

"Everyone, please get a good night sleep," Christian told his followers. "We have a big day tomorrow." Judas worked out the sleeping arrangements for the apostles. Everyone said their goodnights and retired to their rooms.

Christian and the apostles gathered at the cooking fire in the courtyard the next morning. "I've been invited by Rabbi Jarius to teach at the synagogue this morning," he announced. "After that, we'll make our way around Capernaum. Brace yourselves for a busy day." If the Gospels were any indication, today would be exhausting.

Christian and his disciples walked next door to the synagogue and, after a solemn embrace, Christian thanked Rabbi Jarius for the opportunity to teach that morning. "I won't be teaching from the scripture of Moses this morning. I have a new message to share. First thing I'm going to do is ask my disciples to look into their own hearts, to check our own motivations and shortcomings, before we take on this mission." Christian preached that morning and delivered a challenge of introspection of self and love for one's neighbor.

As Christian finished, there appeared in the synagogue a man crying out, "What do you want with us Jesus of Nazareth? Have you come to destroy us? I know you are the Holy One of God."

This was the first time Christian heard that title directed at him. Of all the issues for him to deal with that first morning of his ministry, it had to be a person with an "unclean spirit." Having elicited opinions on this issue at length with Spintronics Atlanta and their CDC consultants, their main theory involved the possibility that the cellular nanites, with their secondary healing affects, may also be able to stabilize chemical imbalances in the brain. If the nanites didn't heal the mentally ill, his fallback was the power of suggestion. Nevertheless, Christian was determined to treat the mentally ill people he encountered throughout his ministry with compassion. He signaled for the man to come sit next to him at the front of the synagogue. He put his arm around the man. "You have all of my attention. Put these other people here out of your mind. See how beautiful the view is from up here and think about how great God must be to have created such beauty." Christian gestured beyond the people to the view overlooking the Sea of Galilee. "Now tell me, why is it you say I am the Holy One of God?"

"I have heard of your miracles: purifying the well, curing the shepherd boy, changing water into wine, and the holy dove that descended on you at the time of your baptism," the man said.

Christian thought, wow that's a pretty good list already; word travels fast in ancient Galilee, even without the benefit of social media. To think he's just getting started with the ministry.

Despite being able to rattle off the list of miracles, Christian could see that the man was suffering from a nervous system affliction and perhaps some kind of mental instability. "I appreciate your acknowledgment of the signs of my ministry. I tell you sincerely that we are all children of God and he loves you very much. What is your name?"

"My name is Jabez."

"Well I see how shaky you are Jabez and I would like to try and help you. To do this, you need to trust me," Christian said. "Will you let me try and help you?

Jabez nodded.

Christian knew no other way, so he pulled out the fisherman's knife from his leather pouch. "This is going to seem strange, but there is healing power in my blood. I'm going to cut my hand and put some drops of my blood on your tongue."

Jabez looked on apprehensively as Christian sliced his own hand. He covered his pointer finger in blood and dabbed the man's tongue with it. Jabez immediately went into convulsions. Christian was no expert, but if he had to guess, Jabez was suffering from a type of epilepsy and Christian had just triggered a seizure.

The seizure eventually abated. Christian was still holding Jabez, though now his head rested on Christian's lap. Jabez was worn out from the seizure. "How frequently do you have seizures?" Christian asked.

"Every once in a while, Lord. I cannot control them."

"It is my belief that my blood may be able to help your condition. Can you do me the favor of stopping by the home of Judas after a week or so? That's where I'm staying. I would like you to let me know how you're doing."

"I can do that Lord."

Christian couldn't be certain what kind of healing power his cellular nanites might have on the man's condition. He felt he had done all he could for him, for now.

After the synagogue teaching, Judas, Simon and Andrew were discussing the man with the unclean spirit. "Do you really think you healed him?" Judas asked Christian.

"I don't know. It's going to be harder to tell with those who have mental conditions. His name is Jabez and I asked him to check in at your place in a couple weeks to let us know how he's doing. Please tell your house staff to be aware of him in case he stops by when we're not around."

"Will do Lord," Judas said.

"The healing would be evident more quickly if we could find some people who are physically injured or ill," Christian said.

"My mother-in-law is ill with fever," Simon said. "She lives here in Capernaum with me and Andrew. Do you think you can help her?"

It hadn't occurred to Christian's until just then that Simon Peter was married.

"Yes Simon, I believe I will be able to help your mother. Tell me also, what's your wife's name and how long have you been married?"

"Her name is Veronica. We got married about a year ago. No kids yet," Simon explained.

"What is your mother-in-law's name?"

"Her name is Ruth."

They left the synagogue and headed for Simon and Andrew's house. Simon's mother-in-law was lying in bed sick with fever. Christian came over to her and sat at the edge of her bed. "Ruth, my name is Jesus. How are you feeling?"

"Oh Jesus, I'm not feeling too well right now," Ruth said. "Simon has told us all about you. He's explained he needs to follow your calling. My daughter Veronica is concerned you're going to take him away for a long time. How long do you think Simon will be gone with you?"

"Ruth, tell you what, let's get you healthy and then we can talk about these other things. Veronica need not worry about being separated from her husband, Simon. She is welcome to join us, just as several other women already have. Now, will you let me try and heal you?"

"Yes, Jesus, I would appreciate that."

Christian's hand was already healed from the morning's synagogue healing. He once again sliced a small cut and placed a drop of his blood on her tongue. "My blood has healing power and I believe it will help you feel better. Just rest here a minute and relax."

The fever quickly left Ruth and soon she was feeling well enough to move about the house and wait on her guests. The remaining apostles joined them at the house where they stayed for a while. Word spread and all manner of people with various diseases and demons were brought to the door throughout the afternoon and into the evening. Christian offered them healing by slicing his hand and exposing the cellular nanites in his blood to theirs. It was exhausting for him. They returned that evening to Judas' house and began to plan their trips to other nearby towns around Galilee.

Christian walked next door to the synagogue early the next morning to speak with HQ in private, using the upper room of the high tower. He relayed to the technician who answered the cubepod what he had observed with the healing effects of the cellular nanites for both physical and possibly mental ailments. The technician, one Christian didn't recognize, assured Christian that he would relay the recent discoveries.

He returned to Judas' house. The plan for the day was to visit the town of Tabigha. According to the *Bible*, Jesus cured a leper there and, in the process, caused word of his ministry and healing abilities to spread further into Galilee. The disciples gathered in the courtyard and together they walked east to Tabigha.

Christian and his disciples arrived in Tabigha within an hour. Christian spent some time there preaching. After his sermon a man suffering from severe skin lesions approached Christian. The leper fell to his knees. "Jesus, I have heard about your healing ability. I know if you are willing you can make me clean."

Christian reached out and held the man's exposed hands. "I am willing. Allow me to help you. Yesterday, I was healing people in Capernaum by placing drops of my blood into their mouths. Since you are a leper, today I would like you to help me prove that contact with my blood on the open sores of your skin will also promote healing. Let's see together what happens with the lesions on your hands and arms." Christian proceeded to slice his finger tip and then drip some blood onto the man's hands and arms.

The man accepted the explanation and stayed on his knees, allowing Christian to treat him. Christian held the man's hands and engaged him in conversation while they waited together for the nanites to accomplish their healing. "What's your name?" Christian asked.

"My name is Uzziah."

"Uzziah, it is good to meet you this morning. History will not record your name, but it will record that after you are cured of this condition you are going to run and show yourself to the rabbi and you're going to tell them who healed you. Can you do that for me?"

"Oh yes, Lord, I would gladly do so."

"Great, just look at your hands, I see the lesions are starting to heal. Let me release your hands and make sure the healing process continues," Christian said.

Christian released Uzziah's hands and they both watched as the lesions on his hands and arms continued to ease in redness and puffiness. Uzziah was getting better.

"Does it feel any better Uzziah?"

"Oh yes, Lord, it is such a relief. I feel so blessed, thank you so much!"

"Great, now get up off your knees and go show yourself to the rabbi."

Uzziah followed Christian's instructions and proclaimed throughout Tabigha that Jesus cured his leprosy. Christian stayed for a while on the outskirts of Tabigha that day, offering his healing touch to those who needed it. Christian and the apostles returned to Capernaum late that evening.

Christian pinged HQ the next morning and his dad answered. "I've started to channel the ministry of Jesus," Christian said. "The healing power of the cellular nanites is quite impressive. I'm able to heal many conditions with my blood."

"Isn't it interesting that a modern medical treatment designed to cure your cancer is facilitating the amazing healing power Jesus demonstrated 2,000 years ago," his dad said.

"You don't think that's a coincidence, do you Dad?"

"Well, let's put it this way, I find it validating. You and I understand it's a side effect of the nanites in your body, but to these people it's mysterious and miraculous. They will begin to worship you just as they worshipped Jesus."

"I know. I'm determined to stay true to myself in this ministry. I'm not going to claim to be something I'm not. If they want to call me Messiah, that's fine, since that title infers the easing of suffering for people in need. I'm going to focus on the message Jesus brought to these people, and I will help them the best I can."

"I think that's wise," his dad said.

"I still have more apostles to recruit. Other than that, no more updates from my end. Anything from HQ?"

"Nope, we're good. Love you."

"Love you, too, Dad."

A few days later, after it became known that Jesus was back in Judas' home, a great crowd gathered so that there was no longer room even to get into the courtyard. Christian stood on a table by the fire pit so that the crowd could see him and hear his words. He noticed Jabez, the mentally ill man, in the crowd and acknowledged him. Christian was in the middle of a sermon about not putting new wine in old wine skins, when four young men propped open a hole in the thatched roof and began lowering a paralytic laying on a pallet down through the hole.

Christian heard Mary comment, "Judas, they're ruining your roof." Judas did not seem amused.

The four young men on the roof lowered the pallet with their paralytic friend to the ground. Christian hopped off the table and sauntered over to the young paralytic man. "Those are good friends you have there. They worked very hard to get you close to me so you can be healed." Christian laid his hands on the young man's legs. "What happened to you to make you no longer able to walk?"

"I took a bad fall and hurt my back. The doctor was able to reset the backbone, but he could not make the feeling return to my legs," the young man said.

"Okay, sit still a minute. I'm going to apply my healing blood to your injured spine. I'm going to have to make a small incision in the small of your back so my healing blood can get to your spine. Is that all right?"

"Yes, do what you need to Rabbi," the young man said.

Christian took out his fisherman's knife and sliced his hand. He moved his hand to the young man's lower back, made a small cut, and massaged his blood into the man's back. His cellular nanites would fix what the doctor could not. He waited a few minutes and then said to the paralytic, "Is there any feeling coming back to your legs?"

"Yes, at first it felt like a bunch of needles all over them, but now it's feeling better."

"All right, when you're ready, see if you can stand up, pick up your pallet and walk." Christian was trusting in both the healing nanites and what was already written.

The young man rose to his feet, picked up his pallet, and walked towards the courtyard gate. The crowd parted as the young man made his way through them. The four men looking down through the hole in the roof were cheering and the people in the courtyard were amazed. Several knew the young man for he was local to Capernaum and they conferred with each other that he had indeed fallen and broken his back.

Christian completed the evening preaching and the crowd slowly dispersed, still astounded at the healing of the paralytic young man. Christian noticed one of the young men who had lowered the paralytic down through the hole in the roof lingering at the courtyard gate. The young man approached Judas. "Sorry about your roof Judas. We couldn't get through the crowd, so we climbed the roof to get my twin brother closer to Jesus."

Christian remembered that Thomas means twin and, on a hunch, said to the young man, "The paralytic boy was your twin brother? Your name isn't Thomas by chance is it?"

"Yes, my Lord. That's correct, my name is Thomas."

What an interesting surprise. Christian hadn't been able to discern from scripture exactly who Thomas was or how he was recruited, but now he knew.

He turned to Judas, "Can we make room for this young man? He is to be one of my twelve apostles."

Judas nodded and quietly whispered, "Yes, Sire."

Christian turned back to Thomas. "I'm glad I could help your brother. Join me and help bring the message of salvation to the world."

"That is why I'm still here, Lord," Thomas said.

Judas arranged for Thomas to share a house with Simon the Zealot.

Mary greeted Thomas the next morning in the cooking area, pulling a hot cake from the stone oven and offering it to him. The cooking area was a popular place each morning. Various apostles came wandering in and asked what the plans were for the day. Judas sided up to Thomas, looked at him, looked up at the hole in his roof, "You going to fix that today?"

"Yes sir, absolutely," Thomas replied. "I'll fix your roof."

Christian shook his head at Judas and put his arm around Thomas. "I had the opportunity to do a lot of odd jobs with my brother around Nazareth. How about I help you?"

"That would be great. Thank you, Lord," Thomas said.

Christian was looking forward to learning more about this apostle of whom the *Bible* says very little, except for after the resurrection when he becomes doubting Thomas for not believing that the other apostles saw Jesus alive. They climbed up the stone steps to the roof, carrying thatch and twine. "I'm glad you've joined us, Thomas. Tell me, is your family from Capernaum?"

"Yes, I have lived here all my life. My father is a tailor in town. You may be wearing one of his tunics right now."

"Well fancy that. I'm glad your brother is well. Tell me about how your brother fell and became paralyzed?"

"My brother, my friends, and I were walking to Arbela to buy some linen for my father. We saw vultures circling a cliff's edge and more eating the carcass of an animal down below. My bother noticed a bundle of wool on the ledge below and decided to climb down to fetch it. He slipped, landed awkwardly, and cracked his spine. It took all four of us to carry him home. He's been paralyzed ever since, until last night when you cured him."

Christian listened to Thomas and could envision the entire scenario. He knew that cliff all too well. "You did a very nice thing for your twin brother last night by carrying him to me. Let's get this roof fixed so Judas doesn't give you any more grief." Christian gave Thomas a big smile.

Christian pondered a chain of connected events. If David's wool hadn't been on the ledge would Thomas' twin brother have avoided his fate to become the paralytic? In which case, would the healing of the paralytic *Bible* story have even happened? Would Thomas have become an apostle? Which came first, the chicken or the egg?

Thomas and Christian fixed the hole in the roof. Next on the agenda was another important apostle to recruit, Matthew the tax collector, the only eye witness author of a gospel in the *Bible*. Christian would want to keep Matthew close. Christian found James, son of Alphaeus, in the courtyard. "Come take a walk with me."

"Sure. Where are we going?" James asked.

"We're going to recruit your brother Matthew. He's important to the posterity of the ministry because of his writing ability."

"Yeah, he's smart, but he's a tax collector, working on behalf of the Romans. He's not just going to drop everything and follow you Lord," James said.

"Yes, he is and you're going to help me convince him."

Christian headed for the commerce district near the shore's docks where the tax collectors were located. After putting much thought into how to recruit Matthew, he decided to be utterly honest with him. He hoped it would work.

James pointed to his brother sitting in the tax office. Christian approached Matthew and leaned close enough to whisper in his ear. "Greetings my friend. You are Matthew, son of Alphaeus. Your brother James was a disciple of John the Baptist. He followed me from there and resides with me and the rest of my apostles in Judas' home. You were born and raised in Galilee and you despise your job as a collector of taxes for the occupiers of your country. You are fluent in both Aramaic and Greek and can write equally well in both languages. The world needs you to record my ministry for posterity. Your destiny changes today when you follow me."

Matthew set down his reed pen, looked up at Christian and said directly to James, "I'm kind of busy right now. Did you put him up to this?"

"No. I told him you're a stubborn asshole, licking the caligae of our Roman occupiers, and that you would be too arrogant to join our humble mission," James said.

Matthew gathered up his reed pens, animal skin parchment, and other belongings. He stood and peered at Christian. "My brother always did have a way with words. I've heard about you. Everyone around here has and I'm in as long as I can disparage my brother in this document you want me to write. Plus, you're right about my weariness of the Roman occupation, but honestly, I loathe the Pharisees even more. May I denounce their hypocrisy as I document your ministry?"

"The pen is mightier than the sword," Christian said.

"That is a clever phrase," Matthew said. "I like it."

Christian wasn't sure what the protocol would be for attribution of quotes to a man yet to be born, in this case Benjamin Franklin. Would Matthew jot it down, he wondered. It would be an interesting phrase to find on a Dead Sea scroll.

Christian and his apostles dined that evening in Matthew's home with other "sinners," and discussed lodging arrangements. The last remaining bedroom was in the two-bedroom house that Judas himself used. "The tax collector may stay in my house," Judas said.

"Thank you, Judas," Christian said.

"Also, Lord, I would like a word with you, alone."

"Of course, Judas."

The two men retreated to a private corner of the courtyard. "I've been meaning to talk with you about this for a while," Judas started. "You have recruited eleven apostles, and I know you are looking for only twelve. I would like to be your twelfth apostle." Judas looked squarely at Christian.

"No," Christian cried, clearly taking Judas aback.

"Why, Lord? Have I not been with you and helped you greatly so far?" Judas asked.

"Judas, you can't be my apostle. It's just not possible that it's you."

"I don't understand," Judas said. "I know from whence you came, and I believe in your mission. I believe in you."

Clearly distressed, Christian said, "I need to discuss this with my father. Let me give you an answer in the morning."

"I look forward to speaking with you in the morning then." Judas graciously retreated to the courtyard kitchen area where Christian saw him continue his duties as host.

Christian climbed the temple tower again the next morning and asked to speak with his father.

"Dad, I'm so glad to see you. I need to speak with you."

"I'm happy to see you too. What's the matter? You seem distressed."

"I am. You know my friend Judas that I've been telling you about, the one whose house is to be our base in Capernaum?"

"Yes, I remember. He's been a big help to you. I've been comforted by the fact that you have such an ally and friend there."

"He wants to be my twelfth apostle."

Silence.

"Dad, he can't be. He's Judas! He can't be the man who betrays me. I've recruited all the other apostles, just as they were recruited in the *Bible*. Oh, and Simon the Zealot was the flute player at the Cana wedding and Thomas is the twin brother of the paralytic that was let down through the roof and healed by Jesus. The only apostle I don't have yet is Judas."

"Maybe this Judas is meant to be your apostle, Christian."

"No. He's a nice guy, Dad. And my friend. I can't put that on him. Judas is known for the rest of the ages as the man who betrayed Jesus. He's reviled. And he kills himself after the crucifixion. Dad, I just can't fathom that Judas, my friend, is Judas Iscariot."

"Son, I don't have all the answers, and I don't envy your predicament. But Judas has been an immense help to you and probably will continue to be, for whatever reason. You're planning to take him with you on your journeys, aren't you?"

"Well, yes, but not as an apostle."

"It looks like you may not have a choice. I know you'll figure this out. Face it, you don't know Judas all that well. He may have ulterior motives for his actions, or not."

"I know you're right, Dad. I just hate the thought of him being *that* Judas."

"Christian, there's a saying that just might be apropos to the situation."

"What's that?"
"Keep your friends close and your enemies closer."

Galilean Ministry

Christian awoke early the next morning and greeted his disciples one by one as they mingled in the courtyard. He found Judas and put his arm around him. "Let's go for a walk."

"I would like that, where do you have in mind?" Judas said.

"It doesn't matter where we walk, the point is for you and me to talk."

"How about we go sit on the terrace of the synagogue?" Judas suggested.

"Perfect."

They made small talk as they rounded the block and took the short stroll to the temple and up the stone flight of stairs. There, overlooking the Sea of Galilee, Christian gave Judas his answer.

"Judas, you asked me yesterday if you could serve as my twelfth apostle. I hesitated to allow you do so because I know it will be a heavy burden to bear. I must confide with you, the path we're riding leads to martyrdom for me and for many of my apostles. You are already my friend and you have already proven to be an invaluable right-hand man. I was perfectly content to leave you in that role. You have a business to run and a household to maintain. Are you sure you feel the calling to do this?"

"Yes Lord, I am set on doing this. There is no place I would rather be than by your side throughout your ministry."

"It is settled then. You are my twelfth apostle. Welcome aboard." They clasped hands. Apparently, it was hopeless for Judas to resist his destiny. Christian felt utterly dispirited.

They walked back to Judas' home and gathered the disciples to embark on a tour of Galilee. They packed what provisions they could carry on their backs to allow them to camp outside if needed. The plan was to find accommodations in the homes of villagers when they could, however, some of the towns were more than one day's walking distance and Christian advised them to be self-sufficient if needed.

"We are about to go on a great tour of Galilee to spread our message around the region," Christian told the gathering. "I tell you with confidence, what we do here will bring hope and redemption not only to the oppressed people of Palestine, but also to millions of people yet born. Let's do this."

Their first stop was a small village just north of Capernaum called Chorazin. The village was located in the hills north of the Sea of Galilee. Most of the village structures were made from the local black basalt rock. Olive trees grew in the volcanic soil of the surrounding hills, supplying the village with a thriving olive oil business. Christian chose to tell the parable of sowing seeds in various kinds of soil because of the especially rocky terrain surrounding the village. He spoke in parables, so the people would understand his preaching through stories with which they would relate.

Christian and his disciples stayed in Chorazin for a couple of days, preaching and engaging with the population.

Their next stop was the small agricultural village of Tabigha where Christian had cured the leper, Uzziah. Tabigha was situated on the north-western shore of the Sea of Galilee, not far from Chorazin and Capernaum. It had several fresh water springs which supported a couple dozen farms and large gardens. Christian was preaching in the town market when Uzziah approached him enthusiastically. "Jesus, I'm completely healed! The townspeople no longer shun me. Look, I'm here in the market today."

Christian embraced him. "I'm very happy for you Uzziah. You are a good man and I'm glad you no longer suffer from the skin disease."

"Lord, there is another family here who could use your help," Uzziah said. "Will you come to their house and heal their baby?"

"Show me," Christian followed Uzziah to a stone house where a young mother presented her infant child to Christian for healing.

"What is wrong with the child?" Christian asked.

In response to this question the baby's mother opened the blanket to reveal the child had no legs, only stubs where her legs should have been. Christian was crestfallen. Missing limbs are not mentioned in the Gospels. It wasn't until this moment that he considered that there would be people he would not be able to help with his nanites. "I will bless your child, but my healing powers will not prompt her legs to grow. I am truly sorry."

"Please try Lord," the mother pleaded.

Christian did try and the result was as expected. Perhaps there would someday be nanite technology that could grow a replacement human limb. He realized this would not be the first healing shortfall of his ministry. How many people with missing or cut off limbs would he disappoint?

Christian and his disciples stayed in Tabigha for just half a day and then headed for Mary's hometown of Magdala. Christian walked with Mary and discussed his inability to heal the baby with her. "It really bothers me that I wasn't able to help that woman's child."

"Look at all the people you did help," Mary said. "Don't be so hard on yourself. People are going to have to understand that there is only so much you can do."

Christian nodded. Mary was right, he wasn't going to be able to heal everyone. He would have to find a way to manage the disappointment for those he couldn't heal.

Magdala was a moderate sized fishing village situated on the western shore of the Sea of Galilee. Its main industries were the processing and drying of fish, flax weaving, and cloth dyeing. He chose Magdala to tell the story of the pearl of great price, where the Kingdom of Heaven was likened to a hidden treasure in a field, which a man finds and sells everything he has to buy the field. Christian explained, "A man's soul is more valuable than everything else he owns."

Mary had countless friends in Magdala and went ahead of the party earlier in the day to arrange for the disciple's arrival that afternoon. The disciples were well fed and entertained that evening, thanks to the hospitality of Mary's friends.

Christian and the disciples remained an extra day in Magdala to rest and refresh themselves.

Christian mapped out the group's next moves. In the morning they'd head for Tiberias, the capital of Galilee, commissioned so by King Herod Antipas. Tiberias was located on the western shore of the Sea of Galilee, south of Magdala. He remembered that this was the city where Mother Mary's husband Joseph died in a construction accident. Tiberias, he knew, was also the middle name of Captain James T. Kirk of the *Starship Enterprise*. He chuckled at the thought.

The group arrived on the outskirts of Tiberias the next day and found it bustling with construction activity. The city was being built around the natural springs that existed in the vicinity and Christian envisioned the elite of society pampering themselves in the spas. He preached outside the walls and attracted a modest crowd of merchants and servants who were there supporting the construction workers. He refrained from entering the city, for this was the home of King Herod Antipas, executioner of John the Baptist, and it was not yet time for blatant agitation.

Christian and the disciples didn't want to stay in the capital city that night due to their general animus toward the Galilean king, so they slept under the stars. They were south of Tiberias, on their way to Philoteria where Christian would preach again the next day. Several of the servant girls who had heard Christian preaching outside the walls of Tiberias followed the disciples to their campsite. Picking up new followers was a common occurrence with each town they visited. On this occasion one of the servant girls was particularly enamored with Christian and situated her sleeping arrangement close to his. As the camp settled down and the disciples nodded off she managed to snuggle under his cloak. Seeking body warmth at night was relatively widespread practice, but Christian promptly recognized a distinction with this girl.

The intensity of the closeness and the subtle undulations of her body communicated copulas intentions. Christian's own arousal reminded him that it had been some time since he had been with a woman. Her hair, draped at his neck, smelled of cumin and mint. Under the cloak, her body was warm and emanated the fragrance of raw sexual desire. It was right there and would have been so easy for him to let what was about to happen, happen. Instead Christian said gently, half kicking himself as he did so, "Stop."

He pulled himself back from the promised land, leaned on his side and whispered to the girl, "What's your name?"

"Delilah," she whispered.

Christian searched for the right words to explain the refusal of her desired intimacy. He struggled because the source of his hesitation wasn't exactly clear to himself. He considered that he was in a relatively open setting near the camp fire and his role as Jesus demanded discretion, of not complete restraint. Ultimately, he thought of Mary.

"I'm in love with another woman," he managed to say to her. In this moment Christian admitted to himself that he felt for Mary in a way he had never felt before, and he wanted to keep his love for her sacred, even though their relationship was yet to be consummated.

Delilah stroked Christian's hair one time and cracked a genial smile. "That is a very lucky woman." With that, Delilah slipped out from under the cloak, rolled a pace away, and curled into a fetal sleeping position.

Christian rolled the other way and pulled his cloak tighter around himself. When he woke up the next morning, Delilah was gone. He stretched and watched as the disciples gathered their belongings. He nibbled on matzah and cheese for breakfast and made his good morning rounds. As he approached Mary and Joanna they suddenly stopped talking.

"Good Morning," he offered. Joanna nodded. Mary ignored him, turning away to pack up her bag. "Everything okay?" he tried again.

"We'll be fine," Joanna replied, "it's girl stuff."

Mary's maudlin disposition continued throughout the morning. Christian pulled Judas aside, "What's going on with Mary?"

"Lord, I suspect you know what might be bugging her. We're an open community in night camps and you must realize how closely your disciples watch over you."

"I did nothing wrong," Christian pleaded.

"No need to be defensive. You get no judgment from me either way," Judas said. "But if it's that important to you, I would suggest you find a way to relay your abstinence to Mary."

"It's important to me, and I will," he nodded.

"Sounds good. Do you love her?"

"Very much."

Christian shifted his focus back to the ministry. He had studied the maps of ancient Galilee and saw that Philoteria was a substantial town of that time located at the northernmost point of the Jordan valley, where the Jordan River meets the Sea of Galilee. It resided on the eastern frontier of Galilee, bordering Decapolis. To the west were the marginally fertile rolling hills of Galilee and to the east was the even wilder terrain of Decapolis, fit for grazing goats and swine. Christian felt obliged to visit and preach in the city, even though no significant biblical events were recorded there. It was all part of building the eminence of Jesus throughout the region.

Christian and the disciples trekked east across the Jordan and into Decapolis. They managed to harness a rather large following, which attracted the attention of the local Roman garrison. Christian was in the middle of preaching when a Roman cavalry attachment rode straight through the crowd and up to Christian. The leader, bearing the Aquila, circled Christian twice, clearing space between him and the crowd. Only Judas remained by his side. "This is an illegal assembly, arrest this man," the Decurion said as he pointed directly at Christian, "and disperse this rabble." He gestured in a waving motion across the gathering of disciples. The Roman legionnaires swiftly dismounted. Two of them went to seize Christian. He had just enough time to snap his leather pouch off his belt and hand it to Judas standing next to him. "Hang onto this for me," he said before the soldiers grabbed him. Judas nodded and made his escape from the center of the crowd. The remaining legionnaires wielded their gladiuses in a broadening circle as the crowd cowered at the blatant Roman intimidation.

It happened so fast. Christian did not expect to be arrested in Decapolis, for that was not documented in the *Bible*. He would have to remain cognizant that not all events were enumerated. In the short term, he needed to deal with his immediate arrest, but he wasn't exactly sure how. The soldiers led him back to their encampment and tossed him into a cave that was serving as a makeshift prison. This was nothing like the county jail Christian spent one night in after a stint of intoxication at Fort Lauderdale. The cave was already occupied by desperate men in various states of depression and starvation. It had no facilities whatsoever: no toilets, no beds, and no privacy. What the cave did have was the wretched decaying stench of human excrement, urine, feces, and vomit emanating mostly from the impromptu latrine of the left cave wall.

Christian found a spot towards the right cave wall and settled down next to the healthiest man he saw. The warrior looking man had a swollen lip and a black eye. The Romans saw fit to leave this man in chains and there the man sat, bound hands and feet, gazing towards the cave entrance. Christian sat quietly for a while before chancing a conversation with the chained man. "Hello."

"Hello," the man replied.

"Been here long?"

"Long enough."

"I'm Jesus of Nazareth. What's your name?"

"I've heard of you. My name is Bar Abbas." Barabbas extended his massive chained hands to Christian. Christian extended both his hands and they shook all four hands together in one fist.

"Looks like the Romans didn't like the idea of me gathering a crowd near their encampment, not that I knew it was here," Christian said. "How did you end up here as a prisoner of the Romans?"

"I'm not their prisoner, at least not yet anyway. I'm a salararius mercenary for the bastards and got into a fight with one of their officers. You should see the other guy," Barabbas smirked. "They probably won't leave me in here long. They know the longer I stew the angrier I will be when I get out."

Just then, a guard appeared at the gate that had been chiseled into the cave entrance and called out, "Bar Abbas, get your ass over here." Barabbas stood, signaled farewell to Christian and shuffled with his chain-bound feet to the entrance. Christian saw them let Barabbas out, deliver a round of chastisement in Latin, and then unbind his chains. Barabbas strutted off towards the encampment, evidently to rejoin the cohort in their services as a mercenary.

Christian languished for another day and a half in the cave with the other prisoners. He spent the time providing what comfort he could to the other suffering prisoners. There was scant food and water offered during this time and no charges were levied against him. Rotting in prison wasn't the plan and Christian began to contemplate what might have gone wrong. Finally, a gruff voice bellowed from the cave entrance, "Jesus of Nazareth, come forth."

Christian obeyed and was grateful to see the guard unlocking the gate. The guard escorted him a short distance towards the encampment, but before they reached the boundary two men on horseback emerged and rode towards them. Upon reaching Christian the elder man said, "Rabbi Jesus, my name is Chuza, manager of the king's properties and more importantly for you, the husband to one of your devoted followers, Joanna." Chuza offered a reserved smile and slight bow. "This is my son Asa," he gestured to the younger man on the other horse. "We managed to negotiate your release, which was tricky because we have no jurisdiction here. We've brought you a fresh tunic. Put this on and then please hop on my son's horse so we can get you out of here. We can talk more later."

Christian needed no further prompting. He accepted the tunic and changed into it. Then he grabbed Asa's outstretched hand and climbed aboard the stallion. Christian noticed the cloth saddle lacked a pommel horn for the rider to hold onto for balance. He watched and noted Asa's riding technique of holding the reins in one hand and with the other, gripping the horse's mane. Chuza and Asa set the horses to a sustainable gallop as they rode away from the Roman encampment. Christian asked Asa, "How are the disciples doing?"

"I believe they've rallied just over the boarder Lord, in Galilee," Asa replied. "They're waiting for you."

The trio arrived to a relieved crowd of disciples on the Galilean side of Philoteria. Chuza, Asa, and Christian dismounted and each in turn were smothered in hugs and kisses. Judas handed Christian back the leather pouch. "Intact and unopened Lord."

Christian nodded in sincere appreciation to Judas.

Next Christian hugged Mary. He held her a moment extra by the shoulders and looked her in the eyes. "We need to talk."

"I would love to talk," Mary replied. "And if it will ease your mind, Judas has already come to your defense about the servant girl."

Christian had just enough time to say, "Excellent," before other disciples crushed him with enthusiastic hugs.

The mood in camp was festive that evening, but Christian caught himself nodding off to sleep by the fire. Several apostles wound up tucking him for an early evening. The disciples rested for a few days in Philoteria before resuming the ministry.

Next, Christian and the disciples tracked southwest towards the plains of Esdraelon and the city of Nain near the border of Samaria. "Nain is an important city for our Galilean ministry," Christian said. "We pass through here a couple of times and both times the people of Nain will witness my healing powers."

"Lord, your foresight is an amazing gift," Simon said. "How is it you know these things?"

"These events are already written, Simon. Just as I knew you and your brother would be fishing on the Sea of Galilee and Mathew would be collecting taxes," Christian said. "So, too, do I know we will encounter ten lepers to be healed on the outskirts of Nain." Such was

Christian's confidence in the written word of the Gospel based on his experiences so far.

The walk from Philoteria to Nain was about a half day's journey through rocky outcroppings and rolling hills of sheep-grazing country. Every time the group passed a flock of sheep Christian would scan the hillside for a shepherd; per chance he would cross paths with his friend David again.

"What are you looking for in the hills Master?" Simon noticed Christian scanning the hillside.

"There's a young shepherd boy I made friends with a while back," Christian said. "I keep thinking it would be nice to see him again."

"Curious, how is it you know we will encounter ten lepers in Nain and yet you do not know if you will encounter your shepherding friend again?" Simon asked.

"That is an astute observation Simon. Some things are written, and some things are not. If the events are not written, I must experience them as they happen, like any other person in Palestine."

Christian knew from his previous trip with James that Nain was on the main travel route between Syria and Egypt. It served as a trading hub as well as a place where travelers could rest. The group skirted south of Mt. Tabor and approached Nain from the east. As expected, as they neared the outskirts of the city, ten men with leprosy were there to meet Christian.

"Jesus, Master, have pity on us." They stood at a distance and called out in loud voices.

Christian approached the lepers with compassion. Just like Uzziah in Tabigha, these lepers lived on the fringes of society, such was the fear of their affliction spreading to others. "Be at ease my friends. The healing power of my blood can cure your leprosy. You're going to have to allow me to touch each of you." He cut incisions in both his hands, grasped each of the lepers one by one and rubbed his bloody palms across their open sores long enough to transfer nanites from his blood. "When you see that your sores are healed, go, show yourselves to the priests in your city temple and show them you are clean."

They followed his instructions and as they went on their way the nanites began to heal their wounds, cleansing them of leprosy. One of them, a Samaritan, came back praising God in a loud voice. He threw himself down at Christian's feet and thanked him.

"Were not all ten cleansed? Where are the other nine? Has no one returned to give praise to God except this foreigner?" Christian mimicked the *Bible* verbatim.

Word of the healed lepers spread in Nain and a large crowd gathered at the city temple to hear Christian's message. The healing of the lepers and the power of his messages swayed many residents of Nain and the disciples were all provided lodging for several days.

Christian took this opportunity to climb part way up nearby Mt. Tabor, solo, to establish communication with HQ. He conducted a normal check-in with the HQ lab tech whose turn it was to hold the cubepod. There were no new instructions, nor was any progress reported on working out the more problematic miracles. He explained to the technician that the disciples were touring Galilee and he would check in as opportunity presented itself. Christian charged the cubepod and headed back to Nain.

Their next destination was Nazareth. This would be Christian's first return to the village since accepting his mission as Jesus. He was looking forward to seeing Mary, James, and their Nazareth friends.

Christian and his disciples arrived at Nazareth around midday. It was a joyous reunion between the Mother Mary and the man she had accepted as her son Jesus. James, too, was glad to see his step brother and they traded hugs and barbs as brothers do. Nazareth had obviously received advanced notice that Jesus and his disciples were on their way because the village center was cleared and prepared for a large gathering.

That night was one of celebration with music and dancing around a community fire. Simon got a chance to show off his mizmar playing skills. James' construction buddies chided Christian to produce more wine for them, just as he had at Cana. He resisted the urge to do so, sighting that there is a time and place for all things under heaven.

Christian and Mother Mary found time to catch up. Christian was sitting by the fire holding the cutting edge of his fisherman's knife over the flame.

"Why do you do that?" Mother Mary asked.

"I'm sterilizing the blade. My healing blood should theoretically prevent infection, but I still think it best to keep the knife clean." Christian avoided mentioning germs and couldn't think of an equivalent word in Aramaic anyway.

"I see," Mother Mary nodded in understanding, then just gazed at him. "We are hearing fabulous tales of your ministry."

"That's good to know. People are in desperate need of hope and they've been quite receptive of our message of a loving God."

"You really have embraced this mission, haven't you?" she asked.

"Yes, I suppose I have. I'm receiving a lot of support from my twelve apostles and the rest of the disciples. I would like you to meet some of them. Would you walk around with me?"

"Jesus, it would be my honor to be introduced to your friends."

"If you're going to call me Jesus, I'm going to introduce you as my mother. Is that okay?" Christian smiled.

"I would love that."

Mary and Christian socialized with the townspeople, the apostles, and the disciples.

Christian approached Mary Magdalene and put his arm around her. "Mother, I want you to meet someone very special to me. This is Mary of Magdala."

"It is a pleasure to meet you," Mother Mary said. "Where did you get that beautiful cloak? It is so pretty."

Mary Magdalene beamed. "Thank you. It's one of my favorites. There's a fabulous textile merchant in Capernaum who gets exotic material from traders who come by camel from Babylon. They have connections further east who provide these exquisite deep reds and purples that I love. Would you like to try it on?"

"Oh, yes, I would be delighted. It's so fancy!"

Mary Magdalene said something about how well it would match her eyes and skin tone and some such other thing sufficient enough for Christian to lose interest in the conversation. Clearly, he was no longer the center of their mutual attention. "I'm going to go crack open a Budweiser," he said, knowing full well they wouldn't be listening to him. Christian allowed his arm to slither off Mary's shoulder, unnoticed, and he left to find Judas.

Judas was sitting at table, cup of wine in hand with the wafting smoke of incense filling the room. Christian sat down next to him and sniffed the air. The aroma was a mix of a woman's perfume and incense. Christian couldn't place it.

"What's that? Where did you get it?" Christian asked.

"It's frankincense, a rather fine resin. Your mother Mary gave it to me," Judas said. "Said she held onto it for a long time, waiting for the right occasion to use it. I guess she's happy you're here."

Christian refrained from making a comment he might regret about it being a gift from the magi and instead managed to give Judas a look that probably resembled a half snicker and half snarl.

"I can't read that expression Christian. What's up?" Judas asked.

Christian paused and gathered his thoughts. "Judas, do you understand women?"

Judas laughed.

"I'm serious."

Judas laughed even more heartily. He reached for an extra cup and the jug of wine. He poured the wine, overflowing the brim and spilling some as he handed the cup to Christian. Judas was grinning ear to ear. "You need a drink in your hand my friend. Enjoy the evening. Your home town is celebrating your return and clearly your family is glad to see you." Christian accepted the cup of wine and the advice. They toasted each other and mingled with friends and family late into the evening.

The next day was the Sabbath. Christian was invited to speak in the town's temple. His friends, family, disciples, and the townspeople gathered for the traditional prayers and readings. He noticed that Mother Mary was wearing a lovely new cloak. Christian did the reading in Hebrew. The grumbling began when he took the opportunity to claim fulfillment of Old Testament scripture by being there with them that day.

"Surely you misspeak," the rabbi said. "We realize our religious language is still new to you."

"No, I understand the language just fine and I meant what I said," Christian said.

"Come on Christian, lighten up," one of his local construction friends said.

"Yeah, what's gotten into you with this Jesus thing?" Another person said.

Christian had read about this happening to Jesus, so he forged ahead as quoted in scripture. "A prophet is not without honor, except in his hometown."

At this, the gathering erupted into chaos and their happy reunion in Nazareth was cut short. Christian took enough time to say last minute goodbyes.

"It was so nice to be able to spend time with you again," he said to Mother Mary and James.

"We feel the same, Jesus. We get occasional reports of your ministry and you make us very proud," Mary said.

"You make us proud indeed, brother," James said. "Be careful, though, not everyone is happy with the message you have to share. We also hear you have your enemies in Jerusalem."

"Thanks for the warning James," Christian said. "It is as to be expected."

Christian hugged them, and he and his disciples were walking over the hill to Japhia within the hour. Christian was ahead of everyone on the road when Judas glided up next to him. "That went well."

Christian just grumbled.

Judas nudged him, "Japhia will be fine and Cana will be even better. Shake it off."

"Thank you, Judas," Christian said. "You're a good friend to me. I appreciate it."

"Thank you, Lord," Judas said. "By the way, I need to get back to Capernaum to tend to some business there. I won't be long and will catch back up with you in a few days."

"Okay, travel safe." Christian added, "While you're there, can you do me a favor and pick up a delicately blown glass for drinking wine? It needs to be from Sidon. Bring it wrapped in a gift box. It's for a friend in Cana."

"One wine glass, got it covered," Judas said and then faded back through the rest of the disciples and headed off on his errand.

The walk to Japhia cleared Christian's head. Most people in Japhia didn't recall Christian's visit prior to him taking on the ministry of Jesus. He had been too distracted by the sacrifice of the dove to engage in much discussion with the locals. He did recall the rebuilt town center and the finely crafted stonework temple in Japhia and wondered to himself if Mary's husband Joseph had helped construct it.

They arrived in Japhia within an hour and were well received by its residents, including the rabbi who Christian remembered sacrificing the doves. Christian stood on the white mortar patio surrounding the tiled temple building and delivered his message of love and redemption. His sermons were better received in Japhia than they had been in Nazareth.

It was burdensome to ask the residents of Japhia to accommodate the party of disciples, as it was simply not large enough. It was also too far to make the walk to Cana that afternoon. They managed to get provisions and then found a place to camp that night, just outside of Japhia. Christian showed off his survival skills by lighting their campfire. Simon and Nathanael went on ahead to Cana to make arrangements with their friends and family for Jesus' visit the next day.

The road to Cana skirted the gates of Sepphoris. Christian thought about the construction work that Joseph had done in Sepphoris and felt an odd sadness that he'd never meet the man, nor serve as his apprentice, as sons often did. The rumble of a Roman chariot told the disciples they were indeed passing close to the fortress city. Simon Barjona and his brother Andrew were walking ahead of the rest of the disciples. They rounded the bend first and stopped suddenly in their tracks.

Christian, Mary and the disciples caught up to them and realized the reason for their halting. On the roadside ahead of the them were the remains of a crucified man still hanging from a cross. Several ravens were perched on the crossbeam, while another pecked at the man's exposed eye sockets. The ravens cawed about impending danger then scurried as Christian approached the cross, followed by the rest of the disciples. The stench of death permeated the air. A swarm of flies buzzed above them, making a meal of the man's rotting flesh. There was a sign nailed above the man's bent head, which Christian couldn't translate. He waved the flies from around his face, turned to Mary and whispered, "What is the meaning of the sign?"

She leaned towards him and whispered, "It is a warning against rebellion by the Zealots."

Christian nodded and said loud enough for all to hear. "God would not have willed this man's life to be taken in this manner. This is the work of depraved men. We must remember to pray for this man, as well as the men who did this to him." Then he asked Matthew, "Do you know anything of the Roman protocol on removing this man's corpse from this tree, for it is being desecrated by the ravens."

"We dare not touch it, Lord. It has undoubtedly been placed here as a warning by the local garrison commander," Matthew replied. "To usurp his authority would yield swift retribution for all of us."

Christian moved to stand between the road and the cross and directed his disciples to move past respectfully. He brought up the rear after the last of them passed, encouraging them with words of God's love for each of them. The omen of the crucified man loomed in their minds as they walked along the road to Cana. Suddenly, a royal official approached them on horseback. Joanna saw the rider and charged out ahead of the disciples.

"Honey, what is it?" Joanna cried to the man.

Christian recognized the man as Chuza, Joanna's husband, from the arrest debacle in Decapolis.

"Something must be wrong for Chuza to have ridden all this way," Christian commented.

Chuza dismounted the horse and hugged his wife.

"Our son Asa is sick," he told her.

Chuza nodded to Mary and then knelt on one knee before Christian.

"Lord, can you come to Capernaum and help my son before he dies? I believe you can save him," Chuza beseeched Christian.

This was another one of the remote healing scenarios where Christian was left to rely completely on faith in the written text of the *Bible*, and to believe that the boy would survive the illness. Christian recalled that in the Bible the boy survives the illness even though Jesus was not present to heal him. "Sir, your faith is a testament before God and man. Go on your way, your son will live."

"I believe you, Lord. I will head back to Capernaum right away. Joanna, your son may yet need you, come back with me."

"Yes dear." Joanna gathered scant belongings and asked Susanna to take care of the rest.

"I will be back as soon as I can," Joanna said to Mary.

"Don't worry, go check on Asa," Mary said.

Chuza and Joanna rode away together.

"Will Asa be all right?" Mary asked Christian.

"Yes, I believe he will, for it is already written that his boy survives."

"Good. Joanna is a dear friend, and her husband is a good man," Mary said. "There's some risk in them supporting us as they do. I would like to think God would reward them by sparing their son his illness."

"I don't think it quite works like that," Christian said. "But that's why it is called faith."

They proceeded into Cana and their arrival was another joyous occasion. Nathanael hadn't been home to Cana since his days of following John the Baptist. His friends were glad to see him and were even more excited by the news that Jesus was coming their way. Simon's friends and family from nearby Jotapata were equally delighted at his return and Jesus' visit.

Christian saw some familiar faces in the crowd at Cana. He recognized the groom and bride from the wedding, Isaac and the voluptuous Sophia, with the latter now visibly pregnant. He recognized some of the servant girls who filled the stone jugs with water for him at the wedding. He saw the headwaiter, Barbelo, as well. He permanently endeared himself to the entire population of this village with his miracle at the wedding.

"Isaac and Sophia, looks like congratulations are in order," Christian said.

"Yes, Lord, they are indeed," Isaac said. "Would you bless the baby please? It would mean so much to us."

"I would be happy to." Christian held his hands towards Sophia's belly for a moment and bowed his head in prayer. Then he turned to Isaac. "And tell me how Rabbi Abraham is doing."

"He'll wish he had been here to see you. He had to go to a meeting in Tiberias," Isaac explained. "He'll be disappointed he missed you."

"Please tell your dad I said hello," Christian said. "Do you think he would mind if we used the synagogue for teaching the good news of our ministry?"

"I'm sure he would be honored, Lord," Isaac said.

The overwhelmingly positive reception and subsequent celebration of Jesus' ministry resulted in the disciples spending a full week in Cana. This allowed time for Christian to provide the healing power of his cellular nanites to the sick in the area.

Christian and the disciples were in Cana for a couple of days when Judas and Joanna returned via horseback.

"How's Asa?" Mary asked Joanna.

"Oh, he's doing fine. By the time Chuza and I got back to Capernaum, his fever had broken, and he was on the mend," Joanna said. "Chuza is delighted with Jesus even more now and Judas was kind enough to arrange for a ride on horseback back here to Cana."

"That's great news. We were worried about you and we prayed for your son. It's really good to know he's going to be all right," Mary said.

"Fill me in on what happened in Capernaum," Christian said to Judas.

"Lord, you've asked me to manage the finances for the ministry and that means that every occasionally, I need to go collect some contributions from our supporters. I swung by Chuza's house to see what he could offer and found that he had taken off to find you because his son was ill. The servants let me in to visit Asa and I did what I could for him," Judas said.

"You healed Asa?" Christian asked.

"No Lord, you healed Asa. If I helped facilitate that, it was my pleasure to do so. I stayed with him until Chuza and Joanna arrived."

Christian chalked up the healing to the immutability of time and the accuracy of the *Bible*.

"I have the glass you asked me pick up," Judas said as he handed Christian a package. "Had to hunt around for it. They're not a common item."

"Perfect. Thank you." Christian accepted the box.

Christian found Mary Magdalene. "Hey, come with me, I want you to meet an intriguing man. I have a gift for him as well, so this should be memorable."

"Gifts are fun, sure I'm coming," Mary said.

Christian and Mary walked to the community hall where the wedding had taken place and found Barbelo preparing for the evening's dinner. "Barbelo, how are you this evening?" The men shook hands.

"Splendid," Barbelo smiled, "it's good for business to have you and your company in town for the week."

"That's what we strive to do Barbelo, support the local economy."

"We appreciate that," Barbelo acknowledged the jest.

"I would like to introduce you to my dear friend Mary of Magdala," Christian said. "Mary, meet Barbelo, headwaiter at the wedding I attended here at Cana."

"Indeed, my claim to fame," Barbelo responded. "It's quite nice to meet you my lady."

"The pleasure is mine, I'm sure," Mary said respectfully.

"And what brings you here this afternoon," Barbelo asked Christian.

"We have a gift for you," Christian said, unveiling the gift from behind his back and presenting it to Barbelo. "We thought you might like this."

"A gift, how nice," Barbelo accepted the box. He opened it to find an exquisitely crafted glass from Sidon. The glass was slightly larger than the one broken during the wedding and was of far greater delicacy.

"How beautiful," Mary gasped.

"Indeed," Barbelo agreed, turning the glass to admire the handiwork. "You did not need to do this Lord. I am speechless."

"Nothing need be said Barbelo. That day was a special day and with this gift, we commemorate it with you."

"I am touched," Barbelo said. "Lord, you and your friends will dine here tonight, on the house, I insist."

"We will accept your generosity Barbelo," Christian said. "Thank you."

As they turned to walk away, Mary playfully turned her head back over her shoulder. "It was nice meeting you Barbelo. See you tonight."

"Likewise, my dear, looking forward to it,"

"What a nice man," Mary said to Christian. "Did you see how he gently caressed and kissed my hand?"

"Nope, hadn't noticed."

"Well, you should pay more attention, Lord," Mary said. "Maybe you would learn something about how to treat a lady."

Christian let that comment pass.

"I knew you would like Barbelo," Christian said. "He's sophisticated, like you."

"I'll take that as a compliment."

"As well you should." Christian offered a slight bow as they strolled, hand in hand.

Dinner that evening included slow roasted lamb, sautéed Mediterranean vegetables, plenty of wine, and a repertoire of mizmar music, complements of Simon. Christian did notice that Barbelo refrained from using his fine glass or china for the gathering.

Towards the end of the week, Christian pulled both Nathanael and Simon aside. "This has been a much welcome visit with your friends and family here in Cana and Jotapata. Please pass along a heartfelt thank you from all of us to all of them."

Nathanael and Simon both acknowledged the gratitude expressed.

"We have more work to do gentlemen. Are you still with me?" Christian asked.

"I can't imagine being anywhere else but by your side, Lord," Nathanael said.

"Neither can I," Simon agreed.

The verbal reassurance was welcomed.

The week's respite was good for the disciples. It was time for them to turn back east and head home in the direction of Capernaum.

Christian had one more visit in mind for them and this was a personal matter.

The juniper and spruce trees spotted amongst the rolling fields reminded Christian of the first time he took this road, walking with David and his donkey, Nikud. This was the longest leg of their journey and by previous experience he knew an ideal place to stop for the day. He found the same ring of stones he and David used for their campfire just off the road. The familiarity was comforting for him as he settled in by the fire that evening. Christian sat next to Thomas. "I have a story for you," he said.

"I'm listening, Lord."

"Tomorrow we head for Arbela. I know that your brother had his tragic fall from the cliffs leading to that town which prevented you from getting there. I, too, had a friend suffer a fall off that very cliff on my way to Arbela earlier this year. My trip would have been just before yours. Those piles of wool you saw strewn on the ledge belonged to the shepherd boy who was with me on that journey. A viper startled the donkey carrying the wool, causing both donkey and my shepherd friend to tumble over the cliff. The donkey died, but fortunately my friend survived. I regard completion of my trip to Arbela as unfinished business. I want you to stick close to me tomorrow. We're going to complete that trip to Arbela together. I refuse to let a damn snake prevent me from completing a journey."

"Lord, I like the idea of making a point to go there," Thomas agreed. "When I see my brother again, I can inform him that we did it for him, also. I like the way you think."

"Yeah, I don't like unfinished business."

The next morning Christian informed the disciples that their next destination was Arbela. There was a slight collective moan from the crowd. They understood, as did he, that the trek would be uphill all the way, and treacherous. Toward midday they were funneling down to single file on the goat trail that led along the edge of the ridgeline. Cliffs loomed ominously to the right. These were Nikud's cliffs and Thomas' twin brother's cliffs, and probably others who suffered similar fates.

Christian considered the chain of events that resulted from the viper striking at Nikud and was reminded to warn the group. "Watch out for snakes!" Christian led the way. Thomas was immediately behind him, followed by Judas and Mary and then the rest of the disciples walking one by one across the cliff's edge.

"Now I see what the fuss is all about. That's seriously a long way down," Judas said.

"Yes, it is. You should try it with a kid cradled in your arms," Christian said.

"You should try it with your twin brother hanging on your back," Thomas countered.

"Boys, you are all my heroes," Mary said trying to validate the testosterone laced banter.

The group completed this journey along the cliffs of Arbel uneventfully. They paused briefly as they rounded the last bend before heading into the trading post of Arbela. The sight of the village that came into view impressed all of those who stood there, staring up at the village houses that scaled the cliff's wall to their right. The doors of several buildings were carved into massive natural outcroppings of limestone and rose as high as they could see. The doors themselves were imprinted with decorative floral motifs and medallions.

"Wow," was all Christian could manage. Thomas, who was standing next to him, was staring gape-jawed, as were the rest of the travelers in their little caravan. "Lord, I had no idea there was such a civilization here," Thomas said. "I had no idea it would be this large," Christian added. "It seems implausible to have such a bustling village with only a precarious route in and out."

"I have heard of the trading at Arbela," Judas said, "but I had never been here before today. Quite impressive."

"Indeed," Mary said, still studying the craftsmanship of the cliff dwellers.

In the village at the base of the cliff were several linen and fabric vendors of many sorts displaying their merchandise. The group slowly made their way through the village. "Look at that tower, Jesus," Judas said, pointing towards the tallest building at the far end of the village. "It appears that they even have a synagogue here."

"Let's see if the Rabbi will help us find lodging while we are here," Christian said.

Christian and the disciples entered the synagogue and were immediately greeted by the rabbi who was working with a few students. When the rabbi heard Jesus' name his eyes grew wide. "Jesus," he said. I have heard of you and your miracles. I am honored by your presence. I know the trip to get here is not an easy one."

"Sure isn't," Christian agreed. "The trip was personally important to me, though, and I am very glad we could make it."

"I can see your passion and the obvious devotion of your followers. Are you staying in Arbela long? I would like it if you could stay and teach us," the rabbi requested.

It was invitations like this that made the ministry most enjoyable for Christian. He and his disciples stayed in Arbela a few days before heading back home to Capernaum. This gave Mary and her friend Joanna time to do some shopping for clothing in the Arbela markets.

"The fabrics here are amazing," Mary told Christian. "They have fine silks and exotic animal hair weavings from the east, and spun cotton garments from Egypt and woven textiles of sorts, the likes of which even Joanna isn't familiar. Joanna obtained contact information from one of the merchants so Chuza can commission woolen carpets for the palace. I was able to pick up a new cloak and we grabbed extra blankets as well. This really turned out to be a fabulous place to visit."

Christian pondered that clothes shopping delighted women of any era. How unfortunate for them there wasn't a shoe store. "That's good to hear, Mary. Nice to know the trip was worthwhile after all."

"We even found a vendor selling some extremely comfortable thong sandals made of bamboo weavings and rice straw. Do you like them?" Mary beamed and twirled her feet one by one to show them off to Christian.

"Amazing."

The disciples made the trip back across the cliffs to Capernaum. They had all heard the stories of Nikud and Thomas' brother by now, which caused a few to peer over the edge looking in vain for bundles of wool.

Back on the road and walking toward Capernaum, Christian turned and took one last look at the cliffs. No vultures were circling at the cliff's edge this time.

Commission

Christian went up the high tower of the temple the first morning back in Capernaum and pinged HQ. Claire's image of her sitting at her desk appeared.

"Claire. Haven't seen you in a while."

"I know. I've been real busy. Everyone misses you. You're all we talk about."

"I appreciate that. Everything okay with you?"

"Yes, going well. Hey, I'm here to relay a request to you from Atlanta. They've been wondering about the idea of tertiary healing powers of the nanites and they would like more data from you. In the *Bible*, Jesus sends the apostles out to minister and, more importantly from Atlanta's perspective, to heal people. Atlanta would like you to do the same thing. Not only are they interested in understanding secondary healing effects from the nanites in your blood, but they want to understand if there are tertiary effects as well. This is a quandary for them since they've not been able to duplicate even the secondary effects in any other subjects. You appear to be an anomaly."

"So, they want me to get on with sending the apostles forth to minister as a lab experiment?"

"Pretty much. But wait, there's more. They want a report enumerated by the success of each apostle."

Christian bit his tongue.

"Last thing," Claire continued. "They've been analyzing the healing you've observed in Capernaum versus the initial event with the shepherd boy. They theorize that the molecular nanites may also be serving as a catalyst. They want to know if you've ingested a lot of molecular nanites since healing the shepherd boy."

"I lived off nanite purified water the entire forty days in the wilderness."

"All right, that might explain it. I'll let them know."

"Tell everyone I say hello."

"Sure will. You take care."

It was good to speak with Claire again, Christian thought. Unfortunately, the commissioning of the apostles has become a CDC field study. Christian liked the original Jesus story better.

Christian followed HQ instructions and sent the twelve apostles out to minister. First, he had to transfer the healing nanites from his blood to theirs, which he did by slicing his left palm and passing the knife down the line, asking each of them to do the same. "With this, we establish our brotherhood," he said. He thoroughly shook each of their hands and they each in turn watched as their hands were healed by his blood.

"As you've received, so should you freely give. Go forth and heal the sick throughout Palestine. Do not accept money. You may accept food and lodging as compensation and stay in villages and towns if you are welcome. Travel in pairs and be sure to support each other, for two are stronger than one. Return here in a couple of months."

Christian thought about what it would be like for the apostles after he was gone. He knew most of the apostles would subsequently be martyred in the name of Jesus. He commissioned them for two months. That would be enough time for the data-hungry Atlanta team and be of sufficient duration for the apostles to get some evangelical experience under their belt. The apostles accepted the commission and began to confer over who was going where. Christian approached Matthew. "I have a special assignment for you. You need to stick with me and take good notes of everything you see and hear. Yours is a special challenge. Can you do that for me?"

"Yes, Lord, of course. I completely understand, and it is my pleasure to do so."

Judas put his arm around Matthew and looked at Christian. "We're a team, *Lord*," he said, heavily emphasizing the formal title.

"Very well Judas, you're with us," Christian said.

Brothers paired with brothers, except for Matthew and James, and Simon paired with Thomas. The apostles ventured off, two by two, to conduct their field studies.

Christian, Matthew, and Judas trekked west along the Sea of Galilee to Bethsaida. They entered the city and a blind man was brought to Christian. The man was begging to be touched by Jesus so that he might see again. Christian took the blind man by the hand and walked the man to just outside the village.

"Now this is going to sound strange, but I'm going to try and heal you with my saliva," Christian said to the blind man. "You are blessed to be part of such an important experiment. I'm going to spit into your eyes, please don't be startled." Christian spit and rubbed his saliva into the man's eyes. "Now, open your eyes and stand still for a minute."

The blind man complied Christian placed his hands over the man's eyes, letting them soak a minute. Then he had the man open his eyes. "Do you see anything?"

"I see men, for I am seeing them like trees, walking about," the blind man said.

The man's vision was blurry. Christian knew from the accounting of this miracle that the healing must have occurred in stages. Again, he laid his hands upon the man's eyes and soon the man could see everything clearly. He told the man to avoid going into the village and instead sent him home. He feared that as soon as word got out he was healing that he'd be mobbed. He had other work to do this day, including proving the hypothesis that his healing nanites were also in his saliva.

Curing the blind man had worked, just as the Gospel described. Christian wanted to close that loop. He turned to Matthew. "Please tell Simon Barjona what you saw here today, it's important that he relay this story to his friend Mark."

"I'm taking good notes, Lord, I promise."

"Great, next we're heading into Decapolis."

"Not again," Matthew said.

"Sounds like fun," Judas added.

"Let's just be mindful of any gathering crowds," Christian said.

They made their way south into Decapolis and came to the hill city of Hippos. The people there brought Christian a man who was deaf and spoke with difficulty. Christian endeavored to cure the man's ailments with his saliva. It was a challenge for him to explain through pantomime, but with definitive hand signals pointing to his ears the man appeared to get that Christian was going to try and cure his deafness.

Christian simultaneously licked both his pinky fingers and stuck them one each into the deaf man's ears. He stood there facing the man making sure healing nanites dripped into the man's ear canals. Next, he spat into his hand and then wiped his saliva on the man's tongue. Christian, channeling the Verizon commercial, repeatedly asked the deaf man, "Can you hear me now?"

Eventually, the man's ears were opened, the speech impediment removed, and the man began speaking plainly. Christian could hear the astonishment in the voices of the crowd. "Truly he is God, for he makes even the deaf to hear and the dumb speak."

"I believe we have stayed in Decapolis long enough," Christian told the other two. "We should leave before I get arrested again."

Upon returning to Capernaum a Roman centurion wearing the full regalia of his rank approached them. Christian thought, oh no, they're going to arrest me again for going into Decapolis. Instead, the centurion removed his helmet and bowed his head to Christian.

"Lord, my servant lies at home paralyzed, suffering terribly," the centurion said.

The scenario sparked the memory in Christian's mind of just such an occurrence documented in the Gospels. He was relieved to see he was back on script. "Shall I come heal him?"

"Lord, I do not deserve to have you come under my roof. But just say the word and my servant will be healed. For I am a man of authority, with soldiers under me who do as I command."

Christian had wondered about this miracle and had talked with the Cape about it. The healing power over distance was a conundrum as the cellular nanites accomplished their healing through physical contact. His dad advised that they trust in the immutability of time and that what was written would come to pass, even if they didn't understand exactly how. It worked with Joanna's and Chuza's son Asa, so he maintained faith that it would also work with the centurion's servant as well.

"Go, and let it be done just as you believe," Christian said.

"Felix culpa. This is a blessed outcome, thank you Lord." The centurion bowed to Christian.

Judas raised an eyebrow. "I will see you two back at the house."

Christian and Matthew navigated the Capernaum streets in the direction of the temple, the beacon for Judas' nearby home. "A bath sure sounds good to me," Christian said when they arrived home.

"Me, too," Matthew agreed.

They relaxed in the baths, washing away the stress of the day. Christian caught himself thinking more and more about Mary Magdalene and dozed off in the bath with a smile on his face.

Later that evening he found some privacy with her by the fire. "Mary, can I ask you a personal question?"

"Yes," she said.

"You're such an incredible woman, on so many levels, that I find it amazing there isn't someone special in your life. Why is that?"

"Maybe I've just been waiting for the right man."

"If I wanted to be that right man, how would I go about accomplishing that?" Christian asked awkwardly.

"I'm a non-traditional woman," Mary said. "Why don't you be the man and tell me exactly what you want."

"I want to get to know you better," Christian confided. "I would like us to spend more quality time together, just you and me. You comfort me Mary. You help me feel safe and you make me happy. Honestly, I get lonely and it would be really nice if our relationship could be more intimate."

"I hear what you're saying," Mary stroked her fingers through his hair. "Please understand, it isn't easy for me to let down my guard. Life's been hard. I've been hurt before and I swore off men several years ago. Honestly, I'm not sure if I could ever be intimate with a man again. I need to hear a certain word from you for me to know this is real. I need to hear you say it and then we can see where this goes."

"I love you Mary," Christian said.

"That's the magic word," Mary nodded as she leaned forward to kiss him. Christian reciprocated and their lips tenderly pressed.

They held each other closely near the fire that evening and talked about their day. Christian shared the story about the centurion's servant and how sometimes he must lean on his faith to believe that things will happen as they are written. "I don't necessarily have to understand how."

"That reminds me," Mary said. "Judas told me to relay a message to you in private. He says he followed the centurion home and made sure the servant was healed. He said you would understand."

"Yes, I think I do understand." Christian would have to thank Judas later.

"Also, Sarah told me that Jabez stopped by the courtyard to let us know he's doing just fine."

"That's good to know as well."

They were curled up in each other's cloaks facing the fire. "It's getting late Christian. We should get to bed," Mary said.

"I'm all alone in my house on the insula Mary."

"We can talk about that in the days to come Christian. For tonight, I bid you farewell, and for the record, I love you, too." Mary smiled.

They kissed again and parted ways for the evening.

Their relationship continued to blossom during the two months the apostles were on their great sojourns.

One day, Christian found a vendor in the Capernaum markets from whom he was able to buy flowers. He purchased an arrangement of chrysanthemums and chamomile with an Egyptian blue lotus as the center piece. He caught up to Mary in the courtyard and presented her with the flowers in the presence of Joanna, Sarah, and Susanna.

"Oh my, where did you get those?" Mary was delighted.

"I found a flower vendor in town." Christian shrugged.

"Girls just love flowers." Mary feigned demurely. "Don't we girls?"

"Wow, the aroma of this Lotus is intense," Sarah said. "I really like it,"

Susanna fawned over the flowers. All the women were giggling to each other and they gently teased Mary about Christian's courtship.

"You two make such a cute couple," Joanna said.

"It's really sweet that you brought me flowers," Mary said to Christian.

"They are an expression of my love for you Mary. I'm glad you like them."

The flowers earned Christian a big hug and kiss from a very happy Mary. Encouraged, he had a conversation with Judas the next day.

"Judas, you've known Mary longer than I have. If you were going to get something extra special for her, something that you knew she would appreciate, what would you get?"

"Well, if it were me I would probably buy her some jewelry. She has an affinity for it, and I know where to find the good stuff," Judas said.

"Are you busy today? Would you mind helping me find something just right for her?"

"I would be happy to. I'm happy to see you finally giving her more of your attention. She's been patiently waiting you know."

"I'm clumsy with this sort of thing Judas," Christian admitted. "I appreciate your help."

"All right, let's go visit a vendor near the docks."

They walked towards the part of town where Christian had recruited Matthew. This area featured open market vendors, just like the town center, but it also included shops selling high quality clothing, pottery and jewelry.

"There's a particular silversmith I prefer. His metal comes from good sources and he does fine work," Judas said. "If he doesn't have exactly what you want, we could probably get him to make it for you."

"All right. I would like to get it today if I could, so hopefully he'll have something that seems right."

They turned down a narrow street one block off the docks and entered the silver merchant's small stone building. Judas introduced Christian to the merchant.

"Joshua, this is Rabbi Jesus. He would like to see if you've anything in stock appropriate to present to a lady."

Joshua was a balding, middle-aged man with leathery skin and a greying beard.

"Nice to meet you," Joshua extended a hand to Christian and the men shook. "Did you have something particular in mind?"

"I don't know. I was hoping to know it when I see it," Christian explained. "May I see what you have?"

"Absolutely." Joshua pulled out sundry long flat drawers of jewelry, including rings, earrings, bracelets, and necklaces.

Christian combed the display drawers until he saw a glistening silver necklace with seven bold silver rings with Hebrew etching. "This catches my eye. Tell me about this piece."

"Those are rings of the seven blessings," Joshua said. "You would want to be very serious about this woman before offering such a gift."

"What are the blessings?" Christian asked.

"Rabbi, they are the blessings of matrimony. I engraved those rings myself, so I know them well. They include: creator of all things, fashioner of man, man in God's likeness, rejoice in children, creator of

Eden, gladden for the groom and bride, and creator of the fruit of the vine."

"Do you think she would like it?" Christian asked Judas.

"Yes, Lord, I think she would love it."

"Does the length of the chain look right? I don't want it to be like a choker. It would be better to have it drape slightly lower," Christian said.

"I have a similar chain of longer length which I can substitute," Joshua said.

"I will take it," Christian said.

"Bill this to me, Joshua. I will square up with you later," Judas said.

"No problem, Judas. I know you're good for it."

"Thank you," Christian bowed slightly. "Thanks to both of you. Do you have something I can put it in?"

"I've a small papyrus pouch, if that works."

"That will work just fine. Thanks again."

"Shalom," replied Joshua.

Christian and Judas strolled back home, having successfully procured another object to demonstrate Christian's affection for Mary. Christian was beaming, and Judas was visibly happy for him.

Christian waited for an opportune moment to present the gift to Mary, which came while the two of them were taking an evening stroll along the shores of the Sea of Galilee. Christian led Mary by the hand to a group of rocks upon which he sat her. He garnered her attention by getting down on one knee in front of her.

"Mary, you've captured my heart. I swear to you this day, my love and devotion, until my last dying breath. I have something for you as a token and symbol of our bond. I hope you like it and I hope you wear it."

Christian reached into his leather pouch and pulled out the smaller papyrus pouch containing the jewelry. He handed Mary the gift. "Judas helped me picked it out."

Mary open the pouch and pulled out the silver chain with the seven silver loops of blessings. She melted into his arms. "Oh Christian, it's beautiful!"

"Will you wear it?"

"Yes, I will. With pride."

He kissed her tenderly as they sat on the rocks at the edge of the sea.

The next day Christian was thinking that he wanted to keep the momentum of the courtship going. He wasn't going to be able to find chocolates in Palestine, but he would endeavor to find sweets a girl might enjoy. He swung by a local baker and asked what they could bake that would be an especially sweet dessert for Mary. He decided on a

Greek plakous cake, with its interspersed layers of cheese and honey. He was able to pick up the dessert later that afternoon.

Christian, Judas, Matthew, and the women were gathered around the fire pit that evening. Christian was pleased to see Mary wearing her new silver necklace.

"That's a lovely piece of jewelry Mary," Joanna said. "Necklace of seven blessings, huh."

"Yes, it's really special." Mary smiled as she fiddled with the necklace.

"I have something else for you, Mary," Christian eased into the conversation. He fetched the cake. "It's Greek plakous cake. I understand it's really tasty. I hope you like it." He presented the tray of triangularly cut cakes to Mary, who was clearly touched.

Mary nodded her head, as if to acknowledge how hard Christian was trying to woo her. She looked up at him and smiled widely. "You had me when I saw you cradling the shepherd boy in your arms. You win me each time you demonstrate tenderness to those you heal, and you have me now, with flowers, jewelry, and sweets. I pledge myself to you." She stood and kissed him, picking one foot playfully off the ground as she did so.

Christian could feel the blood rushing to his face and knew he was blushing deep red. And, yet, it was worth it. Joanna rescued him. "Aw, isn't that cute. Now start passing out those dessert cakes, Mary. There are way too many for you to eat by yourself."

Mary passed around the tray. There was plenty for everyone.

Towards the end of the two months, Christian climbed the stairs of the high tower to have a special discussion with HQ. Cornelius answered the ping. Perfect, Christian thought.

"Ancient Palestine calling Heaven. Are you there, Heaven?" Christian joked.

"Roger, Palestine, this is Heaven, reading you loud and clear," Cornelius said.

"Excellent, we need a special favor down here in Palestine."

"Roger, Palestine, special favors are what we specialize in here in Heaven. Do you need gold? We use it for street pavement."

"Negative on the gold. We need something much more precious. We need to be able to speak to someone very special to me in a language that transcends space and time. Can you help me with that?"

"Roger. There is only one language that does that. What's your preference?"

"Classical."

"Classical music download forthcoming. Is this for a certain special woman in Palestine?" Cornelius asked.

"I'm totally infatuated with Mary but mums the word Cornelius."

"Roger, Palestine. Heaven will comply shortly, and we will tell no one. By the way, please be advised, all cubepod sessions are recorded," Cornelius smiled.

"Just label the discussion something mundane," Christian said.

"Roger, Palestine. This session will be labeled *Something Mundane*. Let me find you something. Sit tight just a minute."

It took a few minutes, but eventually Cornelius was satisfied with the selected downloads.

"Download confirmed. Good luck, Christian,"

"Thank you. Always good talking with you. Take care."

Christian considered the significant role Mary Magdalene had played in the life of Jesus. She was at the foot of the cross when he died, and she was the first to be at the grave when he rose from the dead. For his part, Christian had fallen in love with Mary and he wanted to have something special to share with her when the timing was right.

The courtship of Mary proved successful for him. Mary moved into his house on the insula and her personal servant Sarah moved in with the other servants. Christian's house apparently needed a woman's touch.

"Christian, is this your dirty laundry in the corner over here?"

"Um, maybe," Christian dodged.

"You need to set this outside the door every morning so the servant girls can pick it up and keep it clean for you. How often do you have them come into the house to clean?"

"They come into the house and clean?" Christian saw Mary roll her eyes as she looked into her handheld mirror. He admired the construction of the molten lead on blown glass mirror with gold leaf edges, even as he was chastised by Mary for his housekeeping.

"Yes, but you need to ask them," Mary sighed. "I'll take care of it."

"Thank you dear," Christian said and smiled. He adored this woman. He doubted any of the apostles would be surprised to see that she had moved in with him. If anything, they'd probably wonder what took him so long.

Courtyard Gatherings

The two-month-long commission passed quickly, and the apostles were returning with reports of mixed results. Christian inferred from Judas' report of the centurion's servant that the tertiary healing effects worked reasonably well. Simon reported positive results initially, which eventually faded to more marginal healing and then finally to awkward situations of failure with lepers. The other apostles reported similar results to varying degrees. The consensus was that it was generally exhilarating while the healing powers lasted and then more challenging as their healing success abated. It was not possible for Christian to explain to the apostles that it was not necessarily their faith that waned, but the power of the nanites within them.

Christian climbed the stairs of the high tower and pinged HQ to report results. The Cape team and Atlanta scientists debated about the meaning of the observations. Whatever was going on with the nanites, they didn't have the same kind of staying power in the apostles as they did in Christian. The predominate theory had to do with the affinity the nanites had for his DNA.

He lingered after checking in with HQ to charge the cubepod on the windowsill. He wondered how long the cubepod would last before breaking or wearing out. Hopefully long enough.

The apostles were glad to be back together again at Judas' house. They shared their stories during refreshing baths and gatherings around the courtyard fire. It was during one such bath when Thomas noticed some blotches on Simon's leg.

"What is that on your leg?" Thomas asked.

"Where?" Simon asked. "Oh, that. I'm not sure. I hadn't noticed it before. It's probably nothing."

"No seriously, that doesn't look right," Thomas insisted. "I told you we shouldn't have gone into that leper colony. But, you wouldn't listen. Now look at your leg, you've got leprosy."

At Thomas' pronouncement, everyone leapt out of the baths, except for Simon. The apostles stood naked examining their skin for lesions. Christian understood, despite its propensity, leprosy was not that contagious, in the scheme of things. Infection usually required the transfer of bodily fluid and it was unlikely that any of the apostles could contract it by simply sitting in the bath water with Simon. In the modern era, leprosy was curable through a series of antibiotics. In ancient Palestine, leprosy was curable through application of Christian's cancer fighting cellular nanites. "Everyone relax. Simon will be just fine.

Everyone will be just fine as long as you have me around," Christian said. "So, enjoy it while you can."

Christian sauntered over to the bath where Simon was still immersed. He pulled out his fisherman's knife and sliced his hand so blood would flow.

"Extend your leg," he said to Simon.

Simon followed instructions and stuck his leg out of the tub. Christian gripped Simon's leg and spread his blood across the leprous blotches on Simon's skin.

"Let that soak a while."

Christian walked back around the half wall to sit down by the fire pit next to Mary. Judas looked over and shrugged, "You know we're going to have to scrub those tubs."

Apprehension about using the baths lingered after Simon's leprosy scare, so Judas announced it was time to flush the tanks and replenish to bath water. This was no small endeavor. Word spread around Capernaum that the courtyard bath bucket brigade was once again being summoned. Townspeople, incentivized by goodwill and a small stipend for their trouble, arrived at the gate and assumed position in the bucket passing line, which ultimately stretched from the water cylinder in the courtyard, out the gate, down the alley, and to the artesian well one block south towards the Sea of Galilee.

Judas ordered the cork drain plug at the base of the cylinder to be pulled and water gushed out onto the cobbled courtyard. Slight, imperceptible indents in the cobbled courtyard surface channeled the draining water to the gully in the alley and safely away from the houses on the insula.

Once the water was drained, Judas yelled to the cleaning crew, "Scrub those tubs!"

Shortly thereafter, the first in a long line of water buckets began to arrive, having been delivered hand to hand along the bucket line. The water from each bucket was poured into an opening on the topside of the cylinder and then the empty bucket piled onto a cart. As soon as the cart was full of empty buckets, two boys grabbed the cart and scurried with it back to the well. This process continued until the baths and cylinder were refilled. The entire operation was a sight to behold.

It took most of the afternoon, but the project was completed, and bath water was slowly heating up again. Later that evening, Christian said to Judas, "Well, you're quite the engineer aren't you."

"It took a while for us to get the process down," Judas said. "Now it's just the required maintenance of being a home owner." Christian figured any owner of a modern-day Jacuzzi tub could probably relate.

Christian mused that he was enjoying this stage of the ministry. He established his credentials as a healer and a teacher. The apostles felt empowered and were preaching in the name of Jesus. Christian was regularly accepting invites to public gatherings and people's homes in the areas surrounding Capernaum. And, Judas' home served as an excellent base of operations for their Galilean ministry overall.

Late one afternoon, two camels loaded with cargo arrived at the gate of Judas' courtyard. The camels folded their legs beneath them, bringing riders and cargo nearer to the ground. Judas looked in the direction of several apostles who were lolling about in the cooking area and announced, "All right boys, looks like it's here."

Simon, James, and Thaddaeus enthusiastically headed for the courtyard entrance and began to unload the cargo from the camels while Judas completed the financial transaction with the riders. Each of the apostles assisting Judas carried large feedbags of mysterious content towards the food preparation area by the courtyard stove. Thaddaeus fetched a few smaller bags while Simon and James each grabbed the corked ceramic jugs. They piled the feedbags into four stacks, set the jugs to the side, and pumped their fists in excitement.

"What's all the commotion about?" Christian asked Judas.

"Oh, I promised the boys a special treat a while back while you were in the wilderness. Takes time for deliveries to arrive from Egypt you know," Judas said.

"And the special treat is?" Christian asked.

"We're going to brew some Egyptian zythos," Judas replied enthusiastically.

"What's that?" Christian asked.

"Well," Judas said, "it's an intoxicating brew that I think you're going to like very much."

Christian walked over to cooking area and looked at the markings on the bags. There were large bags of barley, safflower, and salt stacked in piles. Clearly, these were the ingredients for the mash of their homebrew. Next to them were smaller bags of ginger and juniper berry. Christian knew enough about beer to realize that the ancient brew masters used spices and herbs for flavoring before the advent of hops. Judas had selected two classic spices for this purpose and was soon making beer.

The boys were already busy in the cooking area. Simon found a large pot and James ran off to find Sarah and Susanna. The servant girls soon arrived, each with buckets of water. Simon cleared enough room in the stove to boil the water and roast the grain.

Judas provided instructions to the brew crew to accomplish roasting, grinding, and steeping the ingredients in proper proportion to create the mash. They added small amounts of yeast to mashed grain and wild honey to the boiling pot. They boiled the mash for about an hour, then added the spices for the last fifteen minutes of boiling time. This first batch was set aside to cool before being strained and poured into ceramic jugs, which were then sealed.

"How long do we have to wait?" Thaddaeus asked Judas.

"At least a week. Let's get the jugs to a cooler place inside my house," Judas suggested.

Thaddaeus followed Judas inside, then returned empty handed to help start the next batch. The crew prepared several batches of Egyptian homebrew that evening. Subsequent taste testing revealed day seven to be the sweet spot for proper fermentation.

The apostles greatly enjoyed the special treat. Sarah and Susanna had participated in making it and felt obligated to try it.

Joanna came and said, "No way, not me. Been there, done that. That stuff gives me a hangover."

Mary nodded her head in agreement.

Word that Judas brewed Egyptian zythos spread around the town of Capernaum and friends and family came out to try some. Zebedee and Mary, the parents of the apostles James and John, came by the courtyard, as did Peter's mother-in-law Ruth. Suzanna talked her husband Chuza into coming and Chuza brought along his son Asa. Zebedee was able to tell some grand tales, including the story of the full boat of fish Jesus left him with one morning on the Sea of Galilee. Simon the Zealot played entertaining music on his mizmar, but he couldn't convince any of the women to ghawazi dance.

The next night Thomas' twin brother and friends visited. Rabbi Jarius also joined them at the courtyard fire pit to enjoy the exotic brew. That was an evening Christian couldn't quite remember after consuming a few too many cups of beer. Judas explained to him the next day, "I suggested Mary tuck you into bed after you were gazing at the full moon and blabbering something about what it must have been like for a man named Neil Armstrong to walk on it."

"I said that?"

"It was hilarious, Lord," Judas said. "How could I possibly make something like that up?"

"I guess you couldn't have," Christian reasoned.

"You also said something about a mister Trump staking claim to it."

"Let's cut me off at a couple of drinks from now on Judas. I don't want to go down that conversation path again. Ancient politics is bad enough."

"Yeah, that's probably a good idea because you were also babbling in some language none of us could understand. I told them you must have been speaking in the heavenly tongues."

"Oh no, speaking in tongues?" Christian asked.

"Yeah, pretty much," Judas said.

Christian just shook his head and quietly considered the ramifications of his speaking English being interpreted as speaking in tongues. There was a contemplative pause in conversation, then Judas broke the silence.

"You know what I find really interesting about you, Lord? You seem keenly aware of coming events and yet you measure your words carefully when discussing the future. It's as if you know a lot more than you should be able to know or are willing so say. If that's the case, then this must be a lonely quest indeed, for it's far more comforting when we have someone in whom to confide. I just want you to know, you can tell me anything you want. You're not going to shock me with revelations and you may benefit from my observations more than you're allowing currently. I guess what I'm saying is, let me into that head of yours and know that you can trust me."

"Thank you, Judas. I can confide with my father. He gives me comfort and helps me feel like I'm not doing this alone. But still, it's nice to know you're here for me as well."

"I wish I could confide with my father," Judas said.

"Why don't you?"

"He doesn't even know I exist."

"Oh Judas, I'm so sorry. Do you want to talk about it?"

"Not now. That's a story for another time."

"I totally understand." Christian steered to a different subject. "I'll tell you this, man will achieve untold fabulous accomplishments. But, I'm trying to avoid telling fantastic tales."

"So, it is true, a man will walk on the moon?" Judas asked.

"Yes, Judas it's true. Man will accomplish wondrous and terrible things in equal measure, of unimaginable scale. But I will tell you something that I've learned while being here in this time and place," Christian said sincerely. "Whether scratching out a living in Palestine, or thriving in a future world, at our core, man's basic needs remain the same. We seek purpose, we cherish freedom, and we crave love. Our message of love resonates because it strikes a common chord in men's souls and this message transcends generations ancient and future."

"Lord, I just want you to know, when you speak from your heart in this way, your words truly do resonate and what you are doing here is making a difference. I know you've explained that you're following what has been written. I just want to encourage you that you're at your best when you go off script."

"Thank you, Judas. I will take your words to heart."

Christian waited until the beer ran out to have more serious evening conversations. Some of the best times for him were when the apostles gathered together in Judas' courtyard and shared stories around the fire pit. It was during one of these evenings that he decided it was time to let Simon Barjona make his proclamation and earn his new name. He turned to Simon the fisherman. "Simon, who is it people say I am?"

"Some say you are a teacher, or a prophet," Simon replied.

"Who do you say I am?"

"I say you are the Christ, the Son of the loving God."

"Simon, you have made this proclamation just as it was written and so let me tell you what else is written, which we will now bring to fruition. You will henceforward be known by the name of Peter, for you are the rock upon which the church will be built. Congratulates Peter, for you will be honored and revered by millions in the coming age."

"It is my honor, Lord," Peter said with a head bow.

"I'm glad we've finally changed his name," Judas said with a grin. "It was getting confusing with too many Simons. We also have a lot of Mary's and James'. Can we change some of their names, too?"

Christian turned to Judas and shook his head and chided. "Judas, this was supposed to be a solemn moment. Peter has just made an important declaration and the name change imparted upon him is for God's glory, not for our convenience."

"Lord, I do understand the significance. I guess my timing on teasing was a little off." Then Judas turned to Peter. "Peter, Jesus provides you with a great distinction. You are a worthy man. Please accept my congratulations as well." Judas raised his cup in salute, "Mazel Tov."

"Mazel Tov!" came the reply from the apostles.

Pleased at the toast for Peter, Christian pushed on in his agenda for the evening. "With that, now is the appropriate time for me to share with you a prayer that I learned as a child, growing up in a place that is far from here. This prayer is a way to pray to our Father in heaven. I've been looking forward to sharing it with you. Learn it well and teach it to others. By your sharing it, millions will pray in this way."

Christian got on his knees and cupped his hands together. "When you pray, go to your inner room and shut your door. Pray to your Father in secret and he will repay you in secret, for your Father knows what you need before you ask Him. Pray this way." Christian recited the Lord's Prayer.

The apostles were quiet for some time. It was a solemn moment.

"It's a fabulous prayer, Lord. Thank you sharing it," Peter said.

Major Miracles

It was time once again to plan for some of the major miracles from the Gospels. Christian spoke with HQ about how to feed 5,000 people. He already demonstrated he could quickly spawn fish, but that wouldn't help him in the hills of Galilee. Plus, he couldn't figure out how to multiply the loaves of bread.

Both Claire and Dominic were on the cubepod that morning. "We've been working on the bread problem. Our lab experiments show that the molecular nanites will respond to the yeast and will replicate the dough."

"What about baking it?"

That question was answered with silence.

"Are you telling me I need to get someone to bake enough bread to feed 5,000 people in one sitting?" Christian asked.

"Unfortunately, there's no magic trick for that Christian," Dominic said.

"You do realize this isn't the kind of thing I can pull off by myself. I'm going to need some help," Christian said.

"Based on what you've told us, there are people there you can take into your confidence. It's the only way," Claire said.

"Okay, got it mission control. We will figure it out on this end." Christian ended the conversation frustrated. Was this really the best they could do?

Christian asked Judas to join him and Mary in their house on the insula. "Judas, Mary, I need your help with something."

"What is it you need your majesty?" Judas asked.

Christian sighed then said, "Stop it, this is serious. We need to feed 5,000 people this Sabbath."

"That's a lot of people. It will cost a lot of denarii to get the supplies, plus time to prepare," Judas said.

"Yes, that's true. This needs to be viewed as a miracle and we need to feed them bread and fish. Here's what I need you guys to do for me." He described how the events of the day needed to unfold. By his calculations, he needed 500 loaves of bread and maybe a thousand fish. "Listen Mary, we're going to be near Magdala. You have a lot of friends there. Can we impose upon them to bake the necessary bread?"

"Yes, I believe I can get many women of Magdala to help."

"And Judas, I'm counting on you to bring me enough fresh fish for me to work with to spawn more on the hills outside of the city," Christian said. "Don't worry about cooking the fish, they need to be fresh and we'll get the people to smoke them around the fires they build."

"Let me see if I got this, Lord," Judas said. "Sea of Galilee boat docks, water in the barrel, fresh fish in barrel, drag barrel of fish and barrel of water up the hills. That about right?"

"Yeah, I guess, sounds right. One other thing. I'm going to need a horse."

"A horse?" Judas tilted his head slightly and grinned. "All right, that can be arranged."

The evening before the Sabbath, Christian got his disciple's attention in the courtyard. "Folks, tomorrow is going to be a big day. I will be delivering a major sermon just outside of Magdala. Please plan to rise early and be prepared to spread word of the sermon throughout the region, from Hippos to Tiberias. If Mary or Judas asks you to help with something tomorrow, do as they instruct."

Christian and Mary retired to their house on the insula. "Mary, I can't thank you enough for the support you're providing." Mary put her arms around his waist and whispered, "Maybe not, but I'm willing to let you try." She leaned into him, kissed him gently and then with more passion. She allowed her hands to roam down from his waist. "I think it's time to set the loin cloth just outside the door," Christian said. Mary began unwrapping her shoal and suggested, "Hurry back."

Christian obeyed, returning naked to the bedroom, having removed his sandals, belt and tunic along the way. He returned to a vision of renaissance erotica. Mary was lying naked on the wool-stuffed bed, head propped on one arm, hair hanging loosely across her breasts, legs together and curled slightly. Her only adornment was the glistening silver chain with seven silver loops dangling from her neck. Christian was mesmerized. He mused, where does a man start when presented with a masterpiece?

"Do you like what you see?" Mary asked demurely.

"I love what I see, Mary."

Mary's eyes wandered down the full length of Christian's body. She bit her lip slightly and curled her pointer finger in the universal "come here" signal.

Christian obliged. He started with her hair, gently brushing it aside and over her back to reveal Mary's already poised nipples. He rolled her back and dutifully applied his attention to her breasts. He licked the near breast then suckled the nipple fully, gratified by Mary's soft moan. He knew not to leave the woman unbalanced and he artfully repeated the process on the far breast, rewarded by an equally satisfying moan.

Christian moved his attention down from Mary's breasts to her midsection and below. His saliva mixed in completely with her womanhood. To him, she tasted of sweet milk and honey. His tongue lingered there until Mary's groin rhythmically spasmed and the room itself smelled of sweat and sex.

He moved to lie on top of her, kissed her, and whispered, "I can't imagine a man feeling happier than I feel in this moment with you."

Mary's eyes met his and she said, "Can't you?" as she reached to maneuver his manhood where she wanted it. Christian slipped inside her with one steady prolonged motion and they each gasped with the rush of pleasure.

Their love making was full and complete that night, each lost in the wonderment of their love. Afterwards, they cozied together, Mary's head laying against his chest. "That position is still new to me," Mary said. "I find great delight in it. You do things to me that no man has ever done."

"I can tell your body enjoys my attention," he said, kissing her forehead. "I cherish the love that we've found."

There was a calmness about their bed. After a short while, Mary said, "Tomorrow is a big day, we should get some sleep." He had every intention of acknowledging her, as sleep descended upon him.

Early the next morning, Christian accompanied Mary and Sarah to Magdala where her friends were enlisted to bake bread. Her strategy was to divide the labor across as many households as possible. Five hundred loaves across fifty households would be ten loaves each, a doable quantity in the time allotted. This would involve conscripting friends of friends. She's a persuasive and charismatic woman, Christian thought, confident that she could get the job done.

The first order of business was to re-produce enough dough to be baked. Mary kneaded the flour mixture and yeast as Christian had instructed. He cracked open a molecular nanite capsule, spread it on the dough, and waited. Nothing happened. He tried again and again, but still nothing. He was not sure exactly what Houston had accomplished in their bread replication experiments but it wasn't working for Christian and Mary. He turned to Mary, "We have a problem."

"I brought money," Mary said. "Two hundred denarii to buy supplies if we need it."

"You're the best!" Christian kissed her.

"You go on," Mary said. "The women of Magdala will get this bread baked."

That afternoon, a great multitude gathered from the cities in the Sea of Galilee region. The apostles did a fabulous job of spreading the word. The gathering area was uncultivated rolling hills just west of the Sea of Galilee. The hills were typically used for grazing, but today an oppressed people seeking a new shepherd temporarily inhabited them.

Christian felt tremendous compassion for the multitude coming to hear Jesus speak. He started with two basic rules, "Love God, and love one another." Then he enthralled the crowd with the beatitudes.

When he mentioned the peacemakers, he thought of Mother Theresa and Mahatma Gandhi.

Christian decided to take a bit of liberty and borrow from a great American. "I have a dream that one day all of God's children, Jews and Gentiles, Galileans and Samaritans, Romans and Zealots, will be able to recline together at the table of brotherhood and break bread. I have a dream that men of all nations will be able to join hands and sing together in harmony, saying, 'Free at last! Free at last! Thank God Almighty, we're free at last!'" He hoped that Martin Luther King, Jr., would be proud to have his masterpiece of rhetoric shared at the Sermon on the Mount.

The crowd was clearly moved by Christian's words and the disciples were even more in awe.

"How did you like the speech?" Christian asked Matthew, wanting feedback.

"Great, except for the dreaming part," Mathew said. "I might leave it out when I document this. I don't think the Romans will find it inspiring."

Christian was disappointed to learn his channeling of MLK Jr. didn't have the desired effect as he had hoped. "I guess humans aren't ready to hear that message yet," he shrugged and mumbled under his breath.

As expected, it was getting late and the people were getting hungry. The disciples helped by dividing the people into groups and asked them to build cooking fires for they would have to cook their fish.

"How much food do we have?" Nathanael asked, as dusk approached.

"There's a boy here with five loaves of bread and two fish," Philip said.

"Well that's not going to be nearly enough," Nathanael said.

Christian was greatly pleased to see Mary and Judas coming over the ridge leading a small caravan. Mary and her friends managed to bake hundreds of loaves of bread and Judas delivered a large barrel of water and tilapia fresh off the docks. The crowd was heartened at their arrival.

"You two are awesome!" Christian hugged them both.

Christian blessed the food. The disciples distributed the bread. Then Christian sliced open fish until he found one with eggs. He applied the molecular nanites and dropped that fish into the water barrel. The barrel filled with fish in seconds. The disciples distributed the fish and Christian continued the multiplication process until the multitudes were fed that evening. He would later make the subtle suggestion to Matthew that he could omit the caravan bringing the bread when writing his gospel.

This was going to continue to be a busy night for Christian. Next, he needed to walk on water.

First, he delayed the twelve apostles by telling them they each needed to collect a basket of bread fragments from the fields. Twelve baskets for twelve apostles, per the gospels. After which time they were to pile into a boat and head back across the Sea of Galilee, towards Capernaum. While they were doing that Christian needed to book it to the other side of the big lake, hence the horse he requested from Judas. Once there, he would set the cubepod in long distance projection mode.

The boat trip would be about four and a half miles across the lake. He'd wait until the disciples were about four miles across and then fire up the cubepod, projecting a 3D animated image that HQ provided him for this purpose. The projection would appear to be coming towards the boat from across the lake, walking in Christian's direction. At five miles an hour it would take the boat another twelve minutes to approach the opposite shore. This scenario of walking on the water fit nicely with the account in the Gospel of John. If Matthew's account was correct and Peter tried to walk on the water, the instructions to Christian were to wing it.

When the time came, everything worked as planned: the baskets, the horse, the boat, the timing and the cubepod image of Christian walking on the water. Christian heard someone on the boat say, "It's a ghost!" And then things went awry when Peter got brave. The boat sped up as the twelve apostles dealt with the specter coming their way, so by the time Peter climbed out of the boat, Christian was able to finagle closing out the image and wading out to assist Peter. This was a humbling moment for Peter and a source of much entertainment for the rest of the apostles.

Once safely ashore, Judas leaned over to Christian and confided, "Now I see why you needed the horse."

Christian and all twelve apostles returned to Judas' home after their busy day. Suzanna, Sarah and the other servant girls had clean robes and towels ready for them to enjoy the baths. The apostles piled into the stone tubs and recounted the tales of the day. Andrew regaled them with a colorful account of Peter trying to get out of the boat to walk on the water like Jesus.

"Who thought I was a ghost at first?" Christian asked.

"That was I, Lord," Thaddeus admitted, raising his wet arm fully from the bath water and yet maintaining control of the mug of wine in his hand.

"Lord, what you did today was truly amazing," Peter said, striking a more serious tone. "My brother can deride me about trying join you on the water and I suppose it's funny in hindsight, but can you tell us how you managed to walk across the sea? And why? I'm not sure I understand the significance of what you did, and I desperately desire to comprehend it."

"Peter, you, above all, deserve an explanation, I grant you that. First, please understand that when I do these miraculous things it is principally to fulfill that which is written and that which is instructed by my father in heaven. These signs will be documented in the gospels so that future generations may come to believe in the ministry of Jesus and the message of love we bring to the world." Christian paused to make sure all his apostles were paying attention.

"What you witnessed this evening can't be easily explained. There are forces at work here of great significance. Generations from now, when this story is told, thousands will envision what it must have been like to see Jesus walk across the sea, and they'll want to be just as brave as Peter was. They will put trust in their faith. Faith is a powerful force in man's heart. Jesus walking on the water will come to exemplify what is possible with God."

"Thank you, Lord," Peter said. "That helps me understand."

"Peter, you're welcome. Your renown grew tonight."

"Here's to Peter," Judas said, raising his mug.

"Mazel tov," resonated the cheers across the courtyard.

After the baths, the apostles dried off and hung out near the fire pit. Christian was curious about something. "What did you guys do with those twelve baskets of bread you gathered from the hills?"

Mary rejoined Christian and the apostles by the fire. "There were some herdsmen from Decapolis who said they could use the scraps to feed their herd of over two thousand pigs so, we gave them the baskets of bread."

"Ah, I forgot about the two thousand swine story," Christian said to himself, but apparently a little too loudly.

"What two thousand swine story?" Andrew asked.

"Oh, you'll find out soon enough," Christian said. "We're going to have to plan a trip to Decapolis to pay them a visit."

"Do we need to get the baskets back or something?" Andrew said perplexed.

"No, it's not about the baskets," Christian said. "It's about saving a man's soul."

According to the *Bible*, one last trip into Decapolis on the southeast side of the Sea of Galilee remained. Christian knew that this trip involved sending two thousand pigs over a cliff to their death. He had seen enough animals die in the lab back in Houston, so he decided he would switch it up a bit for the sake of the pigs.

"Tomorrow we're taking a trip to Gersenes in Decapolis," Christian announced. "Everyone get a good night sleep. It will be a long day."

There was some grumbling from the apostles. "Decapolis again Lord? Don't you remember what happened last time we went there?" Philip complained.

"Yes, I remember. Don't worry, this time we'll be fine." Christian was banking on there being no mention of Roman cohorts in the *Bible* story about the two thousand swine.

The twelve apostles and Christian climbed into a boat the next morning and set out for the shores of Gersenes. The clouds that morning were dark and some of the apostles looked apprehensive. They nevertheless followed his lead and got into the boat to cross the sea. "When we arrive, there is going to be a crazy man living there," Christian said. "Let me deal with the crazy man. If I ask you to do something, please obey. We can talk about the reasons later."

Christian got out of the boat and started walking towards the tombs. A big, strong, menacing man who lived in the tombs ran out to them, yelling, "What are you doing here! Go away!"

To his surprise, Christian recognized the man. It was Barabbas from the Decapolis prison, but Barabbas was clearly out of his mind, so Christian proceeded cautiously. Christian held his hands up, "I'm not going to hurt you." Which seemed ludicrous to him because Barabbas was twice his size. "I've come all this way because I heard about you living in the tombs and I would really like to help you. Do you remember me from the prison cave?"

Barabbas ceased gnashing his teeth, stopped his advance, and just grunted.

"Would you be willing to talk to me?" Christian asked.

Barabbas nodded slightly and sat down in the sand, folding his legs Indian style.

Christian slowly approached and sat next to him in the same pose. "I know you. Your name is Bar Abbas. You were a mercenary for the Romans."

"You know nothing holy man. Our name is Legion, for we are many," Barabbas replied sternly, drooling as he spoke.

"Legion, you do not belong here." Christian engaged Barabbas' alternate personality. "This is a proud man and a warrior. Your presence in him is a distraction from his pain which he must confront and move past to heal."

"Don't presume to lecture us about belonging here holy man, for you go by many names as well and we know who you are, Holy One of

God, Jesus the Christ, and Christian Naismith. We know what is written and we are amused that you must die."

Christian recognized that while poor Barabbas was delusional, he was astounded that Barabbas had uttered his full given name and had prophesied his death. He logged this for later discussion with his father. "Every man must die, Legion. Why would this amuse you?"

"You are no mere man, oh Holy One of God and your death will be spectacular indeed." Barabbas was wide eyed and grinning ear-to-ear in a demented euphoric state.

Enough of this shit, Christian thought. This guy is starting to piss me off. "My fun meter is pegged with you Legion. How about we exorcise you out of this man?"

"We entreat you not to send us away for this man is strong enough to allow us to live here," Barabbas replied, drool spraying as he spoke.

Christian wondered what had happened since he last saw Barabbas to make him this way. He couldn't know for sure what was going on in Barabbas' brain or whether the cellular nanites might help him, but scripture brought them here for a reason and Christian intended to fulfill what was written.

"I think I can help you in a way that no one else has been able," Christian said. "I know you are a strong person and that is why it takes a legion to possess you. I can help you harness your strength so you can overcome this burden, but I need to touch you to do so. May I have your permission to touch you?"

"We will not hurt you," Barabbas said. Despite this promise, Christian still felt Barabbas flinch and slightly recoil as he laid a comforting hand on Barabbas' shoulder. Christian realized a lifetime of battle and subsequent isolation in the tombs had taken quite a toll on the sanity of the warrior.

Christian turned his head and looked up to Judas. "Do you see that herd of swine on that ridge over there? I need you to take the other apostles up there and when I wave my arms wide, I need you to startle them. Now honestly, it says in scripture that they run over the cliff to their death, but we're not going to do that to them. Instead, I want you to steer them the other way. Just get them over the ridge and out of sight. Got it?"

"Got it, Lord. On your signal we'll scatter the pigs over the ridge and we'll avoid killing them," Judas said and then asked the apostles to come up the hill with him.

Given his condition, Christian dared not break out his knife in front of Barabbas. Instead, he decided to try an alternative nanite transfer method. Christian gripped the man's massive hand. "You're being very brave. Now I'm going to spit on my hands and rub my hands on your mouth. Please allow the spittle between your lips. My saliva has healing power and it should help you feel better."

Christian applied his saliva. Barabbas gradually relaxed.

"See those swine at that ridge? The next thing we're going to do is send the legion of demons into that herd so they won't bother you anymore. How does that sound?"

Barabbas slowly nodded his head.

Christian stood tall, spread his arms wide, waved them up and down and yelled, "Legion, I command you to leave this man and fly into that herd of swine on the hill."

Just then the pigs began to move in mass across the ridge and over the ridgeline. Soon the entire herd was nearly out of sight. Then Christian saw the remnants of the pigs begin to turn around and head back the opposite direction, only to be overtaken and trampled by the stampede of the main herd charging headlong to the sea cliffs. Christian watched helplessly and dumbfounded as two thousand swine thundered over the edge, plunging to their death. It was a like watching a train wreck, both captivating and horrible.

Christian sat back down and gathered his thoughts. He would talk to the apostles about what went wrong later. He held onto Barabbas' hand. "Tell me your name now."

"Bar Abbas," he said with a sigh of relief.

"What happened to you? Another fight with the Romans?"

"Something like that, it's kind of a blur. I think I maimed some of the bastards this time and the Romans left me in shackles a little too long for my tastes. I doubt they'll want me back ever again. I've seen too much battle and bloodshed for any man."

Binding a man hand and foot and letting him live isolated in a tomb is probably not the best way to treat post-traumatic stress disorder, Christian thought. "I'm sorry you had to go through that. It is a shame you've been treated in this way."

"I do feel more at ease since you touched me. I don't know exactly what you did, but my mind feels less 'noisy' now," Barabbas said. "Did you really exorcise a legion of demons from me and cast them into those pigs?"

Christian considered what his response should be. The man had asked a specific question and by his dad's guiding principle, he was therefore ready for the answer. Problem was, Legion was like no other unclean spirit Christian had encountered. Legion said things Christian couldn't explain. "I'm not exactly sure. My apostles were supposed to startle the pigs to give you a visual to focus on and to fulfill text already written, though they weren't supposed to let them run over the cliff. I'll have to find out from them later why the herd stampeded in the wrong direction."

"It was quite a sight," Barabbas observed.

"Yes, I suppose it was," Christian reluctantly agreed. "More importantly for you, my body, blood, and saliva have a healing power which I believe you are now benefiting from. I can't erase your memories of war. You'll have to continue to conquer those demons on your own moving forward. But, the healing I've given you should serve to help you cope. I've received good feedback from others with conditions like yours."

"I understand. You are a good and honest man," Barabbas said. "I have to warn you, though, Legion utterly despises you. He wanted me to hurt you and he showed me what would happen to me if I didn't."

"What did he show you?"

"My death. It was a warrior's death. I fear it not."

"No, Bar Abbas, I get the sense you wouldn't. The good news is, that death won't happen soon. I assure you our paths will cross again in Jerusalem at the next Passover. You will once again be incarcerated and I will facilitate your freedom."

"That's the good news?" Barabbas asked, bewildered.

"Yes, you'll just have to believe me on this one. I, unfortunately, won't be so lucky."

Christian felt compassion for Barabbas and he was tempted to let him return with the apostles in the boat back to Capernaum. Instead, he trusted scripture and told him, "Go to your people in Decapolis. Tell them of the great things Jesus has done for you on this day."

The apostles returned from the ridge. "There were some herders on the hill vehemently complaining about us wrecking their herd. They asked us to get out of here," Judas informed Christian.

"No wonder they're complaining, you guys killed them all. What dumbass sent them running the wrong direction towards the cliffs?"

"It wasn't us," Judas said. "We had them all just about over the ridge and settled down on the other side when something else possessed them and caused them to charge back the other direction. We're lucky none of us got trampled."

"The swine were supposed to survive," Christian shook his head.

"I thought you said it was written that they died," Judas countered. "Maybe you just can't change what happened because it's already written."

Christian baulked at responding to his own mantra mirrored back to him from Judas. He relented and advised the apostles to make their way back to the boat as a crowd of angry local farmers and herdsmen approached the beach.

"Let's get out of here," he suggested.

The apostles returned to the boat, quickly boarded, and headed back to Capernaum.

"You're quiet, what are you thinking about?" Judas asked Christian during the trip back.

"That man back there from the tombs, I expect to cross paths with him again in Jerusalem. The man has nine lives."

"Nine lives?" Judas asked.

"Never mind. Just a figure of speech."

"Hmm," Judas shrugged. "So, what's his name?"

"Bar Abbas. His name is only recorded in scripture once, as Barabbas, in connection with me in Jerusalem, and yet I've run into him twice already in Decapolis."

"I see. You know, Lord, sometimes truths reveal themselves in their own time and place for their own reasons. You did a good thing today and you learned something new. That's how we grow, right?"

"Yes Judas, that is how we grow," Christian said and turned squarely to Judas. "Sometimes I forget you are a master in your own right and I must remember to be open to learn, as well as to teach. Thank you for reminding me of this. You are a wise man and a dear friend."

Judas simply nodded and smiled, exposing pearly whites he had somehow managed to maintain in ancient Palestine.

The waters were getting rough as a storm front was passing over the Sea of Galilee. Some of the apostles were fisherman and had grown accustomed to these turns in the weather, but most were not, and they were quite anxious about the wind and waves pounding the boat. Christian didn't know whether any of them could swim well enough to survive were the boat to capsize. He leveraged his sailing knowledge and his experience growing up on the waters in Florida where he had dealt with hurricanes. He was able to demonstrate calm during the storm and thereby promote courage in the apostles as they crossed the relatively modest sized Sea of Galilee. As they got closer to Capernaum, Christian saw that a crowd was gathering at the dock.

Rabbi Jarius ran to their boat when it docked and said to Christian, "My daughter is at a point near death. Please come lay your hands on her, that she might get well and live."

"Take me to her," Christian commanded.

As they headed towards the temple, a woman confronted Christian and entreated him to cure her. "I've been suffering from bleeding for twelve years and the doctors cannot do anything to help me. If you just let me touch your garments, I know I will get well."

Christian stopped for the woman. "What is your name?"

"My name is Rachelle."

"And where is the hemorrhage Rachelle?"

"Somewhere in my stomach, Lord. No one has been able to figure out exactly where."

"All right, Rachelle, my blood has healing powers. I'm going to slice my hand and put some blood on your tongue." Christian proceeded to slice his finger and drip blood onto her tongue to let the cellular nanites accomplish their healing. "You will feel better soon."

Christian started once again up the street towards Jarius' house. As he got closer he heard wailing. People came out and told Jarius it was too late, that his daughter had already died. Christian rushed in and approached the girl. "What is your daughter's name?"

"Her name is Abby," Jarius' wife replied.

Christian reached out with his already bloody hand and held Abby's hand. He sat and talked tenderly to her for a few moments. This was one of those occasions when the nanites would demonstrate power over death itself. He honored the coaching from his dad and trusted in the immutability of time. "Abby has not died, she is simply sleeping." He trusted the healing nanites would take effect. He opened her mouth and let his blood drip into it.

Abby did recover and news about Jesus' power over death further extended his reputation.

Liberating the man in the tomb from his demons, healing the woman with the internal bleeding, and saving Rabbi Jarius' daughter were individually each fantastic deeds. For them to have been accomplished all in the same day amounted to sensory overload for Christian and his disciples. Some of the apostles were still queasy from the storm on the sea during the journey back from Decapolis and everyone was exhausted. The women made sure the men were fed and then most of the apostles turned in early. Christian was left to share his thoughts with Mary in private. Then, they, too, retired to their house on the insula.

In the days that followed, questions about certain philosophical topics became a consistent theme. The apostles were asking for insight into the significance of baptism and the meaning of being born again.

Christian considered the depth to which he would teach the philosophy of western religion to the apostles. He needed to find the words to communicate the origin and significance of the new message. Baptism was an ancient Egyptian concept which John the Baptist probably picked up on when he grew up there. Jesus extended the concept of baptism to include Greek philosophies of empowerment, permitting the common man to commune with God directly, rather than require the assistance of a privileged intercessory. The combination of these two concepts, wrapped with an overarching guideline of love, made the new covenant powerful, yet dangerous.

Christian gathered the apostles and other disciples around the courtyard fire pit and taught them once again. "I see that you are asking important questions about the meaning of the message we are sharing throughout Galilee. This tells me you are ready to receive instruction with greater discernment. What I share with you now I will share in a plain-spoken manner, not in the parables I have been speaking to the common people. Listen carefully now and you will know truth as I understand it."

Christian saw that the apostles and others were listening intently. "John the Baptist preached repentance in preparation for the dawning of new kind of relationship with God. He baptized with water, symbolizing death and rebirth of the man. John foretold of our ministry where we would baptize people with the Holy Spirit. For thousands of years, people throughout the nations of the world, whether Egyptian, Babylonian, Jewish and others have incorporated a hierarchy of a holy priesthood between man and God. These priests have been the elite of society and privileged in their ability to speak with God and intercede on man's behalf. The message we bring is a new covenant that allows the common man to commune with a loving God directly." Christian went on to explain the impact. "This message empowers the peasant and threatens to render the ruling religious authorities obsolete, which makes it both wonderful and dangerous."

All were quiet for a moment, then Peter spoke. "Lord, how then do we baptize people when we are preaching the gospel and we are not near rivers or ponds?"

"The baptism is symbolic. The important part of the rebirth process is to manifest a change in attitude about oneself and one's relationship with God. To accomplish the rebirth, a man must admit to their weaknesses and yield to a higher power to restore and manage their lives, turning his will over to a God who loves him. The man should then search his soul, ask forgiveness for any wrong doings, and carry out his life moving forward with love and mercy."

"A man's ego is a powerful thing," Peter said. "It will be difficult for many to find the humility to admit they are in fact, powerless."

"Well-spoken Peter. The first step is indeed often the hardest." Christian wrapped up the lesson with this warning. "People will hate you because of this message. They will hate you because the message implies a personal responsibility of which they want no part. Else, they will hate you because they are elite and threatened by circumvention of their leadership role in society. Persevere under these circumstances and believe in the God we are championing."

Road to Judea

I would rather have questions that can't be answered than answers that can't be questioned.
~Richard Feynman

Christian roughly mapped out the timeline of his ministry during the forty days spent in the wilderness. By his calculations, he needed to allow about half a year of ministry time in Judea prior to the fateful Passover weekend when he was to be crucified. He kept to that calendar. He and his disciples were able to continue their ministry unimpeded in Galilee for nearly two years.

The time to wrap up the Galilean ministry drew near, and operations shifted to Judea. Christian climbed the stairs of the high tower to the upper room one last time. He had climbed these spiral stairs often and memorized every crack and crevice. The ascending stairs spiraled left as in castles so that right-handed defending troops could have a maneuverability advantage. He counted sixty-five steps, putting the upper room approximately five stories above the platform level of the Capernaum temple. He would miss the convenience of the temple tower for his conversations with HQ. His ministry in Galilee was a success and he stayed as true to the written biblical records as he possibly could.

He needed to talk to his dad, as the next few months were going to be hectic. HQ responded to his call and he requested to speak with his father.

"What's up, Son?" his father asked.

"Dad, our ministry in Galilee is approaching its conclusion. All the apostles are still with me and they have proven to be faithful. I'm very proud of them. In most cases the events unfolded in a manner consistent with the way they're described in the *Bible*. This next phase is going to get harder, though, as you can imagine. The religious authorities in Judea will rally against me and we know the story doesn't end well."

"It ends with you coming home," his dad reminded him. "I believe whole heartedly in the immutability of time. Trust in what is written. Let the Gospels be your guide and know that I'm fervently praying for you."

"All right, I'll try. I guess one thing I hadn't realized until having lived the experiences here in Galilee is that I seem to be a magnet for people with unclean spirits. On one hand, they don't like me touching them, yet on the other they seek me like a bug to the light. I've discovered that the best way for me to handle them is to respond with compassion and to try to help them through their issues. Do you have any idea what that's all about?"

"No, I really can't say without being there to examine these people. The Catholic Church maintains active exorcists to this day, even though the majority of the cases turn out to be diagnosable mental disorders. What I can say is that maybe they feel like they can trust you, either by reputation or because you really are a genuinely nice person. All I can advise you to do is treat them with compassion. The people coming to you are hurting, either physically, emotionally, or mentally, or all the above. People have all kinds of demons to overcome. It's a natural defense mechanism to attribute destructive feelings to an external projection, especially in that time. The Gospels of Mark and Luke reference seven demons cast out of your friend Mary Magdalene. Have you noticed anything like demons in her?"

"No. Not the way the book makes it sound. I'll figure out a way to ask her about it. The most stunning circumstance was hearing Barabbas address me by my full given name while he was possessed by Legion. It was as if he knew who I really was. Then it was as if the herd of swine got a mind of their own and they stampeded over the cliffs."

"There's no easy explanation for any of that. In our arrogance as men of science we sometimes come to expect things to be explainable in tangible terms and yet we pray. It was noble of you to try and change the outcome of the pigs, but those swine were evidently destined to die, just as the *Bible* said. Let's agree not to discount the spiritual realm in dealing with these poor possessed souls. My advice remains the same, treat them with the utmost compassion." His dad contemplatively folded his hands. "Anything else on your mind?"

"I suppose there is. I haven't been able to help people with missing limbs. I feel bad about that because the people have expectations and they don't understand the limitations of the nanite technology. Is Spintronics working on regrowth of human limbs yet? I guess I'm really just curious."

"We are," his dad said. "It's a natural progression from the molecular nanite work your team was doing in Houston. We haven't mastered it yet, though. Maybe you can help us when you come back home? Interesting that the Gospels never mention Jesus regrowing limbs either."

Christian nodded. He had already made the same observation.

"One last huge item dad. Has Berkeley figured out how to raise Lazarus from the dead?"

"Son, there isn't any technology anywhere on earth that can raise a man from the dead. The anesthesiologists have come up with a poison you can concoct from local ingredients that would render Lazarus unconscious for a time, sufficient to get him buried. Short of that, the next best thing would be faking it with a hologram from the cubepod."

Christian wasn't happy at the idea of faking the resurrection of Lazarus. "There's something about faking it with a hologram that really bothers me. What do we tell his family? 'Oh, just kidding? April fools?' These are real people we're dealing with." Christian considered the implications.

"I realize that Christian. Trust me, it's forefront in my mind as well. The other bit of encouragement I can give you is to remember how tenacious those Berkeley scientists can be when they get hold of a question that can't be answered."

"I love those Berkeley guys."

Christian plodded down the steps of the Capernaum Temple tower for the final time. He paused at the patio level overlooking the Sea of Galilee for nostalgia's sake. Normally, he could see clearly across the lake from this vantage point, but today it was too dark and cloudy. Over the horizon to the south was Jerusalem where his destiny loomed. He heard light footsteps approaching from behind, then felt the grasp of a gentle hand in his. He caught a whiff of lemon mixed with the cool sea breeze and pulled her close to his side. They stood arm in arm together for some time before she broke the silence.

"I thought I might find you here," Mary said. "Speaking with your father again?"

Christian nodded.

"What happens next?" Mary asked.

"This was the easy part Mary. Next, we head into Judea where I must channel the remaining events of my ministry, things both wonderful and terrible. I'm desperately going to need your support now more than ever."

"You have my love and support, Lord, both are unconditional."

They hugged each other and kissed intimately in a rare midday public display of affection on the stone steps of the temple, as storm clouds gathered over the sea.

They strolled together back to Judas' home.

"May I have your attention please," Christian gathered the awareness of his disciples. "I have an important announcement to make this evening. First, let me express heartfelt appreciation to our brother, our host and our friend, Judas, for accommodating all of us in his home for these past two years." Christian nodded towards Judas.

"To Judas!" said Peter.

"To Judas!" echoed the disciples, the salute accompanied with many pats on Judas' back.

Christian waited for attention to return in his direction.

"Be informed, it is now time for us to leave Capernaum and the comforts of the home Judas has so kindly provided. Our mission now transfers to Judea and then to Jerusalem. Be ready. This is our final ministry together." He observed some concerned looks from his disciples at the announcement. "Gather only the belongings you can carry as necessary for hiking and camping. Harness your strength, for the time of great tribulation draws nearer."

The next morning, they trekked southeast through Magdala and past Tiberias, walking the road along hills towards Nain. As they approached the northwest slopes of Mt. Tabor, Christian selected the apostles who were to witness the transfiguration of Jesus. Christian figured imagery from the cubepod would be sufficient to awe the apostles. Peter, James, John, and in this case Judas, accompanied him up the hill. Christian assumed Matthew would purge Judas from much of scripture due to his betrayal of Jesus. Christian turned on the cubepod and conversed with Dominic and Cornelius in a language the apostles didn't understand, English. The apostles thought Jesus was speaking with Moses and Elijah, as the account is written in the *Bible.*

"I see ancient people. What are they saying?" Cornelius asked.

"They think you two are Moses and Elijah. I'm guessing you're Moses," Christian said, looking at Cornelius.

"Very funny. I can't believe we're showing them this technology. Aren't they going to freak out?" Cornelius asked.

"It will be recorded as the transfiguration of Jesus. Berkeley told me one of you will be able to say a phase in Aramaic about how awesome I am," Christian said.

"Oh, I got that," Dominic said. "I've been practicing it with a deep voice. When do I say it?"

"As soon as that dude with the big nose and heavy beard opens his mouth, just go ahead and interrupt him," Christian said.

Moments later Peter said, "Lord, it is good for us to be here to hear you speaking in heavenly tongues. If you wish, I will put up three altars, one for you, one for Moses and one for Elijah."

While he was still speaking, a deep voice bellowed from the bright cloud, "This is my Son, whom I love. With him I am well pleased. Listen to him!"

"Good job. Now they're freaked out. I'll need to go comfort them," Christian said.

Peter, James and John fell facedown, terrified. Judas was the lone apostle remaining standing.

"Who's the one left standing?" Cornelius asked. "He's seems cool and collected."

"That's Judas."

"Iscariot?" Cornelius blurted.

"Not yet. That happens later when we get to Jerusalem."

"I don't remember him being mentioned in the *Bible* as present at the transfiguration," Dominic said.

"He isn't mentioned," Christian said. "Don't worry, the history books will clean it up."

"So, you pretty much know what's going to happen next, all the time?" Cornelius asked.

"Well, not all the details, but the big stuff, yes," Christian said.

"Isn't that surreal?" Cornelius asked.

"I've gotten used to it," Christian shrugged. "See you guys later."

Christian sauntered over and tapped the apostles who had buried their faces. "Get up, don't be afraid."

When they looked up, the 3D image was gone. Peter, James, and John remained aghast and began talking about how Jesus must truly be the Son of God.

"Don't tell anyone what you have seen here today until I've been raised from the dead," Christian instructed them as they were coming down the mountain.

They continued to discuss it amongst themselves, giving Judas a chance to have a private word with Christian. "Did you mean to bring me up here with Peter, James, and John? You've shown me how you communicate with your father, which you used to do alone in the high tower of the Capernaum Temple."

Christian thought that maybe he shouldn't have let Judas see the cubepod in action. "Perhaps I've shown you too much," he admitted as he put his arm around Judas' shoulder. "But, you've become a good friend and I wanted to share this moment with you as well. For what it's worth, you demonstrated yourself to be calm in a startling situation. You didn't bury your head in the dirt like the others."

"I didn't want to miss anything," Judas said.

The group came down the mountain and reunited with the rest of the disciples. There was a man in the crowd who called out, "Teacher, I beg you to look at my son, for he is my only child. A spirit seizes him, and he suddenly screams. It throws him into convulsions so that he foams at the mouth. It scarcely ever leaves him and is destroying him. I begged your disciples to drive it out, but they could not."

"Bring your son here," instructed Christian.

As the boy was coming towards Jesus he was once again thrown to the ground in a convulsion. Christian walked over to the boy and comforted him. He spat on his hands and rubbed the spittle on the boy's mouth, as he held the boy's head in his lap. Eventually, the boy's convulsing settled down enough for him to talk with the boy. "What's your name?"

"My name is Jeremiah."

"Jeremiah, what a strong and proud name. You know Jeremiah, I'm going to go to Jericho soon and it reminds me of how brave Jeremiah must have been to win that city in battle. You know you're going to have to be brave, too, just like he was, to fight through this condition you have. But, I know you can do it and my healing touch is going to help you. I believe in you Jeremiah. Can you be strong for me and for your dad who loves you so much?"

Jeremiah nodded.

"Excellent." Christian handed Jeremiah back to his father.

"Sir, these mental disorders are difficult to assess, but I've seen enough of these cases to convince me that my healing powers do have some positive effect. I will pray for your boy. He seems like a fine child and I know you must love him very much to bring him all the way out here to me. I sincerely wish you and your family the best."

"Thank you, Lord," the father bowed in respect.

The entire group started on its way to Judea. The reputation of Jesus preceded them as they walked towards Samaria. They had countless encounters with ill people whom Christian was able to heal and with people who just wanted to meet Jesus. Christian and the disciples were once again approaching the outskirts of Nain, the city where he heeled the ten lepers.

"Scripture says another important event happens in Nain. Be prepared to help me and to do as I say."

"We will, Lord," came the universal reply.

Christian began to step up the pace and Judas strode up next to him with equal intensity. When he saw the procession of people exiting the city carrying a boy on a gurney Christian kicked off his sandals, dropped his cloak, and broke into an all-out sprint towards the procession. Judas did the same and matched him stride for stride. He reached the boy and commanded, "Put him down."

The men carrying the gurney lowered it to the ground. Christian fell to his knees and checked the boy's vitals, no pulse, no breathing. He could feel from the boy's still warm skin that this was a recent death. Christian expressed his concern in between breaths. "How long has he been like this?"

An older man said, "We were at his side when he breathed his last, just before you arrived. Perhaps if you had been here Master, you could have saved him."

Christian straddled the boy and started CPR. He applied rhythmic and violent downward thrusts. Judas moved around to the other side of the boy and positioned his head to optimally open the air passage. Christian nodded a thank you to Judas. Timing his speech in between CPR thrusts, Christian asked, "What was his condition?"

"He became congested and then he just stopped breathing," the older man said.

Christian needed to get the boy's heart going again and clear the lungs of the pneumonia. "Do you think you can do this?" Christian asked Judas. "Two fingers below the sternum and give the chest a firm downward push. Don't worry about breaking a rib, we'll deal with that later."

"Yes Lord, I can do it," Judas said.

Christian and Judas traded positions. The rest of the disciples caught up to the procession. Christian formed spittle in his mouth, then opened the boy's mouth and performed mouth to mouth resuscitation to get his cellular nanite-laden saliva directly into the boy's respiratory system.

Judas continued CPR. The technique was arduous, and it was a lot to expect a man to keep it up for more than five minutes or so.

"Are you doing okay?" Christian asked Judas.

"I'm good, Lord, you do what's needed."

The boy finally responded, jerking and coughing up phlegm. Judas stopped pressing on the boy's chest. Instead, he firmly grasped him under his armpits and propped him up, resting the boy's upper torso and head onto Christian's lap and chest. The boy's coughing abated. He wheezed through labored breathing for a few minutes. Christian held the boy close and said softly, "What's your name?"

"Daniel, son of Jacob," the boy managed a hoarse reply.

"I take it you are Jacob?" Christian looked up at the older man.

"No, Jacob was my son. He is passed. I am the boy's grandfather. It appears you have brought my grandson back from death. I'm not sure how to thank you for that."

"Hey Daniel, how about you tell your grandpa he can express his thanks by providing a meal for me and my friends and maybe a place to stay for the night. Sound good?"

Daniel smiled and looked up at his grandpa.

"That sounds more than fair to me," his grandpa said. "Please welcome these people into town and let's show them some Nain hospitality. Their Master has saved my grandson and his friends are henceforward mine as well."

Christian and his disciples spent the night in Nain. By morning, Daniel was fully recovered and exhibiting the normal energy of an eleven-year-old boy. This was a pleasant stay for Christian and his entourage. They were fed, rested and had saved another life.

Christian and his disciples headed south the next day in the direction of Jerusalem. It was an exceptionally hot late summer day and they were sweltering in the midday Samarian sauna. Christian endured Houston humidity and the Florida sun, but the arid Israeli heat was uniquely oppressive, and the only real relief would be nighttime. Mary strolled up next to him. "Where are we headed?"

"A town called Bethany in Judea, near Jerusalem," Christian replied.

"Oh, we can visit my sister and brother there," Mary said. "My sister is a bit of a worrier, but she means well. You will like my brother. He's a good man and has a nice home. I'm sure he will let some of us stay at his house and he can arrange lodging for the others."

"That would be nice. His house doesn't happen to have central air conditioning does it?" Christian wiped stringy wet bangs away from his face and feigned a forlorn look at Mary.

"Well I don't know what that is, Lord, so I suppose the answer would be no. Maybe you should ask Judas about it. He's the engineer," she suggested.

"Maybe." Oddly, in the back of his mind the idea didn't seem so farfetched. Then again, he was nearly delusional from the heat stroke. "What are their names?"

"Martha and Lazarus," Mary said.

"Well I'll be damned!" Christian said out loud.

"What's that?" Mary questioned.

"Oh, nothing, it's just I think I know of your brother. But let's just see how things go."

How had Spintronics missed that Mary of Magdala's brother was Lazarus? Christian kept his cool. He needed to consider the ramifications.

"I look forward to meeting your sister and brother," was all he said. He needed to speak with HQ about this new development.

It was several more days' journey before the disciples reached the outskirts of Jerusalem and diverted east towards Bethany at the foot of the Mount of Olives. Mary led them through the village towards her brother's house. Christian noticed a woman scampering down the street towards them and heard her calling, "Mary!"

"Oh, that's my sister Martha." Mary bolted ahead of the disciples and greeted Martha with an enthusiastic hug.

Christian stepped up his pace and reached them as they released their embrace. He saw both Martha and Mary had joyful tears of reunion in their eyes.

"I noticed the crowd coming and I just couldn't believe it when I recognized you in the front," Martha said. "Oh Mary, I'm so glad you're here. We've been worried about you."

"I've missed you, too," Mary said, turning towards Christian. "This is Rabbi Jesus. Do you think he and his disciples could impose upon Lazarus and some of your neighbors for lodging in Bethany for a while? We've had a long journey from Galilee and could use a respite."

"Of course. I'm sure he would consider it an honor. We talk about the new teachings of Jesus often and he'll be delighted to have your followers under his roof, as will I."

Martha and Mary led the disciples to the house. "Lazarus, come look who's here."

Their brother emerged from the house wearing a light tunic, a garment with knotted fringes draped over his shoulders and a huge welcoming smile the moment he saw Mary. The three of them hugged. "Mary, so good to see you," he said.

Mary gestured towards Christian. "Lazarus, this is Rabbi Jesus. I know this is a surprise, but may he and his disciples stay here for a little while?"

"Rabbi, having you in our home would be a blessing," Lazarus said to Christian and smiled. "I must insist you have your followers bath and relax before dining. They will feel better."

"I will ask them to do so my friend." Christian realized the odor of four days' sweat was probably overpowering and Lazarus was making his suggestion diplomatically in a way that would avoid insult.

Lazarus turned out to be a generous host for the disciples. He graciously opened his home to as many as he could manage and helped find lodging for the others, just as Mary and Martha predicted. Christian enjoyed the comradery of the evening and found himself distracted by the thought that Lazarus might be the Lazarus he is supposed to raise from the dead. Martha, for her part, worked diligently in the kitchen to make sure everyone was fed. Christian approached her. "Martha, come join us. Worry about the work later."

"Lord, you and your disciples have completed a wearisome journey. Please allow me to serve you and let my sister rest at your feet, for she's endured a difficult life and it pleases me to see her happy with you."

"Martha, you amaze me. It is written that you are jealous of your sister," Christian said.

"I don't know where that is written, Lord, but the only reason for me to be jealous of my sister is because she's found a man as special as you to care for her," Martha said.

Christian reached out and hugged Martha as she stood in the kitchen and looked back into the adjacent room to see Mary contently watching, smiling wide. Mary tapped the vacant pillow next to her.

"Your sister beckons me once again," Christian said to Martha.

"Go to her," Martha replied.

Christian returned to Mary's side. "She likes you," Mary said.

"You were right about your brother and sister being good people," Christian said.

"I know they are. You seem a little extra emotional, too, this evening. Is everything all right?" Mary gauged Christian's mood swings and sense when he was unsettled.

"Let's enjoy the evening. We're going to have to talk later, but I need to speak with my father about something first."

Christian rose early the next morning to have a long overdue conversation with HQ. Bethany was located just beyond the southeastern slope of the Mount of Olives and the mountain provided a convenient precipice for communicating on the cubepod. Christian headed there and pinged HQ. Claire answered.

"I need to speak with my dad."

"Well good evening to you, too," Claire said.

"Sorry, I'm a little stressed," Christian admitted.

"Sure, I understand. It may take a while for him to arrive. Can we ping you back in a bit?"

"Yes, I'll wait. Good bye." Christian was not in the mood for small talk.

His dad called him about thirty minutes later. "What is it, Son?"

"Lazarus of Bethany and Mary of Magdala are brother and sister. It was right there in front of us the whole time and none of us caught it?"

"Oh my," his dad said.

"Look at the text, Dad. Lazarus has two sisters, Mary and Martha. Mary is the woman Judas gets upset at for wiping Jesus' feet with expensive oil. Tradition has long held that this woman was Mary Magdalene. We cannot let this happen," Christian said emphatically. "We cannot stand by and let Lazarus die."

"I understand," his dad said.

"You understand? Or you agree?"

"Let me talk to Berkeley. Can you call back tomorrow morning?" his dad asked.

"Yes." Christian knew he was being terse. He was stressed. He needed to carry on with his mission. He walked to Jerusalem and appeared in the 2nd Temple courts where people gathered around him. He sat down to teach. The Pharisees brought in a woman caught in adultery. They made her stand before the group and said to Christian, "Teacher, this woman was caught in the act of adultery. In the law Moses commanded us to stone such women. Now what do you say?"

Christian bent down and started to write on the ground with a stick, just as Jesus had in the scriptures. He always wondered what Jesus was writing at this moment. What he decided to write was Lazarus' name in

English. When they kept on questioning him, he straightened up and said to them, "Let the one of you who is without sin be the first to throw a stone." Again, he stooped down and wrote on the ground. This time he wrote Mary's name in English, for she was constantly on his mind. The crowd dwindled away one by one, the older ones first, for they were wise enough to know the conviction of their sins, until only Jesus was left with the woman. Christian straightened up and asked her, "Woman, has no one condemned you?"

"No one, sir," the woman said.

"Then neither do I condemn you. May I ask you your name?"

"Lord, my name is Abigail."

"That is an honorable name, Abigail. Centuries from now there will be tales of a beautiful love story between an influential man named John Adams and his wife who will bear your name. You should carry your name proudly. Here, let me show you what your name will look like for the wife of John Adams." Christian sketched out the name Abigail in the dirt next to the names of Lazarus and Mary. "Those other two words are the names of two people whom I love very much, Abigail, and now your name is in company with theirs."

Christian stood again. Abigail had tears in her eyes as she looked up at him. "Lord, you've touched my soul. I will remember this moment as long as I live."

This reminder of the power of his message and the love that God harbors for each of us was exactly the medicine Christian needed to re-energize and refocus on the purpose of his ministry. "God loves you, Abigail, don't you ever forget that."

Christian grasped her by the shoulders. "I'm glad to have met you here Abigail. You've helped me make a needed attitude adjustment. I wish you well." Abigail bowed and slipped away into the streets of Jerusalem.

Passersby were pressing around Christian. He looked at the names written in the dirt. They were already being trampled. No matter, he grew melancholy, knowing that everything he sees, hears, and touches here in Palestine was already long lost to the ashes and dust of antiquity.

Christian established a routine of walking from Bethany to Jerusalem each Sabbath for the purpose of preaching and healing people.

"This complaint about healing people on the Sabbath is misguided," Christian said to his apostles. "We are going to visit the Jerusalem temple weekly, on the Sabbath, while here in Bethany, making a point to heal someone there each time."

Christian and the apostles went to Jerusalem the following Sabbath. In Jerusalem, near the Sheep Gate on the north side of the 2nd Temple, was the pool of Bethesda. The pool was surrounded by five covered colonnades under which the disabled, blind, and lame would lie waiting for an angel from heaven to stir the waters so they might be healed. Christian didn't understand the myth about the pool, but he nevertheless approached each colonnade and asked, "Who has been here the longest?"

"Sir," a lame man replied, "I have been here thirty-eight years. My legs are weak, and they constantly ache. I have no one to help me into the pool when the water is stirred. While I'm trying to get to the water, someone else goes down ahead of me."

Christian reached down to the man and examined his legs. The man's muscles were atrophied from lack of use. He gently massaged the man's legs as he talked to him.

"How did you become like this?"

"I became sick with fever and body aches many years ago. The sickness eventually went away, but my legs became weaker and weaker until finally I could no longer stand on them," the man said.

Christian thought that perhaps he suffered from severe post-polio syndrome. Conditions like this aren't necessarily understood even in modern medicine because the virus that originally attacked the man would be long gone by now, and yet the leg weakness can get progressively worse.

Christian sliced his hand and explained he was going to have to make a small incision on each of the man's legs to get his healing blood into the man's system. The man gave permission and Christian proceeded to perform the procedure. After a short while, Christian got the sense that nanites transferred from his blood to the man's legs were starting to do their repair work. "Today you are blessed. You no longer need to wait for the waters of the pool to be stirred to be healed. You are cured. Pick up your mat and walk. Go show yourself to the priests and tell them who healed you."

The man was unsteady at first, but he walked better as he got used to having his legs back under him again. The man was so happy to be able to walk again and he openly boasted about being healed by Jesus.

As expected, the Jewish leaders were upset with Christian healing on the Sabbath. Later that day they found Christian in the 2nd Temple and said, "You healed a lame man by the pool on the Sabbath and further you instructed him to carry his mat, which is considered work, also forbidden on the Sabbath."

"You hypocrites," Christian cried back. "You seek to find fault for your own purposes, not for the purposes of God." The response served to further enrage the Pharisees. Christian had accomplished his strategic goal for the day.

There was a man with a withered hand at the synagogue on another Sabbath morning. The Pharisees were there to watch and see if Jesus would heal him. Christian told the man to come forward. Christian massaged the man's arm and hand. Christian sliced his hand and explained to the man, "My blood has healing power. I need to make a small incision in your arm so my blood can heal you. Is that all right?"

"It's fine Lord, I have no feeling in the arm anyway. You won't be hurting me," the man said.

Christian made the incisions and massaged his blood into it the man's cut. "My hand is starting to tingle," the man said.

"That's good, your feeling is coming back. See if you can stretch your hand out."

The man stretched his hand out and was ecstatic. "Praise you Lord! Thank you! Thank you!"

Christian fanned the flames of conspiracy against him by healing another man on the Sabbath.

The following Sabbath, Christian and the apostles again went up the hill from Bethany to Jerusalem. This time they went into Lower City and found a man who was blind from birth. "I will heal this man so that you will see the Kingdom of Heaven is at hand, for even the blind are made to see."

"I'm going to make a healing salve with my saliva," Christian told the man. "I need you to keep it on your eyes for a while and then go wash it out in the pool of Siloam in the southeast corner of the city. My disciples will show you the way. Now hold still for a minute."

Christian spat on the ground, made a clay out of his spittle and applied it directly to the man's eyes. He trusted that the cellular nanites would heal the man's eyes just as was written in the gospel.

"Go wash and when you are able to see, go show yourself to the chief priests and tell them who healed you."

The news of yet another healing on the Sabbath served to further irritate the Jewish leaders. He was pleased to hear later that the man indeed recovered his sight and had testified to it at the 2nd Temple.

Christian and his apostles continued to stay in Lazarus' home in Bethany. He was pensive, waiting for word from HQ about the resurrection of Lazarus. He headed to the Mount of Olives the next morning and pinged HQ. His dad answered. "We've been focusing all our efforts on this problem and you're not going to like the solution."

"Tell me," Christian said.

"According to Berkeley, the best path to success is for Lazarus not to die at all," his dad explained.

"Well that doesn't sound so bad," Christian said.

"We need to fake his death and by we, I mean you, with the help of Lazarus and his family. It requires you and his sisters to lie. He'll apparently have to rough it in the tomb for a few days," his dad explained. "We can knock him out with our poison recipe if needed."

"I can't ask them to do that," Christian said.

"You will have to if you want the raising of Lazarus to be witnessed and recorded. Judging from the consistency of what you've channeled so far versus the written record, if we do not put plans in place to fake his death, then cosmic forces will come into play and he will indeed die."

"And, how would you suggest I convince him and his sisters to fake his death? I just can't fathom it."

"You must convince them by any means necessary. You have complete latitude, including being totally honest," his dad insisted.

"I think I'm going to have to be. Even then, I just don't know if it will convince them."

Christian rushed back to Bethany and sought out Mary.

"I need to speak with you in private," he said.

They found a room to themselves in the house.

"Mary, you've seen that I often know what's going to happen next in the ministry, right?" He was facing her, both his hands on her shoulders.

"Yes, Christian, you're amazing."

"And you've seen that for some things, I have needed assistance."

"Yes, I know."

"Well I'm going to need your help again and this is going to be a challenge." Christian went on to explain what was going to happen to Lazarus unless they faked the story as it is written in the Gospels.

"You're telling me you know what is going to happen to my brother? How do you know what is going to happen?"

"Just as with everything else. It is written."

"Unacceptable. You always say that. I want to see where it's written," Mary challenged.

"It will be written about fifty years from now in a holy manuscript called the Gospel of John. I have the manuscript."

"Show me," Mary looked up at Christian and demanded.

"It's written in Greek. You can't read Greek."

"Show me that you have the manuscript you speak of and show me now."

Christian fired up the cubepod, found the file folder and opened the document. He paged it to the Gospel of John, Chapter 11. "There it is. You must trust me. It says everything I told you."

"No, I don't. My brother will read the Greek manuscript," Mary said.

Christian tried to speak. Mary held up a hand and commanded, "Wait right here."

Oh crap, Christian thought as he closed the display.

Mary returned within minutes, pulling Lazarus along with her.

"Show him what you showed me," she commanded. "Show him right now."

Christian turned on the cubepod and scrolled to the correct file. The Gospel of John presented itself to Lazarus of Bethany. To his credit, he remained calm and read the text.

"What does it say?" Mary asked.

"It tells a story about us. It says I will die, that you and Martha will mourn, and then Jesus will raise me from the dead." Lazarus turned to Christian. "Lord, I am an educated man. I know of the blending of magic and chemistry in the practice of alchemy, and I hunger for knowledge like any other inquisitive man. Honestly though, I don't understand this image before me, or why it says what it says, but I am willing to accept my fate in your hands."

"Mary, now you tell him," Christian sighed.

Mary hesitated.

"Tell him now," Christian insisted.

"He's just a man Lazarus. He doesn't know how to raise you from the dead, so he wants to keep you from dying in the first place," Mary admitted.

"Jesus?" Lazarus said bewildered, looking at Christian.

"The book you see is sacred. I believe that its words will be manifested, one way or another, because of the immutability of time. I'm following my father's instructions to accomplish exactly what's written in this book and what I'm asking you to do now is just as my father has instructed me."

"You want us to fake my death so these words will be correctly written. Do I have that right?" Lazarus asked.

"I believe that is exactly what was done, yes," Christian acknowledged.

"We must convince Martha. Go get her," Lazarus said to Mary.

Christian left the image of the book displayed. What was the use of hiding it now?

Martha entered the room, gawked at the display, listened to her brother and sister and the three of them engaged in an animated debate. After much discussion and argument, they came to agreement to do this deed.

When Martha turned to Christian, she was visibly upset, she was in his face and she said with acrimony, "How dare you! How dare you thrust this burden upon us. How dare you come into this house demanding we orchestrate this charade for the benefit of your ministry. What gives you the right to fool an entire nation that you've raised a man from the dead? Who in their right mind would do such a thing? What kind of person are you? Shame on you. I hate you for this, I hate you, I hate you." She was pounding with both fists onto his shoulders, tears pouring from her eyes.

Christian instinctively extended his arms and enveloped them around her. Her sister Mary did the same from behind her. Their simultaneous hug formed a Martha sandwich. She settled. "I'm sorry," she said. "There are things I don't understand, but you have your role to play and now it appears, so do we."

Just then Judas stuck his head in the door and asked, "What's going on in here?"

"Nothing," replied Mary and Christian in unison.

Enemies

The orchestration of the resurrection of Lazarus continued to dominate Christian's thoughts. He felt compelled to channel the Gospels as written. This would include making more bold declarations that would directly challenge the religious and secular authorities in Jerusalem. The next opportunity to do that came at lunchtime. A Pharisee had heard Christian speaking and invited him to dine. Christian suspected the Pharisee was in league with the religious authorities who were spying on him. After Christian finished speaking, the Pharisee said, "Jesus, my name is Rabbi Gamaliel and I wish to break bread with you at lunchtime. We have many matters to discuss."

"I accept your invitation Rabbi Gamaliel," Christian said. "Are my disciples welcome as well?"

"I'll have room for four more at my table. You are welcome to bring three others," Gamaliel said. "You may follow me to my home."

"Matthew, Peter and Andrew, come with me," Christian said. "The rest of you get some food and we'll meet back up in Bethany this evening."

"Lord, are we to break bread with a Pharisee?" Peter said as they were on their way to Gamaliel's home.

"We won't get that far into the meal Peter, trust me," Christian confided. "The Pharisees are a presumptuous bunch and they cherish their rituals. It won't take much to irritate him. Don't take your sandals off when we enter his home and do not wash your hands in the basin near the table. Just take a seat and follow my cue."

They got to Gamaliel's home where Christian and his disciples dispensed with the formalities and sat directly at table.

"Do you not wash your hands before the meal?" Gamaliel said.

"It is not that which goes into a man which defiles him, it is that which comes out," Christian said.

"Rabbi Jesus, I'm aware of your reputation for wit and sharp tongue, but seriously I'm just speaking about basic hygiene," Gamaliel defended. "Surely you realize these religious customs are routed in practical purpose."

Well, he has me there, Christian mused. But his intent was to provoke the Pharisees and their ilk, so he continued his indignation. He stood up and pointed his finger at Gamaliel. "Listen, you Pharisees clean the outside of your dishes, but inside you are full of greed. You need to take the log out your own eye before you try and remove the speck that is in someone else's. You rue God's purpose while the common man suffers under your sway. Woe to you Pharisee, for your self-righteous power corrupts your mind, and your corrupted minds foster abuse."

"Teacher, when you say these things, you insult us," said one of the lawyers dining.

Christian turned to the lawyer and pressed his point further. "Woe to you experts in the law, because you have withheld key knowledge and because you load people down with burdens they can barely carry and you yourselves show no charity towards them."

"Jesus, I'm not going to allow you to come into my home and condemn us," Gamaliel said. "You're going to have to take this drivel somewhere else. It was obviously a mistake to invite you here and I must insist now that you and your disciples leave."

Christian and his apostles allowed themselves to be escorted out of the house. He considered that this exchange and others like it would certainly inflame the ruling class and he was right. The Pharisees and lawyers even more fiercely opposed him and besieged him with questions in hopes he might be caught saying something that would allow them to bring charges. This was the course of action Jesus had taken and Christian was doing the same. He carried on this routine of accepting invites to dine with Pharisees and often lectured them on hypocrisy and elitism.

Meanwhile, he continued to preach his message to the people. He explained to the people that they no longer needed to offer sacrifice at the temple and ask the religious leaders to intercede on their behalf. He preached tolerance and instructed his followers to abstain from violence. He specifically sermonized, "Whoever hits you on one cheek, offer him the other cheek also."

Christian alluded to his death and resurrection, which were necessary to fulfill scripture and yet uncomfortable for him as he role-played Jesus.

"How long will you keep us in suspense? If you are the Messiah, tell us plainly," the Jews demanded.

"I told you and you do not believe. The works that I do in my Father's name bear witness about me, but you do not believe because you are not among my sheep. I have come to this time and this place to fulfill that which is already written. You are deaf to the new message that God is sharing with you. You reject the message and therefore you reject the messenger."

Upon hearing Christian claim himself to be God, the Jews picked up stones to stone him. "I have shown you many good works from the Father. For which of them are you going to stone me?" Christian asked.

"It is not for a good work that we are going to stone you but for blasphemy, because you, being a man, dare to make yourself God," the Jews answered him.

These claims to deity indeed angered many Jews of Jerusalem and Christian sensed that it was time to leave the area. Christian considered it an odd twist of fate that the Jewish claims against him were essentially correct, he was indeed just a man.

Christian was less than confident about their plans for Lazarus' resurrection. He pulled Lazarus aside. "I don't want to take any chances. I'm going to transfer my healing power to you, just in case you really do get sick."

"You can really do that?" Lazarus asked.

"Yes, I can. Not everything is faked my friend," Christian said.

With that, Christian sliced his hand and asked Lazarus to do the same, and they shook bloody hands, just in case.

Mary and Martha stayed behind with Lazarus in their Bethany home while Christian and the disciples headed east beyond the Jordan River. There they continued the ministry and waited for word from Mary and her sister Martha, as planned.

Christian scouted for high ground and managed to establish cubepod communications. He waited for his dad to come online, relayed all that was happening and expressed his inner conflicts. He desperately sought confirmation and encouragement. Then, he put a vexing question to his dad.

"Dad, does it concern you that the resurrection of Lazarus story appears only in the Gospel of John, the last one written? This is a major event in the ministry of Jesus, so why would it appear in only one of the four Gospels?"

"I've thought about this, especially since we decided to orchestrate Lazarus' resurrection in cahoots with his family. Perhaps the earlier authors knew the truth and glossed over it," his dad said.

"You mean Matthew knows we're staging the event?"

"Either that or he will figure it out eventually. He's not a stupid person and you've asked him to observe and note everything. Peter probably knows, too, and he'll relay that to Mark," his dad said.

"You think they all know?"

"Probably, and they will all prove loyal to you, except one," his dad said.

"This is not a very comforting conversation," Christian observed.

"It's an uncomfortable situation for all of us and you bear the greatest burden. I remain prouder of you than ever. Be strong. I love you."

"Thanks Dad, I will. Love you, too."

Lazarus

Within the month, word came that Lazarus was ill. It was show time.

"We've just gotten word that our friend Lazarus is ill," he announced. "Please pray for his recovery."

They lingered two more days beyond the Jordan, then Christian announced, "Let us go back to Judea. Our friend Lazarus has fallen asleep, but I am going there to wake him up"

Christian proceeded, over the objections of Thomas and Simon who were concerned that the Jews in Jerusalem still wanted to stone Jesus.

"Lord, if he sleeps, he will get better," Thomas said.

"I tell you plainly, Lazarus is dead, and we must go revive him."

They packed up and headed back to Bethany. They were passing through Jericho when a blind man called out, "Jesus have mercy on me." Some of the crowd tried to hush him, but Christian stopped walking.

"Bring him here to me." Upon hearing that Jesus wanted to talk to him, the blind man stood up and headed in the direction of Christian's voice.

"What is your name?" Christian asked.

"Rabbi, my name is Bartimaeus."

"What do you want me to do for you, Bartimaeus?"

"Rabbi, I am blessed that you are here. I want to regain my sight."

"The healing of your blindness outside of Jericho has already been written," Christian said. "Now open your eyelids, so I may spit into your eyes and heal your eyesight to fulfill scripture."

Bartimaeus acceded to Christian's instructions and soon his eyes were healed. Christian took some comfort in knowing that not everything he was doing here was faked. The Lazarus resurrection masquerade was chipping away as his cosmic integrity.

As Christian entered Jericho he recalled a childhood Bible song about a wee little man named Zaccheus who had climbed up into a sycamore tree just to see Jesus. He was still playing the *Bible* story validation game in his head since a book written thirty years after the fact was unlikely to recount events verbatim. He scanned the gathering crowd and sure enough saw a diminutive man perched on a tree limb. He looked up and called out to the man, "Hey Zaccheus! I see you up there in that tree. Come down, we're going to have lunch with you today."

Zaccheus was stunned that Jesus knew his name, but immediately climbed down from the tree and led Christian and his retinue to his home for lunch. Matthew and Zaccheus, as tax collectors, traded commentary on what it was like to collect taxes for the Romans. Matthew expressed that he was much happier now that he was following Jesus and he suggested that Zaccheus do the same. Zaccheus committed that day to give half his possessions to the poor. After lunch, Christian and the disciples left Jericho and headed on to Bethany.

They arrived at Bethany in the afternoon. Lazarus had been in the tomb for four days by the time Christian arrived and mourners came to comfort Mary and Martha at the loss of their brother. Martha and Mary went out to meet Christian. Mary ran to him first, fell to her knees at his feet and was doing an excellent job of crying. For a moment Christian thought Lazarus might really be dead. Martha delivered her line next. "Lord, if you had been here, my brother would not have died. But I know that even now God will give you whatever you ask."

Christian wept as well. "Your brother will rise again. Where have you laid him?"

"Come and see, Lord," Mary said.

Some of the Jews commented on how much Jesus must have loved Lazarus, but others scoffed. "Could not he who opened the eyes of the blind man have kept this man from dying?"

So far so good, Christian thought, but my friend Lazarus is probably aching to get out of that tomb. He approached the tomb. It was a cave with a large stone laid across the entrance. Access to the tomb could be gained by a flight of uneven rock-cut steps leading up from the street. The steps led to a square chamber, which served as a place of prayer. More steps led to a lower chamber where Lazarus would be waiting.

"Take away the stone," Christian commanded.

"But Lord, by this time there will be a bad odor," Martha said, "for he has been there four days."

Christian thought about poor Lazarus having to stay in that dark tomb for four days. It was going to be a relief for him to be free. "Did I not tell you that if you believe, you will see the glory of God?"

Two young Jewish men took away the stone. Christian looked up. "Father, I thank you that you have heard me. I know that you always hear me, but I say this for the benefit of the people standing here, that they may believe that you sent me."

"Lazarus, come out!" Christian called out in a loud voice.

Lazarus came out, his hands and feet wrapped with strips of linen and a cloth around his face.

"Take off the grave clothes and let him go," Christian said.

The Jews who watched the event were amazed and Christian heard one of them say, "Truly this man is the Son of God, for only God could raise a dead man from grave."

Christian, Lazarus, Mary, and Martha stepped back into the square chamber off the street level, out of sight of the other people, and let Lazarus unwrap from the grave clothes in dignity. Martha had a fresh loincloth and tunic for him, plus a stash of food and a fresh skin of water.

"Lord, I'm really glad to see you." Lazarus hugged Christian.

"How long were you in there?"

"We played it straight. I've been in here four days," Lazarus said. "But, I only got wrapped up like this, this morning. I had to do it myself. Did I do okay?"

"You looked like a mummy," Christian said.

"A what?" Lazarus asked.

"Sorry, that was a strange word. I meant to say you looked quite convincing. Good job."

"What happens next?" Lazarus asked.

"Next, there is going to be trouble as word spreads of this miracle. The Pharisees will view it as a threat and will intensify their efforts to thwart my ministry," Christian explained. "You will also be in danger and I'm truly sorry for that. If it's any consolation, I believe you and your siblings will be just fine, but I don't know that for a fact. You should all be prepared to leave Bethany and please remain cautious."

"We understand, and we will be careful, Lord," Lazarus said.

"I can't stay long. We'll head to Ephraim and wait there until Passover. I would like to bring Mary with me this time, if that's all right?" Christian asked.

"Yes, absolutely, she has missed you," Lazarus said.

"Martha did fabulous today," Christian said.

"Yes, she knew her part. She's still upset with you, though," Lazarus warned.

"Yeah, I figured"

There was much controversy over the resurrection of Lazarus and Christian was once again receiving invitations from Pharisees to dine with them to explain his intentions. Christian generally perceived traps in these overtures and elected to refrain from further agitation until the timing was right. The apostles jealously guarded Christian during this time and they were particularly on edge when two members of the Jewish Sanhedrin arrived at Lazarus' door. Christian heard the voices.

"We are here to visit the Rabbi Jesus."

"He's busy right now," Peter said.

"We know he's here. Please tell him Joseph of Arimathea and Nicodemus, son of Gurion are here to discuss important matters with him."

Judas got Christian's attention and said quietly, "I know him. He's a member of the Sanhedrin. We've done business together and I believe him to be friendly to our cause."

"Let them in," Christian suggested. He recognized the name as well from biblical records and it was convenient that Judas was already familiar with him.

Peter opened the door to reveal a tall, thin, grey haired man and another man of stockier build standing in the doorway. Each was wearing the tunic and yarmulke appropriate for Jewish leadership. They bowed in unison to Christian and the tall one, Joseph, said, "We come in peace. Our purpose is to honor and serve our Messiah." Joseph directed his attention to Lazarus. "It is good to see you up and well. Your resurrection is the talk of the town."

"I can just imagine," said Lazarus. "If you are friends of Jesus, then you are welcome in my home." He gestured for them to enter.

The women set the table for six and Christian asked that Peter, Judas, and Lazarus join them to break bread that evening. They removed their sandals and washed their hands in the traditional manner before they reclined at the table. Christian inspected his guests. He estimated Joseph to be roughly sixty years of age. He was well dressed, well mannered, smart and articulate, with strong facial features, a full nose and lips, and full head of grey hair. He wore a signet ring, finely detailed in its craftsmanship, of the ilk Judas proffered. It bore a familiar engraving, an image of the masonic square and compass, but without the G in the center. Christian recognized it as the insignia of the Freemasons. Christian took a moment to recall his history and thought that the insignia was not totally out of place, as origins of the Freemasons predated the time of Christ. Joseph of Arimathea, owner of the tomb of Christ and a Freemason, Christian thought. It made sense.

"Nice ring," Christian said. "The symbols are familiar to me."

"Yes, they pay tribute to the sacred geometry brought to us by the great Egyptian architects," Joseph replied. "I myself commissioned Judas for the design." Joseph nodded toward Judas.

"It was my pleasure, Rabbi Joseph," Judas said. "One of my finest pieces."

"Rabbi Jesus," Joseph said, "we come to you in homage and with many questions. Are you willing to indulge us to greater understanding?"

"Certainly, my father has taught me a man who is willing to ask questions is a man willing to learn truth."

"Your father sounds like a smart man. We as a nation are a depraved people, and Nicodemus and I seek truth on our peoples' behalf, whether they are ready for it or not. Let us first say that based on the signs you've demonstrated, the wisdom and foresight you possess, we truly believe you to be the messiah, or we would not be sitting here."

Christian nodded his understanding.

"What is interesting to us is that you emerged so suddenly from Galilee, on the heels of John the Baptist's execution. There is little known of you prior to the first demonstration of your powers in Cana and it remains a curiosity to us that you burst onto the scene as you did just a few years ago. Scripture explains our messiah would be of clear lineage from the house of David. We know Mary, wife of Joseph, accepts you as her son, and we are willing to accept this as well. What we are wondering is, where have you been all these years?"

Christian pondered the astute observations and the question. He didn't sense nefarious intent in the question. He considered the inquiry reasonable and yet he couldn't honor his father's guiding principles in his response. 'I'm a time traveler from the future and I fell into this role' would not be a good response or, for that matter, fair to these well-meaning men. "Honestly, it took me some time to accept this calling," Christian said. "It wasn't until the wedding at Cana that I truly understood what my role must be." It was as sincere an answer as he could muster.

"We appreciate that's when your ministry initiated, rabbi, and we can imagine the consternation that must have been associated with accepting the calling as messiah for the Jewish people," Nicodemus added.

"Not just Jewish people, all people," Christian interrupted.

"Yes certainly, and that's exactly those kinds of universal assertions we mean to understand," Nicodemus continued. "What we want you to understand, though, is the importance of the question, where have you been? For the Sadducees view you as an imposter. It will be difficult to convince them of your divinity if they are not convinced of your heritage."

Christian realized that this was shaping up to be a difficult conversation.

"Is it not enough that Mary accepts him as her son and that her husband Joseph descends from the house of David?" Judas asked, trying to help.

"No," said Joseph, turning to Christian, "that may not be enough. We advise you to be careful with the religious authorities in Jerusalem. They seek any excuse to bring you down, and we believe we can help defend you if we were to have a better understanding of from whence you came. Can you tell us where you were before you performed your first miracle in Cana?"

"I came from Nazareth," Christian offered.

"We know that much. Where were you before that? We've heard the stories. We know you arrived there a stranger as well," Nicodemus said. "You didn't get that accent from Galilee."

Christian had managed to skirt this level of scrutiny for three years. He hated to seem evasive to these most basic of questions and he still couldn't seem to shake his southern drawl. "I came from another place, far away."

"Lord, we all come from somewhere." Joseph was not dissuaded. "Our society identifies us based on residence and lineage. In your case, both these facts seem nebulous and the Sanhedrin will surely use this against you. I have been all over the known world, from the estates of Herod in Gaul and beyond to the far reaches of China and India. Your teachings indicate to me that you're familiar with religious philosophies east and west, from Vyasa to Plato. You're certainly much more than a stonecutter's son emerging from the Galilean hill country. Please understand, we accept that you're indeed the Christ, but you must understand we're dumbfounded that you're here. It's as if you appeared out of nowhere just three years ago."

"I arrived when the timing was right for me to arrive, to fulfill the mission I was meant to fulfill."

"Defending you will be difficult with those kinds of answers, Lord. When the time comes, perhaps it would be better for you to say nothing at all," Nicodemus said.

Christian realized that wouldn't help, either. He will be damned if he says something and damned if he doesn't.

Just then, the women brought in some mutton, bread, fruit paste and wine. "Let's eat, shall we gentlemen?" Lazarus said.

"That sounds like a great idea," said Peter.

The mood for the balance of the dinner remained cordial. Joseph and Nicodemus clearly didn't gain the insight they sought, but they remained steadfast in their commitment to advocate for Jesus as best they could with the ruling authorities. Though his path was predestined, Christian was heartened by the show of support from these influential men.

"It is kind for you to receive us for a meal like this. You must allow me to return the favor," Joseph said, and scribbled directions to his Jerusalem home on a scrape of parchment and handed it to Lazarus. "The house is located on a hill in the southwest of the Upper City. There's plenty of space for everyone in the upper room, so all are welcome."

"Your offer is most gracious rabbi. Shalom." Lazarus nodded and slid the parchment over to Christian.

Christian slipped the scrap of parchment into his leather pouch.

After dinner and after their visitors left, Judas said to Christian, "They sure were interested in knowing your origins."

"Yeah, they were."

"They asked a lot of questions I've wanted to ask, but I've not wanted to pry," Judas said.

"You already know more about my history than most. If you asked anymore details, I would probably tell you the same thing I told them," Christian shrugged.

"I figured."

Christian spent a few more days in Bethany before he and his disciples said their goodbyes and headed for the relative safety of Ephraim to await Passover.

Ephraim

Christian and the disciples settled into the wooded hill country of Ephraim to the northeast of Jerusalem. It provided a needed respite for them as they prepared for the coming of Passover, which is when they would be returning to Jerusalem.

Mary and Christian were able to find private time together in a rugged stone and wood structure that sympathetic locals vacated for them. These were precious moments for Christian and Mary. Their relationship had progressed from friendship to a sensual and loving one, and now his time was running short. In a quiet moment with their heads on pillows stuffed with hay, cuddled together, he spoke to her. "Mary, there's a mention about you in the book I showed you and your brother that I don't quite understand. I've been waiting for an appropriate time to ask you about it. It may be a delicate subject, but if you don't mind, may I ask you something personal?"

"I suppose," Mary said pensively.

"It's worded awkwardly in scripture, but it says something about seven demons having gone out of you. Do you know what that might be about?"

Mary sat quietly for a few seconds, stretched her neck to relieve some tension, looked up at Christian and said, "Yes I do. It is a subject I have not spoken of with anyone."

Christian waited for her to continue.

"I was raped by seven Roman soldiers. You would not know this story because you were not around then, but many do know it and its notoriety motivated me to relocate from Bethany to Magdala so that I could have a fresh start."

"Mary, I'm so sorry," Christian said tenderly as he caressed her cheek.

"Thank you for understanding. But you do not need to be sad, for you've brought back to me a happiness and dignity I didn't know I would ever find again."

"You've brought me happiness, too, Mary, beyond anything I've ever known."

"Thank you, but I'm not just saying that you make me happy. You've changed my outlook on life. And now that you have asked me, please permit me to fully disclose this dark moment in my life. It has been painful to bear alone, and I must let it go."

"Mary, I'm listening."

"I was young and naïve," Mary began. "One night I allowed myself to drink too much and got into a situation where I was in over my head with a squad of Roman guardsmen. They took turns on me. I still see their faces laughing as each man enjoyed my body against my will. Their skin smelled of olive oil and their breath reeked of garlic. My body responded in a way I haven't allowed my mind to accept. Not only have I suffered the public humiliation of having been defiled repeatedly by a gang of thugs, I've long quietly endured the realization that my body responded receptively."

Christian reached out and Mary allowed herself to be held. Christian hugged her tight. "Our mind and body are not always connected Mary. We have defense mechanisms and reactions in our bodies called reflexes that serve to protect us in ways we don't always understand. You'll get no judgment from me and you need not be ashamed. What those men did to you was wrong and the shame belongs on them."

"I had not been with another man until you came into my life. The satisfaction I have felt with you far exceeds anything I previously thought possible. I trust you've not exorcised demons from others in the same way you've exorcised mine."

Mary managed to flatter and tease Christian in one fell swoop, even while sharing what was obviously a difficult and very private burden.

"No, of course not. Not in the same way, and you have no idea how much it means to me that you felt comfortable enough to share this story with me now." Christian looked into Mary's watery eyes. "So, this is what love feels like. I've always wondered and now, thanks to you, I know."

Christian held her close. There was a long silence and they reveled in the comfort of their togetherness. He felt the moment had come to share a special gift with Mary, one that Cornelius downloaded for him months prior.

"I have something for you. It's a gift sent to me from heaven and now I would like to share it with you."

"Girls love gifts, especially ones from heaven."

Christian reached into his leather pouch and removed the cubepod. He brought up the menu of files, scrolled to the playlist and made his selection. The image switched to an orchestra of sharply dressed musicians seated on a 21st century stage. The song began softly, slowly, with the swaying back and forth rhythm of a bow on a solitary cello. Other cellos joined, followed by violins. The violins deviated to their own rising sequence of notes that filled the ancient home with the exquisite universal language of classical music at its finest. Mary listened and watched.

"They're playing *Canon in D*, a song that will be written 1650 years from now by a German composer named Johann Pachelbel," Christian said.

Mary nodded, still listening. The violins were faster paced now.

The word for 'composer' was loosely translated, but she understood his intent. "The smaller wooden instruments with strings that fill the hall with music are called violins. The larger ones are violas and cellos."

Christian searched his mind for words to describe a piano in Aramaic. "The large piece of furniture with the finger bars is called a piano."

Christian considered his next statement. He wanted to describe Vienna Philharmonic Orchestra, but there was no word for philharmonic or orchestra.

"Those people on stage are a formal music group from a city called Vienna, north of Italia. They are playing the song 375 years later in a great auditorium called the Musikverein Golden Hall located in Vienna. Many consider them the world's finest."

"It's beautiful." Mary was captivated.

The stringed instruments were slowing their pace and coming back into swaying rhythm. Violins, violas and cellos moved as one through the last movement.

"Thank you for sharing that." She smiled. "Will you play it again?"

Mary listened and watched the concert several times that evening. She didn't quiz Christian with bigger questions. She simply accepted the gift of beautiful music. He held her tenderly through the dark hours that night and loved her completely.

The questions came the next morning as Christian sat at a chair and studied text on the cubepod in front of Mary.

"Can you tell me more about the box that shows the images?" Mary was curious.

"Yes, I'm glad you're asking. It's time for me to explain more things to you. It's called a cubepod. It will be invented about two thousand years from now. This is a very special device. It allows me to speak with my father in the time and place where I came from originally."

"You're from another time and another place? These are unfamiliar concepts."

"I'm from your future. This is how I know what things will happen, because for me they have already happened. I'm a time traveler."

"Are there other time travelers like you?"

"I'm the first."

Mary was ready to know the truth. She wasn't afraid to keep asking questions.

"Why did you come here?"

"I originally came here to try and fix a problem we were having with our experiments. I thought it would be nice to meet Jesus while I was here. I've worshiped him my whole life, as have millions of others throughout the ages."

"Did you manage to fix the original problem?"

"No, not really. We did learn some new things, but the main problem remains."

"And you didn't find Jesus here, either?"

Christian nodded.

"You didn't find the man you were looking for and the book compelled you to make him and all the things he did become a reality?" Mary asked.

"That's exactly right."

"You're like a puppet on a string."

"I think we all are. Some of us are more aware of it than others. I'm going to tell you something now that will be difficult for you to understand, but I promise it will make more sense later. When I die, there isn't going to a body here anymore. My body will return to where my father is."

"Why do you have to die Christian? I don't want you to die." Tears welled in Mary's eyes.

"I have to die to get back home. I will wake up there and live out the rest of my life. That is my destiny."

"You're destined to leave and there is no other way?"

"That's the way it has to be."

"So, what's my destiny after you leave?"

"There's very little accounting of what happens to you after I leave. There is only legend. Historians think that you fled the area and migrated to Gaul. We should start working on those plans because it may not be safe here for you after I leave."

"You're so practical Christian. It's both endearing and frustrating at the same time. I would like to think that if two people love each other, they would be able to find a way to be together even if destiny was stacked against them."

"Right now, I don't know how to change this predetermined path. But if there is a way, I promise I will find it." He kissed her and held her tight.

Christian found high ground later that day. He didn't know how many more opportunities he would have to use the cubepod. He would make sure to charge it well after today's use. He provided Mary with basic instruction in its use and would be handing it off to her soon.

He pinged HQ. It would be second shift there. Claire's image appeared. She was wearing her green clover earrings. Then Christian saw that Dominic and Cornelius were with her.

"Hey guys!" Christian was genuinely glad to see them together. "So good to see all of you."

"We've all been working second shift to catch your next check in," Claire spoke first.

"Yes, we have," Dominic and Cornelius chimed in behind her.

"We're not the only ones." Cornelius poked a button on a cubepod in his hand and after a moment, the image of Paul appeared. Christian could swear the image seemed even sharper than usual. As if reading his mind, Cornelius said, "It's the next version of the cubepod. We received beta versions." He was beaming with pride.

"Christian, an honor to see you sir," Paul said with a slight bow. Christian was going to have to break Paul of that habit. "We've been on standby waiting for your next check-in. Hold on, I have some other people coming into the room." Paul panned the camera to reveal a room full of Berkley team members. They smiled and waved, yelling things like, "We love you, Christian."

What a treat this was. Christian was touched.

Cornelius fired up another cubepod. This time it was the Atlanta facility with members of their team. These were the doctors and research scientists who developed the cellular nanite treatment that cured Christian's cancer. They, too, enthusiastically cheered and waved.

The process continued with a third cubepod presenting the Houston team, the developers of the molecular nanites. They clapped in unison, chanting, "Christian, Christian." One of the men from Christian's Houston beer experiments team held up a sign that read 'Make Humanity Great Again!'"

Finally, Claire reversed the camera angle on the cubepod she was holding to reveal the Cape Canaveral team of technicians, doctors, scientists, and engineers who were waving arms, standing on tables and cheering for him. He could pick out individual faces he recognized, even the faces of two technicians he remembered having walked off the job in disgust at the slaughter of the test animals. He couldn't blame them then and he was pleased to see them back.

"We've all been working second shift, for you Christian. We wanted you to know how much you mean to us," Claire said.

Christian, for his part, couldn't hold back the tears. He fumbled through some words that ultimately communicated a sincere heartfelt thank you.

He couldn't remember what his agenda was for this check-in. Its purpose was hijacked by the overwhelming recognition by the Spintronics teams.

Christian sat for a while on the Ephraim hilltop that day. He was charging the cubepod and gathering personal energy for the challenge ahead. Then he returned one last time to the house where he and Mary were staying.

Jerusalem

Passover was approaching, and it was time to head to Jerusalem. Christian had studied Passover to work out the timeline of these last seven days. It was time for him to reinforce the message about the death and resurrection of Jesus.

To his disciples he said, "I'll be delivered over to the hands of evil men. They will condemn me to death and will hand me over to the Romans, who will mock me, hit me, flog me, and then kill me. Three days later you will find my tomb empty, for I will have risen from the dead."

The disciples were deeply grieved upon hearing this. Christian expected as much. He preached scripture as written, saying the things that Jesus said.

Christian noticed that Judas remained more distant. Judas and Christian's friendship transcended Christian's role as Jesus. At first, Christian thought he might have to confide in Judas and explain the role that he must play for the sake of the fulfillment of history. It was a heavy burden Christian had carried for some time. But now, as the crucifixion approached, Judas was already distancing himself. Perhaps Judas was aware of the lie about the resurrection of Lazarus and it didn't sit well with him. The concept that his friend Judas was the man who would become Judas the Iscariot, 'murderer of men', seemed unfathomable to Christian. He couldn't envision Judas betraying him at any price, much less for a mere thirty pieces of silver. Thinking about it broke his heart.

Christian was leading the walk from Ephraim to Jerusalem. He considered the chasm that developed between him and Judas since they migrated the ministry to Judea and he decided to attempt to bridge it. He waited for Judas to catch up to him. "You've been quiet," he said to Judas.

"I've been doing a lot of thinking. I'm mostly just trying to stay out of your way."

"If there's anything you want to talk about, and I mean anything, just let me know."

"I appreciate that, Lord."

"You know I'm doing this to fulfill that which is written, channeling history as my father has instructed," Christian said solemnly.

"Yes, you must do what you must do," Judas said softly. "And now, I have to do what I have to do as well."

"You're entering the city of Jerusalem just when it's packed with worshippers," Judas said a bit too loudly. "You won't be able to control these crowds. Frankly, I'm tired of covering for you and if these people find out you've lied to them, they'll kill you. That's what they do to their false prophets. You know, I was all in while we were in Capernaum. We were making a difference in people's lives in Galilee. But you had to come to Judea and stick your fingers in the eyes of powerful members of society who don't like to be trifled with. They've been watching your every move ever since we got here, looking for you to trip up so they could have something to charge you with. If you were God, they couldn't legitimately charge you with blasphemy. But when they do, who's going to defend you? The people of Nazareth? The women who baked the bread for Mary? The pig farmers of Decapolis? The family of Lazarus? Well I can assure you of this, it's not the man who gave you the horse in Galilee. I'm done."

Christian remained silent. He figured nothing he said or did would make a difference.

"You're going to allow yourself to go down in a blaze of glory just because it is written in that stupid book of yours. You're leaving behind these poor people." Judas sounded exasperated. He gestured to the gathered crowd. "What makes you so sure anything you've said or done will have any meaning after they kill you? You're going to be leaving nothing behind but blood and destruction. Have you no sympathy for them at least, your innocent flock?"

Judas gazed at the silent Christian then looked past him towards the crowd, which continued to grow. He concluded his tirade with a loud and assertive, "This is pathetic. You are pathetic. I'm done."

Judas walked off, not wanting to participate in the triumphant entry of Jesus into Jerusalem.

This conversation served as a reminder for Christian about the immutability of time. Judas was going to betray Jesus for his own reasons. History would do an adequate job of describing what Judas did, but it wouldn't record the real reasons driving his treachery. Christian reminded himself they were just puppets on string. Judas couldn't avoid his fate any more than Christian could avoid his. Jesus must die and Christian with him. Judas was playing his part.

Christian and his disciples approached Jerusalem by way of Bethany. The road was crowded with Jews and their animals making the pilgrimage for Passover. They could see the black smoke of incinerated sacrificed animals rising from the eastern side of the city, where the 2nd Temple was situated. Christian found a boy who reminded him of David the shepherd from what seemed like so long ago. He told the boy, "Go up ahead and find a donkey. Explain to owner that the Master needs it. Untie the donkey and bring it here."

Christian and his disciples rested by the road until the boy returned, leading a donkey. "Lord, it was just as you described," the boy said.

Christian rode the donkey into Jerusalem to fulfill scripture. He lamented he had forgotten how badly these animals smelled and now he was learning how uncomfortable they were to ride. But Christian put on a cheerful disposition and rode the donkey into Jerusalem.

The crowd gathered to greet their Messiah and shower him with worship. Some were spreading their cloaks on the road. When he came near the city walls, the whole crowd was singing joyful praises to God in bellowing voices for all the wonders they saw and heard.

Some of the Pharisees in the crowd addressed Christian. "Teacher, rebuke your disciples. We don't want a riot breaking out in the city during Passover and your crowd is already much too loud."

"I tell you that if the crowd kept totally quiet the stones would start singing." In a sense it was true because he could easily fire up the cubepod and crank some Rolling Stones, he thought.

As Christian approached the city gates, he foretold its destruction, just as Jesus had. He proclaimed that enemies would lay siege to Jerusalem and tear down its walls and massacre its occupants. He knew the Romans would sack Jerusalem and destroy the famous 2nd Temple in the year 70 AD, during the first Jewish-Roman war. Modern day Rome, Arch of Emperor Titus, celebrated the event.

Christian and his disciples entered Jerusalem near the Sheep's Gate and Solomon's Porch, near the 2nd Temple of Jerusalem. The Pharisees took note. Any other entrance would have generated less commotion, but keeping a low profile was not Christian's objective.

The Jewish tradition of offering animal sacrifices at the temple during Passover spawned the necessity of money exchanges and animal vendors in the market next to the temple. It would have been inconvenient for worshippers to travel long distances to Jerusalem and have to bring their own animal sacrifices. Their currency needed to be exchanged for local currency, so they could purchase the animals for sacrifice. From the Jewish perspective, there was nothing sacrilegious about the process. It was a fundamental necessity of Passover.

Christian was perplexed as to why Jesus smashed tables and threw out the money changers, but, it was something he needed to do to fulfill scripture. On Monday, he made his way to the temple market. He entered the temple courts and drove out those who were exchanging money and selling animals for sacrifice.

"My house will be a house of prayer, but you have made it a den of thieves," he cried, lashing out at those around him. His disciples stared on in horror, not having been given a heads-up by Christian. He wanted them to react accordingly for this to play out as he intended. The crowds railed against him and he and the disciples left before harm could be inflicted upon them. They retreated to Lazarus' home in Bethany for the evening to gather for food and lodging with their friends. Judas finally showed up later that night, calmed down from losing his temper.

The next day, Christian was back, preaching in the temple in parables and against the religious authorities. He was fully prepared to debate the Pharisees and handle their challenging questions, which included the familiar conundrum about how Jesus proposed to deal with obligations to both Rome and religion. When Christian replied to them, "Render to Caesar that which belongs to Caesar and render to God that which belongs to God," he wasn't sure if he was channeling Jesus or John F. Kennedy, who said the same thing when challenged about his loyalty to his country versus the Pope.

Later that day Simon and his Zealot friends were anxious to speak with Jesus about a more aggressive strategy of agitation against oppression from the Romans. "Lord, you've entered Jerusalem at just the right time to stir the people up against not only the religious Pharisees who are hypocrites, but also against the Romans," Simon said. "The people of Judea are tired of their dictates and their taxes. You have the support of the people and they hang on your every word. Turn their hatred towards Rome. You will rise up as our king and we will be a free people again."

Christian could not comply with their requests to turn his movement into a revolution. That was not Jesus' purpose, nor was it Christian's.

"Simon, your friendship has given me strength and your continued loyalty is appreciated. I tell you honestly, I didn't come to this time and this place to lead a revolution against the Romans, or anyone else. I'm simply fulfilling what has already been written and my time is almost through. Remember my words and be strong after I'm gone," Christian encouraged him.

Christian retreated to the Mount of Olives later that evening. He spent this time talking to his disciples about the end of the ages and made a point to tell his apostles that he would be retreating here, to the Garden of Gethsemane, each evening. He figured he may as well make it easier on Judas to find him.

Christian and the apostles were invited to dine at a friend of Lazarus' family in Bethany on Wednesday evening, two days before Passover. Mary saw that Christian was stressed and was intent on helping him relax. She brought an alabaster jar of very expensive perfumed spikenard oil to Christian and poured the oil on his head. It was quite relaxing, like a mild analgesic.

When Judas objected that Mary was wasting the oil and that they could have given money to the poor instead, Christian rebuked Judas. "What's gotten into you Judas? Why are you bothering her? This is a beautiful gesture on her part, anointing my body in advance of burial. We've plenty of other money to give to the poor and there will always be more poor people. You're only going to have me here for a brief time longer and you're going to miss me when I'm gone."

Judas was not pleased with this answer. He stormed out. This was the day Judas would be plotting to hand him over to the authorities. He would like to think Judas was handing Jesus over because of having been possessed by the devil. Instead, he sensed that this was personal. Judas had evidently grown weary of certain deceptions in the ministry. Christian couldn't rationalize his friend Judas turning him over for a slow torturous death of crucifixion. He chose to believe Judas simply didn't realize it would come to that.

Thursday

Christian woke up Thursday morning feeling pensive. He cherished the warmth of Mary's naked body lying next to him for a few more precious moments. Any other morning he'd have quenched his desires by making love to her, but anxiety over his impending death consumed him. He slipped out from beneath the covers and avoided interrupting her slumber. He affixed his loincloth, donned his tunic, and made his way to Lazarus' kitchen where he found several of the apostles already gathering around the food.

"Breakfast, Lord?" Martha asked briskly.

"Not this morning Martha, thank you." Christian had no appetite.

"At least drink some water," Martha said, handing him a mug.

Christian took a swig, and then drank the full mug.

"I must not have realized how thirsty I was." He nodded in appreciation.

"How did you sleep, Lord?" Peter was sitting at the table gnawing on a hunk of cheese.

"Not that great. Lots on my mind right now," Christian said. "Speaking of which, tonight is the feast of Unleavened Bread and we need to make arrangements for the meal."

"We can host it here, Lord," Martha said with a sigh, making no eye contact.

"No Martha, I have something else in mind." Christian reached into his pouch and pulled out the piece of parchment with directions to Joseph of Arimathea's house in Jerusalem. "Peter, after you finish your breakfast, follow these directions to Joseph's house and inform him we'll take him up on his offer for the Passover meal in the upper room of his house."

"Yes, Lord," Peter replied. Christian saw Peter grab John on the way out the door and heard him say, "Let's go for a walk."

Just then, Mary strolled into the kitchen.

"Thanks for the help fixing breakfast," Martha said sarcastically.

Mary ignored her protest. She had her own grievance to voice.

"You didn't wake me this morning," she said to Christian.

Christian avoided stating something about erectile dysfunction due to anxiety over his impending death and instead replied, "You looked so content sleeping dear, I didn't have the heart to selfishly wake you."

Mary whispered into his ear, "It's not selfish when you wake me to make love."

"I know," he held her around the waist for a moment. "I love you, Mary."

"I love you, too," she said and kissed him.

The kitchen was quiet. Christian glanced over that direction and saw the disciples there staring at him and Mary.

"I love you guys, too," Christian said.

"But you don't kiss us like that," Andrew joked.

"Do you want me to?"

"Nope, I'm good."

Christian took advantage in the lull in activity that morning to walk through Lazarus' gardens to get somewhat refreshed. He sought privacy and searched his mind for alternatives. He was putting up a strong front, hiding his doubts and fears from his disciples. Deep inside, however, he still hoped for a way out.

Peter and John arrived back in Bethany by early afternoon.

"It's all set, Lord," Peter said. "Joseph says the upper room is all ours and he'll have plenty of food, including the lamb."

"Excellent, thank you, Peter."

Later that afternoon, Christian and the apostles walked through the Lower City of Jerusalem and across to the Upper City where Joseph's house was located. Christian made a mental note that Joseph's house was high enough on a hill that he may be able to get decent cubepod reception, particularly in the upper room. That would not be important for tonight, though.

"Welcome," Joseph greeted them. "It's good to see you again, despite the troubling circumstances."

"We appreciate your hospitality," Christian said.

"My pleasure," Joseph replied. "There is much to discuss, but for now you and your men have the entire upper room to yourselves for the Passover meal."

"Perhaps we can talk after dinner," Christian said and nodded. The upper room was furnished with a large low wooden table and wool stuffed pillows for reclining, as was the custom. Christian and the apostles didn't congregate on one side of table to strike a pose, instead they huddled circular around it. The upper room of Joseph's home was clearly set aside for accommodating gatherings such as this. Large cedar beams stretched directly overhead, and cedar wood flooring covered the room. Windows at either end of the long room provided much needed ventilation.

Christian and the apostles reclined around the table when evening came. "I have eagerly desired to eat this Passover with you before I suffer," he began. "For I tell you, I will not eat it again until I am with my father."

Christian pondered how he was going to conduct this last supper and the meaning that was associated with the body and the blood of Christ. Christianity has fractured over the centuries in disagreement about the doctrine of the Eucharist. Christian decided he'd conduct this last supper with his apostles in a manner that no religion had yet articulated.

Christian planned to infuse the unleavened bread with his skin cells and he planned to infuse the wine with his blood, both of which contained the healing cellular nanites that had worked many miraculous healings.

Christian's last supper really would include his body and blood and he would let the theologians debate it from there. He explained to the apostles that the healing energy of his skin and blood would continue to work in them. With a combination of molecular nanites, laced with cellular nanites from his skin and blood, he'd serve them a healthy dose of healing nanites, which he reasoned would allow them to pass along their healing power, perhaps diluted, but nevertheless sufficient to accomplish many miracles.

The apostles were busy socializing with each other around table. Christian unsealed the molecular nanite capsule, crushed it in his fist, rubbed his palms together and pressed his palms on either side of the unleavened bread. Christian utilized this praying pose to infuse the bread with nanites from his skin. Then he took the bread, gave thanks, and broke it and gave it to them, saying, "This is my body given for you. Do this in remembrance of me."

Next Christian unsealed another molecular nanite capsule and poured the contents into an empty cup. He pulled out his fisherman's knife, sliced his hand and let the blood drain into the cup. He had not consulted with Berkeley on this exercise. He went rogue. He was attempting to get the self-programming of the molecular nanites to accept his blood as the base structure for infusing the target liquid. Lastly, he poured wine into the cup. He raised the cup. "This cup is the new covenant of my blood, which is to be poured out for you."

The apostles were lounging around the low table in haphazard fashion, bracing against the pillows and leaning on one another. They complied with Christian's instructions and passed around the bread and wine and each ate the bread and drank from the cup.

Christian avoided drinking any of the nanite infused liquid, not wanting to compound his suffering.

Various debates arose among the apostles about who was greater. When Peter claimed he was willing to die for Jesus, Christian told him, "I tell you Peter, before the rooster crows you will deny three times that you know me."

The look on Peter's face was incredulous. Christian assumed he wouldn't be around to see this prediction come true, however, he had seen firsthand that the Gospels were pretty accurate in their records of events, so he trusted this would be fulfilled.

"Be ready, for what is written about me is reaching its fulfillment." Christian told them.

Judas arranged to be closest to Christian and leaned his head against Christian's chest for a private conversation. When Christian began to speak about who was going to betray him, Judas interrupted him. "You can dispense with the theatrics."

Christian proceeded to dip his bread into the wine and Judas followed suit at the same moment. Christian looked closely at Judas. "Don't you have an errand to run?"

"I suppose I do," Judas said. "You're anxious to get on with this aren't you?"

"I'm sad and I'm tired. And, what you're about to do isn't helping my mood," Christian said.

"You think I like this role? Which part would you rather play, yours or mine?" Judas asked.

"I'm the one about to walk the plank, but I wouldn't wish this burden on either of us."

"But you did and now I'm off to solidify my reputation. I despise this moment and you are right, I must go now. I must go do what has already been written, as you so eloquently often state." Judas rose and left the upper room, before anyone else. Christian could sense Judas' angst and was truly sorry for his fate.

Servant women were coming up to serve more bread and fruit and pour more wine. Mary came upstairs to offer the apostles water. Christian observed how gracefully she carried herself and how elegant she appeared in the light of the lanterns. He wondered if perhaps history could write its own story and if, instead of crucifixion, he and Mary could simply slip away in the night and head for southern France as legend held that Mary had. He dwelt on the concept. He could pull Matthew aside and tell him what needed to be written about the crucifixion and his subsequent resurrection. After all, he rationalized, what was important about history was what ended up being written, not necessarily what happened. He accepted a refill of water from Mary and said to her, "I'm going to want to talk with you after we get done up here."

"I'll be waiting downstairs, Lord," she said and headed down the stairs. Christian endured the remainder of the meal, distracted in thought, toggling between alternatives.

After the meal, Christian came downstairs and drew Mary close. He spoke softly to her. "Stay close by my side in the coming hours. We may need to move quickly. Be ready."

"I understand, and I will be ready. Judas left early, do you know why?" Mary asked.

"He had to run an errand about which I am now torn."

"All right, he asked me to grab something. Wait here, I need to go get it." Mary raced up the stairs to the upper room. She came back down holding the cup Christian had used at the meal.

Christian cocked his head. He looked at the cup, then back to Mary's eyes. "What did Judas ask you to do, exactly?"

"He told me to grab the cup you used at dinner and to hang onto it."

Christian processed this information and slightly nodded to himself. He needed to talk to Judas again and find out what was in his head. Christian's determination to proceed with the crucifixion would, according to scripture, lead directly to Judas' suicide and the notorious vilification of his name as the Iscariot. Perhaps it didn't need to be that way, he thought again, and here was an indication that perhaps Judas had similar thoughts. Maybe he always had. Christian stood directly in front of Mary and took her squarely by her shoulders. "We need to find Judas before he betrays me. There are other choices we all can make together which may accomplish the same ends." Why in the world they hadn't asked Berkeley to work on a non-crucifixion alternative, just like they had figured out with Lazarus, escaped his reasoning.

"He left a while ago, Lord," Mary said. "Judas could be anywhere in the city by now."

"We need to find him!" Christian grabbed Mary by the hand and they charged out the front doors.

The night was black. Only torch light and random house oil lanterns dimly illuminated the streets of the Upper City. Unfortunately, even at this late hour, the streets were still teaming with Jewish pilgrims here to celebrate Passover. Christian checked the nearby house of Caiaphas; chief priest of the Jewish judicial body called the Sanhedrin and known co-conspirator of the sham trial of Jesus. There was activity, but Judas was not present there. They weaved through the intersections of upper Jerusalem. "He may be with a gathering of men, or even soldiers, I'm not exactly sure. Check any gathered crowd you see for Judas among them. We must get his attention and speak to him in private. It's very important."

Christian dragged Mary past street after street of the Upper City, exhaustively checking each alley. Finally, Mary dug in her heels. "Wait a minute, can you explain to me what the panic is about and what did you mean about Judas betraying you?"

"Okay, this isn't working anyway," Christian conceded. "Sit down with me over here, we need to map out a plan and consider the possibility that we don't intercept Judas in time." They found a seat on a burnished stone bench.

"Lord, this is not like you. You're scaring me," Mary admitted. "You so often know what's coming, it concerns me when you're uncertain."

"Plans may be changing, Mary," Christian said. "We are going off-script. Do you trust me?"

"Yes, of course I trust you."

"I think Judas is playing a role, just like I am, and I suspect he feels compelled to betray me to fulfill scripture just as I have been playing the role of Jesus. Wished I realized this sooner because we may have been able to collaborate better on another way, just as we did with Lazarus."

"How exactly does he betray you?" Mary asked.

"He leads a band of soldiers to the Garden of Gethsemane this very night to arrest me, then be handed over to the Sanhedrin for trial for the crime of blasphemy. This eventually leads to my crucifixion at the hands of the Romans. It's a messy horrid death, which may no longer be necessary if we game it right. If we can get to our friend Judas and reason another path with him, we may be able to spare him his fate as well."

"What will happen to him if we don't?" Mary asked.

"If we don't divert from the current path, I'll end up crucified and Judas will end up dead as well. For these reasons alone, I blame myself for not confiding in him sooner. In hindsight, I see he left me plenty of opportunities to do so. We must tell him that I'm no longer following through with the crucifixion. We will use the power of Matthew's pen to shape the historical record and the three of us will escape Jerusalem. We'll head for Gaul, with Judas and me adopting aliases."

"I don't understand, but I trust you. What do you need me to do?"

"Stay right by my side Mary. The situation may turn ugly quickly. We need to consider the possibility that we don't encounter Judas again until he brings the soldiers to the Garden of Gethsemane, in which case, we may have to fight our way out. Let's get back to Joseph's house. We need to be prepared for the worst and Simon's friends may be able to help us with some arms."

They arrived back at the house to find the apostles and women loitering on the main level. The first person he saw was Peter, standing just outside the door. "Where did you two run off to?" Peter asked.

"We're in a crunch for time Peter. What I'm about to ask you may sound abrupt, but the time is at hand for the homeowner to lock his doors and guard his house, for the thief is coming in the night. Go get Simon and ask if his friends have any weapons and people to spare. We may need to take up arms and be ready to defend ourselves this very evening. We will meet you as normal at the Garden of Gethsemane. Be prepared."

"Yes, Lord," Peter acknowledged, with no objection or questions. Christian considered how quickly all the apostles would fight for him, if asked. He was confident they would.

Peter ducked back into the house and quickly emerged with Simon in tow, bolting past Christian and Mary.

Christian stuck his head in the front door and announced, "Come on folks, it's time to head to the Garden of Gethsemane again. Please be alert for danger this evening and if anyone sees Judas on the way, give me a shout. I need to talk with him."

Christian turned to Mary, took her by the shoulders and squeezed them. He looked her in the eyes. "I love you, Mary." She met his gaze, wrapped her arms around his neck and tenderly gave him a long kiss.

"Stay close," Christian reiterated. He held her hand, pivoted, and then headed back down the dimly lit streets of Jerusalem. They exited the Upper City, walked through the Lower City, past the Huldah gates of the 2nd Temple and out the gates of Jerusalem towards the Mount of Olives. They walked down a steep incline and then crossed the brook of Cedron using a small stone bridge.

Christian took in the beauty of the slopes of the Mount of Olives. He was headed up the western slope to the Garden of Gethsemane for what may end up being an epic battle between his disciples and the mob coming to arrest him. On reaching the gates of the garden, he told the disciples that he expected trouble tonight from the religious authorities. Just then he heard a commotion coming up the hill. Men with torches arrived at the garden. They were Peter and Simon the Zealot and other friends of Simon, each armed with swords. "Glad you made it. Wait here and be alert. I need to go speak with my father." Christian retreated to a higher ground and pinged HQ on the cubepod. His dad's image appeared.

"Dad, I knew it would be you," Christian said.

"Had to be this way," his dad acknowledged.

"I don't know how much time we'll have to talk and there's a lot I have to tell you," Christian said. "When we started a few years ago I was a lot more inspired than what I am right now. I've done everything that's been asked of me. I'm not sure you could ask a person to do any more and I completely empathize with why Jesus asked that this cup be taken away from him, because I've come, in a way, to ask the same of you. I've concluded that following through with the crucifixion is no longer necessary. Judas seems to be aware of this somehow and I think we can work something out on our end. We can get Matthew to write the rest of the story and Judas and I can steal away to southern France, to quietly live out the rest of our lives."

"If you're doubting destiny now, I can't indulge you. Escape would leave you in antiquity for an unforeseen duration. What about the immutability of time? You know that path isn't consistent with the wounds your body apparently suffered."

"The immutability of time be damned. What if you're wrong? We've been working so arduously to make everything consistent with history. What if we don't?" Christian challenged. "Who's to say what's right?"

"Son, I know you're stressed. You're not thinking straight. The immutability of time is like gravity. It isn't a matter or right or wrong, it just is what it is and to deny its existence will not make it go away. And what about your faith?"

"Dad, I told you, we can have Matthew write the whole thing. History will be recorded, just as it was two thousand years ago."

"Christian, I don't understand God's ways any more than you do. Jesus ultimately gave his life for man because he knew he had to be the instrument of God's love. There was no other way, though he dreaded his fate as much as you do now. But there's something else—"

"Dad," Christian cut him off.

"No, listen to me. There are rights and wrongs to be considered and to stay in Palestine, or anywhere in that past existence, would be an injustice to someone who needs you here in present day."

"Dad, really? You'll be just fine, and we can keep in touch with the cubepod."

"Not me Christian, my grandson." He paused. "Your two-and-a-half-year-old son needs his father and if you are at all able to return to him, you must feel the obligation to do so. No bond is stronger than that of a parent with his child. I wish that bond for you and him, just as you and I enjoy our relationship today."

"Claire?" Christian stammered.

"Yes, she is the mother of your son."

Christian wept. He had just started down a course in defiance of history, only to be jolted back to fulfill what he now realized was his true fate. He needed to come home and that meant that he needed to die. "She never said a word," Christian muttered. "This whole time she never said a word. No one did."

"She wanted it this way," his dad said. "She felt you bore enough burden already and that it would have been an unnecessary distraction for you. The only reason I've told you now is that it's apparent you needed this incentive to finish what's been started and come home."

"I'll finish it," Christian said. "I've started some other threads of action that I'm immediately going to have to shut down. My friends are going to be mightily confused. I told them to bring swords to the garden and to be ready to fight."

"Oh my, you're going to have to cool things down," his dad said. "It was a confusing event. I wish there was something I could do to take this cup from you. I am heartbroken at the thought of what's to come, as I'm sure you are."

"I'll do my best." Christian was pressed for time. "I need to go soon. I just want you to know, you've always been an inspiration for me."

"I'm proud of you and I'll be praying for you to get through this." His dad was openly crying.

There was precious little time to process the parallels between his discussion with his dad and Jesus' prayer in the Garden of Gethsemane. He heard people coming up the slope and he had to get to Mary.

He moved quickly to her, removed his leather pouch containing the cubepod and held it out to her. "Mary, here take this. Guard it well."

"What's happening? What about getting away from here?"

"Change in plans, again. All those things I told you we would ask Matthew to write, I'm going to have to follow through with. Believe me, I wish there were another way. I was grasping for another way. There isn't one and I'm sorry. Take these and I'll talk to you from the other side, when this is all over."

Christian handed Mary the leather pouch and its collection of objects, but he held onto the memories as a source of strength to get him through the coming punishment. The pouch was a gift from James to replace the ragged feed sack from Nikud's stable. It's contents included the cubepod, link to home and facilitator of miracles, the fisherman's knife, the bow drill, a few remaining silver coins and molecular nanite capsules. Christian would be on his own from here.

"Oh no Christian, there has to be another way. What about Judas?" Mary accepted the leather pouch and its contents, but she still objected.

"I will deal with that directly."

"I'll guard it and everything in it, well," Mary acknowledged.

Christian turned to see his apostles and other men with swords on high alert to defend him from arrest in the garden. Curiously, the gospels say that Jesus' apostles were sleeping when he returned. Christian's men were wide awake and prepared for battle. He was proud of them in this moment and yet sad for what they were about to witness.

A group of men arrived, with Judas in the lead. They were out of breath, as if they had climbed up the hill slope at an unaccustomed pace. Some of the men were finely dressed in the garbs of the temple, while others were dressed in motley tunics and common cloaks. Some of the men were armed with swords and clubs, others carried torches. They looked like a scene from Young Frankenstein, Christian thought, where the angry townspeople come to burn down the house of the monster.

Christian's men prevented everyone in the mob except for Judas to approach. Judas leaned forward and kissed him on the cheek.

Christian looked squarely into Judas' eyes just inches from his face and said softly, "You've never kissed me before." Christian purposefully deviated from the script. He previously had every intention of saying something about Judas betraying him with a kiss, but he suspected what he said wouldn't matter and what would be recorded was what was already written. Christian followed his own agenda. He wanted Judas to drop out of character because he still wanted to have a frank conversation with him.

Christian maintained eye contact and remained close in the aftermath of the epic kiss from Judas. Was that a look of surprise in Judas' eyes, or expectation? In that intimate moment, it was just he and Judas in the garden, like a slow-motion picture frame. If it's true that the eyes are the windows to a man's soul, then what Christian saw in Judas was above all, compassion. Beyond that, possibly a faraway stare of memories?

"Yes, I have, and I love you," Judas said sincerely.

Christian processed the words. Somehow, they did not surprise him. The words were not what you would expect to hear from this infamous man of historical betrayal, but they were entirely appropriate coming from his good friend Judas at this tragic moment. No, the words themselves did not surprise Christian at all. What did surprise Christian was that the words were spoken in clear, unaccented English.

"I'll be okay," Christian simply replied, also in English.

"I will be too," Judas nodded.

Just then, Peter, who was armed with a sword, struck out at one of the high priest's servants, cutting off his right ear.

"No more of that! Put away your swords." Christian raised his hand, holding up the universal stop signal.

"I now ask you once again to eschew violence my beloved disciples. Stick to being fishers of men from now on, as I have taught you." Then he licked his hand, reached out and touched the side of the man's injured head so that cellular nanites would transfer to the wounded man's ear. As Christian held his hand to the man's ear he asked him, "What is your name?"

The man looked back in disbelief because he could tell his ear was already starting to heal and said, "Lord, my name is Malchus."

"My saliva will heal the wound and you should be able to hear just fine, but I'm afraid this night will leave you scared without an ear Malchus."

"I have a feeling your scars will be far more severe Lord, and I am already regretful of my part in it," Malchus replied.

Christian nodded. "No worries." Then he turned to the mob and addressed them sternly. "Am I leading a rebellion that you have come armed to arrest me? I've been in the temple courts every day this week and you didn't lay a hand on me. But this is the hour when darkness reigns. I will go with you peacefully." He held out his hands and a man with a rope bound them. The mob seized Christian and led him away, back towards Jerusalem. According to biblical accounts, he would be brought first to the house of Caiaphas, Jewish High Priest, who had plotted his arrest with Judas. The Sanhedrin would conduct his trial and the deck would be stacked against him.

Christian was saddened as he approached the walls of Jerusalem and heard a rooster crow, signaling that Peter had completed his three denials.

The temple guards leading the mob paraded Christian back into the Lower City of Jerusalem. The city was packed with Jews who made the pilgrimage for Passover. The mob escorting Christian became pressed together and mixed with the pilgrims in the streets and the crowd intensified with an even larger following as they passed through the Lower City. Christian was being bombarded with questions and insults shouted at him.

"Are you really God?" someone shouted.

"Do some miracles, save yourself!" another man said.

"Call for the angels to come help you, Lord," a woman yelled.

It appeared to Christian that there was mass confusion about what was happening. It was probably difficult to discern if Christian was arrested or being shuffled through the busy city by armed guards for his own safety. Some knew what was happening because they heard some jeers about a trial at the house of Caiaphas. Christian wondered if perhaps this was a big mistake.

As the temple guards funneled Christian into the Upper City of Jerusalem, the accumulated crowd slowly dispersed. The original arresting mob rumbled to within just a few blocks of the house on the hill with the upper room where Christian and the apostles held their Passover meal. There was a bustle of activity around Caiaphas' house, which was more like a small palace, in anticipation of Jesus' arrival. Christian was placed in a holding cell across the street from the house.

He could see out into the street until one of men closed the thatch shade over the window, darkening the room except for lamplight.

The thugs guarding Christian tied him to a bench and placed a feed sack over his head. The first crushing blow caught Christian off guard and he was immediately disoriented. The men were taunting him. They said vile things about his family and mother. Why were they hitting him? The next blow crashed directly onto his nose. The cracking sound he heard of his nose breaking was sickening. The pain shot behind his eyes and across his cheeks. Blood began to flow freely from his nostrils, draining down into his mustache, beard, and mouth. The third blow came from the side. It cracked the orbital socket of his right eye. The next blow came quickly, delivered to the same location. It caused his right retina to tear across the macula, effectively blinding him in the right eye. Instead of seeing shadows through the feed sack, he saw bright flashes and glimpses of the back of his own blood-soaked eyeball. The fifth blow struck directly onto the bridge of his nose, driving it further into his skull. The pain was excruciating. He regretted not letting his disciples use their swords just a few hours earlier. The next blow struck his right cheek and he heard mocking cries laced with profanity. That blow was followed quickly by another to his left cheek, accompanied by loud mocking jeers. They targeted the cheeks for a time, alternating back and forth, purposely turning his head in advance of the blow. The beating continued until the guards were either bored or exhausted. The room smelled of blood and sweat and urine. The feed sack was still draped over his head and it was saturated with blood.

The beating ceased. He didn't know how many times he had been hit. His breathing was labored. His consciousness was returning, with structured thought beginning to reform in his mind. He remembered his cellular nanites and reasoned that they must already be at work, healing his battered face. A horrible thought occurred to him. These guys were going to have to pulverize him, to kill him. His suffering was going to be excruciating. His face was numb. He could feel the holes of several missing teeth with the tip of his swollen tongue. His cheeks were sore. He was thirsty.

Friday

This is not the end, it is not even the beginning of the end, but it is, perhaps, the end of the beginning.
~Winston S. Churchill

Christian could hear commotion outside Caiaphas' house at daybreak. The Sanhedrin was convening for the trial of Jesus. The thugs untied him from the bench, removed the feed sack from his head, and led him into the house. The Sadducees and Pharisees must have been forewarned because they filled the large room at this early hour. They undoubtedly wanted to get on with the day's messy business as soon as possible.

Christian noticed he was receiving odd looks from the Sanhedrin participants. If he had a mirror, he assumed he'd see a displaced nose, a warped eye socket and bruised swollen cheeks. He reasoned that the nanites could stop the bleeding and heal the soft tissue, but they couldn't reset facial bones. He closed one eye and then alternated to the other to confirm that he was indeed able to see out of both eyes. At least his right eye healed itself.

The guards made no effort to clean Christian in advance of the trial. He stood before the assembly humbly soiled in his own blood and smelling of urine. The blood had spewed from his nose, down his beard and into his tunic, staining it a deep crimson red across his chest. Some of the judges gawked, while others averted their gaze.

This was a convening of the Great Sanhedrin, which presided as the supreme Jewish authority. He hadn't expected there would be quite so many judges. He looked around the room packed with scores of men, some with beards hanging down to their navel. He recognized the chief priest, Caiaphas, from observations at the 2nd Temple. Annus, son of Anasus, was present, along with his brothers. Other Sadducee priests and scribes filled the room. Christian saw Rabbi Gamaliel, whom he had so grandly insulted in his own home. Gamaliel was sure to offer a guilty vote. He took some comfort in seeing Joseph of Arimathea and his friend Nicodemus, though their input would be futile.

Caiaphas called the meeting to order. The judges fell quickly into line, terminating side conversations and shifting their attention to the high priest.

Caiaphas put forth the guidelines of the hearing. He first addressed the members of the Sanhedrin. "Gentlemen, we all know why we are here. The man standing before you is the one called Jesus the Christ. He is a teacher. He is a hero of the people. He is a miracle worker. Some say he is a prophet. We are here to try him for blasphemy for his claims to be God himself."

At this statement there was grumbling in the room and unveiled assertions of outrage from the judges.

"We will have order in this court." Caiaphas pounded his fist on the table before him. "We will hear this man out and grant him the fair trial that he deserves under Jewish Law."

Caiaphas directed his attention to Christian. "Jesus, first let me offer my sincere apologies for the treatment you received last night from guards at my house. They took liberties that are not consistent with the practices and beliefs of this esteemed gathering of men. I will personally see to it that the men who abused you last night are properly punished. Henceforward, for your own protection, after these proceedings we will be placing you under Roman guard."

Christian considered how convenient that was, given the end goal was crucifixion by the Romans. Protection my ass, he thought.

Caiaphas paused briefly. He stretched out the scroll before him and continued his opening remarks. "Now, let us get to the matter at hand. Jesus, I have here a signed affidavit testifying to your crime. You are accused of blasphemy before God and man. Further, we have a plethora of witnesses to your repeated claims to being the Messiah. Sometimes you make these claims in cryptic terms or in the form of analogy through your clever stories. Other times you're plainer spoken in your claim to deity, with you and your followers stating outright that you are in fact the Christ, the Son of God. All proper titles, which at their root meaning would make you God himself." Caiaphas let the scroll coil up on itself before he resumed speaking. He clenched the convolved scroll in his hand and pointed it at Christian. "So, let me ask you plainly now, before this court, do you denounce these assertions? Or, are you ready to stake your claim as the Messiah, the King of the Jewish Nation as foretold in scripture?"

Christian's throat was dry and his voice raspy. "If I told you who I was, you would not believe me. And, if I asked you to explain my being here, you could not do it. I tell you honestly, I will soon be back home with my father."

There was grumbling from the Sanhedrin judges about cryptic responses, then a clear question arose. "Are you then the Son of God?"

"You say that I am," Christian stated simply in Hebrew.

The whole of the Sanhedrin burst into uproar. Caiaphas brought them back to order, overcoming their protestations with poundings of his fist and loud reprimands. Caiaphas directed his attention back to Christian.

"Jesus, you know full well we've been watching you carefully over the past few months. We have numerous witnesses we could bring before this court whose testimony would not be favorable to you. We have people from your own hometown of Nazareth who claim outright that you are not who you say you are. They doubt that you are even Jewish. And, I must admit that while you are versed in scripture, you are not versed in our culture. You are cognizant of our history, but you fail to understand our essence. Your story telling rivals Vyasa and yet your origins remain mysterious. Even your accent is like none we've ever heard. If I were to guess, I would say your philosophies tend to be more Egyptian or Greek in origin, or possibly some other western culture we are not familiar with here in Israel."

Christian thought, this is not a stupid man. Did Caiaphas realize how close he was to a truth nobody else he encountered in ancient Palestine was able to comprehend, let alone articulate?

"I personally am intrigued by your philosophies," Caiaphas said. "In different times and under different circumstances, I believe we may have been friends."

Christian thought he might be right.

"Our agents have seen you demonstrate miraculous capabilities that even our sages cannot explain," Caiaphas said. "You've healed leapers. You've made lame men walk. You've made blind men see and deaf men hear."

"He healed a man's withered hand on the Sabbath," a Sanhedrin judge yelled.

Caiaphas turned his attention to the Sanhedrin council and admonished them instead. "I was wondering when this charge would emerge. We're supposed to be the wisest, most learned men in all of Judea here on this council and yet we would allow the closed-minded Pharisees to dictate our judgment about the worthiness of a man to be healed on the Sabbath. Further, we would condemn the man who healed the poor bastard? I tell you this now, we will drop this charge. It is ludicrous and this teacher from Galilee was correct to call you out on it."

Caiaphas nodded towards Christian.

Christian was a bit surprised at the validation from his chief accuser, but he still realized this would not end well. He was learning, though, that his prosecution was neither as cut and dry as scripture recorded, nor was it without merit, at least in his case.

Caiaphas returned his attention to Christian. "Now, where was I? Yes, you've healed people and our sages don't deny that you have, nor do they know how you do it. It also seems that you have gone to great lengths to fabricate other miraculous signs, to what end I cannot fathom.

We have witnesses to the origin of the bread with which you fed a mass of over five thousand men. There are manifold others who would come into this court and openly testify that they saw a man who looked just like you riding a horse around the Sea of Galilee that very night. I don't know what your apostles saw that night, but I suspect it wasn't you walking across the water. Am I right?"

Christian wanted to say something about pleading the 5th Amendment, instead he remained silent. Caiaphas was correct.

Caiaphas noted his silence. "I figured as much. None of this is particularly bothersome to me Jesus. If you want to trick people into thinking you can manufacture food and defy the laws of nature by skipping across a lake, that's fine with me. I don't get it, but that's immaterial to me."

Caiaphas paused, making sure he had the attention of the room. "What concerns me infinitely more are your efforts to defy the laws of God himself with your claims to the power of necromancy. For unknown reasons you felt compelled to demonstrate this power by making a spectacle of your friend Lazarus. I'm skeptical that the man ever died. For how convenient it is that the man you are renowned for raising from the dead just happens to be the brother of a close woman friend of yours. If I were going to orchestrate such a miracle, I would keep those plans close to home indeed."

Christian remained stoic yet stunned.

"Shall I go on?" Caiaphas asked. "I believe I will. It's an honest question really, though I suspect you will not answer, which greatly disappoints me, for it's another reason I wish our circumstances were different. Our agents report you have some kind of magic little box that calls angels to your side. I'm fascinated. What is this box?"

Christian remained silent. No way dude, you're not getting hold of that technology, he thought.

"You indict yourself with your silence," Caiaphas said. "At this point I see no further need for testimony. We have heard Jesus say from his own lips that he is the Messiah. Whether he states it plainly or not here in court matters not. The man is guilty of blasphemy. What further need do we have to deliberate?"

Then Joseph, seated in the front of the Sanhedrin assembly, stood to speak his counter arguments on behalf of Jesus.

"Ah yes, it seems Jesus has a fan in our midst. The court recognizes the esteemed Joseph of Arimathea," Caiaphas said.

"Your honorable Caiaphas, do not your own words, as well considered as they are, lead you to another conclusion about Jesus?" Joseph asked. "You state yourself he is not familiar with our culture and our way of life. How then can we judge him under our Mosaic laws?

Jesus' speech may be acerbic, and I cannot say exactly why he says some of the things he says and why he does some of the things he does, but ultimately his is a message of love and mercy that resonates with the common people. Would it not be better for the Sanhedrin to embrace Jesus as one of our own? Allow him to sit with our scribes and sages to better learn our ways? We would be praised for our wise judgment of him. We could shape his message and collectively rise to an even greater power. Surely, we would benefit more by allying ourselves with a man as inspirational as Jesus, rather than condemning him."

Christian realized through these trial proceedings that perhaps he underestimated the suaveness of the highest echelon of Jewish leadership. Joseph was on target for a wiser course of action for the Sanhedrin. History would judge the Sanhedrin harshly, aside for the lone wise man, Joseph, who stood to defend the case of Jesus at the trial. He once again noted the signet ring Joseph wore. He scanned the room and saw that Caiaphas also wore a signet ring, as did a few others, each bearing unique symbols, though none of them contained the freemason design like Joseph's. Christian's attention snapped back to the trial proceedings.

"Annus, what say you in this matter?" Caiaphas asked.

Annus was the brother-in-law of Caiaphas. They were closely aligned and undoubtedly had conspired in advance of the trial.

"I say the esteemed Joseph has demonstrated once again why it is our honor to have him serving on the Sanhedrin, for he alone speaks up in defense of this man Jesus and he does so with erudite persuasion," Annus said. "Unfortunately, the situation does not lend itself to heeding his advice."

Annus paused and then spoke in a lower voice and slower cadence. He clenched his fists. "Lest we forget the Romans." He looked around the room for effect, then continued. "The crowds have already crowned this man king. If we throw ourselves in alliance with him, we would be declaring rebellion against the Roman Empire. Instead, I say this man is dangerous and we must rule and behave in such a way that keeps maximum distance between him and us, for our own safety. Our survival as a legislative body could well be at stake. Clearly, this is a man standing before us. He does not deny that he has claimed to be God. His own lips betray him, and he therefore condemns himself. Who are we to judge what God has commanded. The penalty of this man's crime is death. There is no other choice."

"We condemn an innocent man," Nicodemus asserted shaking his head, breaking his silence in obvious disgust. Nicodemus glanced at Christian and for a brief instant the two men maintained eye contact.

Christian sensed a bond of compassion and mutual respect in that fleeting moment.

"Enough! I agree with Annus." Caiaphas held up his hands in front of the assembly. "We personally hold no animus against Jesus. He has condemned himself in action and in words."

Caiaphas turned his attention back to Christian. "Jesus, I understand you like to teach in parables. Well I have a story for you. Listen and tell me what you think. A man invites guests over to his house for a meal of sweet dessert cakes. The man takes particular care to use only the best flour of the first harvest, the sweetest goat's milk and the finest spices. As he stirs the mixture for baking he also adds a cup of putrid sheep dung. The man bakes the cakes and offers them to his guests. Would you expect the guests to partake of the dessert, knowing full well that sheep dung is amongst the ingredients?" Caiaphas paused. "No, of course you would not. So clearly you understand that neither does this court find the ministry you've baked to be palatable. Unfortunately, the admirable aspects of your ministry fail to compensate for the sheep dung you've mixed in with it. If you were truly God, your ministry would be pure and I for one would embrace it on behalf of this assembly. But alas, you and I both know you've resorted to artifice over truth, and these impurities defile the entirety of your ministry."

Caiaphas' concluding remarks stung. Christian made no effort to explain or refute the accusations. Any effort to do so would be pointless.

"Debate is over," Caiaphas announced. "We now put the matter to a vote."

The verdict of guilty was predetermined, of course. No argument Joseph mounted would have swayed minds or overcome the corrupt family connections within the Jewish Sanhedrin. Clearly, Joseph was a savvy politician and he must have known the fix was in, and yet he rose to speak. Whether he realized it or not, in so doing he preserved his own legacy as a man of honor in this dark hour.

The vote wasn't even close. The Sanhedrin voted Jesus guilty of blasphemy sixty-nine to two, with the two dissenting votes coming from Joseph and Nicodemus. Christian managed to mouth a Hebrew thank you and slight bow in Joseph and Nicodemus' direction before being pulled away by Roman guards and led to the praetorium, the Roman barracks inside Jerusalem, where Pontius Pilate presided. Two Roman soldiers escorted Christian, each roughly holding his upper arm on either side of him. Coherent thought was returning to Christian's mind as he was paraded towards the praetorium. The guards smelled of olive oil and garlic, adding insult to injury, which infuriated him because the scents reminded him of Mary's ordeal. Even at this late hour, Christian clung to fleeting notions of somehow bailing out of his scripted execution and escaping with Mary.

Caiaphas requested that the guards stop short of entering the praetorium so as not to cause the whole of the Sanhedrin to be defiled in a dwelling place of gentiles just before Passover. They requested that Pilate come to them at the entrance. Christian thought it ironic that this same Sanhedrin could condemn Jesus to suffer death on the eve of the Passover, without fear of defilement.

Christian understood that Pilate was known to dislike his assignment as governor over the high-maintenance Jews. Pilate would likely be further irritated at having to come outside the praetorium to receive the religious leaders of the Jewish faith. Christian's reading of the gospels depicted Pilate as a rather reluctant executioner in Jesus' case. He was about the see how this played out in person.

Christian had often wondered how such a multitude suddenly appeared, aligned against Jesus at the trial before Pilate. His experience before the Sanhedrin filled in that knowledge gap, for the Sanhedrin was a very large assembly and all its members need do was call for a show of strength from extended family and friends.

The hostile crowd continued to gather as a clean-shaven, narrow-faced Roman aristocrat emerged from the barracks. He wore a royal purple tunic embroidered with golden stitching. The golden wreath of laurel leaves about his head stood out in contrast to his short cropped dark brown hair and tanned skin. He stopped at the praetorium gate and stood for a moment with erect posture and arms folded across his chest. The Roman guards paid him reverence by bracing their long spears to the ground and coming to attention, heals together and face forward. His commanding aura told Christian, in no uncertain terms, that this man was Governor Pontius Pilate.

"You better have a good reason to summon the governor in this manner." Pilate grit his teeth as he spoke in a succinctly refined Latin.

"We have found this man subverting our nation," Annus said to Pilate. "He opposes payment of taxes to Caesar and claims to be the Messiah, a king."

Wait a minute, Christian thought, I said people *should* pay their taxes. But it wouldn't matter. The accusation wasn't the crime for which the Sanhedrin would convict Jesus. The charge against Jesus by the Sanhedrin was blasphemy, but Annus knew the Romans would care less about that. He needed to trump up charges that were menacing to Rome itself.

"Are you the king of the Jews?" Pilate asked Christian.

"You have said so," Christian replied in Latin, parroting Jesus.

"That is not an answer," Pilate said. "But, I didn't expect you to say a much different. I must tell you, you should not mince words with the Roman authorities and ordinarily I wouldn't be in the mood to tolerate it, but fortunately, I've been warned that you have a habit of speaking cryptically, so I'll spare you the lecture."

That was sparing me the lecture? Christian thought.

Christian noticed Pontius Pilate also sported a signet ring. It bore a brilliant red ruby with bold black etchings of a spider centered on the gem. The etchings were cleanly and deeply cut, right angled and precisely shaped into what Christian recognized as a Jain swastika. Christian was unaware that this religious symbol of ancient origin been adopted by the Roman Empire. Pilate, obviously, wouldn't equate the symbol with the Nazis, Christian mused, but even if he was told of its 20th Century relevance, Christian believed Pilate would probably wear it anyway.

Christian listened as Pilate, Caiaphas, and Annus argued back and forth about the charges against Jesus and the punishment that was required. Pilate was reluctant to get involved in the religious dispute and finally closed the matter. "I find no basis for a charge against this man. Furthermore, he comes from Galilee, so as a Galilean, this man is under the jurisdiction of Herod Antipas. I know Herod is here in Jerusalem for Passover. Send this man to Herod."

Having been dismissed by Pilate, Christian was once again led through the streets of Jerusalem under Roman guard, this time to the Palace of Herod on the far west side of Jerusalem. He sometimes wondered what Jesus was thinking about as he was marched back and forth between these various judges during his passion. In Christian's case, he was humming *Jesus Christ Superstar* tunes and all he could imagine was a buffoonish Herod character on a boat dock doing the Charleston. Christian recalled in the *Bible* accounts that Jesus says nothing to Herod and Christian planned to do the same. He expected this to be a short and disappointing, one-way discussion and then he would be marched back to Pilate for final judgment.

The crowd arrived at the palace. Christian heard Greek and Latin discussions between the Roman guards and palace guards about jurisdiction, then Christian was led into the palace chambers. Palace guards only escorted him, the crowd remained outside. This would apparently be a private audience.

Christian observed the man sitting on the throne before him. Herod looked to be a man in his mid-fifties, of slender build, with dark skin, dark full beard and wearing well fitted traditional royal Jewish clothing. Herod, too, wore a signet ring on his right ring finger. He saw Herod's ring featured a deep blue stone exquisitely etched with two high contrasting semi-circles arching into one another to form the recognizable image of a fish. Christian reasoned that Galilee's capital, Tiberias, resided on the western banks of the Sea of Galilee and that fishing was indeed an important industry for the region. It was possible that this image had previously been associated with Galilee and then was later adopted by the followers of Jesus, who primarily initiated from Galilee. Herod was genuinely pleased to have Jesus visiting him. "Come in, please, and sit down."

Herod gestured for Christian to sit in one of the chairs facing the throne. Then he signaled to the guards to leave and shut the doors, leaving only the throne's chamber attendants in the room with him and Christian.

Christian collapsed into a chair. It was his first opportunity to sit since the early morning hours. He hung his head and gazed mindlessly down at the ornate woolen carpet of the throne room. Then he felt himself being inspected by Herod. What Herod saw was a beaten and bloodied man. Christian's ordeal was just beginning.

Herod signaled to one of the attendants. "Bring this man some water and food and fetch some clean robes for him." Then he turned towards Christian. "You look a mess, Jesus. I've been wanting for some time to have the opportunity to meet you and for that moment to come now under such tragic circumstances is truly unfortunate, for we have much to discuss. Judas warned me it might be difficult to draw you into conversation because of the written guidance to which you adhere, which is why I've arranged for this private setting. There is no one here who would dare divulge the words uttered within these royal chambers. It is my hope that we will have a chance to speak freely under these conditions."

Christian was not yet moved to speak. Christian observed the finely crafted ring, the offer of hospitality, the mention of Judas and the privacy of the meeting. The manner of this discourse was not what he expected.

"You don't realize the respect you've garnered from my household. The very rug you're dripping blood onto was crafted by a vendor that your follower Joanna befriended in Arbela. It's of yak wool, cured and dyed by the nomadic peoples of the eastern plains using vinegar and urine. Lovely, don't you think?"

Christian listened, glanced again at the vibrant carpet, silently agreed, but reserved comment.

Water, fresh fruit, savory cheese and fine new clothes arrived for Christian. "Walk him through the palace baths before you dress him again, he deserves that much at least." The attendants led him through to an adjacent cleansing room and walked him through the bath waters.

They helped him change into new garments, brought him back to the throne room, and filled his cup with the fresh water of the palace. Christian's swollen tongue and parched throat absorbed one cup and then another of the refreshing liquid. Christian appreciated that Herod patiently waited as attendants tended to his needs.

"I hoped to meet you while you were preaching in Galilee and even heard you were coming our way, to Tiberias," Herod said. "I was in town that week, supervising enhancements to our bathing facility for travelers, just outside of one of the royal spas. You would have enjoyed using it. Then it was reported your disciples had camped on the edge of town and left. I don't know why you chose to skip coming into town that day and I have regretted missing you ever since."

Christian was regretting it now, too, but he still only offered the king silence.

"You know, it was only a couple of years ago that I learned that the builder Joseph of Nazareth had another son named Jesus. It was as if you just dropped onto the map, from nowhere. My palace offered Joseph's son James work on the capital construction projects, but his mother would have none of it. I cannot say I blame her after losing her husband so tragically. Had we known of you we would have offered you work, too, of course."

Christian nodded in acknowledgment that King Herod had his attention.

"Your father saved many people that day in Tiberias when the keystone of a supporting arch of the eastern facing porch slipped during its placing. Joseph was high up into the scaffolding and close enough to the placement to recognize the danger. He bellowed desperate warnings for every construction worker in that section of the building. There was no way for him, or his immediate crew to escape the collapse, but due to his early recognition and loud alarm every man at or near ground level was spared being crushed by massive basalt blocks. Your father was a hero."

Christian was moved by this story and felt tears well in his eyes. Mary had not told the story quite this way.

"You've never heard this story, have you?" Herod asked.

"No, I have not, and I sincerely thank you for sharing it," Christian finally replied.

"Indulge me and let me tell you another."

Christian nodded.

"When I was a young man of not quite twenty years, three fabulously dressed sorcerers, or magi, showed up at this very palace. They announced to my father that a great king was born in Judea and that they were here to pay homage to the new king. Now, I don't know what these sorcerers expected, but Herod the Great was not a man inclined to yield his kingship to anyone, including his own sons, except by his own death. The idea that these fortune tellers would even suggest the idea was an outrage to him and he loosed his wrath throughout Judea. No Jewish infant child near Jerusalem in those days would have been safe and honestly, I can't blame any parent who took precautions to save their babies by sending them away from Judea during those dark times. So, Jesus, son of Mary and Joseph of Nazareth, I can understand why those who cared for you were compelled to have you leave Judea thirty years ago and unfortunately the catalyst was the tyranny of my own father. What I don't understand is why you came back. May I ask you why?"

Christian wasn't braced for this question. He was expecting to go through the motions of a familiar Passion play, but this was not in the script.

"Your Majesty, I'm so far down this path, it seems too arduous to explain how I got to this point. I'm not sure I could explain it in a way I would fully understand myself. This path was thrust upon me and it is near completion," Christian said. "Honestly, this conversation is a most pleasant surprise."

"It is a pleasure for me as well, and long overdue. I am sorry the circumstances are so tragic indeed and you appear to already have been the subject of some abuse. Your nose appears to be broken."

"Yes, I'm sure it is. It doesn't hurt anymore, though."

"Well that's good. Though I'm afraid I cannot save you from the Romans. Judas forewarned me not to try and he says the events surrounding your conviction here in Jerusalem this Passover will have severe and far reaching consequences. I'm not sure what all of this means, but I respect Judas greatly and value his wisdom."

"That's the second time I've heard you mention Judas. How do you know him?"

"Judas is an important business man from our trade hub in Capernaum. As king, I like to get to know our important citizens. I met your father in the same way. He was doing fine work for us in Japhia. The exquisite tiles on the Japhia Temple are largely his handiwork. It was because of his demonstrated skill there that we asked the Romans to allow him to join our construction crews on the royal facilities in Tiberias. If you remember, under my father's rule, Galilee had no official capital. When the torch of leadership was passed to me, I endeavored to change that so the people of Galilee would be better served. One of the first things I did was to commission Tiberias to be the capital. I wanted the best people available to perform the necessary construction. The Romans begrudgingly released Joseph from his construction duties on the Roman fortress of Sepphoris after I promised their leadership unlimited access to the spas of Tiberias. Likewise, Judas has been an asset in the development of trade from the frontiers of Babylon to the east to Egypt to the west. Judas has provided us with lucrative trade routes we had not even envisioned. I hate to see him go as well."

Christian's mind turned to Judas and his traveling. He was all over the map, had well placed connections and demonstrated foresight. Things didn't add up.

"Judas told you he's leaving?" Christian asked.

"Yes, Judas explained that he must leave because of what happens here this Passover. He asked me to do him some favors. He's asked that his house in Capernaum be deeded to the apostle you call Peter. He also requested that the apostles be provided safe harbor in Capernaum after you and he are gone."

"And, you agreed to this?"

"Yes, I agreed gladly. These will be dangerous times for your followers in Judea. I will offer them security in Galilee until the day I die. By the way, I'm led to believe you could probably give me an idea of how soon that might be, but let's leave that to be discovered. I don't think I want to have that bit of knowledge."

Christian recalled that Herod had about ten years more to live, but he kept that to himself. Christian was honestly surprised at the personable discussion he was having with the King of Galilee. He wondered if he might be able to solicit an explanation for Herod's most notorious crime.

"I've avoided you until now because I've held a grudge over your execution of John the Baptist," Christian said.

"I was afraid you might bring that up," Herod groaned. "Listen, John wasn't even preaching in Galilee, he was preaching on the edge of the wilderness in Peraea. No reasonable thinking man would have thought him a threat to my kingdom and yet, against my better judgment, I permitted his arrest. John had haters in my court. Through corruption and my own drunkenness, I allowed myself to become boxed into ordering his execution. I greatly regretted the decision then and I still do, to this very day. Do you not think that I learned my lesson through that episode? You sojourned nearly two long years in my own backyard throughout Galilee and never once did soldiers under my sway impede you. Further, did I not allow my royal steward Chuza to finance your ministry through the active participation of his wife Joanna and even bail you out of a pinch in Decapolis? Your troubles with the Jewish authorities began when you took your show on the road to Judea."

Christian agreed with the truth of the observation and offered, "Your Majesty, history will not judge you kindly."

"Judas told me that, too. I've accepted that between you and him, there are forces at work here beyond my comprehension. I've already yielded to higher powers, as have you. It is my understanding that I cannot save you and I must order you back to Pilate. Is that your understanding as well?"

"Yes, that is correct."

They ended their meeting with the understanding that what was said in the palace chamber that day would remain hidden. It was bitter sweet for Christian. He would take the conversation to his grave.

Herod walked with Christian out of the palace and stated to the Romans guards, "Inform Governor Pilate I can make no judgment against Jesus." The Roman guards and the waiting crowd escorted Christian back to the gateway of the Roman praetorium. Pilate stepped outside the praetorium once again.

"Pilate, the crimes this man has committed require punishment to death," Annus said. "Under Roman control, we have no ability to execute criminals in this way and we once again turn to Rome to pass this judgment."

"You've already brought me this man as one you claim was inciting rebellion," Pilate said. "I examined him and found no basis for the charges against him. Neither has Herod, for he sent him back to us. As you can see, he has done nothing to deserve death."

Christian stood listening to the familiar dialog and to the shouting from the crowd. The idea that any crowd of civilized people would become this bloodthirsty for a crucifixion was revolting.

Pilate indeed played the part of the reluctant executioner. Christian found it interesting that Pilate refrained from saying anything about the new robe Herod provided. Pilate ordered the guards to fetch another prisoner. A squad of Roman soldiers returned with a wild-eyed muscular warrior bound in shackles.

Pilate gestured to the man standing on his left. "Shall I free the criminal Bar Abbas?" Then he gestured to Christian. "Or shall I free your king, Jesus?"

Christian and Barabbas simultaneously turned to each other in recognition.

The crowd repeatedly shouted out that the criminal Barabbas should be released and that Jesus should be crucified.

"You fools," Barabbas raged. "Free the Lord Jesus!" But, his voice was drowned out by the cast of hundreds in the crowd.

Pilate vacillated, but having made the offer, he honored it and indeed ordered Barabbas released. Barabbas, for his part, was completely enraged and the Roman guard dared not unshackle him in that state.

"You sons of bitches," Barabbas yelled. "I'll not fight for your freedom ever again. Do you hear me? You stupid people don't deserve it."

It took an entire squad of Roman guards to contain Barabbas and physically drag him from the scene.

"I won't forget you Jesus." His last exclamation echoed across the courtyard.

This left Christian standing alone before Pilate, waiting for him to pass judgment.

"Well Jesus, it looks like you have at least one fan. Fascinating to see. For it seems the self-righteous condemn you, while the criminals embrace you. You're an enigma," Pilate observed.

"I still find no grounds for the death penalty against this man," Pilate said to the crowd. "However, I will have him flogged to satisfy your cries for his punishment."

Well there it was, Christian thought, and this was going to hurt.

Two soldiers bound Christian to a nearby wooden post. They tore his fine robe and let it drop to his feet. Christian stood in only his loincloth, bracing for the terrible crack of the whip. He expected this was going to hurt. To his horror, he saw there were two soldiers with multi-tailed whips in hand ready to mete out his archaic punishment. They were close enough for him to see that the whip tails contained small pieces of metal and bone sewn into them to exact even more severe punishment. The two soldiers would take turns.

The first lash ripped into his right shoulder blade across his spine and down the left side of his back. The shock of the impact was followed quickly by the sharp sting of metal and bone tearing through the outer layers of his skin. The next lash ripped laterally the opposite direction across the left shoulder blade to the right side of his back. It, too, was shocking and painful. The third lash of the whip followed the track of the first, ripping deeper through the flesh, causing him to writhe in agony. The fourth lash followed the track of the second, ripping flesh in an alternating pattern. There was already a rhythm developing to the punishment. The fifth lash struck lower and more heavily sideways across his back with a strand of metal in the whip reaching around into his right arm pit and tearing away a chunk of flesh clear through the muscle tissue. The sixth lash struck upwardly from lower left back through to the nape his neck and the rhythm he thought he found was lost.

It was worse not knowing what to expect next. The seventh lash bit severely into the bone of his right shoulder blade, exposing it briefly before the wound filled with blood. The eighth lash fell heavily on his lower back, decimating previously untarnished skin. He recalled the meaning of sarcasm, ripping of flesh, in Greek. The flesh on his back was being ripped apart. He was sorry for being sarcastic with Claire. The next lash was so strategically positioned under his right shoulder blade he literally felt his skin rollup towards his outstretched and bound arms. His right upper back was now fully exposed for the next alternate blow. The alternating blows continued. His internal chant became ripping of flesh, ripping of flesh. There would be no mercy for him in these moments and no amount of work from healing nanites could ease the pain of the abuse his body was enduring. As the alternating lashing continued, he was ready to die, hoping to die. It would be relief from the next lash. He wanted death to come before the next lash. The sound of the lashes changed from sharp cracks to more like dull thuds and they cut ever deeper into the flesh of his back. His mind couldn't comprehend this pain. He wondered whom that poor bastard was they were whipping. It sounded horrid.

Christian felt the binds being cut loose and he collapsed to the dirt. His body had suffered serious trauma. The pain remained severe and the blood loss was so significant Christian thought even the healing nanites wouldn't be able to keep up. His back was now raw flesh and the back of his rib cage was exposed to the bone. Pilate cradled Christian's head in his arms, leaned towards his ear and talked to him gently. "Do you know why scourging includes just thirty-nine lashes Jesus? I'll tell you. Theory holds that a Roman soldier should be able to kill any man with forty lashes. So, a punishment of 39 lashes constitutes the maximum punishment short of a death sentence that can be administered. Mind you, I've seen men die from receiving the kind of beating you've just endured. You held up rather well, considering. The strong minded usually do. Alas, it is no matter. This crowd isn't satisfied with your scourging. I'm going to have to allow the execution by crucifixion to proceed. This isn't the outcome I would have wished for you. Your friend Judas warned me it would come to this. That is some friend you have in him. He has paid me thirty pieces of silver to have my guards do you a small favor to ease your suffering on the cross."

Pilate had bloodied his hands from holding Christian's head so close in conversation. From his vantage point on the dirt, Christian saw Pilate wash his hands of the blood as Pilate made the fatal pronouncement. He pondered what favor Judas had arranged.

Roman legionnaires rustled Christian to his feet. They draped his robe over his shoulders and escort him to a holding cell in the Lower City of Jerusalem. The flesh on Christian's back, shoulders and sides was horrifically bloodied and sore. He couldn't tell if he was healing or not. He was thirsty again.

Christian heard the streets outside the cell bustling with the noise of a gathering crowd. His cell door opened and in a mocking gesture, one of the soldiers roughly planted a crown of thorns on his head. Numerous thorns punctured his skull to the bone, dealing another humiliation and dose of pain.

Christian was led to an alley and there the cross beam of the cross on which he would be crucified was placed on his bruised and bleeding shoulders and strapped to his outstretched arms. He was woozy from the lashing and realized it would be difficult to catch himself if he stumbled.

Soon into his harrowing death march, his weakened state combined with the heavy weight of the beam exhausted him and he fell to the ground. Pain shot across his forehead and behind his eyes as he reinjured his broken nose. The guards roughly rustled him back to his feet and mercilessly urged him onward.

Christian rounded a narrow street corner and encountered the familiar face of the Mother Mary. She was wearing the cloak given to her by Mary Magdalene over a year ago. In a moment of clear headedness, he realized Mother Mary must have traveled hastily to make it here to Jerusalem from Galilee. There was no time for words.

Christian was noticeably laboring with the cross so the Romans recruited an onlooker to carry the beam on Christian's behalf. Christian was relieved to get some assistance. The crowd was funneling its way through the narrow streets of the Lower City when Christian saw Veronica, Peter's wife, step into the street. Veronica bravely caused the procession to stop while she wiped Christian's disfigured face with her veil.

The cross beam was returned to Christian's raw shoulders and he fell again shortly thereafter. The guards were not at all sympathetic and struck his lacerated back to urge him onward. Christian exited the city and saw the faces of women he recognized. There was Martha, Susanna, Sarah, Joanna and Ruth, Peter's mother-in-law, just outside the gate. Martha was wailing.

"Jesus, I'm sorry for what I said. I love you. We all do," Martha cried out.

Christian could manage no reply. He was climbing uphill and his burden was heavy.

Christian arrived at the hilltop, succumbed to utter exhaustion and fell once again. The guards roughly stripped his robe off his back, ripping caked dried blood off his mangled flesh, re-exposing the grotesque wounds of his scourging. He was bleeding again, and he was thirsty. The cross beam was unlatched from his shoulders and attached to the vertical beam. He was laid flat on this back, arms extended, hands spread. There was little pause before he felt a large construction nail being hammered through his right wrist. He cried out in pain. It was unfathomable for his brain to process this level of agony. The left wrist was driven through in the same way, with equally excruciating pain. Then both feet were nailed. The cross was raised, beginning the process of Christian's hanging until death. He was delirious.

Christian saw the two other criminals hanging on crosses to his right and left. He recalled from scripture that there were conversations, but he lacked the coherence to engage in them. His beatings and the pain were beyond anything he anticipated. The guards were mocking him. He was slipping in and out of consciousness. He contemplated the possibility that despite the severe beating, his healing nanites might not let him die, at least not quickly. His arms were exhausted. He was laboring to even breathe. Christian could feel the blood pooling in his lower extremities to the point of numbing pain and yet he was unable to move them to affect circulation.

Someone poked a sponge soaked with sour wine into his face. Christian rejected it. Awakened, he looked down and saw Mary Magdalene, Mary the wife of Zebedee and lastly, Mother Mary, standing next to Judas at the foot of the cross.

"I will take care of Mother Mary. She will come live in my house in Capernaum," Judas yelled up to Christian.

Christian nodded in understanding, as best he could. He could not speak, but his mind was taking in the scene. He remembered the Gospel of John, and the mention of "The disciple whom Jesus loved." Historians thought that was John, the fisherman son of Zebedee. John was a good man, but he would not have been capable of writing the Gospel of John. Now Christian understood that there was indeed another apostle, in addition to Matthew, who would be able to write a first-hand account of Jesus' ministry and who would be inclined to obscure his identity in the process. He realized Judas was the disciple whom Jesus loved. Christian managed to disassociate his mind from the pain of crucifixion for just a few moments of coherent thought. No, he was not delusional. He could now see clearly the clues strung out before him. The apostle Judas would stage a well-publicized horrible death and a new man would emerge. This man of vision would assume a new name and new purpose. Christian savored his love for Judas as death approached.

Christian heard something spoken in Latin from the legionnaire about orders from Pontius Pilate and then he felt the cutting slice of a blade at the base of his right calf and then also on his left. The bleeding was profuse. He felt the blood rhythmically flow from the wounds. It was a relief. The nanites would not be able to keep up with the exsanguination. He would soon bleed to death thanks to the Roman legionnaire who severed Christian's posterior tibial arteries.

Christian heard Judas say, "It's over Christian, you can go home now."

Christian reminisced about the precious time spent with Mary Magdalene, Judas, and all the disciples. He had done his utmost to fulfill scripture, but now he was ready to go home. He was weakening. He was no longer thirsty. He felt his heart palpitating. His vision tunneled. His hearing quieted. His pain faded. At last, in the blackness and the silence and the profound stillness, he died.

Resurrection ~ 2025 AD

I would give anything I own. Give up my life, my heart, my home. I would give anything I own, just to have you back again, just to touch you once again.
~David Gates, Bread

A flicker of awareness stirred in his mind. He heard a slight buzzing noise and a rhythmic high-pitched beeping. Self-awareness slowly returned. The agonizing suffering was gone, replaced by the dull pain and weakness of atrophied muscles. He recognized voices. He was thirsty again and hungry, too. Christian's body was stirring to life after three years of hibernation and his mind was coming to life after three years of moderate coma. Any kind of recovery from coma of this duration was rare. It could take years for the patient to regain the ability to walk or talk. Christian's body was different. It was sustained by the cellular nanites coursing through his veins. Now that his consciousness has returned, his body would restore to normal strength again quickly as he resumed activity and began to exercise.

Christian's first visitor was his dad, soon after he regained consciousness. Christian was propped up in his hospital bed. His dad reached for his son's hand and squeezed it tightly, then he leaned onto the bed and gave him a big hug. They talked for a while and caught up on three years of life events at the Cape. Christian was the center of his dad's attention the entire time. The other major development for his dad was his life as a grandpa. His dad obviously took it easy on sharing too much about that until Christian could get re-acclimated and meet his son himself. They would have more time to talk as he got stronger.

"Son, it is so good to see you again, awake like this," his dad said sincerely. "I'm so relieved. It's been a nightmare. Your broken body remains the single most traumatic image I hope I ever have to see in my life. It is one I would not wish upon any other parent. And now, your safe return finally supplants that sadness. It is so good to have you back."

"I'm sorry you had to see that."

"You were pretty beat up. We took the liberty of fixing your battered face while you were comatose. Surgeons reconstructed your nose, repaired your orbital socket, corrected your jaw misalignment, reset your broken cheekbones, and fitted you with a full set of dental implants. Your cellular nanites managed to seal the skin around the nail wounds in your wrists and feet. We left the scars there. We can talk about whether you want to deal with them cosmetically, or not. We surgically repaired both Achilles tendons so you'd be able to walk again. The flesh on your back was shredded to the rib cage. We performed a series of skin grafts and your cellular nanites helped heal you there, too. You still have significant scarring the length of your back."

Christian listened to his father bluntly enumerate the wounds of the epic beating. It sounded disgusting to fix, much less endure. He suppressed flashes of memory and kept his reply more placid. "I'm glad you guys fixed me up. The scars seem kind of funky, but I may get used to them, we'll see."

"What do you remember about what happened the last three years?" his dad asked.

"My memories are scattered. It's as if I've had a very lucid dream, but I can't exactly remember the details. I clearly remember the initial transport, with you and Claire by my side, but after that I'm not really not sure I remember events clearly."

"Completely understandable. Could be shock effect from the coma. Hopefully your recollections will improve," his dad said as he squeezed his hand." Good to see you back with us. Is there anything I can get for you?"

"Maybe a newspaper to read and can you ask the kitchen to fix me something. I've had a craving for a cheeseburger."

"You got it. Let me find you a paper and I'll place your order," his dad said with a smile.

His dad came back with the Sunday copy of the *New Your Times*, still in newsprint after all these years despite repeated earth friendly efforts to digitize everything. Christian could understand why; there was something about having the paper in hand that felt comforting. "Your order has been placed. Enjoy it. Love you."

"Thanks Dad, love you, too."

Christian absorbed the newspaper's content. He read the headlines, the world news, the business, the sports, the arts, the comics, the advice column, his horoscope, and even did the crossword puzzle. Trump's third term was extended indefinitely due to world turmoil. A third term for an American president seemed so unconstitutional. Christian felt so out of touch. Still, it was amazing that such a simple thing as reading a newspaper could provide consolation for the homesick time traveler.

As he convalesced, he had numerous conversations with his father and heard all about the extended drama as it played out from HQ perspective. He reiterated the story of initial shock at his returned condition, then the waiting, the discoveries and revelations, the data downloads, and subsequent communications and the periodic reports HQ received of his imitation of Jesus' ministry. And now, with the miraculous disappearance of his body from the cave, they both understood that faith in the resurrection story would remain intact. The staff, his dad told him, was disappointed to hear that Christian's memories of playing the role of Jesus were lost to antiquity.

He was happy to hear that Spintronics continued to thrive and expand operations. Christian's father leveraged deep pocketed investors to purchase a highly regarded scientific research division based out of upstate NY. Thus, Spintronics secured its fifth site in Christian's absence.

It took a couple of days for the medical staff to clear Christian for other visitors. Once cleared, the first people through the door were Dominic and Cornelius. They exchanged cheerful greetings and hugs with Christian.

"We've been waiting a long time for this day. It's awesome to have you back. Talking to you on the other side of the cubepod just isn't the same," Dominic said.

"I know you don't remember, but you'll see when you listen to the archives, between Dominic and I, we dominated the air time with you. He wouldn't even yield the cubepod for the first week. We had to practically pry it from his fingers," Cornelius said.

"Not a doubt in my mind. I know you guys must have given me great support. Our friendship literally transcends space and time and I appreciate you so much," Christian said.

They caught up on three years' worth of details from the lives of Dominic and Cornelius back at the Cape. As soon as Christian was able, they promised, they'd head out for beers.

The Children

The next day, the door to Christian's recovery room opened and Claire stuck her head into the room.

"Hey Chipmunk," Claire said with a big smile and usual liveliness.

"Well look who it is, my favorite biologist," Christian said.

"It's good to see you awake," she said. "Those were long years. Talking to you back there in Palestine and seeing your hibernating body here at the Cape was taxing."

"I can't believe you guys kept that from me for so long. My dad's rules about signaling readiness to receive information by asking questions drives me crazy sometimes."

"Yeah, he's pretty strict about that. Speaking of which, I know your dad felt compelled to tell you our little secret, so if you're ready, I have someone I'd like you to meet."

"I'm glad I found out. It helped me make the right decision."

Claire stepped out of the room and then nudged the door open again, entering holding the hand of a two-and-a-half-year-old boy. The boy came tentatively into the room holding onto Claire with one hand and in the other a handful of over-sized playing cards. Claire led the little boy to Christian's bedside.

"Christian, say hello to your son, Judas."

"Judas?" Christian looked at Claire and then back to the boy.

"Judas, hello," Christian said, extending a hand for the boy to grasp. Judas waved his cards and shyly said, "Hi."

Christian gave Claire a big smile.

"Well hello there, Judas. It's really nice to meet you," Christian said. "What's that you have in your hand?"

"Play cards," little Judas said as he held out his hand. "I like pictures. I pretend I this one," he said as he held out the jack of clubs.

There in the palm of little boy's hand lay the tell. The center of the card contained the picture of a man adorned with a jeweled crown. It wasn't Judas Maccabee, but it may as well have been. Large 'J's' were imprinted in the upper right and lower left corners and large club symbols were on the opposite corners. The image was the mirror version of the signet ring worn by the apostle Judas. Christian thought about the things the apostle Judas knew and said at the time that didn't quite make sense. He remembered what Judas said about having kissed him before and that he loved him. Christian fought back tears as the puzzle was fitting together in his mind. Perhaps this was not the first time he had met his child.

"Hey Judas," Christian said. "You know what would help me feel better right now?"

"What?" little Judas asked.

"Can you give me a little kiss right here?" Christian said, pointing to his cheek.

"Okay."

Claire picked him up so he could give Christian a kiss.

"Thank you, Judas."

"Okay little chipmunk, let me take you back outside to grandma," Claire said. "Then I need to speak with Christian for a few moments."

Claire escorted little Judas out the door.

Claire came back in the room a minute later. "I wanted to tell you myself about Judas. It's the kind of thing a man should know. It's just that circumstances were so incredibly awkward. I gave your dad permission to tell you if conditions warranted. I hope you're all right with the name. I was moved by the information you were relaying about the friendship you established with Judas in Palestine. His name's been so maligned, I figured it was about time somebody started to pay tribute to it again. Your dad's been super supportive. He flew my mother in from Lebanon and made arrangements with the State Department for an extended Visa."

"It's a fabulous name. He seems like a wonderful boy and I'm glad your mother has been here to help."

"Christian, I can tell you're being reserved and I understand why. You've come back from a traumatic experience and I'm not expecting you to instantly step into the role of fatherhood. What we need you to do right now is focus on getting yourself fully healthy. You've been through quite an ordeal. We all have. We can talk about the logistics of co-parenting later. Does that work for you?"

"Yes, Claire, that works for me just fine. Thank you for coming to visit, for introducing me to Judas, and for giving me the time to re-acclimate."

Claire leaned forward, gave Christian a little peck on the cheek, and then left the room.

Christian gathered sufficient strength to walk and generally function independently within a few more weeks. He was taking regular walks, exploring the grounds, often taking time away from others to clear his head and sneak a cigarette. It became his routine to seek solitude, away from the charged atmosphere of the HQ staff who were still excited about his return. He shied away from answering any of their questions about what he remembered.

He caught up with advances in nanite research with his dad. He missed the random brainstorming and intellectual banter that had characterized their relationship for so many years. In a sentimental moment, Christian made a special request.

"Dad, is the companion cubepod still here at HQ."

"Yes, of course."

"May I see it?"

"Now, why would you want that, it's practically useless without its paired companion."

"I just want it for a souvenir," he lied. "I figure I've earned it."

"A souvenir it is then. I'll have a technician bring it over."

The cubepod arrived that afternoon and Christian was anxious to use it. He scouted the grounds during his cigarette breaks and knew where he could find privacy for extended periods of time. He settled into a seldom-used auxiliary building on the edge of campus. He turned off the auto record function on the cubepod and pinged the companion cube which was with Mary.

There was no answer right away, but then an acknowledging ping occurred. He attempted to sync communications, but reception was marginal. He waited for Mary to find a hilltop, just as he instructed. Within an hour there was an incoming link request, and, with his acknowledgment, there appeared the 3D image of Mary Magdalene. Christian switched to his fluent Aramaic and they exchanged tearful greetings. They talked, across the distance and across the ages, they talked as only devoted friends and lovers can. And they updated each other about new developments.

"Christian, you made it! I'm so glad to see you alive. And well?" Mary asked.

"Yes Mary, indeed I am alive and slowly feeling better."

"It was a shock when we went to your tomb only to find the stone rolled away and your body missing. We found the wrappings of course, and in place, just as you described they would be, like an empty cocoon. Sometime you're going to have to explain to me why you have to time travel naked."

Christian chuckled. Yes, he would certainly do that.

"Thank you for sending your friend to comfort me there at the cave entrance. He told me not to seek the living among the dead and reminded me that you said you would rise again. I took the message as confirmation that you made it and I was hoping to hear from you soon."

"What did he look like?" Christian asked. He was curious about the unknown visitor.

Mary didn't quite have all the right words to describe what she saw, but she tried. "He was a tall, young man with radiant skin and he was wearing a dazzling white robe and he spoke clearly to me."

"Did you touch him?"

"No. Why?"

"Just wondering. Let's talk about this more later. How are the apostles and the rest of the disciples?"

"They're scared and scattered now that they've lost their shepherd."

"Yes, I can understand that. It must have been traumatic for them. Listen, do me a favor, gather them back into the upper room of Joseph's house. Bring the cubepod and ping me when they're gathered there. I have an important message to deliver to them. Tell me how you're doing, Mary. We didn't have much time there to talk at the end."

"Yes, you surprised me when you handed me the pouch with all of your stuff in it. You and I had just started making other plans, plans that I would have preferred to this. And, we have an unfinished topic to discuss."

"The distance does not change the love I feel for you Mary. I've been anxious to get back in touch with you."

"Beyond our love Christian, is yet another life at stake," Mary said, "for I am with child."

There was nothing Mary could have said to make him feel any more like a heel for leaving her. Not only did Christian leave Mary behind in Palestine, he left her pregnant. As if her life wasn't hard enough, now she was to be an out-of-wedlock mother in an ancient society, left to raise a child alone. Tears welled in his eyes. He came back to modern society out of a sense of obligation for one child, only to discover he had dual responsibilities.

"Mary, I'm so sorry I can't be there for you now." They both were crying. "You need to make arrangements to leave Galilee. We need to get you and the baby as far away from there as we can. Tell no one of the baby until you get to a safer place. You'll have to head for Caesarea, find passage by boat, and sail the great sea past Rome to a place called Gaul. It's modern day southern France, but no matter, it's Roman controlled and safely away from the turmoil that will be coming to the Asia Minor region. Gaul is the place I mentioned to you before, where legend says you traveled."

"I remember Christian. I still have people here who can help me obtain safe passage. I'll do exactly as you say, as it would be folly for me to question things you already know will happen."

"Mary, you are an amazing woman."

"You're an amazing man, Christian. Will I ever see you again, I mean in person, actually be with you?" Mary asked through her tears.

Christian paused, this was a perceptive woman. He didn't know the answer. It was yet another revelation, after all this time playing Jesus, working miracles and knowing in detail what was to come, had he developed some sort of God complex? In this instant he was reminded that he did not know the future. He was not God. The laws of physics prohibited him from knowing the space-time stamp of events that had not yet happened in his frame of reference.

"Honestly Mary, I don't know. I certainly hope so. In the meantime, we can keep in touch through these cubepods."

"I suppose that will have to do for now," Mary said dolefully.

"For now," Christine said and nodded.

"It may take a few days to gather your disciples," Mary said.

"I'll await your ping. I love you, Mary."

He pursed his lips and leaned forward for a virtual kiss. She reciprocated. He closed his eyes, cherishing the moment. He heard, "I love you, too, Christian." The room darkened slightly as he opened his eyes and saw that her image was gone. It was then that Christian saw his dad at the door of the room, leaning casually against the doorframe. How much had he seen and heard?

"Before you ask, I saw enough. I couldn't understand all of it, but I'm pretty sure I got the gist," his dad admitted.

"Son, I have to say, that had to be one of the most romantic scenes ever played out across the ages. I didn't have the heart to interrupt it."

Christian bowed his head, appreciating his dad's discernment.

"From what I can tell, you gamed it right. While I knew there was something not quite right about your apparent lack of memory, I also suspected you had your reasons." He maintained brief eye contact with Christian. "Your body not only endured the crucifixion, but all of the events leading up to it, from the moment it was initially transported. Assuming those amazing cellular nanites of yours managed to keep your brain's neurons intact, those memories must have resided there."

Taking a breath, he pressed forward. "Perhaps you've already suspected, but I will confirm for you, Atlanta hasn't been able to duplicate the success of the cellular nanite cancer treatment to nearly the degree of success observed in your body. Upon hearing about your demonstrated secondary healing abilities in ancient Galilee, we circled back to the other early experimental patients and there are no such properties exhibited. It could be a side effect of the time travel, or something genetic, we don't know."

"I remember more than I've let on thus far, that's true. I'm still sorting things out and I need time do that. I won't carry on the amnesia act forever. I'll talk when I'm ready, I promise. What else did you hear?"

"I saw her put her hand on her belly and thought I understood her say she was with child. I take it you didn't know, or else you might have made a different decision," his dad said. "Regardless, at this point, I think it's wise to keep future cubepod conversations secure. Knowledge of your bloodline in antiquity could be problematic with consequences unknown, given its apparent uniqueness, lending credibility to crusades for the blood of Christ and the Holy Grail"

"Honestly, events are happening so fast, I haven't had time to process all of the ramifications. Until I understood more about the situation, I just felt it best to remain reserved about what I shared."

His dad nodded then grinned wide. "You keep procreating, making me a grandpa," he said cheerfully.

After everything Christian had been though, the nuggets of wisdom in his dad's speech and his ability to sense his mood once again reminded him of how awesome his dad truly was. "Hey Dad, one last question. I'm not exactly sure what may have gone on here over the past three years, so I was just wondering, did you send anyone back to Judea, circa 30 AD, around the time of my crucifixion?"

"No. Why do you ask?"

"Mary described some rather odd visitors at the tomb."

"I wondered what that was about, but I couldn't quite pick up what she was saying."

Christian relayed what Mary told him.

"What do you think?"

"Sounds to me like someone besides us has the space-time coordinates of ancient Palestine."

About the Author

After 25 years at IBM, J. D. Morrison decided to follow his passion and began to write. His books span the genres of sci-fi, contemporary YA, psychological thriller, and the paranormal. All defy the status quo, shatter paradigms of accepted truths and give voice to taboo topics. Morrison has a bachelor's degree from the University of Maryland and master's degree from Syracuse University, both in engineering. Besides writing, he enjoys playing guitar, spinning and achieving his obligatory 10,000 steps per day. He is married to his muse and editor, Jena. Together they have five children and two grandchildren. He lives in northern Virginia with his wife and two cats, Black and Decker.

ALL THINGS THAT MATTER PRESS

FOR MORE INFORMATION ON TITLES AVAILABLE FROM
ALL THINGS THAT MATTER PRESS, GO TO
http://allthingsthatmatterpress.com
or contact us at
allthingsthatmatterpress@gmail.com

If you enjoyed this book, please post a review on Amazon.com and
your favorite social media sites.
Thank you!